He scooped her up and carried her back to the room he'd shared with Charlie, ignoring her protests as he fumbled clumsily at her clothing. Then she was in a tumbled bed that smelled of oil and sweat. She tried to close her ears to the things he was saying, her senses to what he was doing.

"David, you're hurting me—"

He finally fell away to lie in drunken slumber. Amantha stared at the ceiling, thinking of green meadows, a shepherd's cot—of a man who loved her gently, sweetly, on a fragrant, grassy bed.

What had happened to the laughing boy she married?

RED WIND BLOWING

Aola Vandergriff

FAWCETT GOLD MEDAL • NEW YORK

A Fawcett Gold Medal Book
Published by Ballantine Books

Library of Congress Catalog Card Number: 84-91056

ISBN: 0-449-12432-0

Manufactured in the United States of America

First Ballantine Books Edition: October 1984

For Dad

Author's Note

Though the background of my story is authentic and carefully researched, any names, any resemblance of the characters to persons living or dead is purely coincidental. This is a work of fiction, based on a single sentence spoken to me by an elderly lady many years ago.

"I came to the oil fields from England, to join my husband. And, my dear, I found he had become a very rough man—"

You, Oklahoma,
With a red wind blowing;
Black blood flowing
From crimson wounds . . .

A.S.

BOOK I

Amantha

Prologue

The flight was called, the last passengers shuffling down the ramp leading to the plane. Phil Huttling, standing to one side of the gate and fussing with his valise, began to get nervous.

What if his informant had been wrong, and the old bitch didn't appear? He'd be out a bundle and have nothing to show for it but a first-class ticket to Oklahoma.

There were still a few latecomers. A trim, pretty woman had reached the desk. Good-looking legs, Huttling thought automatically. His gaze moved on to a white-haired female with a cane, then snapped back as he heard a name.

"Everything's in order, Mrs. Carmody," the agent said. "And we're running right on schedule."

"Thank you." The woman's voice was sweet, cultured, with a trace of an English accent. Carrying only a purse and a briefcase, she went through the gate. Huttling adjusted the lapels of his trenchcoat, cupped his hands over his hair for an instant to settle it in the style he affected, and followed.

He had pulled it off, he thought exultantly. There were only the two of them in first class on this night flight. This beat the hell out of trying to outshout his fellow reporters! By God, he was going to get an exclusive!

Taking a seat across the aisle, he studied Amantha Carmody, the guiding spirit of Carmody-Forbes Oil. Back in the thirties she'd taken hold of a small wildcat operation and had built it into a textbook corporation. She'd refused to gamble, to diversify as most companies did. As a result, Carmody-

3

Forbes's stock was steady as a rock, and she still held firm control.

Her briefcase was already open, and she studied a page of notes. Huttling couldn't see her face; only the soft curve of a cheek. She had to be somewhere in her sixties—but he'd follow those legs anywhere!

The stewardess went through her emergency procedures routine, and the gigantic plane moved along the runway. In a few moments there was the pressure against the back of the seat, the initial breathlessness of wheels lifting from the ground. Then they were airborne, circling, the no-smoking and seat-belt signs no longer engaged.

Huttling released his belt and moved across the aisle, seating himself beside his prey.

"Mrs. Carmody?"

Amantha Carmody's mind had been far away, enmeshed in the facts and figures before her. "Yes?" she said.

He placed a hand on her arm. "I would like to ask a few questions. Your interview with the president—"

Now her head came up, eyes meeting his; young eyes, set in a face that made only one concession to age—a softness that would feel like velvet to the touch. But there was something in her gaze, a blue intensity, that almost staggered him with its forcefulness.

"I have no comment," she said coolly. "Now, if you will excuse me—"

Huttling tried for a disarming smile. "I already have the facts, ma'am. The topic was oil. And I'll quote you!"

He took a clipping from his pocket and began to read.

"Mrs. Amantha Carmody, first lady of oil, met today in heated discussion with the president of the United States. She believes this country has exhausted only thirty-nine percent of its resources, with another twenty-four percent in reserve. With sufficient incentive, thirty-seven percent more can be produced. Using enhanced recovery, steam stimulation, chemicals, another hundred-fifty to two-hundred-thirty-five billion barrels can be brought to the market . . ."

Amantha Carmody lifted a staying hand. "I have read the

4

article. And you will note the president did not agree, therefore there is no point in pursuing the matter."

"But there is," Huttling insisted. "I need the personal angle. Is Carmody-Forbes in trouble? And why did they send a woman to do a man's job?"

"Carmody-Forbes is solvent. And this has always been my job. If you will excuse me—"

"Aw-w," he wheedled, "don't be that way! Let's forget about business and talk about you! You're a mystery woman, you know! Just about every gal in the country would like to trade places with you! They'll want to read about what you eat, what you wear. What about the men in your life? Is it true that you and Thorne Greenberg were lovers before your daughter was—"

With an almost imperceptible movement Amantha Carmody beckoned to the stewardess. "Miss—Susan, isn't it?"

The girl, concerned over the harrassment of one of her favorite passengers, smiled.

"Yes, ma'am."

"Please aid this gentleman in finding another seat. I find I need more working space. And I should like a pot of tea, if you please."

Phil Huttling found himself moved to the rear of the first-class section. He sat glowering at the back of the seat that concealed Amantha Carmody as he downed drink after drink.

Who the hell did she think she was, anyway! One of these days he just might be sitting in Walter Cronkite's chair! And Carmody-Forbes might need a friend—especially if this latest scoop he'd heard was true!

He grinned savagely as he realized she might not know it yet herself. Maybe he'd have the pleasure of clueing her in!

Rising to his feet, he wavered down the aisle, leaning to breathe the scent of scotch into Amantha Carmody's face.

"Don' like career wimmen," he said, truculently.

"I don't imagine you do." Her flat statement was tinged with distaste.

"But I'm gonna do you a fav—favor. Gonna tell you a

5

shecret! Your damn comp'ny's gonna faw down around your ears. Know that, hunh? You know that?''

Amantha drew back from the jabbing finger with which he punctuated his words.

"Greenberg's gonna call a special meeting of the board," he said triumphantly. "And, lady, you're gonna get dumped! When it hits the headlines, you're gonna need people like me! Might as well go out in style—"

"Thank you for your concern, but I'm afraid your information is faulty. My partner and I control the majority of stock—"

"Thass it!" He was drunkenly gleeful. "You an' Forbes! Way I hear it, the man is selling out! You're on your own, baby!"

There was not a flicker of apprehension in the woman's composed face. Her blue eyes drilled into him. "If you are quite finished, I have a great deal of paperwork to go over."

"You damned icicle! You—"

"Come, Mr. Huttling!" The little stewardess was at his side, leading him away. "You should resume your seat. We will be landing before long."

Amantha was deaf to his mumbled objections as he was propelled toward the rear. That one concentrated moment of self-control had drained her. Her face was void of color, the heart beneath her Givenchy suit clenched like a fist.

She had expected Thorne Greenberg to try to oust her. After all, it wasn't the first time.

But, Charlie?

Dear God, not Charlie Forbes! Never Charlie!

The seat-belt light went on and she fastened the apparatus with mechanical fingers. She was no longer Amantha Carmody, businesswoman extraordinaire; confidante of presidents and kings. . . .

She had gone back in time; back to the terrors of a girl-mother, whose husband had left her in England—either through circumstance or design.

Coming to find him, she'd felt like this; trembling with doubt—and the fear of ultimate betrayal.

She closed her eyes, and the plane became a train, rushing backward through more than forty years.

Chapter One

The train took a curve like a huge segmented worm, its whistle hooting mournfully. Amantha Carmody, sick with the rocking motion she'd endured for hours, looked at her sleeping son. He lay in the opposite seat, head in his nanny's lap.

She wished she, too, could sleep away the hours of the journey. But her worry about what awaited her at the end of the trip, coupled with nervousness at her strange surroundings, kept her awake.

Too, there were the Indians.

Amantha cast a sideways look at the figure across the aisle. An enormous copper-colored man overflowed the seat, a blanket about his shoulders. His long greasy braids were interlaced with strips of bright cloth. And he was intoxicated. Once, weaving his way back to his seat, he stumbled, falling on her. A strong feral scent, coupled with the stench of whiskey, mingled with the odor of coal smoke that permeated the car.

Sensing her fascinated gaze, the Indian opened one slitted eye. It glittered balefully and she shivered, looking quickly away. Nanny Goforth, who had been her own nurse-governess and was now young Peter's, was certain they'd all be scalped. It was her opinion that terrors lay beyond the train windows, now blank with rain; that naked Indians on horseback would surround them, pinning them with arrows.

It was probably the naked part that upset Nanny. Nanny was most awfully proper, even now in sleep. She sat stiffly upright, leaning away from the seat, her horse-face rigid, lips tightly clamped over buckteeth. In one hand, her furled umbrella was gripped, ready for action if needed.

In contrast, Peter was completely relaxed, his blond curls resting against Nanny's angular lap. Amantha yearned to take him beside her and renew her quivering confidence at the feel of his warm little body in her arms.

But Nanny would not approve. She would regard it as an invasion of her province.

Amantha wished she hadn't had to bring her along. She'd only done so in deference to her newly widowed mother's wishes. Nanny Goforth would be another surprise for David. An unpleasant one. He'd never liked the woman.

At the thought of her husband, Amantha's painful uncertainty returned. Her fingers, in slightly soiled gloves, were knotted in her lap. She forced them to relax and wiped a circle on the steamed window. The rain still slanted down. Ahead, the train whistle sounded lonely in the night.

She flinched as a hand touched her shoulder.

It was only the conductor. He was nice, friendly, but he'd been rather a nuisance since he learned his passengers were British. He'd assured her the Indian was harmless. "Just got hisself a snootful." And he'd warned Amantha against conversation with two overly painted women at the rear of the car.

"Got Reno Street writ all over 'em," he judged. "Ain't in your class a-tall."

Though his language was difficult to comprehend, his meaning was clear. Nanny was scandalized and Amantha was unable to control a blush.

"Next stop, Oklahoma City," the conductor said now.

"We're going to be on schedule?"

He repeated her last word, moving his lips in an effort to duplicate it. *Shed-you-all*. Then he chuckled paternally. "Yep. An' that man o' your'n 'll be waitin'. Betcha he's in a tizzy!"

He wandered down the aisle, still wagging his head at his passenger's odd speech. Amantha watched him go, wondering what kind of vehicle a tizzy might be.

"He's quite wrong, you know!" Nanny was awake, her face set in forbidding lines. "David Carmody will not be there when we arrive!"

"I'm sure he will." Amantha's tone was defensive, and Nanny Goforth pounced.

"If he wished you to come to him, he would have sent for you. You know my opinion of that young man! I consider him a charlatan!"

Amantha knew Nanny's opinions. She voiced them loudly and often. David's manners were crude, his language uncouth. He was not a fit husband for a girl with a proper upbringing.

"I know how you feel," Amantha said quietly, "but you must remember, David is different because he is an American. I must demand that you—you treat him with respect! You've hardly had time to become acquainted—"

"Nor have you, Amantha! You married a man you hardly knew. He left you behind. Mark my word, he has forgotten you. He will have another woman—or women!"

Amantha put her hands to her ears. "Please, Nanny! I won't listen to this!"

The older woman sniffed. "I will have no back talk, Amantha. I consented to this dreadful journey only through duty, not to you, but to your dear mother!" She turned her gaze to the window, and Amantha sighed.

All her life the word *duty* had taken precedence over love. She'd spent her childhood bounded by duty's chaste utilitarian walls, not knowing there was more to living—

Until David.

Though the coach was hot and steamy, she shivered. What if Nanny were correct in her assumptions? Perhaps David had found someone else. An American girl, who wore furs, cloche hats, painted her lips. A girl with long silken legs. . . .

Amantha smoothed the skirt of her tweed suit. It seemed appropriate at home. But she knew that in America its old-fashioned cut, her sensible walking shoes, and small round hat with flowers on its brim made her look like a peasant.

And after all, this was 1929, nearly five years since he left her. Sufficient time for a man to forget. If she could only have returned to the States with him! But there had been the fall; her broken leg, the pelvic injury that caused the doctor so much concern. And she had been pregnant.

They were to be parted for only a little while, just until the baby was born. But Peter's delivery was difficult. Then there was her father's illness, her mother's insistence that she stay until the end. She had a duty—

Dear God! Duty again! She had a duty to her husband! She might have rebelled despite her affection for her father, but David's letters counseled patience.

"Don't you dare think about coming until you and the kid are strong enough to travel," he'd written in the beginning. *"You're too damn precious to me!"* Then, when she'd informed him of her father's terminal illness, *"Sorry as hell to hear about your dad. I know you'll want to stick around until it's over."*

It took years to be over. In that time there were fewer communications, no money. Amantha and Peter existed on her parents' charity. When her father died, her mother expected Amantha to move with her into the dower house; her brother, Ian, and his new wife to occupy the manor.

But Amantha received an inheritance of five hundred pounds.

She used it for fare, wiring David only after she reached New York, not giving him time to send an answer. She would arrive in an alien place with three pieces of luggage—her own, Nanny's, Peter's—and a worn trunk containing some old linens and the family silver her mother insisted she take to her new home.

David would be waiting for her. He had to be.

Amantha drifted into a memory of the first time she'd seen David Carmody, with his tumbled black hair and blue, amused eyes. Son of a Tulsa oil man, he was doing a year at Cambridge to please his mother. He came home with Amantha's brother, Ian, for a holiday; a visit that was to be repeated until, shortly before term's end, against stiffly polite parental opposition, David and Amantha were married.

Two days before they were to sail for the States, they rode across the meadows; acres of softly mounded grass. It was to be a farewell pilgrimage, saying good-bye to the crumbling ruins of a tower silhouetted against the blue sky; the fat lambs grazing against a hedgerow in the distance.

David looked unusually serious as they paused to survey the scene. Her heart stopped at his words.

"I don't know how to say this, honey, but . . . maybe we've made a mistake. Getting married, I mean."

"David!"

"Hey, don't get me wrong! It's just being with your folks this last week, everything so damned old and holy! Great-Great-Grandfather's codpiece; Great-Aunt Fannie's slop jar!"

He issued the ludicrous statements in a parody of her mother's thin, informative voice. Amantha laughed in spite of herself. "Mum's grand tour! I've quite memorized it, you know. But what does it have to do with us?"

"We live in different worlds, honey. And looking at all this green stuff—hell, mine's even a different color."

"My word! And what color, if you please?"

He squirmed uncomfortably in his saddle. "Well, red, I guess."

She laughed again, mentally transposing the scene before her; red meadows, a red lamb, a red David.

"I love you, David," she said.

Had he been trying to convey his true feelings on that long-ago day? Trying to dissuade her from accompanying him even then? Did he feel trapped when she insisted she loved him and wished only to live with him, wherever it might be?

Trapped or not, he wheeled his horse toward a deserted shepherd's cot. It stood to one side, walls tumbled, thatched roof open partially to the sky. He dismounted and reached up for her.

"I want my girl! Oh, God, Amantha!"

She'd backed from him, cheeks pink. "Here? In the day? Oh, I say, David! It isn't done, you know!"

He grinned. "I keep forgetting you're my prim little English rose! Can't hug you in public. Can't get you alone because the Woozeleys or the Gooseleys have come to call—"

"Worcesters and Gosdens," she corrected him, but his voice rose, overriding her own.

"I reach out to touch you and somebody shoves a goddam cup of tea in my hand. I need some loving. Hell, even Nanny Goforth's beginning to look good! I just might—"

She put her hands to his lips. "David, you silly fool!" Her voice faltered as his fingers went to her hair, removing pins, letting it fall in a shimmer of ash brown. Her knees went weak as he led her to the ruined cottage. They made love sweetly and naturally on a carpet of grass. Through the ragged thatch, she could see the blueness of the sky and a small white cloud—like a fat lamb in a hedgerow.

Amantha remembered every detail of that day. It sustained her for a long time. Because, on the way back to the manor, as Amantha raced ahead of David in pretended flight, her mount stumbled and she took her disastrous fall; the fall that kept her from accompanying David on his journey home. He had been forced to return at his father's command.

"I'll send for you as soon as you can travel. That's a promise. It won't be long. A few months—"

Those months had lengthened into long and lonely years.

The train seemed to be slowing. Nanny shook Peter awake, adjusting his blue velvet jacket over his frilled shirt, brushing at the matching short breeches that revealed rosy knees. She didn't speak, but her expression said she knew her efforts were all for nothing.

Amantha wiped a circle of mist from the window. She could see only the rain and a faint glow in the night as the clatter of wheels slowed, steam brakes hissed, and the mournful whistle signaled the train's arrival.

She looked once more at her watch. One o'clock in the morning.

David, please be waiting for me! David—

Chapter Two

*A*mantha *remained in her seat until the car emptied. The* Indian lurched down the aisle, followed by the cheap-appearing women the conductor cautioned Amantha against. Two well-dressed men passed. With their suits they wore big hats and cowboy boots. Their voices were raised in profane conversation. One of them was grumbling about a lease. He thought he had it in the bag, but a goddam spook hangin' around the court-house got there first with the most.

Hell, he'd break it up, oversell, and nobody'd do a god-damn thing about it.

The incomprehensible words trailed into the distance, and then there was only silence.

"Well?" Nanny asked, brows raised.

Amantha rose reluctantly, taking her case and Peter's. Nanny followed with her own and the child. The conductor, waiting at the let-down step, reached up for the luggage, happy to oblige the young woman he'd enjoyed talking to.

She was looking past him, staring at the empty platform, her face cold and frozen. The conductor frowned. Nobody there. Y'd think the sumbitch'd be on time, little lady from a strange country and all!

Hefting the luggage, he carried it to the long wooden building, then returned for the trunk. His passengers waited along the wall, not speaking. The child clung to the older woman's skirts. His mother looked shrunken and lost.

Skeert to death, he thought compassionately as he searched for something to say.

"Yessir," he told Amantha, "this yere's your new home!" He pointed out a few yellow squares of light visible against the wet sky. "Them's skyscrapers. Over there's the Skirvin Hotel. And that there is—"

They weren't listening. Oh, hell! None of his business, but he couldn't leave them standing like this. "Your man knowed for sure you was comin'?"

"I sent him a wire."

"Then he'll git here. Prob'ly stuck in the mud, somewheres. Yessir, betcha that's it."

"Yes." Amantha's eyes were glazed, but she spoke in a polite, remote tone. "Thank you. We will wait."

And he was gone.

"I told you," Nanny Goforth began.

Amantha raised a staying hand. "He will be here," she said icily. "Take Peter and go inside. See if there is a message at the ticket window."

Nanny was accustomed to giving orders, not receiving them. But something in Amantha's tone sent her scurrying to obey.

Amantha waited with the luggage, the depot wall at her back, a voice in her head crying, "David! David! David—"

A shambling figure passed, an old man, drunk and mumbling to himself; a pair of young lovers, carrying on a bawdy courtship with slaps and shrill giggling; then a pasty-faced, shifty-eyed man.

"Waitin' fer someone, lady?"

"My husband," she said firmly.

He went on his way, but she was left trembling. Reared in the English countryside, she had no experience with city life. She knew, intuitively, that she should not be here at this hour, alone, and she was terrified.

When a ramshackle truck pulled to a halt at the curb, two unkempt men climbing down from its cab, Amantha was careful to look away. Let them pass me, she prayed. Dear God! If she could only be invisible—

"Amantha?"

She whirled to face the man who'd said her name, eyes wide with shock. It was David's voice, but this man was older, unshaven, wearing workman's clothing, streaked with filth. The dark hair David had worn in an artfully rumpled way was uncut, a wild shock through which he ran his fingers as though in despair.

"David?" she asked timidly. Then, "Oh, David!"

She moved toward him, her cry of delight faltering as she saw his face. It was obstinate, closed against her, as if he were forced into a situation not of his liking.

And indeed he was.

David Carmody had finally succeeded in putting his young English wife from his mind. He'd still planned to send for her when he got things straightened out, but this sure as hell wasn't the time. He was tired. He and Charlie had been working twenty hours a day. Tonight they'd decided to take a break, stopping by Merk's for a sociable drink or two after the evening tour.

And there was that goddam wire! Somebody'd carried his mail out from town.

Too stunned to think, he'd had a few to brace himself. His irritation built as Charlie drove him in to the station. She had no business showing up like this! He rubbed his eyes. Dammit, he couldn't even remember what she looked like—

When he saw the tiny, dowdily dressed figure against the depot wall, his jaw dropped. Good God, he must have been out of his mind, over there in England.

Charlie nudged him forward. He said her name, and she turned. He stood frozen for a moment, overwhelmed by a sweet flood of memories. How could he have forgotten that flowerlike face, those eyes like Texas bluebonnets? He drew a ragged breath, his features softening.

"David?" This time, his name was a plea.

She watched his face alter, moving from obstinacy to surprise to wonder. The magic between them was still there. Oblivious to his friend, Amantha moved into David's arms. His mouth found hers, and she gave herself to his kiss. Unshaven stubble scratched her tender flesh. But it was all right! He smelled of alcohol and the oil that stained his clothing.

But he was David, he was here, and he still wanted her!

Thank God! Oh, thank God—

15

Nanny Goforth had a nose for trouble. Waiting uneasily inside, she finally decided she'd had enough of these surroundings. Amantha had made a fool of herself, coming to this desolate, wild country! The sooner she faced up to it, the better off they'd all be. She would insist they hire a conveyance to take them to a hotel where they might bathe and sleep.

And then they could consider returning home!

Dragging the complaining child, she went to the door, blinking in the darkness.

"My word!"

Her young mistress was in the arms of a—a most unpresentable man! Another stood by. She was being attacked—

Nanny Goforth charged, forcing her big-boned figure between Amantha and David. "Fiend," she shrieked. "Release her! I shall call a bobby—"

Amantha caught at her flailing arms. "Nanny! Stop! It's David!"

"Oh, my word," the older woman gasped. "My word!"

David Carmody was equally astounded. He scowled at Amantha. "What the hell is she doing here?"

Amantha explained that Nanny served as nurse-governess to their son.

"Goddam," David said fervently. "Oh—goddam!"

"And this is Peter." Amantha set the child who had followed Nanny from the depot before his father. David stared at the boy in disbelief.

This? His son? Velvet suit, frills, short pants; blond curls like fat sausages hanging to his shoulders. His kid—a goddam sissy?

Well, that would be remedied! There were more pressing problems now. Like what the hell he was going to do with them all!

He turned to his companion, a lanky, gray-eyed man who waited unobtrusively in the background.

"Looks like I got a bucket of worms, Charlie. What the hell do I do now? Any suggestions?"

"Put 'em up at a hotel for the night?" Charlie offered. "Give us a chance to git the place cleaned up." He pulled a huge watch from his pocket and frowned at it. "Two in the mornin'," he stated gloomily.

Dave Carmody scowled. They couldn't transport more than three in Charlie's truck. The kid could sit on his lap. But there wouldn't be any room for that damned old biddy. Why the hell had Amantha dragged her along? By God, if she thought she was going to be living in an English-style manor, she was in for a surprise!

He wondered how Amantha would feel about a shot-gun oil-field shack consisting of three rooms. He and Charlie just batched it. The place was a mess. And now he had a wife—and a nanny for his sissy kid.

He set his jaw.

"Take the old woman and the kid over to the Black," he told Charlie. "My wife will go out to the camp with us. Hell, she might as well see what she's up against."

Amantha paled. It appeared she was to be separated from her son. "David—?"

It was Charlie who answered. "The Black's a purty good hotel," he said gently. "Not in the runnin' with the Skirvin or the Biltmore, but t'ain't bad. And it's only for tonight. Give you an' Dave here a chance to talk things over."

"No," Amantha said, shakily. "No—"

Nanny found her tongue and moved in front of Amantha, arms spread protectively. "We must remain together. For all we know, these men may be murderers, thieves, or—" she swallowed hard, her face splotched with red as she mentioned the unspeakable, "—or white slavers! In this lawless country—"

"Oh, for God's sake!" David growled. "Charlie—"

"Please, Nanny," Amantha said softly, trying to stop the older woman's tirade, "let me talk to David."

"Talk all you want to," Nanny Goforth snorted. "But don't listen! Not unless you want to be found dead in a ditch!"

Small Peter, terrified at the harsh voices around him, began to sob, burying his face in Nanny's skirt. David looked at his son, dressed in that silly getup—and now crying like a girl! An expression of distaste crossed his features. Amantha saw it and felt a twist of pain. David's friend was right. She and

17

her husband—this stranger with David's eyes—must have time for a private discussion.

"Peter rarely cries," she said, her head high. "He's exhausted from our journey. And Nanny is overly protective. You must remember, we are in an unknown place. If we could stay together, it would be—"

"We can't. Go ahead, Charlie. Load 'em up."

The older woman glared at David, then turned to Amantha, who gave an almost imperceptible nod. "The man will take you to the hotel, Nanny."

"Just remember, I told you," Nanny said haughtily. Stiff-backed, she walked to the rattle-trap truck, lifted Peter in, and climbed in herself, refusing Charlie's assistance.

Amantha watched with a sinking heart as the vehicle clattered away, then turned to David. He was staring at her, his blue eyes alight with desire that made her blush.

"David—"

"Don't talk." His voice held a rough edge. "I know this is a helluva place to meet after all these years. But, dammit, you're my wife! Come over here!" He drew her into the shadows. "I want to hold you—"

She stiffened a little. This was a public place. Then his lips claimed hers and she melted against him.

"Oh, David, David!"

He slid calloused fingers along her smooth throat, snagging them on her lace-trimmed blouse. I'll have to be careful, he thought. I'm just drunk enough to take her right here! How could he have forgotten what the touch of her did to him? How could he have put it from his mind? He needed her! God, he needed her!

But he didn't need three additional encumbrances right now, not when he was so close to his goal. So what in the hell could he do with her? Give her a good night's loving, send her home to England, ask her to wait a while longer?

"David, what is it?" She had sensed his confusion. He forced a grin.

"Just thinking how much I love you. Wishing we were alone."

18

"It has been so long." The blue eyes tilted to his sparkled with tears. "I have missed you, David."

"And I've missed you." It was true, though he hadn't realized it. For a moment he felt like the boy he'd been when he wooed and won her; well-dressed, carefree. He looked down at his oil-soaked clothing, seeing himself for the first time. He'd even smudged her white blouse.

"I'm sorry. I didn't have time to change."

"It doesn't matter, David. It doesn't matter!"

She was in his arms again. He revelled in the feel of her slender body against his own, stroking her with work-hardened hands, kissing her until she was dizzy.

It was going to be all right! In the morning they would collect Peter and Nanny and be a real family. When David got to know his son, he would love him as she did.

The journey was behind Amantha, along with her fears. She was in her husband's arms. He wanted her—

Her David—

Chapter Three

*T*he *idyllic renewal of their love was not to last. Charlie* returned and they joined him in the cab of the truck. And with his coming, David seemed to change. It was as if he regretted the tender moments they'd spent alone. He reached among the jumbled tools on the floorboards and came up with a mason jar. Unscrewing the top of it, he offered a drink to his friend, who refused it, then lapsed into a morose silence as he sipped away.

Charlie's face was red. He was embarrassed for the woman's sake. He knew David's problems, but she'd walked into this mess cold. He wished he knew how to help her.

"Reckon we ain't been proper introduced," he said in his soft drawling voice. "Me, I'm Charlie Forbes. Me an' Dave here's been pardners for a coon's age."

"I'm pleased to meet you, Mr. Forbes."

"Charlie," he corrected with a grin.

"Charlie, then." She smiled, not really seeing him, turning to her husband.

"Where are we going, David? Is it far?"

He grunted sourly, and she flinched. His attitude in front of his friend was so . . . different. Was he ashamed of her? She supposed she wasn't beautiful by American standards—

Charlie answered for him. "Not too far, way we figger it. Ol' Lena'll git us there." He slapped the wheel affectionately. "She's a 'twenty-five T-Model. Never let me down. Got her bad side, though. Slow starter. Dang nigh busted my arm once—"

He talked on, and Amantha sat quietly. David had shut himself away from her. Their magic moments were gone. What could she have said or done?

"David, perhaps you shouldn't drink—"

"A nagging wife already, by God," he exploded. Then his voice softened. "Sorry, sweetheart. I'm tired. And I've got some thinking to do."

"It's quite all right," she said stiffly, hiding her hurt. She turned to Charlie. "Where are we?"

"This here street is South Robinson. The bridge we come across is over the Canadian. Ahead of us, here, is Capitol Hill."

"Where the capitol is?"

"No, ma'am. It's north and east. This here's oil country."

She let the puzzling statement pass. A peculiar smell in the air had intensified. She jerked up straight at the sight of skeletonlike structures silhouetted by burning flares. Below them, mud ran red, like blood. The area teemed with workmen, some shirtless, demonic in the lurid light.

"Oil patch," Charlie explained laconically. "Take some gettin' used to. Got four, five close to camp."

"Camp?"

"Where you're gonna live," he explained. "Me an' Dave work for Tremenco Oil. Got their own housing. Ain't much, but it's a roof. Work the evenin' tour." He pronounced the word, in oil-field fashion, as *tower*. It was only later that Amantha would learn its true spelling.

"Then you should be working now? I've taken you from your jobs?" Let that be the reason for David's moodiness. Please God, let there be a reason!

"No, ma'am. Evenin' tour's from noon to midnight. Mornin's Dave an' me work over to Drumright, on a wildcat we got shares in."

Sensing her confusion, he stopped. "Ain't ol' Dave wrote you about it?"

"No—He didn't mention it." That was better than confessing he hadn't written at all for a year.

"Better let him fill you in, then."

They drove on in uneasy silence. David slept, chin on

chest, empty glass jar in his hand. None of this was real: the oil patches straight from Dante's *Inferno;* the fact that she was seated in a jolting truck between a semiliterate man and a drunken husband, heading for an unknown destination; Nanny and Peter lost somewhere in the city behind them. . . .

They turned into an unpaved road, the Model-T slithering from side to side, throwing her against David, against the driver's lanky frame.

"Hang on to your hat," Charlie shouted above the laboring engine. "Only ten, twelve more miles."

Amantha sat immersed in the tangle of her thoughts, and Charlie was silent as he concentrated on keeping the vehicle on the road.

They stopped at a low frame building with a sign that read Merk's Gas and Groceries. The store was closed, its windows dark. From a shedlike extension behind it sounded the stamping of feet, laughter, music.

"Tell me why you lie-yi-yi to me," the words to the tune wailed through the night, *"You honky-tonk an' slip around on me-ye-ye—"*

David spoke for the first time, coming instantly awake. "What the hell you doing, Charlie?"

"Thought mebbe Missus Merk would open up and sell us some milk or something. Nuthin' in the house—"

"Forget it."

Charlie shrugged. "Suit yourself." He reentered the cab and they were moving again, David lapsing into a belligerent silence.

Within a mile or two they turned into a lane that led through flat terrain. On the horizon flares burned, derricks apparent as they neared. In the midst of them stood a collection of narrow buildings almost obscured by rain. Charlie pulled up before one of them and shut off the engine.

"Home, sweet home," he said wryly.

David revived enough to carry Amantha to the house, sliding and stumbling in the red mud. Setting her over the threshold, he called to Charlie to bring her luggage. Amantha looked in stunned silence at her new home.

The structure was long and narrow, one room wide. The

front room was floored with linoleum. Ragged lace curtains drooped at the windows; a torn shade hung crazily. Against an oatmeal-papered wall sat a sprung sofa. Another chair leaked cotton stuffing. The small enamel heater evidently hadn't been lit for a long time. The room was damp, with a smell of mice and mildew. Through a door Amantha could see a grimy sink overflowing with dirty dishes.

David sank into a chair, evading her eyes. It was Charlie who, after bringing in her suitcase and trunk, knelt to light the heater.

"Guess I better be goin'," he said, rising to his feet.

"Hell, no," Dave said. "We're gonna have a party, celebrate! Sit down, Charlie! Talk to m'bride!" He staggered into the kitchen for glasses and came back with them and a filled jar.

"Merk's best bootleg booze," he said. "Cheers."

Charlie Forbes made only a token display of drinking. "Ol' Dave's in hawg heaven, you bein' here," he drawled, smiling at Amantha. "Don't usually tie one on like this."

She sensed that he was trying to comfort her, making excuses for his friend. And, for the first time, she saw him as a person: tall, lean, slow-moving; a nice face, kind eyes—

But she wished he would go home! She must get David to stop drinking, talk to him—

A terrible thought entered her mind.

She excused herself and went through the filthy kitchen into a room with two dirty, tumbled beds. It was true, then! The man, Charlie, lived here—with David.

Surely she would not be expected to sleep in the same room!

She opened the rear door. It led to a cluttered porch. At one side was the sanitary convenience; a tiny room with a leaking toilet, a soiled shower, a sink grimed with oily residue. Amantha turned the tap. It ran a thin stream of rusty red. When it cleared a little, she rinsed her hot face.

She would not live like this! She would not bring Peter here! And Nanny, after having an apoplectic fit, would write her mother and Ian straightaway!

She marched back to the front room. "David—"

The front door slammed open as she said his name, and Amantha gasped in astonishment.

A girl stood there, an Indian girl in full ceremonial dress. The beaded doeskin of her costume was drenched with rain, black hair plastered against copper cheeks. She was beautiful—

And intoxicated.

"They told me at Merk's," she mumbled. "I came to see—"

Charlie was on his feet. He moved toward the girl, putting an arm around her. "Come on, Rosie. I'll drive you home."

The girl struck out at him. "No," she said, her dark eyes fierce with concentration. "I want—"

"You want to go home." Charlie shepherded her outside, turning to say, "See you folks in the mornin'."

The door closed behind him.

Amantha looked at her husband. "Who was that?"

His face was red. "Just Rosie. She hangs around Merk's."

"But—what was she doing here?"

"Hell, I dunno. Ask Charlie."

"Charlie lives here, doesn't he?" David's silence was answer enough. "Well, where is he going to sleep?"

"He'll find a place to bed down."

"With that—that Indian?"

"Dammit, Amantha, he's a grown man! What difference does it make?"

"He's brought her here, hasn't he, David? To this house! I don't mind being poor, David. But you've got to remember I have certain standards. I won't have people of low moral character around Peter."

He stared at her, then gave a whoop of mirthless laughter.

"By God, you sound just like Nanny!" He rose to his feet. "Well, my prim little English rose, it's about time you got what you came for!"

He scooped her up and carried her back to the room he'd shared with Charlie, ignoring her protests as he fumbled clumsily at her clothing, ripping her blouse. Then she was in a tumbled bed that smelled of oil and sweat, enduring a brutal lovemaking that was akin to rape. She tried to close her ears to the things he was saying, her senses to what he was doing.

24

"David, you're hurting me—"

He finally fell away to lie in drunken slumber. Amantha stared at the ceiling, bruised, violated, thinking of green meadows, a shepherd's cot—of a man who loved her gently, sweetly, on a fragrant, grassy bed.

What had happened to the laughing boy she married?

Once, she thought dully, she'd promised to go with him anywhere. And here she was, in his red world. The flares from the oil wells flickered in the room, dancing on the ceiling, making highlights on David's sleeping face.

He looked like the devil himself.

Perhaps he was.

"No," she moaned, half aloud. He moved at the sound and threw a heavy arm across her. She lay still, imprisoned, trying to justify his actions to herself.

Everything would be better in the morning. It was only a question of cleaning this house, getting rid of David's undesirable friends.

This was David, David, whom she loved. If this were his world, she would have to make the best of it.

Curling close to him, pretending the five-year gap in their lives did not exist, Amantha fell asleep; the scent of oil in her nostrils, the rhythmic sound of a pumpjack in her ears.

Chapter Four

*A*mantha woke to a man's shout. *"Set them tongs, damn you!"*

She sat up. The voice that seemed to have originated in the room had carried from a drilling rig, some distance away. It was morning. Somehow she'd slept through the unquiet night.

A faint, lemony light seeped through the ragged shade at the window, pointing up her sordid surroundings.

She looked at David. He slept with one arm thrown above his head, brown chest bared above the soiled sheets, looking absurdly young.

As for herself, she felt old; aching from her long journey and his rough lovemaking. She longed for a hot bath, clean sheets.

Tears filled her eyes and she blinked them away. There was much to do, and she must prepare the place before Peter and Nanny arrived.

She thought of home, of Cook, and of the cleaning women. Amantha had never learned the arts of housekeeping. Her family was far from wealthy. They maintained no second home in London as their neighbors did. But, as her father had inherited from his, the positions of service had been passed down among the tenants in his domain.

Amantha's home had been self-sufficient, though she hadn't realized it until now.

Slipping from bed, she surveyed the remains of her clothes on the floor; rumpled, torn, the blouse beyond wearing. Her case was still in the front room, but she dared not pass through the house as she was. The sound of male activity outside was loud in her ears.

Donning her skirt, her jacket in lieu of the torn blouse, she hurried to her luggage. She selected an old lawn dress with soft sleeves that would push above her elbows; clean underthings, a handkerchief that would serve as washcloth. Then she went back to the convenience, noting with dismay that there was no lock on the door. Swollen with the damp, it didn't quite close.

Amantha washed at the rusty tap. Then, refreshed, if not clean, she dressed. There was no clothes cupboard in the bedroom, only a series of hooks, most of them festooned with faded work clothing. Making space for her own, she tiptoed into the kitchen.

She'd had an idea of fixing breakfast, but there was no way to begin. There was no soap. The dishes in the sink were coated with grease. The small icebox in a corner was dark and evil-smelling, containing half a bottle of soured milk, a few bread ends, a partially peeled hard-boiled egg.

At home there would be tea, scones, a myriad of dishes on the sideboard, kept warm beneath silver covers.

She would not think of home.

A battered coffeepot stood on the stove, a can of coffee beside it. She rinsed the pot and studied it. There were markings on the side and on the basket it contained. It appeared the lower part was for water, the upper for coffee.

She filled it, quite proud of herself—then realized she did not know how to light the stove, or how long coffee should boil before it was done.

She rinsed two cups. A towel, hanging above the sink, was evidently used for drying, but it was gray and sour-smelling. Amantha set the cups on the table, wet, removing a stack of paper covered with figures and sketches. The table was littered with crumbs. At least the towel would do to brush them away.

She reached for it, and a large insect, amber-brown, ran across her hand. In horror, she saw the wall was swarming with the things.

With a small scream, Amantha backed into the center of

the room, the ugliness of it all sweeping over her, drowning her.

The incessant noise! The mud, the filth!

Charlie, with his Indian mistress!

David, intoxicated, his brutal treatment!

Nanny and Peter—How could she bring them here?

She put her hands to her face and began to cry.

"Amantha—"

David stood in the doorway, barefoot, clad only in a pair of trousers. His black hair was tousled, his face pale. His eyes were troubled and filled with pity.

She ran to him and he held her against his heart, soothing her. "I'm sorry, sweetheart! I'm so goddam sorry—"

When her sobs had subsided, he led her to a chair and padded across to the stove. Hefting the coffeepot, he saw what she'd done and made a small sound of approval. He lit the stove, set the pot over the flame, and went back to the bedroom. When he emerged, he was dressed in clean, faded, blue work shirt and trousers.

He poured a cup of bitter black liquid for each of them, then sat down opposite her, running his fingers through his hair.

"God, my head hurts!" He attempted a smile. "I don't go for more than a couple of drinks as a rule. But, last night—I don't remember much about it," he confessed. "I didn't . . . hurt you?"

"No," she lied.

"I was scared as hell," he said simply. "I wasn't going to send for you until I could give you the things you're used to. Another year, maybe two. Then you show up on my doorstep, complete with kid and Nanny. I didn't see how I could handle it. Still don't, goddam it."

"If you didn't want me here, why did you marry me?"

Again, he ran his fingers through his hair in a gesture of frustration. "It was different then. Oh, hell, Amantha, it's a long story."

"I should like to hear it," she said evenly.

He leaned forward, propping himself with his elbows, fingers at his temples.

It was, indeed, a long story.

David's father was wealthy, a self-made, self-taught man; his mother a product of an exclusive school back east. They'd been constantly at war over their son's upbringing. His dad figured work and experience were more important than education. His mother insisted upon schooling, a smattering of culture.

To the point when he'd gone to Cambridge, David's mother won out. Then he had blown it, marrying an English girl.

Amantha's face flamed. "I don't see—"

"Dad had a wife picked out for me," David said roughly. "An oil tycoon's daughter. Hell, it wasn't going to be a marriage, but a merger!"

The old man withdrew his allowance. If David wished to send for his bride, he would have to earn her passage. He would have to do it as his father had, starting at the bottom of the ladder; roustabout, roughneck. . . .

He took every shitty job his old man handed him, sticking around for his mother's sake. She died, leaving him enough for a stake.

"David, you didn't tell me."

"Didn't have time," he said grimly. He'd walked out of the house and come here, determined to beat his dad at his own game; he'd make him look like a piker.

This place was lousy with oil. All you had to do was get it out of the ground. But it took expensive equipment, big rotary rigs in the fields around the city.

He and Charlie worked the rotaries on the evening tour, living on twenty dollars a week, socking the rest away. They usually left the camp at three in the morning and drove to Drumright, where they worked a cable rig on shares. A buddy of Charlie's had a little piece of land. He, Charlie, and two others had picked up an old rig, cheap, and skidded it in. Until a month ago they'd been changing off, two to a shift. But then they ran into a problem.

"We got into what they call redbeds," David said morosely. "You see, you put down a twenty-inch casing, but the redbeds are—well—cavey. Have to go down with an underreamer, clean it out. Damned thing's stuck down there. The other two

29

quit on us, and we bought up their shares. Charlie and I have been working like hell—''

If they could free the tool, if the wildcat well came in, the proceeds would be divided three ways. His share and Charlie's would be enough to accomplish the job they'd set out to do: put down a rotary on some land that was Charlie's, free and clear, leased to nobody.

When that well came in, they'd purchase another, then another. . . .

"It will. Charlie's got a nose for oil, and he owns the land. I've got the know-how. And one of these days—well, the sky's the limit! You can visit your folks wearing diamonds and furs! And that's a promise!''

She didn't want them, Amantha thought drearily. She wanted David, Peter, a small neat house. And David's letters had mentioned none of this. Even in the beginning, he hadn't shared his problems or his dreams.

"I didn't want you to have to come to something like this, Amantha. But I'm glad you're here.'' David cocked his head to one side, looking like Peter when he'd confessed to naughtiness—and knew he'd be forgiven.

There was a knock at the front door. David answered and returned, grinning. "It was ol' Charlie. He stayed the night with the Springers, next door. Said I was welcome to his truck, to pick up Nanny and the kid. Anna's coming over to help you clean up some. No rush. I got a couple of other errands to run.''

Who was Anna? And how could the two men make such a decision without consulting her? To have another woman see this—this chaos! For a moment Amantha was rigid, then she sagged. She must be sensible. She had no idea where to begin.

Peter and Nanny were coming to this dreadful place. She needed help.

Chapter Five

The mystery of Anna was solved on the heels of David's departure. She was announced by a crashing at the rear door.

Amantha hurried to answer it. Beyond the screen was what appeared to be a large box with legs, a broom and mop leaning at angles. The box was set down with a bang, revealing a woman behind it; a gaunt little creature with hair in tight, knobby braids, bony cheekbones, and inquisitive eyes.

"You're Dave's wife. Hell, you don't look like his type. I'm Anna Springer."

Without waiting for an invitation, she pulled off muddy boots and walked barefoot into the house.

"Reg'lar boar's nest," she said cheerfully.

From the box she produced a plate covered with a white towel, and a jar, similarly wrapped, and she carried them through the bedroom to the kitchen.

The plate, when she whisked the towel away, held scrambled eggs and—scones?

"Biscuits. And this here's coffee."

The aroma from the liquid she poured out of the jar was wonderful.

Anna lifted the lid of the pot on the stove and sniffed. "Wheee-ooo! This'll rust your pipes! Hafta boil it out once in a while. Now, you—" she pointed a bony finger at Amantha, "set and eat! I'll get started."

She returned to the screened porch for her cleaning supplies and set to work like a whirlwind.

Water was boiled, a bar of soap appeared. "This here's

31

Crystal White," she said chattily. "Some uses Fels naphtha. Glad I brought some clean rags. This goddam dishrag's died! Never get rid of them damn roaches, not with the Skaggs in camp! But we can fix it so they won't feel so to home! Brought some carbolic acid solution to wipe down the baseboards and cupboard. Lye water on the floor—"

Within an hour, the kitchen was shining. And in that hour Amantha learned how to use the stove and that the icebox should be cleaned periodically with "sody-water." The instructions included the drip pan from which Anna vigorously scrubbed dried scum.

"Men," she snorted. "When it comes to keeping clean, pigs got more sense!"

Like a small, ugly wren, Anna flitted from room to room, chattering as she worked. Amantha watched and listened, fascinated. Everybody, Anna expounded, knowed Dave had money. But he was a goddam tightwad! Amantha oughta make him buy her one of them new e-lectric gy-rators. They was fifty-nine fifty at Montgomery Ward's. No sense using a rub board, unless she had to. Amantha oughta take them whorehouse curtains down. Shades was only fifty cents apiece at Freeman Langston's. Sears had a sale on housedresses—

Sheets were whisked from the beds. Anna inspected the striped ticking carefully. "At least you ain't got bedbugs," she said, vaguely disappointed at not discovering a new challenge. "This stuff's gotta be washed, the blankets aired, but ain't no use 'til the sun shines."

Amantha opened the chest of discards from her home in England. There were soft linens to replace the soiled sheets. Ragged blankets were supplanted by down-filled quilts. Anna's eyes popped at sight of the magnificent silver service—for which they could find no place.

She disappeared for a time and returned, wagging a small drop-leaf table. "Got it at a junk sale," she puffed. "Two bucks. Damn thing's just in my way."

She polished it diligently, covering a cigarette burn with a doily from Amantha's trunk, and placed the silver service in the center.

Massive, priceless, it dominated the small front room.

Frayed upholstery was whipstitched, covered with Amantha's two shawls. Curtains were mended, still on their rods.

"Just making do," Anna said determinedly, "till you get something better."

As they worked, Anna gave a vitriolic rundown on the neighbors. Earl Skaggs was a roughneck. Him and his woman, Edna, lived common-law. Edna was jolly enough, but a lazy slob with the filthiest house in the row and a passel of red-headed kids that would take anything not nailed down.

Maybelle Mitchell, married to a tool dresser, was something else! Anna stopped working and posed, little finger thrust out, speaking as though her mouth were filled with warm treacle.

"Ah wouldn't be wheah ah am, if mah grandaddy's plantation wasn't destroyed durin' the Civil Wah." Anna gestured to the right, simpering. "On one side, ah'm kin to Gennul Lee. On the othah"—she pointed to the left—"to Jeff Davis, bless his sweet soul!"

Amantha understood little of what she was saying, but she couldn't help laughing at her exaggerated actions.

"You oughta do that more often," Anna said pointedly. "Ain't no flies on Dave when it comes to the ladies."

Another incomprehensible statement.

Anna finally leaned her mop against the back porch and threw the mop water into the yard. "Now you're gonna have company," she said sourly. "Watch!"

Almost immediately, a woman and a young girl appeared at the front door. Edna Skaggs and her daughter Florrie. Plump, blowsy, smiling, they were almost identical, except for age. Edna carried a hot peach pie that gave forth a mouth-watering aroma.

"Canned them peaches myself," she beamed as she proffered her gift to her new neighbor.

"Worm to ever jar," Anna snipped. "Florrie, take them shoes off! We just mopped this floor!"

No sooner had the guests been admitted and seated on the sofa than another knock sounded. Anna answered the door.

"Maybelle," she said. "Good of you to wait 'til we got

33

through cleanin'. Don't know what the hell we'd of done with a little help.''

Amantha strove to make up for Anna's rudeness. "You must be Maybelle Mitchell,'' she said enthusiastically. Then, looking at the plate the woman offered, "What lovely little biscuits!''

Maybelle's childlike features clouded as she looked at her gift uncertainly. "These are cookies.''

Amantha was confused. Scones were biscuits. Biscuits were cookies. Would she ever be able to communicate with these people? She opened her mouth to apologize for her ignorance, but there was no need. Maybelle had seen the silver service. With a squeal of delight, she hastened to inspect it. Little fingers on each hand extended, she spoke in her treacly voice.

"Mah goodness! It's so lahk mah ol' grandmama's! A fam'ly heirloom? It is?'' Another girlish squeal.

"Ah could tell you had breedin' the minute ah laid eyes on you. So nice to have someone heah of mah type, someone who can undahstand—''

"I think we all understand you, Maybelle,'' Anna interrupted. "It's standin' you that's the goddam problem!''

Maybelle puckered again, then chose to pass her words off as a jest. "Oh, you!'' She waggled a playful hand. "Always spoofin' little ol' me!''

Anna allowed the guests exactly fifteen minutes, then herded them out. Dave would be home soon. Wouldn't want his house full of gossiping old hens. They left, reluctantly, and Anna sagged against the door she closed behind them.

"Wheee-ooo,'' she gasped. Then, "Well?''

"They seem very nice. And I appreciate their welcome.''

Anna made a face. "I'd better take my own advice and get the hell out of here.'' She waved away Amantha's thanks. "Forget it. Got myself a new boarder, so I gotta go start Charlie's supper.''

"Anna, wait.'' Amantha stumbled over her words, wondering how to put what she was going to ask. "What is Charlie Forbes really like?''

"Everbody's friend,'' Anna said, her sharp voice softening a little.

"I received that impression last night," Amantha said, flushing. "An Indian girl came to the door. She was quite intoxicated, and Mr. Forbes took her home. The—the relationship is rather irregular, according to David, and I'm concerned that—"

Anna's birdlike eyes were snapping, her knobby cheekbones red. "Hell," she said finally, "don't make a federal case out of it. Charlie ain't a married man." Picking up her box of supplies, she left without further ado.

Amantha was disturbed at their parting. Anna had seemed both angry and embarrassed. Amantha didn't blame her. She'd had no business asking questions regarding the morals of David's friends.

But it did seem that Charlie Forbes was going to be a part of her new life—whether she liked the notion or not.

Amantha wandered through the house, trying to see it with Nanny's eyes. It looked much better now that it was clean. But it was a far cry from what Nanny was accustomed to. She'd have to sleep on the sagging sofa in the front room, until they could work out a better arrangement.

The asthmatic sound of Charlie's truck alerted her. David was home. Nanny and Peter would be with him. For a moment she stood rooted, unable to trust her trembling knees. Then the door flew open and David entered, carrying a block of ice.

"Get this in the box. I'll bring the rest of the groceries. Pete's carrying the bread."

Amantha flew to do his bidding, then turned back. In the doorway stood a small boy in overalls, a boy who looked older than Peter Carmody, his features thinner.

Peter, in cheap new farm boy's clothing, his blond curls shorn.

Amantha couldn't find her voice, but stood staring at the child who was a stranger to her. David passed through the room again, kissing her on the nape of the neck.

"Looks good, doesn't he? By the way, I got rid of Nanny. Old bitch flew into me for taking my own kid to the barber. I palmed her off on a guy who had a gusher come in. His wife thinks having an English nanny'll improve her social life."

"David! No!"

"David, yes," he grinned impishly, mimicking her tone. "Old girl was happy as a clam. Sent you this." He fumbled in his pocket, producing a note covered with Nanny's firm writing.

"I considered returning to England," it read, *"but feel it my duty to remain nearby. Therefore, I have accepted another position and intend to write your dear mother, telling her the reasons for my having done so. I am including my address for future reference. Do not contact me until you have come to your senses and rid yourself of that dreadful man."*

Oh, Nanny, Nanny!

Amantha's eyes glistened with tears. She pitied the old, domineering woman, alone in a strange land, stubbornly clinging to her sense of duty like a dog to a bone. And with her pity, Amantha felt a sense of guilt. Guilt at the wave of relief that swept over her. She was free! Free to be herself, free to love David, to care for her own child as she'd always wished.

And, whatever dire indictments were in the letter Nanny wrote home, she had not seen this poverty-stricken little shack that would be Amantha's home. She could not blame David for this—

Amantha wiped at her eyes, feeling as if she were torn in two. She supposed she had one thing in common with Nanny. A sense of duty. And now her loyalties must be divided.

Dave passed her, whistling, on his way back to the truck for another load. Amantha relieved Peter of his burden and knelt, arms around him, her cheek wet against his cropped hair.

"Peter—"

"Pete," the child corrected her. "Dad says my name is Pete, Mum. I shall be his helper." Wriggling away, he was out the door to join David.

Amantha had never felt so lost, or so alone.

Chapter Six

The days that followed were bittersweet ones. David's first act was to remove the couch from the front room to the back porch. It was replaced with Peter's bed, giving them privacy in their bedroom. Again, David's lovemaking was sweet and tender. Amantha knew, helplessly, that she loved him enough to bear this life—or any other that he chose.

She saw little of him. He came in after midnight, leaving before dawn. After he had gone, Amantha would go to Peter's bed and hold him, telling him tales of England; of a visit to London, when she caught a glimpse of the king; of Buckingham Palace; of royal coaches drawn by horses with nodding plumes.

She talked of home with its green meadows and hedgerows; herself a little girl in a white dress with blue-ribbon sash, playing lawn games with her brother, Ian.

Peter listened gravely. He was a mannerly child—too mannerly, according to David—and she wasn't certain how much he remembered. But she had a desperate need to impart something of his background to him, to prove he was born in surroundings better than his present ones.

Later, in a flurry of guilt, she would scrub, cook, and clean in an effort to make up for what seemed like disloyalty to David. She prayed the sun would shine, the muddy yard would dry. And when it did she longed miserably for the rain.

The only tree in camp stood at the rear of the Carmody compound. It was here the men from the nearby rigs gathered to eat their lunch. Their language was too foul for Peter's ears. And Amantha's laundry tubs were situated on a bench against the rear porch. Rubbing bar soap over soiled clothing, scrubbing against the corrugated washboard, Amantha heard the men sniggering. Her skirts blew as she hung flapping sheets on a sagging line. There were lewd comments from the watchers.

David was equally amused at her complaints. "Hell, honey, give 'em a treat!"

She insisted that they loaf somewhere else. He refused to deprive them of the only shade. She begged for an electric gyrator, such as Anna mentioned. He reminded her of the need to save money.

If the wind blowing her skirts embarrassed her, she could get a pair of boy's pants at Freeman Langston's for a dollar. . . .

Amantha, reared as a docile child in a serene, well-ordered world, wanted to rail out at her husband; to tell him he was much too miserly; to show him her bleeding hands where she'd scrubbed the skin away on the corrugated board.

Instead, she smoothed her limp hair back in a gesture of hopelessness. David had not sent for her. She had come along on her own, increasing his expenses, upsetting his timetable.

She swallowed her angry words.

It was Peter who suffered most on the long hot days. He, for all his haircut and overalls, was a strange bird in the flock of Skaggs children who fought, screamed, and played violent, tussling games. His first excursion outside brought him a bruised eye and a bleeding nose.

David's reaction was one of disgust. The red-headed child who struck his son was younger and smaller. Pete needed a few lessons in self-defense. Peter did not agree. He cried, further angering his father. Amantha sided with Peter. It precipitated their first quarrel.

Worst of all, Anna Springer sided with David. "Hell," she snorted, "It's dawg eat dawg around here. Kid's gotta learn!"

But then Anna was childless. She couldn't possibly understand.

When the hazing didn't stop, Amantha finally went to Edna Skaggs with her story. The big woman heard her out, placidly chewing at the twig that was always in her mouth, conveying the snuff that stained the creases to her chin.

"I'll talk to Curtis," she said. "Ask him not to hit Pete no more. But you know how it is. Boys will be boys."

Maybelle Mitchell was sympathetic. She and her man had only one child, Chauncey. He was down south in a military school.

"Ah've suffahed," Maybelle said, clasping her heart. "But evahthing heah is so rough an' tacky, ah couldn't see bringin' up a chile in these surroundin's. If you-all would like to send Petah theah, ah have some influence. Mah cousin, once removed, on the Davis side—"

"Thank you, Maybelle. David wouldn't allow it, I'm certain."

Maybelle nodded. "He is a tightwad, ain't he? You'd think with all his money . . ." She wagged her head, sadly.

Another reference to David's money. How much did he have? Enough to maintain a better standard of living? Amantha put the thought from her.

For the rest of the week she remained in the house, keeping Peter with her.

She did not see Charlie Forbes, due to the rigid working schedule he and David maintained. In the early dawn there would be the chuffing sound of his truck, the honking of a horn, and David would join him for the drive to Drumright.

From what David said, he and Charlie came perilously close to a quarrel. A statue, to be called *The Pioneer Woman*, was to be unveiled at Ponca City, with a big ceremony. It was Charlie's idea to take the day off and drive them all up in his truck. It was time Amantha got to know something of her new land.

David flatly refused. They'd lose time on the Drumright rig and a day's pay from Tremenco. Charlie was a damned fool where money was concerned.

Despite her distaste for Charlie's company, Amantha was disappointed. Suddenly it seemed imperative to get away from the noise of shouting, swearing men on the surrounding rigs; from the sound of pumpjacks pounding at her temples.

Anna came to her rescue. Once a week, she appropriated

her husband's Model-A and shopped in the city. Every woman needed a day on the town once in awhile. She enjoyed showing her shy little British friend the sights: Reno Street, with its upstairs rooms and loose women; the boarded window places, masquerading as dance palaces, that were really speakeasies; the Trianon, more respectable, where one danced above Utterbach's type shop on California Street. Men hitching jerkily along California, panhandling; 'jakelegs,' victims of bad rum.

Amantha, Peter on her lap, gazed with awe as they drove along Main, with its stores both plain and fancy; Kress's, John A. Brown's department store, the Criterion Theater; the new Midwest, still under construction; Montgomery Ward at the corner of Main and Walker.

Ward's was having a sale. Housedresses a buck apiece. Anna suggested they take a look.

"Perhaps another time."

"Dammit, honey, in a month or two it'll be hotter than the hubs of hell! Damn near everything you got is wool! You-all are gonna need some cotton dresses."

"I'll manage with what I have."

"Dave don't have to know," Anna argued, damning him for being a skinflint. "You can save it on your groceries. Look, Dave's been buyin' Louis coffee, thirty-nine cents a pound. You can get Standard Special for nineteen. He won't know the difference! Then, if you buy your compound— shortenin'—in bulk, it's only ten a pound, where—"

"I have sufficient clothing, Anna."

"Oh, hell, forget it!"

Anna drove up Broadway, pointing out the Huckins, the Skirvin, and the new thirty-three-story Biltmore. Then she went on to the majestic state capitol, which looked out on Lincoln Boulevard. Afterward she criss-crossed the residential areas behind it, seeing Amantha's eyes widen at the mansionlike homes that bespoke gracious living.

"I'm quite amazed," Amantha admitted. "I had presumed the rest of the city to be like—well—"

"Like the dump we live in? Don't kid yourself, honey. But

speaking of dumps, we better get our groceries and head for home.''

''Wait, Anna—''

There was an odd note in Amantha's voice. Anna looked at her curiously.

Amantha took a folded paper from her purse, reading off an address. ''Would you know how to find this place?''

Anna pursed her lips. ''We're in the right neighborhood.'' She looked keenly at Amantha. ''Didn't know you knowed anybody in town.''

''I don't,'' Amantha stammered. ''I would just . . . like to see the house.''

Anna wasn't dumb. If Amantha wanted to keep her lip buttoned, it was her business. Anna skillfully steered the shabby little car through the streets of the wealthy area around the capitol. She finally parked across the street from a mansion built in the southern style, with sweeping steps, and white pillars reaching two stories, framing an ornate door with an arch of colored glass.

''There she is,'' Anna said in a slightly awed tone. ''Now, I call that one helluva house!''

Amantha studied the facade of Nanny Goforth's new home. At this hour she would be putting a small child down for a nap, giving lessons in manners and deportment to an older one. Nanny's days were rigidly disciplined.

For a moment she felt a wave of nostalgia for the past, where nothing changed, when there was time for rest. She had felt safe and secure. . . .

She did not wish those years back, but she still felt a twinge of guilt about Nanny. There was no doubt that she was better off here, but she wished she could talk to her. Explain—

She bit her lips surreptitiously and pinched some color into her cheeks.

''Anna, tell me honestly, how do I look.''

Anna's gaze turned from the mansion to her friend. ''Well,'' she said judiciously, ''you're a little peaked. And it's no damn wonder, wearing that outfit in this heat.'' Her angular face softened in a grin. ''I reckon you do purty good for the wife of a damn oilie—''

41

The wife of an oilie, living in a shotgun shack in the oil patch. Nanny Goforth was living much more comfortably than she. It was time to stop worrying about what couldn't be helped; she must devote her attention to her husband and her son.

She had done her duty to the best of her ability.

Amantha settled back, giving her friend a wan smile. "I guess we'd better get on with our shopping."

Anna put the car in gear, still mystified at Amantha's desire to see this one particular house. For a minute there, she acted like she was thinking about going in. Well, if her new friend wanted to talk about it, she would. If not—what the hell! Right now, they'd head to Kanaly's for groceries.

Under Anna's excellent tutelage, Amantha learned the art of economy buying. One purchased oleo, two pounds for twenty-nine cents, rather than butter. Each package of the white lardlike substance contained a packet of coloring. When mixed, it made a suitable spread.

A picnic ham at sixteen cents per pound was a better buy than steak at seventeen and a half. The meat made several meals, and the bone could be boiled with beans, noodles, and the like.

Apple butter for Peter at twenty-three cents a quart. Oatmeal. Sugar. Rice. And puffed cereal, inexpensive because it was made right here on the west side of the city, shot from guns that boomed day and night.

Flour. Salt. Baking powder. Yeast. The list went on.

For vegetables they went to the public market on Exchange. Later the stalls would be laden with local produce. Now they bought only vegetables that were keepers: potatoes, onions, turnips, and winter squash.

Amantha was ecstatic at the quantities she'd purchased so carefully. Finished, she still had five left of the twenty she could afford to spend. Anna, frugal herself, did an unprecedented thing.

She bought a toy from a dispirited hawker; a small furry rabbit that leaped at the pressure of a bulb. She'd seen the longing in Peter's eyes, echoed in his mother's, and known Amantha wanted to buy it—but didn't dare.

"Hell," Anna growled, pressing it into the delighted boy's hands. "You're only a kid once."

On the way back to camp, Anna chattered away about the state capitol; how the state seal was stolen from Guthrie in the night and brought to its new home. Peter played with his new toy, and Amantha was silent.

"Someday," Amantha finally said, "when David strikes oil, we're going to buy one of those beautiful houses we saw today."

Anna kept her eyes on the road and her mouth shut. She couldn't tell this poor child that her dreams weren't likely to come true. For one thing, putting a well down was always a gamble. For another, even if Dave brought in a gusher, he wasn't going to be satisfied. Every cent he made would go right back into a damn hole in the ground!

Anna had known too many of them.

She removed one hand from the wheel and reached out to touch Amantha's; a rare gesture of affection on the part of tough little Anna Springer.

"Look," she said. "There's Charlie's truck. What the hell they doing home this time of day?"

Chapter Seven

*D*ave Carmody and Charlie Forbes were grinning like monkeys. They'd done it. They had dislodged the errant underreamer from the Drumright hole, and now they could begin drilling again. The joke was on their former partners, who hadn't had the guts to hang in there.

They'd taken leave of their Tremenco tours, because this was a night for celebration. "Put your glad rags on, honey," David exulted. He lifted Amantha from her feet and swung her around. "We'll get these groceries in."

Blushing, Amantha fled to dress.

Most of her wardrobe consisted of utilitarian woolens suited to the cool, damp British countryside. She donned her one dressy dress, gray-blue, bloused at the waist, and small matching pumps. Then she went to meet David and Charlie. They wore clean work clothes, hair slicked down, still sparkling with water.

Amantha paused, puzzled. Were they going as they were? David's dancing eyes darkened as he studied her. "Hell, sweetheart, don't you have anything fancier than that?"

"She looks real nice," Charlie drawled.

Florrie Skaggs, Edna's teenage daughter, who was to stay with Peter until their return, gawked at Amantha.

"I think she looks real classy," she pronounced.

The compliments failed to soothe Amantha's feelings. The damage had been done. Some of the enchantment had gone out of the evening.

She kissed Peter good-bye and they left the house. Amantha

grew increasingly nervous as they traversed the rutted lane and turned onto the road. Would they go, perhaps, to one of the large hotels she'd seen today? Surely the men wouldn't have worn work clothing if this were the case. Perhaps it was acceptable at the Trianon.

She thought of the speakeasies, disguised as dance palaces, studding Reno Street. Ah, please—not a place like that.

Charlie turned into the drive at Merk's and shut off the engine.

"Here we are," David beamed. He swung Amantha from the seat and led her into the still-open store. Charlie followed.

"Hello there, Mrs. Merk," David addressed a frowsy woman behind the counter. "Anything going on?" Without waiting for an answer, he moved through a rear door into an enormous shedlike room. A jukebox in a corner belted out the melody of "I Got Rhythm." Men in dirty work garb and women in bright housedresses and ankle socks moved erratically to its beat.

Amantha felt overdressed, out of place. "David—"

He'd forgotten her. "Hey Dave," a man shouted over the music. "Heerd you done it!"

David clasped his hands above his head in a winner's gesture. "You're damn right." His friends crowded around him with congratulations. And David, flushed with pleasure, launched into an explanation, trying to speak over the racket, finally giving up.

"Hell, can't hear myself think!"

"Then let's go out back," a man winked. "Get a drop of something to celebrate with."

"Sure thing. Come on, Charlie. You're in on this, too."

Charlie put a staying hand on David's arm, and David flushed. "Goddam! Almost forgot. Daisy," he beckoned to a cheap-appearing girl, "look after my wife, will you? Introduce her around."

Daisy, after a grudging attempt or two, left Amantha standing against a wall. She stood there trembling, anger at David's thoughtlessness growing in her by the minute, grateful that the atmosphere was dim enough to conceal her flaming face.

It was perhaps ten or fifteen minutes that she stood alone,

though it seemed like hours. She jumped when a voice beside her said, "Hello, beautiful."

A tall, tanned young man looked down at her. In contrast to the others, he wore a white shirt and dark trousers. Seeing her expression, his face changed.

"Forgive me. I assumed you were like the rest." He waved a slender hand that bore the now familiar stains of an oil field worker. "To use a stereotyped phrase, What's a nice girl like you doing in a place like this?"

"I'm waiting for my husband," Amantha stammered.

"Then the bigger fool, he," the newcomer said with distaste. "I wouldn't leave my mother alone in this crowd. Tell me, do I detect a British accent? Indeed? I was in London several years ago. Lovely city. But forgive me, I haven't introduced myself. I'm Jeffrey Saunders. And you are—?"

"Amantha Carmody."

"Well, Amantha, would you care to dance?"

She turned up a helpless palm. "I'm not accustomed to this type of dancing. I'm not certain that I could."

He smiled. "Wait."

Leaving her, he went to stand by the nickelodeon. When the music ended, he inserted a coin. The soft, sweet strains of "Pennies from Heaven" filled the room.

Astounded at her own behavior, Amantha let him lead her on the floor. This was what David had brought her here for, wasn't it? Saunders was an excellent dancer. They moved gracefully among the sweating mob attempting to double-time it.

The song ended and the song she'd heard on that first night began.

"Tell me why you lie-yi-yi to me—"

Amantha shivered and stepped away from the tall man looking down at her. "I don't think—"

He nodded with understanding. "Not your kind of music, is it? Let's wait this one out."

He guided Amantha to the wall, where he leaned beside her, smoking a cigarette—not hand rolled, but tailor-made. It was nice to converse with someone of his type, he told her. He'd only been in the oil fields for six months—since the time his old man lost his second million. She reminded him of the girls he'd dated in college.

"Wait—"

Catching the nickelodeon at the right time, he selected "April Showers" and returned to take Amantha in his arms. Off-guard, she relaxed completely, hearing only the music.

He danced her into a far corner. Suddenly the hand that pressed so decorously against her back pulled her closer, the other sliding the length of her body.

"All right, doll," he said in an odd, guttural voice, "let's get out of here! There's a grove of trees down the road a ways—"

"Let me go! What are you doing!"

"Don't be a fool, sweetie! We've gone through all the preliminaries. Now, it's time for some action. You want it as bad as I do."

Amantha's face was flaming. "My husband—"

"Doesn't exist. Like that fake accent. I know what you are, babe! A hot-pants little townie, looking for some excitement. Well, I went along with you, and we've fooled around long enough. Come on—"

He jerked at her arm and she opened her mouth to scream, David's name forming on her lips.

"Good God!" he swore, covering her mouth with his hand. She bit deeply into his palm, and he released her.

She ran through the rear door in search of David.

He and a group of men were holding forth beneath a tree. David had a glass jar tipped to his lips. She ran toward him, tugging at his sleeve.

"David—"

"I'll be in in a minute," he said, shaking her grip loose. "In a minute, dammit!" He turned back to his audience. "Now, the next thing we did—"

She backed away. Charlie was instantly beside her, his gray eyes studying her face.

"What is it, Amantha?"

"I want to go home."

Without another word, he led her around the building and helped her into his truck. "I'll go back for Dave, if you want."

47

"I just want to go home."

He went through the intricate motions required to start the motor, then climbed in. They drove the distance in silence. Reaching the camp, he stopped.

"Want to talk about it?"

His voice was kind, reassuring, and she burst into tears, the tale of her humiliation spilling into the truck's dark, oil-smelling interior.

"Jeff Saunders," Charlie said slowly. "Con man. Worked the leases for a while until he got caught cheatin' the company. Yep, I place him now. Reckon we better get you on in."

He escorted her into the house, where another shock awaited her. Peter was tucked into bed, but Florrie, left to watch him, had found David's jar of bootleg whiskey in the cupboard. She'd helped herself and was grinning foolishly, tipsily.

It was the final note in an evening filled with ugliness. Amantha put her hands to her cheeks. "Get out of here! Leave my house! Do not ever come here again!"

"But Miz Carmody—"

"Trash," Amantha wept. "Oil field trash! I've learned what it's called since I've been here! You're trash! David's trash—"

"Hush, Amantha!"

The sternness of Charlie Forbes's voice stopped her tirade.

"Don't say things you're gonna be sorry for. Now, I'm taking Florrie home, then you an' me are gonna have a little talk!"

They left her standing, every nerve vibrating with rage and repugnance. She, too, would go home. Everyone said David had money. She would insist on enough for her passage and Peter's. He owed her that much!

Charlie returned, the new firmness still in his tone.

"You're gonna listen to me, Amantha Carmody. First off, we're gonna talk about Dave.

"I ain't sayin' Dave done right, treatin' you like he done tonight. You gotta remember, he ain't used to bein' a husband yet. Takes time. And he's plumb wore out! We been workin' around the clock, mebbe three, four hours sleep a night. Froze our tails off in January, gonna fry in July. This thing with the stuck reamer could of blowed his plans sky-high. He's some set up, tonight, I can tell you!''

"I know, Charlie, but—''

"If I was you, I'd keep my mouth shut," he said, overriding her voice. "Dave's gonna be sorry enough in the morning. He needs you, Amantha.

"And then there's Florrie . . .

"Florrie's snagged in a trap. She looks like her ma, which ain't sayin' much, but she's got something Edna ain't. Florrie's smart. Smart enough to know there's more to life than what she's gettin'. Her folks ain't married, an' everybody knows it. She had to quit school to help with them kids. Ain't no hope for her, no future. She thinks you got class. Way I see it, Florrie needs you, too. You can do some good there—or some hurt. It's up to you.''

David needed Amantha.

Florrie needed her.

Amantha hadn't thought of being needed, but of needing. . . .

Always, there had been her mother, her father, her brother; distant, undemonstrative, but there. They had seen to her basic needs. And there had been Nanny, laying out her clothing, setting her bedtime, instilling her prim English manners . . .

Everything had been calm, settled, predictable.

Now it was up to her. She had to make a life for herself, for Peter—and for undependable, hard-working David. She must be the one to do the caring, the nurturing. She had to grow up.

Charlie was gone, and her face was wet with a rain of tears as she made her way to bed. She was still awake, still pondering Charlie's words, when David came in. He was carrying his shoes, moving with exaggerated stealth, stumbling into things.

She pretended sleep.

In the morning David was, as Charlie said he would be, embarrassed, guilty, and contrite. He hadn't meant to leave her standing the previous night. "Time got away from me. Why the hell did you leave like that?''

She was tired, she said, and he seemed to be occupied.

"A little drunk, too," he confessed. "I don't remember much—except the damndest thing! I guess ol' Charlie must have tied one on, too. Never saw him fight before."

"Charlie? Fight?"

"You bet he did! Beat the hell out of a guy named Saunders. Said he didn't like his face."

Charlie—Saunders—Dear God!

"I don't want to talk about Charlie," David said, reaching for her hand. "I want to talk about us. I'm sorry I left you in the lurch like that. Forgive me?"

Amantha looked at the man who wasn't accustomed to being a husband yet; the man who had frozen in January and would fry in July; the man who went on three or four hours sleep to achieve a dream. That dream had almost gone glimmering when he ran into trouble on the Drumright hole. And she could destroy it now, if she walked out on him.

Man? David was no more grown up than she. He was a boy, a boy whose blue eyes pleaded for forgiveness and understanding.

"I'll never do anything like that again," he said huskily, "and that's a promise."

"It's all right, David," she whispered. "I love you."

Now she only had to make her peace with Florrie Skaggs.

Chapter Eight

Florrie appeared at the door the next day, face swollen, eyes red. She didn't know what got into her last night. She guessed it was seeing Miz Carmody dressed up for a party. Florrie hadn't been away from the camp since she left school. Got to thinking about doing nothing but keep care of kids and, well—she took a sip of Dave's whiskey. Made her feel better, so she took another.

"It's all right, Florrie."

The girl burst into tears and Amantha put her arms around her. Finally, Florrie got her emotions under control.

"Wisht I was like you, little and purty—and nice. You said I was trash last night, and I guess I am. You know, my folks ain't even—"

"It makes no difference, Florrie. It's what you are that matters."

"Yeah, sure. A big fat slob. I don't dress right or talk right. And lookut my hair."

Amantha looked. It was the peculiar orange-red that was characteristic of the Skaggs family. Frizzy, encrusted with dirt, it looked like a fright wig. But perhaps something could be done.

"Would you like me to help you arrange it?"

Florrie looked blank, and Amantha hastened to clarify her statement. "Cut it a little, comb it differently?"

Florrie's face shone. Amantha quailed at the job she'd volunteered for. "First," she said stoutly, "we'd better wash it. It'll be easier to style."

51

She set to work, heating rainwater from the barrel under the eaves. Running over to consult Anna, she returned with homemade lye soap. "Cuts the dirt," Anna said, "and gits rid of cooties." At Amantha's uncomprehending expression, she said, "Oh, hell, just use it. Wrench it good with vinegar."

The rain barrel was half empty before the water Amantha poured over the girl's head ran clear. Then she set to work with her sewing shears until she could run a comb through the tangle, finally shaping it all into a cap of soft waves. Florrie's face looked thinner, her blue-gray eyes larger.

Viewing herself in a mirror, Florrie wept. "Oh, Miz Carmody, I cain't believe it."

"Cannot believe it," Amantha corrected her. "A girl as pretty as you are should speak properly."

Thus began the improve-Florrie program. The girl idolized Amantha and was constantly at her heels, aping her mannerisms, her speech. Suggestions as to proper diet helped. Florrie would never be petite, but she began to bloom. Peter was able to play outdoors once more. Florrie guarded his well-being carefully, smacking the bottom of any small brother who attempted to bully him.

Because Florrie worked so hard to prove her new trust-worthiness, Amantha left her to watch over Peter while she made a trip with David and Charlie to the Drumright well.

It was exciting, rising before daylight, leaving the Tremenco camp with its burning flares. They drove through soft darkness, and Amantha envied the silent, sleep-sodden men their daily journey. The air smelled of sweet grass. Then, again, the sulphurous scent of oil became intrusive.

A farmhouse stood to one side of a winding, bumpy lane. On the other, stark against the sky, was a partially open shacklike building. Above it rose a derrick, made of wood. Small, makeshift, it bore no resemblance to the Tremenco rigs.

"There she is," David said proudly.

This was the much-talked-of Drumright well. This was what David had invested his time and money in; what he based his dreams of future wealth on; driving here every day, depriving her of a husband, Peter of a father.

David climbed from the truck and walked toward the rig. Charlie paused. It was Amantha's first sight of their project. She should be shown around.

"Sure," David called back. "If she's interested."

Amantha frowned at the drilling rig that was her rival.

"I am," she said. "I am!"

Charlie helped her from the cab. "Guess it's sorry-looking, compared to what you've seen."

"Not really," she lied.

"The rigs around camp are rotary. Got to go down six, seven thousand feet of sandstone and shale. But cable works good here, maybe better. Them rotaries go too fast, go right through the oil sands before you catch it. But with cable, you get the chance to smell it, taste it."

Reaching the rig, he helped her up three steps to a splintered floor. "Cellar under here. Eight by eight square, twenty feet deep—"

Amantha looked gingerly at the warped boards beneath her feet. "To hold the oil when you find it?"

His low, lazy laugh sounded. "No, ma'am. Just to accommodate the pipe. Comes in twenty-foot lengths." He went on to explain the workings of this type of operation. The hole wasn't as much drilled as pounded out with a bit attached to a drilling string. The drilling string was a heavy length of steel "jars" attached to a cable, providing the weight to force the bit into the ground. The hole was kept empty, except for a little bit of water. They'd drill down a few feet, then remove the debris with a bailer, an open bucketlike tube with a valve at the bottom. Then steel pipe, or casing, was put down to keep the hole from caving in, growing progressively smaller.

Charlie tilted his head upward and pointed. "That there's the crownblock, with the sheaves for handlin' the drillin' line, the sand line, and the casin' line."

He led her to the engine house, displaying a grease-leaking engine. "Rebuilt that ourselves," he said with satisfaction. "Figger it'll last out till we're done."

Then to the derrick floor. "This here's the Samson post. That there's the walkin' beam, connected to the pitman and the crank—"

"Charlie!" David's voice cut him off in mid-sentence. "Get the hell over here. Got to set some casing!"

Amantha moved to sit on the runningboard of the truck. A red sun rose to limn the wooden derrick with a pink glow, then shot higher to blaze down with a white-hot heat. Amantha's face grew damp with perspiration, and she brushed vainly at a swarm of stinging midges. Something in the long grass irritated her, and she scratched at her ankles, alarmed to feel welts rising on them.

On the derrick floor the men worked, shirtless now, their bronzed bodies slippery with sweat: David, stocky, square-shouldered, tireless as a machine; Charlie, slim, long-waisted and slow-moving, somehow keeping pace with him.

"Fry in July," Charlie had said. And, dear lord, it was only June.

David shut the rig down. He and Charlie mopped their faces and donned their shirts. It was time for the trek home. But first they stopped at a small café where a hard-faced waitress called the men by their first names, joking with them familiarly. Amantha stared in dismay at the fat meat floating in the stew.

When they let her out at home, hurrying off to their second job, Amantha went straight to Anna. The welts that rose on her ankles were red and angry. Now the ailment seemed to have reached her waist. It itched awfully, and she felt feverish. She was terrified that it might be some disease she would carry to Peter.

She received no sympathy from Anna.

The wiry little woman took one look and began to laugh. Chiggers. Redbugs. Impossible to avoid in Oklahoma. Little critters that burrowed beneath the skin to lay their eggs. Anna produced a small bottle.

"Take a sody water bath, then dab this on. Cuts off the air and they die."

That night, Peter abed, Amantha stood in the yard and watched the well being drilled nearby. She'd thought it an ugly thing, but compared to what she'd seen today, it was an object of beauty. Clean, structural steel, five steam boilers furnishing its power, bright yellow hoist, a proper crew—

And David had pinned his hopes on that pathetic rig near Drumright. He was killing himself—and Charlie. How could he hope to compete with this?

She put a hand to her face. Still a little feverish. She had obeyed Anna's instructions, and now each welt was properly covered with a coating that felt dry and scaly. The thought of a hundred little creatures dying beneath her skin made her ill.

Even a day's outing had brought misery. She hated Oklahoma, she hated oil and everything to do with it.

Sighing, she went into the house. Tomorrow was the day for laundry. She must get it done before the oil crews sought the shade of her tree.

In the morning she was still feverish and light-headed from the many bites, but she doggedly began to heat water when David and Charlie left for work. By ten o'clock the laundry was done. She pinned the last sheet to the line, her cheeks turning pink at comments borne on the wind, coming from the derrick floor.

Then suddenly there was a rumble that seemed to shake the ground beneath her feet; a hissing, spewing sound, followed by a bellowing roar.

A geyser of oil flung tools into the derrick, a length of casing went flying into the air like an arrow, twisting and turning. Then she could see nothing. Oil spread on the wind in a black, greasy cloud.

Abandoning her laundry, Amantha ran for the house. She closed the windows—too late. Her curtains were black and sodden, the house spattered and reeking, also dark, since the spraying well blocked out the sun.

A banging at the door announced Anna, her knobby features urgent under the oil that smeared them.

"For God's sake, don't light no fires! I was skeert you might have something on the stove—"

Amantha went white. A fire in this deluge could send the camp up in flames. If she'd still been heating water—

"The others," she said weakly, "Maybelle—Edna—"

"Knows what to do," Anna finished for her. "They been around the oil fields a long time."

It was nearly a week before the well was capped; the

tremendous vibration, the gas pressure coming from the mouth of the well, resisted the efforts of the company engineers. During that week, Amantha's linens hung limply on the line, black and dripping.

No food could be cooked. Unable to start the truck for fear a spark might ignite the flowing well, Charlie and David pushed it, by hand, to a spot some distance away. They lost a morning's work bringing home edibles that need not be heated. Canned pork and beans. Bread, peanut butter, bologna. Tins of peaches.

When the well was finally capped, Amantha surveyed the mess hopelessly. Then, as Anna said, she discovered there was no need to worry. A clean-up crew moved in, washing down the outsides of the houses, repainting them inside and out. A mannerly official gave Amantha a check for five hundred dollars to replace her household goods.

David was elated. "We can clean up enough stuff to get by," he said. "This goes in the kitty."

Amantha plucked it from his fingers. "It's mine."

"Dammit, we're in this thing together. I live here, too. If we can use it to build our future—"

"It's also my future, David, and Peter's—"

"I should think you'd want to do your part."

"I am doing it, David. But I will not sleep on beds without sheets, or live in a house without curtains at the windows."

That night he did not come home.

From Anna she learned he'd had Charlie drop him off at Merk's. He was to pick him up at the usual time and they would head for Drumright.

"You two had a scrap?"

Amantha didn't answer. Instead, eyes sparking, she said, "Isn't tomorrow your day for the car? Would you mind taking Peter and me to town with you? I want to spend my oil check."

So that was the way the wind blew! If Anna had other plans, she shelved them promptly. Amantha'd finally got some gumption. And she'd better spend that money while she had the chance.

She did.

There was a new chair and sofa from Harbour Longmires; a carpet for the front room, to cover the worn linoleum. She bought shades at Freeman Langston's, then curtains, sheets, new pillows and cases from Ward's. There was enough left to buy three summery cottons for herself, shirts and trousers for Peter, and sundaes at a soda fountain. The last purchase was a framed picture, depicting green meadows and fat lambs. It reminded Amantha of home.

They carried what they could. The larger items were to be delivered the next day. Again David did not come home. By nightfall, with the help of Anna and Florrie, everything was in place. The little shack looked homelike, attractive, and the feel of cool new sheets in the hot night was heaven.

Toward morning Amantha heard Charlie's truck. She lay holding her breath until her front door opened and closed. David was home. It was going to be all right. She feigned sleep as he undressed and climbed into bed, lying stiffly away from her.

The sound of Charlie's horn woke her. The few hours had passed too quickly. There was David's coffee to make, his Thermos to fill.

She half rose, then realized he still slept.

"David—"

He only twisted and muttered at her touch. His flesh felt hot. He was burning with fever!

Leaping up, she pulled on a robe and ran, barefoot, to the door, beckoning Charlie inside. He left the truck running and ambled toward her, then hurried his step as he saw the urgency in her gestures.

"David's sick! Awfully sick, Charlie."

"Figgered as much last night. I'll have a look at him."

He went to the back room and she made coffee, hands shaking. She could hear Charlie speaking, David's mumbled answers. Maybe he was coherent now.

Charlie emerged, looking grave. "Flu, I guess. Feller on the evenin' tour went off sick the other night. Oughta have a doc, but cain't get one out here. Dave says he'll jump outta the truck if I try to take him in. You know how Dave is, figgers it'll cost him."

Amantha thought guiltily of the five hundred dollars she'd spent so lavishly. It meant so much to David that he stayed away from home. Maybe if she'd seen he was becoming ill, caught it in time—

"I'll go talk to him."

"Best leave him sleep," Charlie said gently. "If I know Dave, ain't nobody gonna change his mind. Needs rest more'n anything. And you hadn't oughta get exposed yourself."

"I'm already exposed, Charlie. Sleeping in the same bed."

"Reckon you're right. Best thing's not to overdo. And there's young Pete in there to think about. If you don't mind, I'll stick around awhile."

"Thank you very much," she said. "Please sit down." She placed a cup of coffee before him, then unaccountably burst into tears.

Chapter Nine

*A*mantha *found herself being seated, a warm, consoling* hand on her shoulder, a surprisingly clean handkerchief pressed into her hand.

"I'm sorry," she whispered. "It has just been so hot." She paused, choked with embarrassment.

"Got a sayin' here. 'If you don't like Oklahoma weather, wait a minute.' Guess ol' Dave told you how it was in January, snow knee-deep, everything shut down. Cost the city forty thousand just to clear the streets, men workin' around the clock."

"No, he didn't mention it." In fact, other than a few love words at night, they'd talked very little. She didn't realize how little until now.

"Didn't tell you about the big shot then?" He settled comfortably in his chair, drawing a pipe from his pocket. "Like to smoke this when I talk. Don't have time on the rig. You mind?"

She shook her head. He tamped tobacco into his pipe, lit it, and puffed for a moment, reflectively, before he launched into his story.

It was cold. So cold ice glistened on the rig, and work gloves froze to the metal. So cold the men lit a fire, then laid a piece of sheet metal over the coals. When their feet got too numb, they'd stand on it for a while.

And there was this air-jammer—know-it-all—who liked to throw his weight around. Somehow, he made it out from the office. Must of needed an audience pretty bad, because he called them down off the rig. He stood on the only warm spot, in his twill peg-tops, his mackinaw, and the finest thick-soled boots Charlie ever saw. He gave the shivering men around him a pep talk, throwing in a few criticisms as he went.

"We was all goldang mad till we seen the smoke." Charlie's mouth quirked at one corner. "Begin to curl up from them boots. Nobody said nothin', but it was beginnin' to get innarestin'. Guess he was so doggone proud to have our attenshun, he didn't smell nothin' burnin'.

"All of a sudden-like, he begin to dance. Tried to untie his boots, but I guess they was double-knotted. Grabbed out his shiny-new Case knife and cut through laces, tongues an' all. Yanked 'em off an' made a beeline for his car in his sock feet. Never come back."

His mouth quirked again. "Wasn't so doggone cold after that. Sorta warmed up the day, you might say."

His warm, lazy tale, and the dry way he told it, put Amantha at her ease. When he went to look in on David, she realized he'd talked on, giving her time to regain her composure.

David would never have thought to recount the story to her. Since the morning after her arrival, had she and David ever talked at all? There had been his criticisms of the way she'd brought Peter up, making him a sissy, he'd said. And, of course, the urgent need to cut corners and save money—

Charlie returned. "Sleepin'. Some feverish."

"Charlie, the well at Drumright. Do you think you'll find oil?"

He looked surprised and took a long time tamping his pipe before he answered. "Mebbe so, mebbe not. Figger there's better'n a fifty-fifty chance."

"Is it worth it? The two of you killing yourselves on a gamble like that, scrimping, saving—just to gamble some more?"

"It's what Dave wants." He grinned, deprecatingly. "Me, I'm too easygoin'. Just a lazy ol' country boy. I'd be proud to lease my land, take my one-eighth, and let somebody else do the work. Or if I was set on puttin' down a well myself, I'd git some folks to go in on shares. Everbody'd make a pile if she came in, wouldn't lose so much if she didn't.''

Amantha leaned forward. "Charlie, if this isn't what you want, why do you let David do this to you? Tell him you've changed your mind!"

Charlie's sandy brows rose above puzzled gray eyes. It was clear he hadn't considered such a course. "I guess because Dave's my friend. He's got lots of drive. I ain't. Mebbe we're good for each other."

Amantha looked down at her hands. "I wish I could say the same. I suppose he told you I took the money the oil company paid for damages, and spent it."

"Women needs things. Looks real homey now."

"But if I had not, David might have been home these last nights. He might not be ill."

Charlie snorted. "Don't ketch flu tom-cattin' around. Wouldn't let it worry me none."

A moan from the next room brought him to his feet. He went into the bedroom and placed his palm on David's forehead. Amantha, hovering in the doorway, saw his face turn serious.

"Fever's riz. An' he don't look good. I'll go git Anna to set with you. Gotta run into town."

Anna came bearing Watkins's camphorated salve and some chamomile tea. Charlie returned with a thermometer, aspirin, and a small Sterno stove, which he set to boil, adding a few drops of benzoin. Maybelle arrived with chicken soup and an "asafetida" bag for Peter to wear around his neck, warding off contagion.

Amantha held the evil-smelling thing at arm's length. "Does it actually protect him?" she asked Charlie.

He shrugged. "Mebbe so, mebbe not. Cain't do no harm."

Around Peter's neck it went. The small boy stood big-eyed at the door between the kitchen and the front room, forbidden to come any farther.

For three days David worsened, tossing and mumbling. His feverish mutterings betrayed his worst fears.

"Biscuit cutter's shot to hell, Charlie. Gotta get a new bit." Then, "It's a dry hole, dammit! A dry hole!" And later, apologetically, "Guess I'm tired, Charlie. You'll have to take over for me. I'm gonna sit on the lazy bench awhile."

And gentle Charlie, who never used profanity, slapped David's face with a hard hand. "Hell, no," he growled. "You ain't gonna give out on me! Git your lazy butt in gear, you hear?"

"Sure, Charlie. Sure."

Charlie's face was drawn with sleeplessness. For three days and nights he hadn't left his friend's side. And Amantha saw an expression in his red-rimmed eyes that terrified her. Despite his calm exterior, Charlie was afraid!

David was going to die.

Amantha had taken brief periods of rest at Charlie's insistence, napping on the new sofa in the front room. This night she refused to leave even for a moment. She sat at one side of David's bed, Charlie at the other, neither of them daring to meet the other's eyes. David's frantic tossing had ceased. Now there was only a sound of ragged, labored breathing.

"We've got to get a doctor," Amantha wept.

"We done everything there is to do. Doc cain't do no more. It's up to Dave now."

"How do you know so much about it?" Amantha didn't intend a harsh edge to her voice, but it was there. Charlie flinched and seemed to shrink.

"My folks had it during the World War. My ma and pa, my two sisters. Doc told me what to do, and I took care of 'em."

His voice trailed off. Amantha didn't ask the question that was in her mind. The answer was there in Charlie's sagging frame.

It was nearly midnight when someone pounded at the rear door. Amantha tiptoed to the back porch to find Edna Skaggs outside the sagging screen. She held a dishpan filled with a concoction, the aroma of onions so strong that Amantha was staggered.

"Heerd Dave was wuss. These here is onions, baked down slow in lard. Put 'em on his chest while they's still hot. Would've been here sooner, but they just got done. Cured one of my kids, onc't. Hope it h'eps. Put some warm rags over top to hold the heat in.''

Amantha took the pan and thanked her. She carried it into the bedroom, feeling a wild urge to laugh, recognizing it as the edge of hysteria. "What do you think, Charlie?"

She should have known what he'd say! "Might do some good, might not. Don't hurt to try."

They covered the sick man's chest with the nauseous mess, then with a towel. The room was stifling with the odor of onion, benzoin, and camphorated salve. Mingled with it all was the smell of fever.

There was nothing to do but pray.

Amantha jerked from a dream in which she searched for David and couldn't find him. The room was gray with light, and Charlie's hands were beneath her arms as he lifted her to her feet. She dragged back as he tried to lead her, stumbling, toward the front room.

"He's all right. Fever's broke. He's gonna get well."

Charlie helped her to the sofa and drew a blanket over her, tucking her in like a child. His rough fingers pushed a lock of hair away from her tear-wet cheek.

Now, in her dreams, there was only the face of Charlie, gentle and kind. She slept for a long time.

Chapter Ten

David, convalescing, was a difficult patient. He demanded pencil and paper, figuring lost money, lost time. Charlie had to restrain him when he decided to dress and go back to work.

Amantha began to feel a slow simmering anger toward him. If Peter behaved in such a manner, she would chastise him! And David had never ventured a word of apology about the nights he didn't come home.

The backbone of her anger was broken when she found him lying, eyes closed, papers covered with figures scattered on the sheet that covered him. His lashes were wet, tears of weakness running down his sunken cheeks.

"David—?"

"I've got to make it, Amantha! I can't fail now! I've got to show my dad—"

"You will, David. You'll make him proud of you."

"Proud, hell! All I want to do is show the old bastard! Prove I'm a better man than he is! I'll break him, like he tried to break me!"

Amantha closed her lips against what she knew would be unwanted advice. Surely his father wasn't as black as he was portrayed. When David was better, she'd try to convince him he should attempt a reconciliation. But not now, when he was too weak and nervous to think properly.

When David recovered enough to sit in the front room, visitors came; Leroy Springer, Anna's husband, was first. He was a small round-faced man with baby blue eyes that watered as he looked at David's yellowed features and fever-burned lips.

"Goddam," he kept saying, scratching his head. "Goddam! The missus said you was purty bad off, but goddam!"

Earl Skaggs, Edna's common-law consort, was not the raffish character Amantha had pictured him to be. He was tall, thin, with a mournful horse-face and a perpetual worried expression; neat, where Edna was sloppy. He stood, turning his hat in his hands, with little to say.

Maybelle Mitchell's Henry was the biggest surprise. A small, nut-brown man, his face a road map of wrinkles; he was rough, illiterate, with a lewd sense of humor.

"Shee-ut, man," he said to David. "You-all look like somp'n th' cat dragged in—or kivvered up. Mebbe," he cast malicious eyes toward Amantha, "bein' home all this here time, you're just pussy-whipped."

Embarrassed, Amantha retired to the kitchen to replenish the coffeepot. It seemed that all she did lately was make coffee, wash cups.

And it was so hot. Her head ached, the heavy weight of her hair being almost unbearable. Peter, playing on the rear porch, was hammering at something.

Noise.

Never-ending noise.

Dear God, she was dizzy. Perhaps she was finally catching David's flu.

The coffee she poured looked black and greasy in the cups. She escaped to the rear yard, where she leaned against the porch wall, head spinning, nauseated. The sun beat down pitilessly, exposing the red earth, dry and cracked now. Oil stains burned through the fresh white paint on the shacks.

Anna, hanging clothes in the next yard, saw Amantha's white face and hurried over.

"You sick? No wonder, all them damn men in the house! Come on over. I'll make a pot of coffee."

Amantha shuddered and turned away. Anna studied her with measuring eyes.

"How long you been porely, like this?"

"A week or two. I think I'm just tired."

Anna snorted. "Hell, you oughta know better. You had one kid. . . ."

Amantha paled. "Anna, you don't think—"

"Think? Hell, honey, I know! I been looking at Edna Skaggs through half a dozen! You kept track?"

Amantha admitted she hadn't. All she'd had on her mind was David. Dear God, of all the times for this to happen!

"I've got to write Mum for my medical records," she whispered, half to herself. Then, "Oh, Anna, the doctor I had with Peter said—said—"

Her voice trailed off. He'd said it would be impossible for her to deliver again, unless under optimum conditions. He said another lying in would require special care. . . .

She would require a specialist.

There would be medical bills.

Baby things to buy!

A baby in this dreadful place!

Anna had waited long enough. "Said what, Amantha?"

"Nothing," Amantha babbled. "Nothing." She gripped Anna's wiry arms with feverish hands. "Please don't say anything to David. I've got to find a way to tell him."

"He's the daddy, ain't he? Hell, ain't something you done all by your lonesome."

Amantha's face went red, then white again. "Just don't say anything—please."

Anna left, fuming. Damn Dave Carmody, anyway. She'd promised Amantha to keep her mouth shut, but she hadn't said anything about keeping it secret from Charlie. If push came to shove, Charlie could handle Dave!

The next morning Charlie drove into town. He returned carrying a small wooden cabinet with a rounded top. Taking it into the Carmody shack, he set it down, plugged it in, and turned a dial. The strains of music it emitted brought David from the rear of the house, where he had been shaving. He stared at the object, face grim beneath its lather.

"What the hell's that, Charlie?"

"Weddin' present," Charlie drawled. "Just now got around to it. Zenith. Figgered it'd keep Amantha company."

"I thought we agreed neither of us would buy anything that

wasn't a necessity? That goddam thing sure as hell doesn't come under that heading!''

Charlie sat back on his heels, his gray eyes hard and dangerous. "Supposin'," he drawled, "I didn't spend none of our mutual funds? Supposin' I sold a couple of things off the home place? Things my grammaw left me? Old oak sideboard, a clock . . .''

He uncoiled, rising to his feet, a lean whip of a man, menacing in his quietness. "You figger I cheated you out of somethin'? That stuff was passed on down to me, just like my land was. Might figger I don't want no oil messin' up my proppity.''

David's face was livid. "I'm sorry, Charlie. Sometimes I forget your heart isn't in this thing as much as mine is.''

"That's why I still got one," Charlie said laconically. He headed for the door, and Amantha followed him.

"Thank you," she whispered. "It's a wonderful present.''

Charlie's lean face softened in a smile. "Then it's worth it.''

The next day David and Charlie resumed their work routine. Amantha turned dials. The General Electric Symphony Orchestra. Walter Damrosch conducting; the Gillette Orchestra . . .

"Oh, Peter," she said, hugging her son close. "Oh, how lovely! Peter—listen!''

The Zenith was a lifesaver in the days that followed. Since David seemed to regard the radio with animosity, it was turned on only in his absence, becoming something of a bond between mother and child. The soft music seemed to soothe Amantha's nerves, holding her dreadful nausea at bay.

And it was hot. So hot that the leaves on the tree in the yard hung dispiritedly; so hot that the Skaggs children, who could withstand anything, remained indoors. The ice melted in its box, the drip pan spilling over before Amantha could catch it; food turned bad too quickly. Ice wagons didn't visit the isolated Tremenco camp, so Anna made a daily visit to Merk's, bringing home small blocks carefully wrapped in newspaper and blankets. Occasionally, Amantha and Peter rode with her.

And there, Amantha saw a familiar face.

She clutched Anna's arm as they pulled in front of the small store-roadhouse. "Who is that?" she gasped, pointing at a very pregnant girl with long black hair and classic Indian features. "Is it—?"

Anna's knobby cheeks burned red. "Name's Rosie," she said curtly. "Ain't been around for a while. Reckon I can see why!"

"But, she's Charlie's—"

"Dammit, Amantha, don't go jumpin' to no conclusions! Not when you don't know what the hell you're talking about!"

She spun around to the side where ice was kept in a small shed, packed with straw. It was clear she considered the subject closed.

They returned to camp to find an oil-sprayed truck parked before the Carmody house, two black-faced men grinning at them from the cab.

"It's David!" Amantha said, thunderstruck. "And Charlie!"

"Know where we could pick us up a couple of good-lookin' dames?" David called out. "We're a pair of hell-raising oil tycoons, from Drumright—"

Amantha stumbled from the Model-A. David climbed out of the truck, his teeth showing white in an exultant smile as he grabbed her and whirled her in a crazy dance.

"We've done it, baby! We've finally done it! Blew the string right through the derrick! Just got the damned thing capped—"

The well had come in! David had realized his dreams! They would be able to buy a decent house, to pay for a baby. . . .

"I—I'm so pleased!"

"Pleased!" He grinned at her teasingly. "Pleased! God-dam it, is that all you've got to say?"

She took a step backward, squared her chin, and drew a deep breath. "David, I have a surprise for you, too. I'm . . . pregnant."

Incredulity washed the happiness from his eyes. "You sure? Could be you're wrong." There was such hope in his voice that she shivered.

"The baby should be due in February."

"Goddam."

There was a dead silence as she stood trembling before him, her eyes welling with tears. Then David Carmody forced a smile. "It'll work out," he said. "Don't worry about it. Reckon havin' a kid can't cost too much."

"But you're happy about it, aren't you?"

"Yeah, sure. Look, Charlie and I are taking off the rest of the day. Figured we'd run over to Merk's and spread the news about the well coming in. You ready, Charlie?"

"Sure," Charlie said quietly, not looking at Amantha.

Then they were gone, gone with their blackened faces, their oil-soaked clothes that were the badges of their success.

Anna's face was red with anger, embarrassment, and pity for her friend. "Don't let it getcha down, honey. Dave'll come around. You just picked the wrong time."

"The wrong time? Is there a right time? I kept it from him when he was ill, when he was tired, discouraged. I thought with the well coming in—"

"That don't mean nothin'. Sometimes it takes three, four months to pay back what you got in it. Depends on the well. Price of oil is down. Charlie was worryin' the other night. Said they might have to work for Tremenco a while longer."

Amantha's eyes were dull. A sudden gust of hot wind kicked up red dust around her. "A while longer! And I will live in a shack and have a baby!" She held out reddened hands, nails torn to the quick. "I will wash clothes, fight insects, listen to the words Peter picks up from the Skaggs children! The rain, the heat, and now the wind! There's an inch of dust on my kitchen table! Oh, Anna, I can't bear it!"

"Things could be worse," Anna told her.

That night, at nearly midnight, David and Charlie had not come home. Anna, worried over Amantha, had joined her. The heat was still suffocating, and they placed two kitchen chairs at the side of the house to catch a faint breeze. They were sitting there when Charlie's truck drove up. Amantha started to get to her feet and Anna put a staying hand on her arm.

The men were arguing.

"You don't know what the hell you're talking about," David shouted. "You never had a kid!"

"I know what Anna told me," Charlie insisted. "Anna's skeert Amantha's got some kind of problems. You got to get her checked over; she's gotta have this baby in a hospital. I don't give a damn what it costs!"

"Edna has her kids at home."

"Amantha ain't Edna, you goldang fool!"

"This is my business, Charlie, so butt out!"

"And your business just cost you three hundred bucks," Charlie reminded him. "I seen you pay Rosie off, remember."

"I paid her to get the hell out of my life," David growled. "You want her showing up at the door, telling Amantha she's carrying my kid? Besides, I owed her—"

"And you owe Amantha."

"She's got a roof over her head, hasn't she? Food on the table? I love her. She knows that."

"I'd like to wring your goddam neck," Charlie said in a voice like sleet.

"You're welcome to try."

Charlie turned and stamped back to the truck. David went in the house.

Amantha hadn't moved while the conversation was taking place. Now, she made only a small, hurt, whimpering sound. Anna's strong hands gripped Amantha's arms.

"Amantha?" She gave her a little shake. "Amantha, listen to me! This ain't the end of the world!"

Amantha's eyes were glazed, her mouth open in shock. "It's the end of my world. I'm leaving him, Anna. I'm going—home."

Anna's bony fingers bit into her flesh. "You listen to me, Amantha, and you listen good! David's been workin' his tail off for five years! Where was you?"

"I was injured, having a baby—"

"Takes nine months. What did you do after that?"

"My—my father was dying—"

"And he had him a wife, didn't he? David didn't have none. He worked twenty hours a day, then come home to this pigsty. While you was livin' in the lap of luxury, waited on hand and foot, mebbe he needed somebody to put their arms around him and say, "Honey, you're doin' good!"

"He—didn't send for me."

"Mebbe he couldn't afford to, not an' get a start. But I reckon you could of found a way. There's always a way."

Amantha remembered her mother saying, "You're not well enough to go yet, dear." Then, "Your father is ill. Your duty is to him." Nanny had been adamant in her disapproval of David, backing her mother. But her father . . .

Her father had said, "You're a married woman, Amantha. If you want to go, I'll pay your way."

And she had said, "Not yet. . . ."

Tears began to flood her eyes, washing down her face, and Anna's grip relaxed.

"David's a man," Anna said. "Us women gotta keep a close eye on 'em. Sometimes these things is our fault. Which reminds me, I better get home to my old goat."

She left and Amantha stood for a long time, waiting until the tears stopped flowing. Then she went into the house, undressed, and crawled in beside David.

He turned to her. "Missed you," he said drowsily, "Where have you been?"

"Visiting with Anna. Talking about how proud I am of you and your well."

His arms tightened around her. "And I'm proud of you, sweetheart. I'm sorry I didn't sound happier about the baby. It was a shock, and I guess I must have acted like a damn fool. It's going to be all right."

"Of course it is," she said cuddling closer. "Oh, David, I love you!"

He made love to her, gently and sweetly, and she forgot the heat, the poverty of her surroundings. This was David. If he had been unfaithful, so had she, in a way. From now on, she thought, smiling in the darkness, she would keep a close eye on him. What was it Anna had said? She kissed his sleeping cheek. "Honey, you're doing good," she whispered, laughing a little at the odd sound of the words she uttered. She was proud of him! And now she knew where her duty lay. She felt almost sorry for Rosie!

When morning came, the alarm, set on a pie tin to enhance its sound, shook her awake. She lay for a blissful moment, savoring the memory of the night, then swung her feet to the floor. Next door, Charlie's old truck chuffed—and died. He was having trouble getting it started.

David began to dress, and Amantha put the coffeepot on. Then there was a terrific pounding at the front door. David swore and padded toward it in his bare feet.

Charlie stood in the doorway, a sheepish grin on his face. "Ol' Lena went and done it, this time," he said. "Died on me, and when I tried to crank her up . . ." he held out an arm that dangled oddly above the wrist.

"Done gone an' busted it, for sure."

Chapter Eleven

*T*he well at Drumright proved to be less productive than its initial spurt indicated. It settled down to one hundred barrels a day. David sold it to a green easterner at a reasonable profit and took on a new working schedule, splitting a shift with an elderly man who had had a recent heart attack. He worked one well from six until noon, then hitched a ride to a second job on the evening tour, saving gas.

Charlie, ashen-faced, his arm in a sling, spent much of his time beneath the tree at the rear of the Carmody house, entertaining Peter with tales of cowboys and Indians; of the pioneers who had settled this red country. Several days after his injury, he came up with an idea.

He couldn't start his truck alone. Couldn't handle the spark and the crank at the same time. But if Amantha could control the mechanism from within the cab, he could crank the goldang thing with his left hand. Nothin' to steerin'. He'd tell her when to shift. Why didn't they give it a try?

Their first attempts were ludicrous. Amantha was inept. When they made it as far as Merk's, Charlie bought frosty bottles of Nehi. Amantha quelled the thought that David would consider it a waste of money and drank it down, smiling.

Each day they went farther afield. They traveled to the Municipal Airport, where Braniff and Bowen airlines flew an Oklahoma City–Fort Worth–Dallas route; on another day they visited the Northeast Zoo, where Peter was enthralled at the sight of monkeys, bears—and Luna, the elephant, with her constant swaying, looking like a fat lady in wrinkled drawers from the rear.

In October, the air bright and blue, Charlie and Anna loaded a basket in the rear of the truck. Charlie said, mysteriously, that he had a surprise.

They said good-bye to Anna and drove over a rough red road, turning into a lane that became nothing more than tracks leading across a sun-dried rolling meadow delineated at one side by a long strip of trees.

"This here's my place," Charlie said simply. "Far as you-all can see. Down there's where we're gonna put the first hole."

They took the basket and walked down a path that sloped gently to a creek. There were towering pecan trees banked with scarlet sumac; the jackoaks were beginning to turn—

"It's lovely!"

"Oughta see it in the spring. Redbuds, dogwood, all kinds of wild flowers."

The path led upward to a small log cabin, so skillfully placed that it looked as if it had grown there. Beyond it, a fence formed of saplings enclosed small neat areas, a shedlike barn, a chicken house.

"My grandfolks' place," said Charlie. "I growed up here."

He told her of his people. Once owners of large properties in Tennessee, they'd moved on to Arkansas after the Civil War. Then, dogged by ill luck, losing two daughters to malarial fever, they'd come here during the opening of the Cherokee strip. Charlie's grandparents had staked out the allotted quarter section, his uncles and his father claiming adjacent quarter sections for themselves.

His uncles married city girls and sold off their land to their father. Then there was the epidemic of Spanish influenza that took Charlie's family. His grandfolks took him in.

Now the land was his. His and David's.

"You can't drill for oil here! Oh, Charlie, don't spoil it!"

Charlie looked at her oddly. "Granpap was still alive in 'twenty-eight, when everybody was talking about the Discovery well. He took me out fer a walk. Had him a witchin' fork. He said, 'Boy, you ever want to drill yourself a well, you start right here.' Reckon that's what he wanted me to do."

Peter had gone outside and was clamoring for them to follow. They walked on downstream through the bright autumnal foliage, following a creek that ran like a red ribbon until it reached a deeper pool. Here, they sat on a carpet of fallen leaves.

Charlie produced a knife from his pocket and, with Amantha's help, cut a slender sapling. In his pocket he had a ball of fishline, a hook buried in it. Finally they managed to construct a fishing pole. Charlie and Peter blundered comically about in their efforts to catch grasshoppers for bait.

Soon Peter sat on a clay bank watching the stick that served as bobber in fascination. Amantha leaned against a tree and Charlie stretched beside her, talking lazily of his life as a child; of coming here to fish as a little boy; of how he'd tamed a squirrel so that it would come and sit with him. It stole biscuits from his pocket and sat on his shoulder to eat them, holding them in its tiny handlike paws as it nibbled.

A screech from Peter brought Amantha to her feet. He'd caught a rainbow-colored fish. Charlie fashioned a stringer, inserted it into the fish's gills, and lowered it into the water.

Peter fished until it was too dark to see the bobber. Charlie built up a fire on the clay bank and let it burn down to coals. He cut several more thin twigs and produced weiners and marshmallows from the basket, showing the enthralled novices how to roast them.

Amantha watched him, his head close to Peter's as they squatted over the embers. Above, the stars winked on, and the soft air was filled with fireflies.

The beauty of the day wasn't spoiled by a flat tire on the truck when they set out for home. They somehow changed it, using Charlie's good hand and Amantha's inexperienced ones. Peter slept through it all, his fish resting in the picnic basket. Seeing Amantha in the headlights, face and hands blackened, dress covered with red dirt, Charlie groaned.

"Now you see why I'm a ol' unmarried man. See what happens when I take a lady out?"

"You're a very nice man, Charlie. I think this has been one of the happiest days I ever spent."

A long, awkward hush followed her words. Then Charlie moved to open the door and help her in. He was quiet for some time, then his normal, lazy voice broke the silence as he launched into one of his humorous anecdotes, putting her at ease.

It was after twelve when they reached home. David had already come in from the evening tour; dog-tired, grease-smeared, and worried about her absence.

Amantha told of the day's outing, her eyes glowing, explaining about the flat tire that delayed them. He listened, frowning.

"I don't think it's a good idea to be running around in that truck—not in your condition," he said stiffly. Then his arms went around her.

"Amantha, sweetheart! One of these days, there's going to be time for us! There's a place I want to take you—"

He's jealous, she thought, wonderingly, jealous of Charlie! Lifting a hand to touch his cheek, she stood on tiptoe to kiss him.

"I won't go out anymore," she said contritely. "I love you, David. I love you so much—"

As he held her, she felt the movement of the child within her. David's child. From now on, she must think only of the baby.

Two days later Charlie Forbes went back to work. His cast had been removed, and he was relegated to timekeeper on a single shift, but money was going into their drilling fund again. David's spirits lifted. Maybe they'd be able to start on their own in the spring. He'd lowered his sights and was beginning to look for used equipment. Once again the table was littered with papers and figures.

The days passed slowly and pleasantly. Amantha no longer felt the nausea that assailed her in the beginning. But always, at the back of her mind, was a nagging worry. An answer to the letter she wrote to her mother arrived, filled with grim concerns about Amantha's "delicate condition.' Enclosed was an equally depressing report from Doctor Wellington, insisting she procure a good physician without delay.

It was nearly Christmas when Amantha approached Anna, asking her to explain the workings of a pawn shop. She intended to pawn her silver; use the money to pay for a doctor, a hospital stay, baby things.

Anna was aghast. If Dave Carmody was so damned tight—

"It isn't David," Amantha said. "It's something I want to do. And I don't want David to know."

"Oh, hell!" The knobby little woman looked as if she might cry. "How much you think you'll need?"

"Maybe two hundred dollars."

Anna's lips tightened. "I got it. Been saving for new furniture, but you're welcome—"

Amantha refused. They finally settled on a trade. Anna would lend her the money and keep the silver until Amantha could redeem it.

"Be worth it," Anna said with satisfaction, "just seein' that bitch Maybelle Mitchell's face!"

After the silver service was moved next door—David didn't notice it was gone—Anna drove Amantha into town to see a doctor, and to pay for hospital arrangements in advance.

There was enough money left for soft flannel, which would be made into diapers and sacques for a February baby; and for a roasting hen, cranberries, and pumpkins to make into pies for the holidays.

On Christmas day the laundry smell of the shanty had vanished, buried beneath the scent of spice and baking things. There was even a small tree.

"Next year," David said, "we'll have a bigger one. All the way to the ceiling. And that's a promise!"

David and his promises! Smiling, she hugged him. How lovely it would be if his dreams came true! But she was happy with a tree that was here, that was real, that was not a dream.

The crowning delight of the day was the gift of a handmade cradle. It had been Charlie's, and his father's before him. He presented it with an expression of shy pleasure, and it sat near the tree, needing only a baby to make the scene complete.

That night Amantha lay in David's arms, thinking of the wonderful, magical day. All the ugliness of the ending year was erased as they loved each other tenderly, sweetly, and the days ahead seemed filled with promise.

Chapter Twelve

*A*mantha maintained her serenity through the early days of the new year. The radio talked of hard times. The price of oil was dropping. Governor Murray planned a distribution of free seeds and commodities. Marshal Joffre died. Will Rogers passed through on a charity tour.

Only words gathered from the air and passed on through the Zenith.

Then, on February 14, after David had gone to work on the evening tour, Amantha sent Peter for Anna. Anna despatched a man working on a nearby rig to look for David.

David had gone on an errand to town. He had not yet reached Hughes Tool Company, his destination. No one knew where to reach him.

It was Charlie who came at Anna's urgent summons; Charlie who drove a white-lipped Amantha to the small hospital in Capitol Hill.

Two hours later Charlie sat in a waiting room, the ashtray beside him filled to overflowing. He leaped to his feet as a nurse approached carrying a small bundle. She put the baby in his arms, assuming the haggard man to be the father.

"A beautiful little girl. She's going to be tiny, like her mother."

Charlie looked down at the baby's face, crumpled like a wild rose. Throat clogged with emotion, he tried to speak and failed. Then, "Amantha—she all right?"

"She's doing very well. You may see her in a few moments."

She took the infant and he sank back, weak with relief. He had been praying.

Amantha, when he saw her, was exhausted, but ecstatic.

"She's real purty, Amantha."

"Thank you, Charlie."

Embarrassed and awkward in the hospital atmosphere, Charlie turned his hat in his hands, searching for something to say. At that moment, there was a commotion in the hall outside.

David, in his soiled work clothes, his black hair standing on end, pushed past two protesting nurses. "She's my wife," he shouted angrily.

Seeing Amantha, David was blind to anything else. His face broke up like a crumbling dam, his blue eyes welling with tears, his mouth quivering. He knelt beside Amantha and buried his face against her breasts, weeping in harsh, rending sobs.

"When Anna told me, she scared the hell out of me! If anything happened to you, Amantha, goddam it, I'd die! I love you so much—"

Charlie backed from the room.

Downstairs he found Peter and Anna. Anna had driven David in. Charlie left the keys to his truck at the desk for David and rode home with them.

David was with Amantha now, and that was how it should be. But for once Charlie was not his good-natured easy-going self. He guessed he was getting old.

Charlie had taken Amantha to the hospital. Five days later, he took her and the baby, Meggie, home in Anna's Model-A. David had borrowed his truck for some mysterious errand.

Amantha was oddly quiet on the trip, and Charlie was sorry for her. He mentally chastised her thoughtless husband. If this was his wife—

Setting his jaw, he put the thought away.

They reached the camp to find the truck already returned, but David was not in sight. Anna met them at the door.

The Carmody house was cleaned and polished, smelling of cooked food and lemon wax. Amantha put Meggie in the cradle Charlie had given her and left Peter admiring his little sister to follow Anna, who beckoned importantly.

David stood grinning on the back porch. Beside him stood a new electric gyrator, gleaming green and white.

"David!"

"That's why I sent Charlie to get you," he beamed. "Picked this up this morning. Wanted it to be a surprise."

"Oh, David!"

Amantha began to cry, tears of happiness that washed away her hurt.

It was so like David! It hadn't dawned on him that she only wanted her husband, wanted to bring Meggie home as a family. Instead, he'd given her something he thought a greater gift; something he had paid for with blood, sweat, and tears; with a piece of his dream.

"You like it?" he asked uneasily.

"I love it, David! It's the nicest present I ever had."

David was wild about the baby. Coming in from his tour after midnight, his first stop was at the cradle, where he would stand, a big man in soiled work clothes, marveling at the miracle of Meggie.

Peter was doting and possessive of his little sister. Then there were bursts of jealousy. Of late he'd grown taller, big-eyed, thin, his plump babyhood behind him. He seemed to stand back, as if resigned to be relegated to second place.

Amantha thanked God for Charlie, who, not due at work in the morning hours now, gave the boy the companionship he needed. She could see them from the window; faces solemn and absorbed as Charlie taught Peter how to whistle through a blade of grass held between the thumbs, Peter trying to emulate him.

She wished the problems of the world could be so easily solved. Yesterday, going into the city for groceries with Anna, she'd seen long lines of men at the soup kitchen the VFW established at the north end of Robinson Bridge. An army of beaten men, shuffling forward to accept charity. The news spoke of poverty and hunger. A man was sentenced to five years for stealing a loaf of bread to feed his family.

Amelia Earhart, the noted woman flier, appeared at the fairgrounds to demonstrate the first autogyro to come to Oklahoma, netting $3,800 for the Milk and Ice Fund.

81

Wiley Post, a fishing friend of Charlie's, and Harold Gatty, circled the globe in Post's plane, the *Winnie May;* a record time of eight days, fifteen hours.

England seemed suddenly nearer.

Oil dropped to fifteen cents a barrel.

Governor Murray dispensed $6,000 of his own money to feed the hungry. The capitol lawns were plowed and divided into vegetable plots for the needy.

The governor went to war with Texas over toll bridges spanning the Red River, sending troops to the scene.

Then he went to war with the oil interests, regulating production. Oil was cut to a five percent allowable. Some producers were reduced to running "hot oil," bootlegging it in an effort to survive.

There was a rumor the banks were in trouble. David and Charlie withdrew their mutual funds and kept them in a locked tin trunk beneath the Carmody bed. David slept with a revolver under his pillow, and a Winchester was placed on brackets near the front door, out of the children's reach.

On November 4, the oil fields shut down entirely for ten days. November 5, the banks closed. The Zenith, on November 8, carried the news of Franklin Delano Roosevelt's election to the presidency; it was a landslide victory, and he vowed to end the depression.

April brought fresh winds and a whisper of good news. The state legislature enacted House Bill 481, a proration law, creating a proration staff within the Corporation Committee. Both large oil producers and small ones found the rulings fair and equitable after their long battle to survive.

But relief came too late for small Tremenco. Always a hard-luck operation, operating on the edge of bankruptcy, they were unable to meet the loans against their company. It went into receivership, closing down. David and Charlie, the Springers, the Mitchells, and the Skaggs, all were handed pink slips on the same day.

"I'm tired of working for some other sonofabitch," David said. "Hell, Charlie, let's go for broke!"

"Broke?" Amantha asked, her eyes frightened.

"Take a gamble," Charlie grinned. "Start our own company! Put down our own goldang well!"

David still had the money he'd inherited from his mother. And for a number of years he and Charlie had added most of their wages to the kitty. When Tremenco equipment was put up for sale, David bid on an old but serviceable rig. For very little more, the company threw in the shacks that comprised the Tremenco camp. The other residents, out of jobs, agreed to work for David and Charlie at half their old wages.

The small houses were to be removed to Charlie's property. It would be a week before they could get down to the actual drilling, and Charlie volunteered to oversee the removal and get the new camp set up.

Between them, David and Charlie had hatched a plan.

The Springers, with Florrie's help, would look after Peter and Meggie. Charlie said he'd loan David the truck. By God, he and Amantha were going to have a honeymoon!

"But David," Amantha began, "hotels are very expensive. And I have nothing to wear—"

David threw back his head and laughed. "We're going to sleep under the stars! And as far as clothes, nobody's gonna see you but me. You don't need to wear any," he added, teasingly. Amantha's face flamed and Charlie hastily averted his eyes.

Later, as she packed food—picnic stuff, David had said— she looked out across the red fields of the oil patch and shivered. David's idea of a honeymoon out-of-doors was a strange one. And it was torture for her to leave the children. But he'd been working too hard for too long. He needed to get away.

They left at dawn. Soon they were in country that began to show traces of green. The morning air was fresh and clean. Head against David's shoulder, Amantha listened as he extolled the beauties of the place they were going to—deep in the Wichita mountains.

It was evening when they neared their destination. The mountains brooded above them, crests red with the setting sun. Then they were on narrow roads that were scarcely more than trails. At last, in a cup of the mountain, there was a sound of water ahead; a small lake in the hollow, fed by a waterfall; a clear pool tinted by the last fading light. The lake was framed by granite boulders, moss green beneath the falls that sheathed them in silver spray.

"Oh, David!"

"Thought you'd like it." He wore a look of satisfaction as he explained that he and Charlie found this place some years earlier, when they were prospecting around the Anadarko Basin. He'd thought of her then—

David built a campfire and sat, leaning against a tree, cradling Amantha in his arms. His cheek was against hers, and they were content to remain silent, absorbing the beauty around them—beauty Amantha had not known existed in a flat, red land.

They talked about what they would do when their wells came in; the home they would buy. The cottage Amantha dreamed of grew larger in her imagination. She added another room or two. Then she forgot it when he rose to spread their blankets and said her name in a special way.

Around them a small wind rustled in the foliage; the coals of their fire were reflected in the night-dark water of the lake, as if it retained a fragment of sunset. Then David stood above her, heavy-shouldered, slim-waisted, his head haloed with stars.

His calloused hands touched her flesh, bringing fire to run along her veins.

"David, David!"

"This is enough, isn't it?" he asked intensely. "The two of us, like this. The sky for a roof. Do we need anything more?"

"No, David."

It was true, she thought. Nothing else mattered. Only this, and the children who were the fruits of their love. Even they were forgotten as she went back to a time before they existed; to a shepherd's cot on another continent, miles and years away.

After their coming together, she slept in an enchanted

dream. It did not end when she woke to a sound. Morning quivered on the lake's surface. Tendrils of vine were strung with diamond dew. A doe with two fawns at her side drank at the water's edge; gold-bronze, framed against mossy boulders sheathed in silver.

The doe raised her head and looked at the intruders with curious, liquid eyes. Then in perfect unison, she and her little ones seemed to soar as they leaped gracefully into the underbrush.

"David, did you see!"

He was not looking after the deer, but at her face, bright with enjoyment.

"I saw," he said.

All day they wandered hand in hand, climbing granite boulders, looking down into creekbeds with clear pools and clean-washed sand. Birds darted through jackoak thickets. A lizard surveyed from a rocky projection with ancient eyes.

"Mountain boomer," David explained. The creature was considered poisonous because of its pulsing yellow throat, but in fact, it was harmless.

They shared their lunch with squirrels and jays; their evening meal with an inquisitive raccoon who remained at a distance and daintily washed his food at the lakeside before nibbling at it.

Again they slept, clinging to each other. In the morning the deer had returned. This time they maintained their picture-book pose a moment longer.

"I think they know we're leaving. They're saying good-bye," Amantha said.

As the animals arched in graceful flight, David cupped his hands to his mouth and called after them.

"We'll be seeing you again before long! And that's a promise!"

Amantha was sleeping when they returned, not to Tremenco Camp, but the new Carmody-Forbes patch mushrooming on Charlie's property.

When she woke they were on a rutted trail that ran through

a sun-bleached meadow. Ahead were the little shacks, still sitting crookedly on concrete blocks. There would be difficult times ahead, and there was much to do.

But she'd come home.

Chapter Thirteen

Despite her renewed relationship with David, summer at the new oil patch was a horror. It was some time before electricity could be brought across country from the main road. The gyrator stood silent, while Amantha returned to the washboard. The Zenith was mute.

Worst of all were the hazards Amantha feared for the children. Meggie crawled beneath the leaning shack and had to be coaxed out. Her mother shivered, thinking of spiders and snakes. Small privys had been erected behind each house, and mud daubers built nests beneath their eaves, terrifying as they buzzed and circled, though no one was ever stung. Peter followed the Skaggs children as they raced around the dikes enclosing the slushpits. A child, falling in, would drown in liquid mud.

Amantha kept her children in the house. The part of the creekbed behind the camp had become a dump for garbage and tins. The air hummed with flies that found their way through unaligned windows and torn screens. Mosquitoes buzzed at night. And the heat was almost beyond endurance.

David had never been happier. He worked from daybreak until long after dark, dropping in at odd times for meals. And since he was happy, so was she.

One day they would strike it rich. And then they would buy a home. A real home. Amantha dreamed through the days, laughing at herself occasionally.

She was getting as bad as David! Perhaps she, too, had caught the oil fever!

There was so much to laugh about, now! She looked out the window, seeing Maybelle Mitchell heading for her privy, mincing along with her face averted; the picture of a southern lady out for a stroll.

How much she had changed, seeing humor in a situation she once would have thought mannerly to ignore. Her mother would be shocked at her now, and Nanny would just die. . . .

She had a brief moment of homesickness as she thought of her proper mother and her rigid old nurse. In spite of their unbending attitudes, she loved them. But this was her home now; her family. She'd never made an attempt to contact Nanny, knowing she wouldn't fit in. David had been right in finding her another position.

She saw David and Charlie coming across the field, and whirled to check the pie in her oven. It was brown and crusty, the juices bubbling from its slitted cover. She'd timed it just right. . . .

The electrical lines reached the patch. Again the gyrator thumped and rumbled with heavy work clothing; the Zenith bringing in news from what Amantha had begun to think of as "outside." Then, in September, Peter started at his new school. Amantha walked with him to the road to wait for the school bus, watching as he climbed aboard, a very small boy in a blue sweater and gray flannel knickers and cap, carrying his lunch pail.

He came home that night, with a black eye, his trousers torn, and his Thermos broken.

"The boys didn't like me," he whimpered. "They think I talk funny. They called me a sissy."

Charlie, who had stopped by with a message from Dave, took over.

"What does the other guy look like, Pete? You slug him?"

Peter shrank back. "Mum says it's not nice to fight."

For the first time Charlie looked at Amantha in anger. "Your mum's wrong this time," he said gruffly. He got down to his knees and assumed a fighting pose. "Hit me," he ordered. "Goldang it, boy, this here's somethin' you gotta learn if you're gonna git along around here—"

Peter punched at him, ineffectually, as Charlie blocked the blows. Finally, he slipped past the man's guard and landed a good one.

"There you go," Charlie grinned. "That's all there is to it." Then he frowned at Amantha. "Tomorrow," he said, "I'd send him to school in overhauls—"

Amantha was silent. She hated the thought of violence, believing that gentleness and kindness won friends. But perhaps she had been wrong.

The next morning Peter dressed himself as Charlie had directed and insisted on walking to the bus alone. Amantha knelt to kiss him good-bye.

"What shall I do if somebody hits me today?" he asked.

Amantha brushed back a lock of hair that strayed over his forehead as she sought for an answer.

"If somebody hits you," she said, trying to remember Charlie's words, "slug him! Slug him good!"

Evidently Charlie's antidote worked, because Peter was happily settled into school within several weeks. Then, in the first days of November, came the miracle.

With a hiss and a sigh, followed by a roar, David's well erupted in a geyser of oil. Amantha ran to the scene, seeing the workers capering like crazy fools, their clothing slick with the product of their labors.

David rushed to meet her, an ebony David, only his eyes and teeth glinting in a blackened face. "We did it," he cried exultantly. "Goddam! Look at that! Isn't she a beauty?"

Amantha agreed. This wasn't just an oil well! It was a little house! A piano! Music lessons for Peter! Warm winter coats, shoes. . . .

She didn't learn how wrong she was until evening. "Hell, honey," David said, "I'm sorry! I thought you knew. We're going to put our profits into another well. Then, someday, I'll buy you a mansion! And that's a promise!"

David's promises! She laughed, but her laughter hovered at the edge of tears.

"It's okay, isn't it?" He was looking at her anxiously, and she put her arms around him.

"Anything you want," she smiled, "is—" she stumbled over a word that was alien to her, "—is okay with me!"

After a brief celebration they began to drill again.

There was no time to finish the foundations beneath the shacks or renail walls into their proper position. Amantha puttied windows, their frames warped and drafty, and grimly endured an invasion of field mice who had little difficulty entering the structure.

David was in the house much of the time, Charlie running the crews while his partner was immersed in paperwork, a job he detested. Irritable at being cooped up while others did the work he loved, David was even testy with Meggie, who persisted in chattering while he figured.

"Dammit," he would shout, "Amantha, can't you keep that kid quiet? I wish I had an office—"

Amantha would forgive him when he stumbled to bed, his eyes red-rimmed, his tension leaving him as he found solace in her love.

They brought in another successful high-producing well in December. David's elation was tempered by the fact that he now had to pay top wages. Still, he gave a generous amount to Amantha to spend at Christmas and she had a glorious time choosing gifts for everyone.

Opening her own, she found a book of English poetry from Charlie. Her eyes were damp as she leafed through it to find old familiar favorites. David's gift was a small square box. She saved it until last.

A ring! A circlet of gold starred with a huge glittering diamond.

For a moment she was too stunned to react. She needed a warm coat, shoes, so many things. And the price of this would have paid for them over and over.

But she saw David's eyes shining with pleasure. She couldn't spoil it for him. She made a show of appreciation, and he slipped it on her finger and kissed her.

"Now, we're engaged."

All day she had to display it, hating the way it pointed up her small work-roughened hand. But she understood his pride in the gift, in being able to afford such a jewel for his wife.

Christmas over, she asked him to put it with his cash and his ledgers. It was too precious to wear every day.

Then the new year came. "Our best year ever," David promised. As if driven by his will, the new wells went down without problems. But the racked house was impossible to keep warm. Chill winds seeped through every crack in the walls and filtered in around the warped windows. And Meggie caught a cold that developed into croup.

For days, as January moved into February, the house was filled with steam from boiling kettles. Paper bubbled on the walls to hang in shreds, leaving bare spots of lath and plaster. The house smelled of medication, and Amantha, sleepless for many nights, was pale and hollow-eyed.

She longed for spring.

Spring, when it came, wore an ugly face. More drilling rigs had moved in. The once-grassy meadows, gouged by wheels and heavy equipment, were an expanse of raw, red earth, pocked with slushpits. The dust of the small area joined the plowed fields of the state, taking to the wind. For days the air was sepia-tinted, dust blowing into the houses to lie in ripples across the floors, despite sheeted windows.

The men on the rigs wore bandanas to cover their faces. Sometimes they were so blinded that all work had to cease.

The news the Zenith carried seemed in keeping with the weather. Poverty, crime, and violence seemed the order of the day. Farmers and sharecroppers were leaving the state in droves. Lines at soup kitchens extended for miles.

There is going to be a war, Amantha thought. I feel it!

Her fears faded when letters from home carried nothing more disquieting than a rumor regarding an affair between an American divorcee and the beloved Prince of Wales.

In July E. W. Marland was elected governor. There was little fanfare over his election. There was more excitement that July, when John Dillinger, the criminal, was shot to death one evening.

The news of the assassination of Premier Dollfuss was of little moment.

Because the rains finally came!

The blessed rain, settling the red dust and cooling the parched earth that had been so long without water.

Chapter Fourteen

The deluge seemed like a gift from God after the worst drought in history. But it soon became as miserable as the dry, choking winds had been. Rain fell in sheets, turning the oil patch into a sea of red mud. At last it drove the men indoors. David chafed at the delay.

"I'd rather have the dust," he said dismally. "My God, we're all half-drowned! And that damned mud! Slipped on the platform and almost broke my goddam neck!"

Amantha teased him into relaxing. That night, after putting Peter and Meggie to bed, they sat together over a cup of hot cocoa, listening to the rain on the roof.

"We don't do this often enough," Amantha said.

"We'll do it more," he said abstractedly. He was looking about the kitchen, seeing it as if for the first time. The out-of-plumb window, ruined wallpaper, pans set in various spots to catch drips from the leaking ceiling.

"I haven't been very good to you," he said suddenly. "I don't notice things a woman would. And I've been around the oil fields so long I've forgotten what a nice house is like. Charlie offered to let us have his cabin, then he would move in here. Maybe I should have taken him up on it."

"I'm happy here, David."

Surprisingly, she was. The rain gave a feeling of security, of being shut in, away from all the concerns that plagued her. For the moment they were a real family; the children sleeping soundly, David all to herself.

He reached for her hand, trailing his fingers along her

cheek in a loving gesture. "I've made a lot of mistakes," he said. "Maybe I've had my priorities all wrong. You're one helluva good wife. If you asked me to give up the oil business right now—"

"I'd never do that."

"I know." David turned her hand palm up and kissed her fingers one by one. "I know. And I'm going to make it up to you some day. When I get things squared away, we'll have a nice home, travel. And every time it rains, we'll sit like this, drinking cocoa, growing old together. . . ."

"I'd like that," she said.

"We will, and that's a promise." He yawned and stretched. "Don't know what happened, but I'm so damned relaxed I can't keep my eyes open. What do you say, shall we hit the sack?"

Amantha rinsed the cups and they went to bed. She lay warm in his arms, listening to his dreams. Outside there was a glow of rain-wet flares. A pumpjack banged away in the distance. They'd come a long way since she arrived in Oklahoma; a shy British girl, who came to join a man who wasn't the boy she remembered; David, not too sure he wanted her, intent on reaching success.

Their lives had stabilized. They had both changed. Perhaps she most of all.

David had stopped talking. She felt the stirring of his need.

"I thought you were sleepy," she teased.

"I was. But I got to thinking about the years ahead of us; of the nights we've missed being together like this. I—I guess I want to make up for lost time. That is, if you have no objections—"

"None at all," she whispered as his hand began to caress her.

"I love you," he said huskily. "Sometimes I forget to tell you. And sometimes I get so tied up with the patch that I forget to show you. Well, it's going to be different from now on. I promise you. . . ."

His mouth touched hers and she felt it open like a flower. She slipped her arms about him, feeling the smooth warmth of his flesh against her hands. And then, her own need an

94

unbearable ache, she went to him with all her heart, all her body, all her soul.

"David, oh, David, oh love—"

Afterward, drugged with love, she lay listening to the rain, thinking of David's words. She'd grown accustomed to his promises, accepting them without expectation. But tonight they'd been sincere and heart-felt. There would be hard years ahead. She'd learned not to believe in miracles. But things were better. They'd grown close. And someday, as he'd said, they'd drink cocoa on rainy nights, grow old together.

There was nothing more she wanted from life.

Finally, Amantha drifted into sleep.

She woke to David stumbling about, swearing as he tried to get his feet into wet boots. Someone was out there fooling around the wells. He'd heard a strange car. It wasn't the Springers' jalopy, or Charlie's truck. Could be some damn thieves stealing tools. . . .

"I'll take care of it," he ordered. "Go back to sleep."

Amantha lay back, smiling, as he hurried from the house. She was certain it was his imagination. But his trip outside might provide certain benefits. He would return, fully awake, chilled from the rain—and she would be there to warm him.

She frowned. Now that he had gone, she did hear a motor running. She rose, with a vague premonition of trouble, and searched for her slippers, then flinched at a noise that sounded like a gunshot.

David's pistol was still beneath his pillow. He hadn't taken it—

She hurried into the front room. The Winchester was still on its rack. It's only a backfire, Amantha told herself as she made her way to the door. Her knees were weak and shaking, her mouth dry. She could see headlights near a derrick, like two dim yellow eyes diffused by the pouring rain. A figure was delineated briefly by a flare.

It was not David!

Her harsh, indrawn breath was swallowed by the wind and rain. And then she was running, slipping on the wet porch, sliding in the mud. Her slippers were gone, her gown soaked and plastered against her body as she stumbled toward the

95

flare-lit scene. She could hear the vehicle's engine race as its driver sought to free it from the muddy terrain. Then the wheels found purchase and the car roared toward her, slewing sideways as it came.

She saw the face of the passenger, illuminated by burning gas. A face from hell—unmistakably Indian, copper-colored in the torchlight, eyes and mouth black circles of fear as the car bore down on her.

Amantha threw herself to one side and the vehicle was gone. She rose and stumbled on, covered in mud, her hair soaked with rain. She heard herself making a small whimpering sound as she approached the well.

A shadowed form lay at its foot.

"David? David!" Her voice rose to a scream.

"Da-ya-vid-d—"

She reached the spot where he lay face down and fought to turn him, incomprehensible words spilling from her lips in short gasping sounds.

"It's all right, David. He's gone. Wake up, David! David, please, you're frightening me-e-e—"

She managed to turn him. His upraised face was coated with muck that filled his eyes, his nostrils, his open mouth. She looked in horror as mud bled away with the rain. His open eyes reflected the light of the flares.

"David?" It was a timid whisper. "David!" Her fear was overcome by an irrational anger. "You can't! You can't die! You promised me! You promised—Oh God, you promised!"

His head lolled in her arms and she began to tremble. Had those animal sounds issued from her lips? She must get help! Help! But she couldn't leave David lying here like this.

She threw back her head and screamed.

"Charlie! Char-r-lie-e!"

Charlie Forbes had heard the sound of an engine when it first turned into the field. Feeling vaguely uneasy, he rose and dressed, thinking to go check it out. Then he cursed himself for being a fool. Yet it was possible some Skaggs or Springer relative had come in from out of state. He'd look like a fool, rushing out to see what was going on.

He sat down to pull off his boots, but a premonition still

nagged at him. It took him to the porch where he stood peering into the rain. He was still reluctant to cross the little creek. It was running full. The crossing must be made on a log that served as a bridge upstream. Even if the car held a trespasser, David could handle it. He turned to go back in.

And then he heard the shot.

In Charlie's mind there was no mistake about it. He knew a gunshot when he heard one. He ran for the bridge, crossing the red torrent with cat-footed caution, then ran again. He heard the grinding of gears as a car shot onto the road at the far end of the patch, and dashed on without stopping. Reaching the Carmody home, he paused to get his bearings. And he heard his name, a thin wail that cut through the sheeting rain like a knife.

Amantha!

He found her lying across the body of her dead husband, protecting him from the rain, her thin gown stained a deeper red than the flare-lit Oklahoma clay. The derrick rose above her black and skeletal—a monument to the dead.

Chapter Fifteen

*I*t was still raining two days later when the body of David Carmody was laid to rest. Amantha, white, eyes darkly circled, still had not wept. She stood, stiff-backed and tiny, beside Charlie, until the coffin was decently covered. Perhaps this was why the sight of red, running mud repelled her on her arrival from England. Perhaps she had sensed it would come to this.

The man who killed David had not been caught. Probably he never would be. The sheriff and Charlie had reconstructed the crime. The murderer had been stealing drip gas for his car. A bucket and funnel attested to that. A jar, evidently kicked from his car, contained a few drops of whiskey, indicating he was drunk. And the face that was seared indelibly in Amantha's mind was that of an Indian.

He hadn't meant to commit his senseless crime, Charlie believed. Trapped in theft, he'd been frightened out of his sodden wits and reacted instinctively. It seemed improbable that he'd hit his target, or that the gun he left at the scene had fired at all. It was an old .44-caliber Smith and Wesson. One handgrip was completely gone, the other hanging, half-broken away. The front sight was knocked off, the gun itself pitted with rust.

The statistics did not matter to Amantha. David was dead.

"Amantha?" Charlie tugged at her arm, and she followed him to his truck, not looking back. They were the last to leave, the remainder of the small cavalcade now headed toward home. Amantha climbed into the truck and sat, face frozen, gloved hands knotted in her lap.

"Amantha—" Charlie began.

Her mouth twisted wryly. "Spare me your words of wisdom, Charlie. I know you mean well. But this isn't the time."

"I just wanted to say I'm here. You-all got anything needs doin', I'd be mighty proud—"

She turned that new level look of hers on him. "You can make train reservations for me, and take us to the station. I'm going home to England."

Charlie's jaw dropped in dismay. For a moment he lost control of the wheel, and the car slithered sideways on the mud road. Righting it, he turned to Amantha.

"Goldang it, you cain't! This here's your'n! Ol' Dave'd blow his top if you walked out on what he done! He—"

"David is dead. The children and I have to go on living!"

Charlie scratched his head in exasperated frustration. He couldn't let her run out on Dave like that. And he couldn't break through the barrier she'd erected since he was killed. She was like a woman of ice.

She'd thaw, he thought morosely. Give her time. Dave's death had knocked him, Charlie, off his pins. Had to be a durn sight worse for her. Despite his attempts to reassure himself, he felt a sharp gnawing of fear. Pete was his little buddy. And Meggie—goldang it, he'd been the first to hold her. It was like she was his own. And Amantha—

He wished he was dead in Dave's place.

Contrary to Charlie's hopes, Amantha set about packing. First, she opened David's trunk, where his money and ledgers were kept. It contained more money than she'd ever seen in her life.

She ran her fingers through greenbacks, neatly fastened with rubber bands. There was enough here to buy a little house. To David, it would have represented another rig. His eagerness to succeed had been his own undoing.

She took out David's ledgers, opening the first, running down the rows of neat figures. He had kept track of every expenditure. *Work gloves; fifty-nine cents. Shirt and pants: three fifty. Can of Prince Albert*—the list ran on and on.

Until, finally—*Amantha: twenty dollars, groceries,* announced her arrival into his life and his ledger.

Her finger moved on down, stopping dead at an entry that read, *Rosie: three hundred.*

Amantha slammed the book shut and held it in her arms, rocking back and forth. In her mind she could see them together, David and his Indian mistress, the words of the tune played over and over at Merk's screaming in her brain—

"Tell me why you lie-yi-yi to me—"

He hadn't truly lied. He hadn't!

"You honky-tonk and slip around on me—"

The girl threw herself at him! Anna said she did!

"I love you warm, I love you su-sweet
And you tomcat down on Reno Street—"

I loved him, Amantha thought. Dear God, I loved him!

"Tell me why you lie-yi-yi to me-ye-yee—"

And she still loved him. Would love him always. The tears came now, flowing freely, tears that no one would ever see.

She put the ledgers back in place and went on with her packing. They would leave the day after tomorrow. That would give her time to tell the children, get them accustomed to the idea, and to have a business conference with Charlie. The latter was not going to be easy.

That night she didn't sleep. Suddenly the green meadows of home seemed alien, too many miles, too many years away. The thought of leaving Charlie left a wound. He, like everything else in her life, was a reminder of David. But she hated this land that had taken her husband from her; his cruel red world, its veins pumping oil.

"David," she whispered into the darkness, "Help me—"

There was no answer.

In the morning she pulled on a ragged housedress she intended to leave behind and a pair of ankle socks and tennis shoes also to be discarded. Her good shoes were still wet, covered with mud from the cemetery. She hadn't been able to bring herself to touch them, but it must be done.

She pinned her hair loosely, in deference to her aching temples, then took the children to Anna's. It would be better that they didn't watch the packing. Five years of living must be compressed into two pieces of luggage; that was all she could manage to carry. Everything must be listed as to whom it should go. The children's outgrown things to Edna Skaggs, pregnant again. The framed picture with its English scene to Anna. The Zenith—

She touched the radio with reverent fingers. It had been her close companion. Of course it must return to Charlie. The gyrator—

A knock sounded at the door. She hurried to answer it and looked straight into David's eyes.

No, not David's. This man's eyes were the same shape and color, but they were cold and calculating beneath the gray hat that shielded him from the rain. His square-cut body was clad in an expensive overcoat that matched the hat. His stance, too, was familiar.

"You the English woman?"

His eyes swept over her, assessing her from head to toe, taking in the ragged dress, the white socks, the tennis shoes. Her knees went weak.

"I am Mrs. Carmody," she managed. "David's wife. You are his father? Won't you come in?"

He stepped inside. In one swift glance he scanned the poverty of the house, children's beds in the front room, peeling paper, pans set to catch the drip.

"I've been kept informed of David's operation here," he said disdainfully. "I was under the impression that he was doing better than this." He indicated his surroundings with a gloved hand.

"David was doing very well. He—we chose to live here on site." Her chin was lifted now, blue eyes beginning to spark.

"He's done more than I expected of him. But I didn't come to talk about David. I—"

"Mr. Carmody, you do know that David's—"

"Dead? Yes. That's why I'm here. I'm aware that a woman isn't capable of handling a business—even a two-bit operation like this one. Not at a profit. So I have a proposition—"

"And I have a partner," Amantha interrupted, her voice cold with anger. "I do not think—"

Again that wave, dismissing anything she had to say as not

worthy of consideration. "Forbes? Checked him out. Seems like his main credential is that he's a good ol' boy." He drawled the last words, making them sound like an insult as he opened a briefcase and removed some papers. "He won't be hard to handle. Now, here's my offer—"

Amantha listened in disbelief as he set forth his terms. As she must know, he was a widower. He needed a housekeeper, someone to keep his home running smoothly. He would give Amantha and the children a home, in return for which he would take over the management of the field here and set up a decent corporation along the lines of his own.

One day, after a proper upbringing—unlike Dave's—Peter would be his heir. If she would sign here—

"No!"

All the memories David told her of his childhood, the hatred that marred his life, rose before her and sounded in the vehemence of that one word.

"My dear woman, you really have no choice."

"I have many choices, and I assure you, yours is the last I would consider."

"Now, wait a minute!" His lips smiled, but his eyes were angry. "You haven't heard me out."

"It isn't necessary. The answer is still no."

The smile faded, the man's mouth going taut and hard. "You're making a mistake. I'm not without influence in this state. I can break this penny-ante operation. Get custody of the kids. They're my grandchildren."

With a swift movement, Amantha lifted the Winchester from its place on the wall, pointing it at him.

"It's loaded," she said in a whisper. "Now get out of my house! You won't get your hands on David's property unless I make a mistake. And I do not make mistakes! One step toward trying to take my children, and I will kill you! If you do not leave now, I shall shoot you where you stand!"

David's father shoved his papers hastily into the case and backed from the pointed weapon. Outside, he whirled and ran for his car. Charlie, guessing at his identity, had listened outside Amantha's door. He grinned, watching the intruder speed away, tires flinging mud on his shining limousine.

Then he entered to face Amantha. Her pallor was gone. Her face was pink with fury.

"I am not leaving, Charlie," she spat. "I have changed my mind."

Charlie leaned against the wall, rolling a cigarette to still his trembling fingers. "Didn't think you'd run out on us," he said calmly. "Never figgered you would."

Her hands were still clenched, but her voice was level as she asked a question.

"Charlie, how can we start a corporation?"

Charlie looked at her in surprise. "Lord, girl, I dunno. Reckin we'd have to git ourselves a lawyer."

"Then, I suppose," she said, her eyes narrowed in thought, "we'd better start looking for one."

Chapter Sixteen

C*harlie asked around and came up with several prospects.* The likeliest was a young attorney, Thorne Greenberg. He was just out of school, beginning his apprenticeship with Kerr-McGee. He was ambitious, certain that he could bring a small company to the top. He agreed to look over their holdings, and, if satisfied, was willing to begin at a minimum salary—along with ten percent of Carmody-Forbes stock.

"Only problem," Charlie said, "goldang it, I don't like his looks! Too durn slick to suit me."

Amantha didn't agree with him. Knowing they must appear to be important in order to entice Greenberg from his present job, she set up their first meeting. They would talk over lunch at the Skirvin.

Thankful it was winter, Amantha dressed in her good tweed suit, worn now, but still serviceable, along with a slightly frayed blouse that brought out the color of her eyes. Charlie, at her insistence, had donned a rusty black suit with sleeves too short for his long arms, and a tie that he swore was strangling him.

Still, Amantha felt shabby as they entered the plush hotel and were ushered to a table covered with snowy linen. Charlie, too, was uncomfortable. When Thorne Greenberg arrived, impeccable in well-tailored garments, Amantha's heart sank. This man couldn't possibly be interested in their little operation—

Charlie introduced them, and Greenberg's manners were as impeccable as his attire. He sat down, and Amantha studied him covertly over her menu. Tall, slender, his black hair lay close to his head, as shiny as patent leather. His eyes were brown, gleaming with intelligence—but she had the feeling one would never know what he was thinking. Perhaps that was what bothered Charlie.

Their orders given, he got immediately to business. Amantha liked that. And during the course of the luncheon, he agreed to go over their books and set up a workable system.

In turn, Amantha stated her wishes. She and Charlie would retain fifty percent of the stock between them. She would like to set up a corporation like the now-defunct Marland Oil Company, in which employees received benefits and would have the privilege of buying stock if they wished. She intended to improve their living conditions, to beautify the ruined land after the drilling was completed, as Marland did.

"Marland went bust," Charlie said gloomily.

Greenberg had studied the Marland case. It was a textbook company that had gone down through profligate spending and cronyism. It would be a challenge to succeed where Marland failed, and it would damn sure be a feather in his cap.

"That doesn't mean it cannot be done." Greenberg's voice was silky. "Of course, this may be a long-term project, depending upon what I find regarding your financial situation. Newer management techniques stress the security of the worker. But, if you two do not agree—"

"Amantha's the boss. I just handle the drillin'."

Greenberg studied the small woman who faced him across the table. Even the dowdy garments she wore failed to hide a flowerlike beauty and a poise many of the newly rich tycoons' wives would envy. He thought of her sitting across the table from some of the hard-nosed oil men she'd have to deal with.

He had an idea she could handle it.

"There is one more thing," she said quietly. "No person of Indian descent is ever to be employed on Carmody-Forbes property. Not in any capacity, as long as I am involved with the business."

"Looky here, Amantha!" Charlie said angrily, "You can't blame—"

"I believe the lady is within her rights, after her recent

tragedy," Greenberg said in a mild voice. "If she should change her mind at a later date—"

"I shall not," Amantha said.

Greenberg knew of Carmody's death. He had no way of knowing of the drunken Indian on a train—Amantha's first glimpse of a red man—nor of Rosie. But it would not have mattered. He'd caught a glimpse of steel in the slight English woman that intrigued him. With her determination and his expertise, they could go far—providing, of course, that their operation had a strong enough financial base.

To his surprise, further research indicated that Carmody-Forbes was sitting on a gold mine, a seemingly inexhaustible good grade of oil. David, unbeknownst to Charlie, had leased a number of surrounding areas before they'd even started drilling, at an unbelievable low price. The stash in the chest David kept beneath the bed amounted to more than Amantha guessed. In addition, she turned up a bankbook. There was an account he hadn't mentioned.

Amantha felt a swift surge of anger. Here, she and the children had lived in poverty, and all the while they had been rich. Then her anger dissolved in pity for the man she'd loved and lost; the man who had to prove his worth to his father; who wanted so much that whatever he had wasn't enough.

She thought of the gray-suited, hard-eyed man who appeared at her door after David's death. Now she could understand.

We're going to make it, David, her mind whispered. Maybe it won't be exactly the way you would go about it, but one day—we'll show your father! We'll show the world! And that's a promise!

Thorne Greenberg drew up the papers for incorporation. He also prepared a budget that included some extraordinary expenditures.

The oil field shacks were to be replaced with more permanent structures. Health and death benefits would be provided for the workers, along with an option to purchase company shares. An office was to be leased, furnished, and maintained in the city.

And he'd taken the liberty to list a number of large homes

in the capitol area that were for sale. He would help Amantha in selecting the furnishings, and also her clothing from an allowance set aside for that purpose.

Amantha, looking at the sum, was staggered. "I don't understand—"

"It takes money to make money," he explained.

The structure of Oklahoma City society was made up of old families, many of whom had come here after the Civil War; those who had made the run when the territory was opened— and the newly rich.

She must make a name for herself among these people. She would be entertaining; attending luncheons, dinners, benefits; dealing with oil men, refineries, suppliers; surrounded by wives who would be able to estimate the clothing she wore to the penny. In all these circles, it was class that counted. There were few women in her position, that of operating a large and wealthy corporation. She must take advantage of that, and make it count.

"I had thought," Amantha stammered. "I had thought—"

Dear God, what had she thought! That she would sit at the kitchen table as David did, adding up columns of figures?

"There is a dinner next week," he went on, inexorably, "of the Independent Petroleum Association. Your name has been entered as a member. I've made an appointment for you at a beauty salon, and we must find something suitable for you to wear. . . ."

"Perhaps Charlie could go instead," she said, looking to him for help.

"You are management," Greenberg said firmly. "Charlie— sorry, old man—but Charlie is regarded as labor. The way this is set up, there's a definite division of responsibilities. Now if you wish changes—"

"Don't reckon that'd work," Charlie said with a painful grin. "Me, I ain't much for tea parties. That oughta be Amantha's job."

"Good." Greenberg smiled at Amantha. "Suppose we count on tomorrow for shopping?"

"I don't think you need to—"

His brilliant eyes swept over her. Today she wore the same tweed skirt and a much mended sweater.

"Forgive me," he said quietly, "but I think I do."

When he had gone, Amantha's cheeks were stained with red. "He's brilliant—but insufferable!"

"And he's right," Charlie said, avoiding her eyes. "I reckon you better do what the man says."

A week later Amantha stood before an admiring audience that consisted of Anna, the children, and Charlie Forbes. She wore a long gown of dark blue velvet, cut low in a sweetheart line to bare her creamy shoulders, fitted tightly to flare a little below the hips. Small velvet heeled pumps completed her ensemble. The whole costume had the effect of understated elegance. A fur-lined matching cape of velvet was draped over one of the rickety kitchen chairs, to be donned when her escort arrived.

"Well," Amantha asked, breathlessly, "what do you think? I'm not sure I can handle these heels."

Charlie looked at the tiny woman, her blue eyes wide with excitement, ash-brown hair smooth and shining from an expert hairdresser's hands.

"You look almighty purty, and I reckon you can handle anything."

There was such reverence in his voice that he blushed and began to collect Peter, Meggie, and Anna, shooing them out before Thorne Greenberg should arrive.

Left to herself, Amantha thought blissfully of the previous week. She and Greenberg had located a site for the Carmody-Forbes offices—and a huge mansion-like home near the capitol. Tonight she would make her first appearance on behalf of the new corporation. She closed her eyes, imagining the scene: well-dressed men like Greenberg; women in beautiful gowns and jewels—

Jewels!

Amantha went to the chest beneath her bed, removing the ring that had been David's Christmas gift. She slipped it on. Her hands, after a week of creams and lotions, were presentable again. It glittered there, this seal of David's love, like a star.

"I'll make you proud of me tonight, David," she whispered. "I promise."

Then Thorne Greenberg arrived, complimenting her on her appearance, helping her into his rented limousine.

From behind the curtains of Anna Springer's shack, as Amantha's children hugged close, Charlie Forbes watched Amantha and Greenberg drive away. And he knew that this night would put more than miles of distance between himself and his dead friend's wife.

Chapter Seventeen

*D*avid Carmody had refused to socialize with the various oil-men's organizations. He prided himself on being a "working stiff," earning his way through the sweat of his brow. Still, the company heads who comprised the Independent Petroleum Association had heard of him and his phenomenal successes just prior to his tragic death.

The fact that his wife planned to succeed him, and had, in fact, set up a corporation, titillated their curiosity. Amantha, entering the dining room, was the focus of all eyes.

She also came as a shock.

Whatever they expected, it was not this fragile, poised little woman with eyes like blue stars. As Thorne Greenberg introduced her, one rough, tough oil man after another succumbed to her charms. Their strong, male, protective instincts came to the fore as they vied to help the bereaved little widow.

"The oil business ain't no place for a lady. Look, you need any help, you call on me. This here's my private number—"

"How you getting your oil to the refinery? Tank trucks? How much they charging you? That's too damn much! I'll do it for half—"

"You can tie into my pipeline—"

"Don't you trust him, Miz Carmody! He eats little girls like you for breakfast."

They were big, burly men with soft drawling voices, and manners that were courtly and gallant. Amantha liked them. At dinner she found herself seated at the head table, and accepted it as though it were her rightful place. If a few overdressed wives cast poisoned glances in her direction, it didn't matter. She listened, taping every word she heard into her retentive mind.

She was introduced as a new member of the association, invited to serve on the committee for the upcoming Pageant of Petroleum Progress to be held sometime in the future. And, though the state was dry, there were plenty of flasks in evidence. Before the evening ended, she was the recipient of a great deal of maudlin sentimentality. She had a fervent farewell from every man in the room as she and Greenberg left the gathering.

"Allow me to compliment you," Greenberg said as he assisted her into the limousine. "You've got them eating out of your hand!"

"They were very kind."

"Don't let them fool you, Amantha. This is a dog-eat-dog business."

"I would like," Amantha said, reflectively, "a complete dossier on each of them. A copy of their holdings, their financial status, their methods of dealing; anything regarding their personal lives. . . ."

Greenberg's jaw dropped. "Good God! I haven't got access to that sort of—"

"There are ways," she reminded him. "Surely you know people in banking. There are courthouse records, the newspapers. And, if necessary, you can always pay some small stockholder to divulge information."

"But—dammit, why? I don't—"

"I cannot afford mistakes. By avoiding those they've made, I can protect Carmody-Forbes. And nobody's going to try to take us over if I know where the bodies are buried!"

"Do you know what you're saying?" he sputtered. "You're talking about bribery! Blackmail!"

"You misjudge me," she said in a tone of injured innocence. "I just like to be informed. And, by the way, I would like your dossier, also. And a complete rundown on my father-in-law's operation, near Tulsa. Do you suppose you could provide a series of charts, showing our standing as far as other corporations are concerned?"

111

"Right now," he said angrily, "we're just peanuts! Give us a year or two; time to float a loan for expansion, and—"

"No loans."

"But Amantha!"

"No loans. See that there are sufficient reserves to handle any emergency. And I would like to see a five-year projection, based on our present situation, as soon as possible."

They had reached the oil patch. He helped her from the car and walked her to the door, his mind still reeling with a new discovery.

This was not going to be as easy as he'd thought. He'd expected to hitch his wagon to the Carmody-Forbes star and go with it to the top, using Amantha Carmody as window dressing. But it was clear the lady had a mind of her own, one of the shrewdest he'd ever encountered. He'd listened to her tonight, giving the proper answers to the proper questions, skirting any that might give away their own business secrets.

He wouldn't be allowed to do the wheeling and dealing he'd had in mind. It was going to be a slow, tortuous process. Unless—

Unless he could talk her into a different kind of merger. And why not? She was a damn beautiful little thing, a widow, and he was unmarried. Maybe, if he went slowly enough, she might be relegated to a woman's proper place.

Inside the shack, Amantha looked around, seeing it as only a dim memory. She went to the kitchen table, fingering the stack of books on business she'd been studying this last week. Tonight they had paid off. She had listened to the talk around her, understanding most of it. Before long she would be as knowledgeable as anyone. She had moved into a new world; a world in which names like Kerr, McGee, Urshel, Phillips, were commonplace. And to the list, she'd added David's name!

The new Carmody-Forbes offices on North Broadway would be painted, paneled, and carpeted within a matter of weeks. Tomorrow she would start interviewing people to staff it.

And her house—ah, the beautiful house Thorne had found for her! It had a mansard roof, its exterior looking like an

English manor. And even now, in the winter, she could imagine its lawns and gardens. . . .

A slight frown creased her forehead as she thought of furnishing it. She'd wanted a cozy, British atmosphere, but Thorne insisted the lower floor be modern, with polished hardwood floors, a bar, a grand piano, wide expanses for entertaining.

He'd hired a decorator to see to it. She thought, forlornly, that it would not seem like a home.

And worse, there was nothing here that she could take with her. Only Charlie's Zenith. And that, if it embarrassed Thorne Greenberg, could be hidden in her room!

Of David, there would be only memories, two children, and a ring.

If they had only made the move earlier, David would be with her. Why, oh, why, had he been so insistent on doing everything the hard way? If he were watching now, would he understand what she was working toward? Or would he think she had failed him?

"I'm trying, David," she said, sitting down at the table, leaning her forehead against the cool leather bindings of the books that were her guides. "I'm trying. Maybe my way is different, but we're going to make it! Just believe in me."

A knock at the door brought her to her feet. She opened it to admit Charlie Forbes.

He'd just stepped over to tell her the kids were asleep. Anna tucked them into bed and suggested she leave them there till morning.

"Thank you, Charlie."

He shifted from one foot to another. "Well, how'd it go?"

"Very well." The glow returned to her face. "I made many friends."

"Figgered you would."

"Charlie, I—it just isn't right! You're not an employee! You're co-owner. You should attend these—"

He shook his head, grinning his slow, crooked grin. "Me, I'm just a ol' country boy, and I like it that way. Never had a hankerin' for sassiety. Figger that's for someone a mite purtier'n me."

113

"But—Peter's going to miss you when we move to town. You're—all he's got."

He flinched at her words. He'd been worrying some about that himself. Pete had been quiet since Dave was killed. Too quiet. Durn it, the kid needed a dad! And with Amantha so goldang busy—

He'd decided to have a talk with her about Pete, but now wasn't the time. No point in giving her anything else to worry about.

"Got his mother, ain't he?" Charlie said. "Boy'll make new friends, more his kind. Nope, I'll just stick around and watch the operation—"

"Charlie." Amantha's face had gone white. "Charlie, if there's any theft going on, you won't—"

He knew what she was thinking. The same picture was in his mind: David Carmody, lying dead in the rain and mud, flares reflecting off his unseeing eyes.

"I ain't no hee-ro, Amantha," he said quietly.

"I couldn't—couldn't bear it if anything happened to you, Charlie—"

He took a step forward, then stopped himself. This was Amantha Carmody, his friend Dave's wife. She'd worked and slaved for a long time, but she was on the way to being a great lady now. Too good for the likes of him. . . .

"Just don't fergit me," he said raggedly. "Just don't fergit me. And now, goldang it, what does a feller hafta do to git a cuppa coffee around here?"

Chapter Eighteen

In 1936, on the nineteenth of November, a Pageant of Petro- leum Progress was held in Oklahoma City, coincident with a meeting of the Independent Petroleum Association of America.

At the festivities accompanying the occasion, special recognition was given to a small, poised, beautifully gowned English woman. Amantha Carmody moved graciously through the ceremonies and receptions, occupying the Carmody-Forbes limousine in a parade.

As an attraction, an instant gusher was brought in for the benefit of visitors. Using controlled timing, gas was piped into a small producer and, through high pressure, a stream of oil was sent over the crown block.

The event was covered by photographers for national newsreels. Paramount and Fox-Movietone were on hand to film the spectacular. When the films were shown at local theaters, they attracted large crowds.

Oklahoma City was proud of its own.

And perhaps the proudest viewer was Charlie Forbes. He sat through all the showings for two nights running, just to catch a glimpse of Amantha Carmody. And finally he managed to wheedle Amantha into allowing him to take the children to see the newsreel.

They sat beside him now, Peter stiff and mannerly, Meggie crowing with delight at seeing her mother on the screen.

"Mama's pretty," she laughed, clapping her hands.

"You betcher boots," Charlie grinned.

But mingled with his pride was a pang of regret. Amantha

115

was no longer the lost little stranger who arrived in the city on a rainy night. Nor was she the laughing girl who sat on a creekbank with him, watching as Peter fished for the first time in his life—

And the last, come to think of it.

Amantha had a thing about the oil patch. She'd never been back to see what was going on out there, just took Charlie's word for it. And as far as Pete was concerned, she didn't want him to dirty his hands in the business. He was enrolled in a private school, and when he was old enough, she planned to send him off to school in England.

The newsreel ended. Charlie reached out, putting his arm around Peter's thin shoulders, wishing there was some way to break through his polite facade.

"That's it," he said. "It's over. S'pose you-all could set through the show agin?"

Meggie set up a clamor to stay, but Peter shook his head. "Thank you, Uncle Charlie. But if we are late, Mum will worry."

"Reckon you're right."

Charlie rose reluctantly, lifting Meggie in his arms, leading the way from the theater. Amantha'd been overprotective ever since the kidnapping of the Lindbergh baby, and was extra-careful now that she'd become so well known. He appreciated the boy's consideration for his mother but, goldang it, Pete was too good. He was just a kid. He needed to bust loose once in awhile!

They reached the truck, and Charlie carefully rearranged the towel he'd brought to cover the seat. Wouldn't do to spoil the children's clothes.

"Why don't you get a new truck, Uncle Charlie?" Meggie asked, after he'd gone through the involved process of starting the engine.

"Reckon I'm a critter of habit," Charlie grinned. "I like somethin', I kinda stick with it. Ain't much for changin' things."

He drove them home and stopped before the door. Amantha's car was gone. Probably she'd run back to the office for some late-night work. A maid stood waiting in the doorway as the children said their good-byes. Charlie put out a staying hand.

"Say, Pete." He cleared his throat. "Been thinkin' about fishin', lately. S'pose you'd like to go along?"

"Oh, yes!" The boy's face was alight for a moment, then it settled into a noncommittal expression that almost—but not quite—covered disappointment.

"Of course," he said cautiously, "I would have to get Mum's permission."

And probably Thorne Greenberg's, Charlie thought wryly, along with the rest of the goldurn board!

"Well," he said, forcing a grin. "Thanks for goin' with me. See you—"

He waited until he saw the maid usher them in and close the door behind them, feeling sorry for young Peter Carmody. Then he grinned and shook his head.

These kids had everything: a beautiful home, the back garden filled with toys and swings. Amantha was already talking about putting in a pool and tennis courts.

Charlie thought of his own childhood; of walking along the crick in his patched overalls, barefoot; the way the warm dust felt squinching through his toes. . . .

Maybe he had a touch of sour grapes. He had to face up to the fact that these kids were out of his class. Amantha, too.

Thinking of Amantha, he pulled out his pocket watch, then put the truck in gear and headed downtown.

If he hurried, he'd get there just about the time the movie ended—and the newsreel began again.

BOOK II

Peter

Chapter Nineteen

In the exquisitely appointed conference room of Carmody-Forbes, the leading stockholders were already assembled and waiting for the president of the corporation. Amantha, usually punctual, was late.

Her chair, at the head of the long shining table, was empty. Still, her power was such that voices were kept low, and an occasional glance was slanted in that direction as though seeking affirmation.

Charlie, in from the field in his clean work clothes, lounged back in his chair and grinned. Amantha had the Injun sign on them, fer sure. If these folks knew how many times she'd fallen apart on him these last years, scared she was making mistakes, scared she was neglecting the kids—

The last time was when the bombs started dropping on London. He'd held her then, and she cried on his shoulder.

The memory made him shift uneasily in his chair. He'd come pretty close to making a darn fool of hisself that night. Wasn't till he got outside and cooled off that he remembered he wasn't in her league a-tall!

Amantha went right back to business as usual, like she intended to win the war all by her lonesome. He was goldang proud of her for that. He didn't think much of her hunting up Nanny Goforth, hiring her back so she could handle her work with a free mind. Wasn't that Amantha's old nurse didn't take good care of the kids. She was just too set in her ways. And she didn't know a goldurn thing about raisin' boys.

And now lookut what had happened! When Amantha heard

about it, she wasn't gonna to take it sittin' down, that was fer sure! Charlie wasn't looking forward to the cozy little chat he'd promoted for tonight. . . .

"Mister Forbes!"

Thorne Greenberg's voice brought him out of his reverie. Charlie swallowed his irritation. He still didn't have any use for the man, and he was pretty sure the feeling was mutual.

In that he was correct. In spite of Greenberg's hail-fellow, well-met attitude toward what he privately thought of as "the working class" he was forced to maintain a reasonable relationship with Charlie Forbes. The man, after all, was a majority stockholder.

At least, Greenberg thought, until I can get my hands on enough shares.

Greenberg was an ambitious man, and he had several options. Unbeknownst to Amantha, he'd been summoned to a conference with her father-in-law, a stocky bulldog of a man who had a going corporation near Tulsa.

"Break her," the elder Carmody said, slamming his fist on his desk. "Don't give a damn how you do it. Fix the books! Tell her the company's sinking! Get her to take out loans. I'll buy 'em up—"

He was to be well paid for his services, including a whopping block of stock and a job for life.

To date he'd failed in his mission. Amantha was too shrewd in her dealings, keeping account of everything to the penny. And as Carmody-Forbes became more successful, he began to wonder if his interests weren't better served here.

For instance, there was Amantha herself. She was a beautiful woman, and he was irresistibly drawn to her. Marrying Amantha had been his best bet. But she put him off in those earlier years, the memory of her husband too recent. And since the war began, America finally getting into the act, she'd been oblivious to him—except in his professional capacity. Greenberg had a notion that this gray-eyed, lanky red-neck was in some way an obstacle to their relationship. The idea was ego-shattering.

Now he forced himself to be genial.

"You didn't seem to be listening," he said. "We were discussing our contribution to the war effort."

"Didn't know the meetin' took up," Charlie said laconically. "Amantha ain't here yet."

"There isn't any reason we can't talk about it." Exasperation lay beneath the thin veneer of Greenberg's suave words. "I was just saying how vital our business is at this time. The military needs oil for machines, planes, tanks, and trucks; to produce tuolene for explosives; the butadiene constituents of synthetic rubbers; aviation and diesel lubricants; specialty products such as chemicals and cutting oils."

He paused for emphasis, knowing he had the attention of the board.

"And, good God! Think of the demand for high octane! This is the opportunity of a lifetime—"

His oration bothered Charlie. Didn't matter that there was American kids over there gettin' killed. The feller was in hawg heaven, counting his profits.

"Don't reckon Amantha's gonna go fer gougin' the guvment," Charlie put in mildly.

"I said nothing about gouging! And Amantha's a sensible woman. There's no reason we shouldn't expect our share!" Greenberg reddened at Charlie's quirked brow.

"Now, see here, Forbes! You're choosing to twist my statements. I'm a firm believer in patriotism. I'm taking all steps toward doing my best for my country!"

"You joinin' up?" Charlie sat up a little straighter. "Goldang, Greenberg. Didn't know you had it in yuh! Congratulations!"

He extended a calloused hand across the table, and Greenberg recoiled, stammering a little.

"I didn't—I mean, I'm not!—My work is classified as essential—You don't understand—"

Charlie filled his pipe and took his time tamping it. "Reckon I do," he said, grinning ruefully. "They give me the same bull when I tried to enlist. But I figgered that classified crap was fer them that pumped the oil out—didn't know they give deferrments fer bee-ess'n."

Greenberg's face flamed. The damned hayseed was trying to make a fool of him. "Now, see here—"

The entrance of Amantha Carmody saved the day. The men rose to their feet, Charlie lazily uncoiling last of all, and Amantha took her chair.

She tapped her gavel and the meeting began.

Charlie let the motions of business, the minutes of the last meeting and financial reports waft by him. He'd never liked this part of it. Didn't give a durn, about who moved to vote on what. It was enough to feast his eyes on Amantha Carmody. His mind went back in time, seeing a small, dowdily dressed girl in the depot; remembering the way she looked when he brought home the Zenith; the days when a wooden cradle filled her eyes with tears of happiness; when an electric gyrator was the answer to her dreams.

He had to admit it was good to see her, shoulders straight, in command of the situation.

She did look peaked, though. The wild-rose color that stained her cheeks had drained away. It bothered him. Mebbe she was working too hard. Or mebbe she'd got wind of what he had to say to her tonight. . . .

"Now," Amantha said crisply, "is there any new business? Yes, Thorne?"

Charlie hunched his shoulders and shifted his position, enduring Thorne Greenberg's endless monologue. Stuff a cork in his goldang mouth, he'd bust, he thought.

Finally, Greenberg was through and Amantha took the floor again.

"I have an announcement to make," she said quietly. She set an official-looking document before her and began to read.

President Roosevelt had appointed Secretary of the Interior Harold L. Ickes as petroleum coordinator for national defense. Ralph Davies of Standard Oil would be his deputy. They were to organize units dealing with the problems of production, refining, and transportation; conservation, foreign oil resources, research, and information.

Amantha folded the paper, and raised her eyes to the listeners.

124

"I," she said simply, "have been appointed to their committee. I shall be making frequent trips to Washington."

Her words fell into an awesome silence. It was broken when a stockholder cheered.

"Hot damn! This puts us in the big time!"

The meeting broke up without the usual formalities, as the board members crowded around Amantha, congratulating her. Only Thorne Greenberg and Charlie stood back.

Charlie was frankly worried. The war had taken Amantha from her home and kids too much already. She was doin' enough, by golly. Mebbe when she heard what was goin' on right under her nose, she'd turn this down.

Greenberg was upset. After all, he fronted for the company. With his expertise, he would be able to parlay it—and himself—to the top on the national level. He should have been the one. . . .

Amantha had managerial ability, he'd give her that, but she didn't have his vision.

Yet she had been called, and not he.

He could rebound from his disappointment if he could win Amantha for himself. He thought of going to Washington, Amantha as his wife. He would have the opportunity to show what he could do. And she would be an asset, socially.

When the room began to clear, Greenberg made his way toward Amantha, his white teeth gleaming in a broad smile as he held out his hand.

"I waited for a clear spot," he said. "I was so overcome with your news, I didn't know what to say. I still don't, for that matter! I think it's superb."

"Why, thank you, Thorne."

Amantha's eyes were unfocused, her graciousness automatic.

"I think we ought to celebrate," Greenberg continued, enthusiastically. "Just say the word and I'll reserve a table; pheasant, champagne, the works. I'll call for you at eight—"

"Too bad, Greenberg." Charlie's drawl sounded behind him. "The lady's busy tonight. Goin' to see a play at Northeast High. Pete's got the lead part, and I'm takin' her."

Amantha managed to conceal a fleeting look of dismay. In

125

her struggle to get through this day she'd forgotten the play—and Charlie's insistence on accompanying her.

Dear Heaven, she didn't want to see anyone tonight. She only wished to be left alone. And Charlie hinted he wanted to talk to her regarding the children. She wasn't in the mood for any advice, however well-meaning! But she had to remember he had their interests at heart. Dear Charlie—

"Sorry, Thorne," she said gently. "Another time."

When they were gone, Charlie back to the field, Thorne to his office, Amantha gave instructions to Dodie, her secretary.

"Please see that I'm not disturbed."

Then she went to her inner sanctum, closing the door behind her. For a moment she stood, leaning her head back against the cool paneling, letting her tears flow. She had survived the ordeal. And none of them guessed that Amantha Carmody's heart was breaking.

Crossing to her desk, she opened a drawer, placing the letter from the President inside and taking out another that arrived in the same mail.

It was from her sister-in-law in England, Ian's wife.

Ian was dead, shot down near Germany on a bombing mission.

Amantha's mother suffered a stroke upon being informed. Though she still lived, her mind was affected; thus the letter from another's hand.

The lovely old house Amantha remembered was now a refuge for children from bombed-out London. At present, carpenters were putting up partitions in the salon. . . .

It was gone. All gone. Her father, brother, mother—her childhood home—David, who had wooed and won her there.

Her past was effectively erased. She might have been born this minute.

Except for my children, she thought fiercely. I have my children.

Nothing could take that away.

Amantha, who had only wept twice since David's death—once at the death of King George, and again when Edward, Prince of Wales, renounced his throne for an American divorcée—wiped her eyes and set her jaw.

There was still work to do.

German submarines were playing havoc with oil tankers. Railroads and trucks were unable to meet the military and eastern seaboard needs. A big-inch pipeline was being laid with incredible speed, an average of nine miles a day.

But it wasn't fast enough. Amantha's desk held a plethora of orders that could not be filled without sufficient transportation.

For the moment there were no answers. She rubbed her aching temples and left work early.

It was an unprecedented action. Her secretary watched her go, in disbelief.

Chapter Twenty

*B*y the time Charlie arrived, Amantha's nerves were at the breaking point. Ian was dead. And she had left her vital work unfinished to attend a high school play. She paced the floor, a small, slender woman wearing a dark dress and a single strand of pearls.

Charlie Forbes sensed her tension when he arrived and set about alleviating it.

"Durn it, Amantha, set down! We got half an hour yet. World ain't gonna come to a end if you relax a minnit!"

It already has, Amantha thought dazedly. It has for me.

She obeyed, sitting stiffly. Charlie lounged across from her, lighting his pipe, spilling crumbs of tobacco on the carpet.

"Where's the kids?" Charlie asked from behind a cloud of smoke.

"Nanny's helping Meggie dress. Peter didn't come home. It appears they're running through one more rehearsal. Charlie, how long do you think the play will last?"

"Couple of hours, I reckon."

"I wonder if you'd mind bringing Peter and Meggie on home in your truck?"

Charlie's face was glum as she explained she'd left some work undone. She intended to have Ryan, the chauffeur, drive her straight to the office when the affair was over.

"Mebbe you better quit thinkin' about work and start worryin' about your kids," he said jerkily.

128

"Don't be silly, Charlie! There's a war on, remember?"

"Kinda hard to fergit," he said. "But they's other things that's important, too. We're gonna have to have a talk—"

Amantha forced a smile, folding her arms in mock exasperation. "All right, Charlie, let's talk! It's about Peter, right? Now, let me see! He should be allowed to go to public school. I've already allowed that."

Then, in a parody of his drawl, "That kid oughta have him a old model car to work on, git hisself dirty once in a while. Nanny Goforth is too goldang strict. Boy his age hadn't oughta have a shofer drivin' him to school—

"Which is it, this time?"

"Wisht it was any of 'em," Charlie said morosely.

"For Heaven's sake, Charlie, say it, whatever it is—I'm too tired to play games."

"You ain't gonna like this, Amantha." Charlie swallowed and ran his finger inside his collar. "Pete wanted me to tell you—there's this girl—"

"A girl?"

"Pete and her got a case on each other. He said I could tell you about it. But he wanted you to see her first. She's in the play—"

Amantha felt a knot in her stomach. Nanny'd voiced dark suspicions; lipstick on Peter's shirt; a line in the *Norseman Scroll*, the school paper—

"Peter and Joylene," it read, *"are the latest woosome twosome."*

She'd ignored it. It seemed alien to her son's character. And after all, Peter was not an unusual name. The "lipstick" was probably showcard color. He'd mentioned working on posters for tonight's affair. . . .

Dear God in Heaven! What was she worrying about! She laughed, with an edge of hysteria.

"Charlie, this is absurd! Peter's only sixteen! Just a child! I suppose he might have a romantic fancy for some little friend, but it can't be more than that!"

"All I'm askin' is that you stick around home tonight. Give the kid a chance to tell you hisself. I reckon he needs some advice."

129

"Of course, Charlie!"

Her initial concern had given away to amusement. Poor old Charlie, always making mountains out of molehills. When Peter had measles, the man had hovered around his sickbed like an old woman!

"Just standin' in for Dave," he said.

She wanted to reach up, to smoothe that worried frown from his tanned forehead. Charlie had always tried to fill David's shoes as the family protector. She wondered if David would have taken parenting as seriously.

Meggie was clattering down the stairs and Charlie Forbes reached for Amantha's wrap, settling it around her, his traitorous hands lingering a little in the gentlemanly act. Peter had moved to a secondary position in his mind. It was Amantha who mattered most; Amantha, as fragile as a dandelion puff; who already carried too great a load for one little woman to handle.

She looked so goldang pale tonight. This thing with Pete could break her up in little bitty pieces.

Charlie wished he could tell her the whole story, but that was Pete's job. The kid had to face up to the situation like a man.

He only hoped that he could help her put those pieces together again. Now, he just wanted to hold her—

Amantha looked over her shoulder, perplexed at his slowness, and he felt his face flame. Meggie's entrance dissolved his tension and he turned to her in relief.

"Well, young lady! You're purty as a speckled pup! Ready to go out among 'em?"

Meggie was ready. A little blond bundle of giggles and enthusiasm, Meggie was always ready for anything.

When they reached the auditorium, Amantha felt another pang of guilt. This was her first time setting foot inside Peter's school. She'd received invitations to attend PTA, but somehow she'd always been busy on those nights; conferences with out-of-towners, special meetings, dinners. . . .

She was on a treadmill, and she couldn't let down. Not until the war was over.

Charlie found four empty seats in a row, and they sat.

Amantha looked over the crowd, seeing scrubbed young faces; parents beaming with pride. The audience ranged from the privileged living in the capitol area to oil field types in their faded work clothes. They had all come to see their children perform.

"Bet Bob's scared as hell," a father in front of her chuckled to his wife. "Know I would be, gettin' up in front of all these folks—"

"He's only got two lines, Harry. And we've gone over them every night—"

Amantha froze. Was Peter nervous? She hadn't thought of that! And who had listened to him memorize his part?

She had no idea what the play was about!

I'm failing them all, she thought. Ian, David, Peter—

The orchestra was tuning up. Everyone stood as it launched into the school song.

"Crimson and silver gray, we're flashing to vic'try—"

It ended in a rousing cheer, and students and parents sat down once more. Amantha sank back as the plaintive notes of the play's theme heralded the opening curtain.

It opened to reveal a ballroom scene, exotically costumed youngsters dancing to the theme music. Then, with a flourish of drums a pompous butler announced the arrival of the prince.

Amantha caught her breath as Peter strode from the wings, the picture of royalty. Ian, she thought dazedly. A young Ian.

Meggie suffocated a small screech of delight with her palm. Charlie placed his rough hand on Amantha's.

"Ain't he a jim-dandy?"

Amantha had to admit that he was. She watched and listened, enthralled, to the interchange of stage conversation. Then her heart stopped.

A girl had stepped forward.

Rosie!

David's Rosie!

Just so had Rosie stood in her beaded Indian garments on Amantha's first night at the Tremenco camp. The tawny rounded face, dark eyes, long black hair—

She approached Peter, placing a gloved hand on his ex-

131

tended arm. Amantha looked at her program. The girl's name was Joylene Cloud.

The school paper! *Peter and Joylene—a woosome twosome— David and Rosie—*

No, Amantha thought dully. No. There was a buzzing in her ears and she shook her head to clear it. Charlie had a tight grip on her wrist. She made herself relax.

For her the play dragged on interminably. At the end the prince renounced his throne.

"I do not wish to wear a crown. I only want your love."

There was a concerted sigh as Peter kissed Joylene. A whimper issued from Amantha Carmody's pale lips. And in the brief silence that followed, she heard the whispering behind her.

"They been practicin' that one!"

"Didja know Joylene's pregnant?"

"Shee-yut! He ain't man enough!"

"Maybe he had some help."

Amantha took one look at Charlie's face, seeing the guilty knowledge written there. He knew!

The curtains drew across the scene. There was tumultuous applause and they opened. Peter and Joylene, hand in hand, bowed an acknowledgement. Finally the orchestra broke into the strains of the school song and everyone stood.

Amantha pulled free of Charlie and forced her way through the standing row, hurrying down a side aisle toward the front, Charlie and Meggie behind her.

Charlie caught her arm. "Where do you think yer goin'?"

"Backstage!" she hissed. And then she was gone.

The cast was still assembled, laughing, congratulating one another, when Amantha burst into their midst. Peter's face reddened as he dropped the arm that encircled Joylene's waist.

"Mum!"

"Come, Peter, we're going home."

"But, Mum—"

"I said come, Peter. I will brook no nonsense."

Her appearance was almost frightening: face ashen, lips

132

tight. Peter Carmody looked beyond her, seeing Charlie and Meggie.

"Better do what she says, Pete," Charlie drawled. "Reckon she ain't feelin' too good."

Peter followed his mother, Charlie, and Meggie to the waiting limousine. They rode home in silence.

Amantha sent Meggie to bed, then asked Nanny, Charlie, and Peter to join her in the den. There she moved to sit behind her desk, appearing to gain strength from her position.

"I have decided to send Peter to a private school in Washington. I will make arrangements for him to transfer, immediately—"

Peter's young voice cracked for the first time in weeks as he stepped forward. "I won't, Mum! I absolutely refuse—"

"You have no choice in the matter."

"Amantha!" Charlie tried to interrupt, but she silenced him with an imperious hand.

"You will remove that ridiculous costume, and you will pack, tonight."

"It's Joylene, isn't it? You know about Joylene?"

Amantha's silence was answer enough.

"Well," Peter said savagely, "you're not going to send me away! I'm going to marry her, whether you like it or not! She's—she's—"

Amantha was on her feet, her desk chair crashing to the floor. "I won't hear another word from you, Peter! God in Heaven! The girl's a—a conniving little opportunist! An Indian! They're drunks, whores! Murderers! And you—you!" her voice rose to a shrill pitch—

"You're no better than your father!"

She stopped short, appalled at what she'd said. The room seemed to echo with her words. Charlie and Peter looked stunned.

Amantha's voice, when it came, was almost a gagging sound.

"Go to your room, Peter! Go to your room!"

Peter looked at Charlie, who nodded. He turned on his heel and went upstairs.

"Follow him," Amantha ordered Nanny Goforth, "and lock his door."

Peter, divesting himself of his royal raiment, heard the key turn in the lock.

He went to the door and tried to turn the knob, tempted to shout and batter the door down. Changing his mind, he donned slacks, a shirt and sweater, his tennis shoes. And, finally, he stood for a moment taking a last look at the room that had become a prison; the room Nanny still referred to as a nursery. A narrow bed, bookshelves with every book he'd ever owned; a silly toy he'd had most of his life—a small furry rabbit attached to a bulb. When one squeezed the bulb, it hopped.

He touched it with a remembering hand, then turned to the window. Raising it, he unhooked the screen and crept out on the branch of a tree. He'd often thought of doing this, but hadn't, due to a fear of heights. He wasn't afraid now. Somehow it didn't seem to matter anymore.

Cautiously, he made his way to the ground, where the shadow of the tree lay black against winter grass.

And he was free.

Chapter Twenty-One

The evening ended for Joylene Cloud when Peter left. She still smarted from the look Mrs. Carmody gave her. As if she were dirt. She was tempted to leave the school. Instead, she changed into a skirt and sweater, and, head high, rejoined the rest of the cast.

In answer to the queries regarding Peter's absence, she said his mother was ill. If she recovered, he'd be back.

Her words were met with grins of disbelief. It was clear everyone knew Mrs. Carmody decided Joylene wasn't good enough for her little boy and dragged him home.

No one was more surprised than Joylene when Peter appeared in the doorway. She ran to him and he drew her outside, where they stood shivering in the chill air. There, holding her close, he told her his mother's plans to send him away in the morning.

"Pete, no!"

"I'm not going. I've left home and I won't go back."

She was silent for a moment, her dark eyes stricken. "What are you going to do?"

He didn't know. He wanted to marry her, get a job, a house of their own. But his mother would use any means to stop him when she learned he was gone. Maybe if they ran away, hid out until they were old enough—

"You really mean it, Pete? About getting married?"

"More than anything in the world!"

"Wait!"

Joylene reentered the school and returned, her dark eyes

glowing. She'd talked to one of her friends, whose sister eloped with a GI. At Wichita Falls, across the Texas border, there was a justice of the peace who didn't ask questions.

"But that's—"

"A couple of hundred miles," she beamed. "And, see—" she held out her hand. "I scrounged enough ration stamps for gas—"

"But I haven't a car."

"We'll take my uncle's. He leaves his keys on the hall table, so there's no problem. He'll be mad as the devil, but he won't report us to the cops. I'll leave a note."

Peter was silent as they walked together toward the place she lived, baby-sitting small cousins in exchange for room and board during the school year. It was there, in the family's absence, that they had consummated their love; a lonely, misfit boy who rode to school in a limousine and an Indian girl, homesick for her mother in Anadarko.

With that consummation, Peter had become a man. But now he had to admit that he was scared. Scared to death.

Don't let him be sorry, Joylene prayed, looking at his somber face. Please don't let him be sorry! I'd just die—

"Pete, are you sure this is what you want? Your mom's rich. You'll be giving up an awful lot."

He smiled, his lips trembling a little as he quoted a line from the play.

"*I do not wish to wear a crown. I only want your love.*"

It's like the Prince of Wales and Mrs. Simpson, Joylene said to herself. Romantic and beautiful. She thought of her mother and father in Anadarko. With their house full of kids, they were concerned only with shoes and groceries. And then there was her uncle who sat around in his undershirt, drinking beer and reading the paper while her aunt complained.

Her life would never be like that. She and Peter would always have this wonderful, warm closeness.

"*I'll be loving you*," she began to sing, "*always—*"

He stopped and pulled her to him, kissing her in the darkness, running his hands over the soft, well-developed body that held his child. And he knew he would never be sorry.

It was she who finally drew back. There was no knowing how long his absence would go undetected. They must hurry.

Her uncle's gray Nash was parked at the curb. Joylene slipped inside the house and filched his keys. As an after-thought, she scribbled a note and left it by the telephone.

Tiptoeing out, she handed the keys to Peter. He looked down at them in confusion.

"I've never driven—"

"It doesn't matter," Joylene said. "I have."

Joylene slid behind the wheel and they were away. She couldn't help giggling a little at the thought of a girl driving herself to her own runaway marriage.

"What are you laughing at?" Peter wanted to know.

"Nothing. Nothing at all." She smiled at her helpless little-boy groom, feeling a warm wave of maternal affection. "I'm just happy, that's all."

Taking one hand from the wheel, she curled her fingers in his and they settled back for the long drive.

Peter's absence was not discovered for some time.

After the boy was sent to his room, Charlie tried to reason with Amantha, who was angry beyond rationality. "You punishin' Pete," he asked, "or Dave? You still got Rosie on yer mind after all these years?"

"That remark was inexcusable!"

"Well, I ain't apologizin'. It's about time you got yer thinkin' straight. Could of been a white chippy Dave picked up at Merk's—"

"But it wasn't," she said icily. "And, if you remember, it was a drunken Indian who murdered David."

"They's plenty Injuns kilt by drunk whites," he reminded her. "Goldang it, Amantha, git back to the point. We got us two kids here, Peter got the girl in trouble, an' we got to figger out what to do about it!"

"Is three hundred dollars still the going rate? Or is this one more expensive? Give her whatever she asks for, get her out of town!"

Charlie looked stunned. Then he said, "How you plan to

buy Pete off? Girl didn't do it all by her lonesome! Dammit, Amantha!''

Charlie never used profanity. And he was looking at her as though he didn't like her.

"Stop hammering at me, Charlie! Oh, God! I can't take anymore today—"

Amantha burst into tears, harsh racking sobs that tore at her throat. Then Charlie was beside her, his arms around her.

"Amantha, honey—don't—"

Once started, she couldn't stop. She poured out the story of Ian's death, her mother's illness, the taking over of her old home; her guilt at neglecting her children; business pressures due to the war. . . .

"I can't take anymore! I can't—"

Charlie held her, too shaken to do more than murmur little incomprehensible words of comfort and love. When she began to quiet, clinging hard to him, he dared to hope. Finally she pulled away, wiping at her ravaged face.

"I don't know what I'd do without you, Charlie. Don't ever be angry with me. I need you."

"And Pete needs a pa," Charlie said cautiously. "Amantha—if—"

"He needs David," Amantha wept. "We all do! Oh, Charlie, why did David have to die! And Ian—"

Charlie retreated to his chair and sat studying his hands, trying to hide his emotions. Goldang it, he'd almost done it again. He changed the subject.

"Why don't we sleep on this. Things'll look better in the morning."

She shook her head. They wouldn't. She must talk to Peter, tell him she was overwrought, that she didn't mean the ugly things she said. There could be no question of Peter marrying that girl, but they would try to work this out, come to some sort of understanding.

Together they climbed the stairs to Peter's room. Amantha called out the boy's name. When there was no answer, she opened the door.

Peter's costume lay in a heap on the floor. A blast of chill air stirred the curtains of the open window.

Peter was gone.

Amantha's anger returned, this time under icy control. She whirled and went downstairs, calling the school.

There was no answer.

Then she searched the telephone book, swiftly running her fingers down the Cs. Clare—Clemm—Cloud—

There was only one. She dialed the five-digit number and a sleepy man answered, irate at her question.

"Who? Your son? Here? Why the hell would he be here? It's four in the morning!" And, finally, "Rachel, see if Joylene's in yet. There's some nut on the phone—" A pause, and the telephone began to crackle as Joylene's uncle exploded in a blast of profanity. Charlie saw Amantha go white.

"A note? They've gone away to get married? I—I see. They stole your automobile? I assure you, Peter wouldn't—"

The telephone crackled again and Amantha slumped as if all life had gone out of her. "I understand—"

Then her lips tightened. She reached for a pencil. "I would like a description of the vehicle, please . . . Gray Nash . . . 'forty model . . . And the license? Thank you—"

She hung up, searched for another number, and dialed again.

"I would like to report a theft," she said. "My son is involved."

Chapter Twenty-Two

*P*eter *and Joylene arrived in Wichita Falls in time to* interrupt the justice of the peace's breakfast. He had not shaved, and there was egg on his stubbled chin. The young couple watched, fascinated by the bobbing blob of yellow as he read the service. Then it was done and they were outside on the walk, a signed and witnessed certificate in Peter's hand. It had been so swift, so simple in comparison with the enormity of their elopement, that it didn't seem real.

A cold wind swept the streets of the Texas town, picking up trash and slapping it against their ankles. Joylene was shivering. Peter was uncertain, feeling he was supposed to take charge somehow. He reached to take her hand.

"Well, Mrs. Carmody," he laughed, self-consciously, "I think a wedding breakfast is in order."

They found a small café and sat at a table in a secluded corner, exchanging shy glances as they tried to look like they'd been wed forever. Joylene, with an eye to their finances, ordered short stacks and coffee. The cakes were bitter with soda, the coffee leftover, strong and black. It didn't seem to matter. They scarcely touched the food. The excitement of their adventure wore off, and now they must review their situation.

They had to return the car to Joylene's uncle. They would have to go home and face whatever recriminations awaited them.

"I'll need to find a job," Peter said uncertainly.

He felt wretched, the responsibility he'd taken on growing

in his mind. It all seemed easy last night. Now he was a family man. He must find some way to pay rent, to put food on the table. He wondered what kind of work he might be fitted for.

"I can work, too," Joylene offered. "I can wait tables—"

Peter looked at the slovenly, yawning waitress clearing another table and shivered. "No," he said, "we'll find a way to manage."

Maybe, he thought, Mum would forgive him. If she'd only allow them to stay until he found something to do! Until the baby was born—

"I have my headright," Joylene said, "my tribal money. It comes in quarterly."

He stared at her, seeing the Indian features, her dark eyes and long black hair. His heart sank. He loved her just as she was, but her words pointed up the fact that they could expect no help from his mother.

He was frightened, but Joylene was also afraid. It was up to him to reassure her. He cupped her hand in his.

"It will be all right," he said. "I promise you. It will be all right."

They paid their check and went out, shivering in the cold. The heater in the car didn't work. Peter sat close to Joylene, an arm around her shoulders as she drove out of town. They had not gone far when a small explosion sent the car sluing sideways. Joylene fought it to a stop at the side of the road.

"A flat!" she said disgustedly. They both climbed out and surveyed the blown tire.

"Well, I guess you'd better put on the spare."

Peter looked at her blankly.

He had never changed a tire.

She showed him how to set the jack, to use the lug wrench. When they finished, they were both exhausted, streaked with black.

They looked at each other, then suddenly began to laugh; irrepressible howls that bordered on hysteria. They were laughing at themselves, at their ridiculous wedding day: the dismal ceremony; the seedy café; the flat tire; a bride and groom with dirty faces, heading home to face the music.

"At least," Joylene finally sputtered, pushing her hair back with a blackened hand, "things can't get much worse."

Peter kissed her, loving this girl who made him laugh as he'd never done before. Life with her was going to be so wonderful—

A passing car honked in salute to the lovers and they sprang apart, realizing they were visible to others. They were putting the damaged tire in the trunk when a police car pulled up behind them. Peter fumbled and the tire fell to the ground. They waited, frozen with fear.

"He did it," Joylene whispered, terror in her dark eyes. "My uncle called the cops. Oh, Peter—"

"Shhh!" Peter's voice was trembling. "Let's try to bluff it out."

He righted the tire once more and tried to smile at the approaching policemen.

"It's all right, officers. Just a flat. We're ready to move on."

As one man noted the license plate, the other questioned him.

"Name."

"Peter Carmody. And my wife." Peter thrust the marriage document forward as proof.

"Driver's license?"

Peter and Joylene looked at each other. They had none.

Their questioner snapped his book shut. "We got 'em," he said to his companion. "Take him on in the squad car. I'll drive the stolen one and bring the girl."

He had his hand on Joylene's wrist. She began to struggle as Peter was led away.

"He didn't steal anything. I took the car. It's my uncle's and I borrowed it. I left a note. If he says Peter stole—"

"Don't tell me your troubles, sister. We're taking you into Lawton. You can make a phone call—"

Charlie Forbes was in Amantha's home, sitting near the phone when it rang. Amantha had gone to the office, her face still set in a frozen mask. Charlie chose to remain behind. He grabbed the telephone, to Nanny Goforth's chagrin, breathing a sigh of relief at the sound of Peter's voice.

He listened carefully, then asked to speak to the desk sergeant.

"I'll take responsibility," he said. "Just hang on to 'em till I get there."

He wondered if he should call Amantha and tell her the kids were in custody. He decided against it. Nanny Goforth could handle that little detail.

Late in the afternoon Peter and Joylene were free.

The major charge, theft, was dropped. A call to Joylene's uncle elicited that he did not wish the girl prosecuted. He only wanted his car back. Joylene was not to enter his house again.

The minor charge, driving without a license, was forgiven with a fine. Charlie paid it. He also employed an off-duty policeman to return the Nash to the Cloud home, since Joylene was not allowed to drive.

On the way back, jammed into Charlie's old truck, they were quiet. Charlie, for Amantha's sake, tried to talk some sense into them.

They was dang fool kids, jumpin' smackdab into livin' before they knowed what it was all about. The marriage wasn't no good, them being under age. He figured Amantha already had Greenberg settin' it straight. There was a place where girls had babies and put them up for adoption—

"Joylene is my wife," Peter said stubbornly.

"All I'm sayin' is you oughta make peace with your families. Grow up a mite. Then, some day, if this is still whatcha want—"

"She's my wife, Uncle Charlie!"

"Then how the devil you gonna keep care of her?" Charlie snapped.

There was no answer, and he drove on in silence. Amantha had been adamant. Peter could come home, but she would not have that girl in her house. Charlie couldn't go against her, but he durn sure couldn't let these kids starve.

"If yer gonna play growed-up," he said finally, "yer gonna have to face the consequences. I'll loan you a couple

143

of hundred. Loan, I said. And I'll help you find a place to rent, help Peter git a job. From then on, yer on yer own—''

It was late night when he left them in a light-housekeeping apartment in Capitol Hill. The apartment consisted of a living-sleeping room and a tiny dark kitchen. A bath was shared with two other apartments. The landlady provided sheets, pillows, a ragged quilt, and some pots and pans.

Peter surveyed it gloomily: the sagging bed, peeling paint, a tear in the wallpaper showing layers of various prints that had graced the room over the years.

"It's rather dreadful, isn't it?"

"It's our first home," Joylene consoled him. "Don't talk about it that way!"

He put his arms around her, then flinched at the sound of a dripping tap.

"Listen to that."

"Don't worry about it, sweetheart. You can fix it tomorrow."

"I'll try. I've never done it before."

"I have." Joylene's loving voice was tinged with exasperation. Then, seeing his face turn miserably red, she hugged him.

"It isn't a leaky faucet," she laughed. "It's a waterfall! And this is a tropical island and we're on our honeymoon."

She spun away from him and snatched up a towel, wrapping it around her middle. Then she shook her black hair until it hung wildly about her face, and swayed her hips seductively.

Peter began to grin. "I like the sarong," he said judiciously, "but it might look better without the sweater—"

She peeled it off and stood facing him, her shoulders golden in the light, her lips slightly parted, eyes glowing in the excitement of their game.

But the game was over. Peter's clear blue eyes were shadowed with emotion.

"I love you, Joylene," he said quietly. Then, in a voice taut with desperation, "I need you."

This was not their first coming together. Before, they had been a little guilty; awed, frightened, finding their way. This night there were other elements; they were man and wife, free to indulge in passion that shook them to their very core—

144

And they were two lost children, yearning to comfort and be comforted.

Tomorrow, with its frightening decisions, was still hours away. In the meantime, there were kisses to be exchanged; the warmth of body against body; the opening of one to the other like a flower. . . .

When Peter finally slept, his face buried against her breast, Joylene gazed into darkness for a long time. She could have sworn Peter's face was wet with tears.

Gently she smoothed his fair, silken hair. He was her husband, her love, her little boy; her prince who couldn't drive a car, fix a flat or a dripping tap.

What could he do?

The future was suddenly dark and frightening as she held him in her loving, protective arms.

Chapter Twenty-Three

*W*ithin two days, Peter had a job. Charlie vouched for him, finding him a position as "boll weevil," or helper, on a well. He was to work the second tour. Approaching the well on that first afternoon, Peter had a dim memory of a long-ago conversation with his mother.

He asked if he'd have to work in the oil fields when he grew up. Never, she told him. One day he would be president of Carmody-Forbes.

Well, he'd blown it. He set his teeth and moved ahead to sign in, the new overalls and pristine dinner pail proclaiming his amateur status among the other jostling men.

It was a bright blue day with a freezing wind that cut to the bone. Wearing a jacket, Peter was soon soaked with sweat. He removed it and was chilled.

The workmen had a new butt for their jokes: a scared kid still wet behind the ears. They pulled out all the stops.

Peter had a hard time differentiating between legitimate commands and false ones.

"Git me a left-handed monkey wrench, dammit!"

He ran himself ragged, looking for a tool that didn't exist, then found himself in trouble for not doing what he should have been doing instead.

Squatting during the break to eat his supper, he discovered somebody had defaced the shiny black pail. Lewd pictures and words were scratched into it.

He couldn't stop the tears that brimmed; tears of fatigue and frustration. He dragged his sleeve across his eyes.

He could not work with these people. There had to be something better!

Peter closed the pail and rose, walking around the derrick floor to where the boss driller and tool pusher were eating, their backs to him.

"Amantha Carmody's kid?" The tool pusher's voice was incredulous. "You gotta be kiddin'!"

"Charlie Forbes said so. Give 'im the job on Charlie's say."

"I be damned! One thing fer sure, he ain't got the balls his old lady's got. Don't reckon he'll stick it out."

Peter backed away and returned to his supper.

He stumbled home at midnight, clothes filthy, hands grease-blackened, blistered, and bleeding. He knew, with a sense of humiliation, that he didn't earn his pay that day. Nor would he, if he maintained the same standards of ineptness.

"Got two left hands," a co-worker grumbled. "And his goddam fingers is all thumbs."

To Joylene, however, he was her husband come home from a hard day's work. She cleaned the grimy little apartment until it was shining and made a midnight meal for him.

Peter was too tired to be hungry. All he wanted was a bath; to take his aching body to bed. He tried to make a show of pleasure as he sat down to lumpy gravy, heavy biscuits, scorched carrots, and a pie with a crust like leather.

"It all tastes awful, doesn't it?" Joylene asked in a small voice.

Manfully, he tried to comfort her. But they went to bed and lay apart, Joylene's feelings hurt, Peter too tired to care.

The situation did not improve. Peter tried doggedly, but the working of things mechanical was beyond his comprehension. His slender body had not been toughened by labor or sports. And Joylene was unaccustomed to loneliness. Maybe if she went back to school. . . .

"Don't talk like an idiot!" Peter exploded. "You're pregnant, remember? And we can't even afford carfare!"

"If you think I'm going to be stuck in this place when you're gone all day—"

Joylene stopped, her eyes rounding.

"Peter! We're fighting!"

They made up, each begging the other's forgiveness. But their togetherness did not last long. Peter returned one night to find her absent. He went through a few minutes of hell. Maybe it was the baby—a miscarriage; this neighborhood wasn't too safe. Perhaps some man—

When she came in, her eyes were shining. She'd taken a bus downtown and gone to the movies. Greer Garson—

He shouted at her, his relief turning to anger, making him say all the wrong things.

They could not afford movies! They could not afford these! He pointed to a stack of movie magazines with lurid covers. Joylene would have to grow up!

"Grow up!" Her voice rose almost to a shriek. "I stay here by myself, cook for you, wait up for you! And do I get any thanks?"

"I'm sorry. I'm—tired, I guess."

"Well, I get tired, too. Tired of living like this!"

She fled to the kitchen and he followed her, turning her to face him. The big dark eyes were glassy with tears. He kissed them away.

"It's all my fault," he said huskily. "I've been so worn out. But, sweetheart, I love you! Please love me—"

"I do, Pete. I do!"

They went to bed and she clung to him. He felt his passion stirring in spite of his exhaustion, and their love was new and wondrous once more.

Joylene solved two problems: what to do with her lonely days, and how to put some money aside for when the baby came. She found a job waiting tables.

Peter was unhappy about it. It didn't seem right, he said gloomily. He was the man of the family. It made him feel like a failure.

"I'm doing it because I want to," Joylene argued. "I have people to talk to—and look what I brought you!"

It was a copy of the *Daily Oklahoman* left discarded at a table.

Long after she was asleep, he read the Help Wanted ads. There seemed to be nothing he could do.

For a time their life seemed to be brighter. Peter felt an ache of resentment when he learned that with tips she was bringing in more than his salary. But Joylene was happy and cheerful, dispensing gossip from the café, loving him with a new abandon that made him catch his breath.

"You're wonderful," she insisted after a session of lovemaking.

Peter couldn't resist a wry grin. At least there was something he was good at.

And, finally, he was developing a sense of humor.

Joylene's working shift was from seven in the morning until late afternoon. Peter's tour at the well was from three until midnight. He would rise to a cold house, prepare his own breakfast, pack his own lunch, and grimly endure his day of hell.

At night, for a time, she was waiting to greet him. Then the long hours combined with pregnancy began to take their toll. Always Peter found a meal prepared for him and a discarded newspaper to read. Joylene would already be abed, asleep, dark hair swept across a face that, once the color of amber, had grown thin and pale. Her swollen ankles would be propped on the rolled-up quilt.

His heart ached at the sight of them.

Finally, Lon Talbott, the boss driller, had a talk with him, settling down beside him with his dinner pail. Peter couldn't help feeling a little flattered until he began to speak.

Pete wasn't doing too well. Oh, he wasn't gonna can him. But the guys were raising a little hell. Needed somebody that'd jump when they hollered frawg—

"I move as fast as I can."

"But you got butterflies, kid. An' you genr'ly move in the wrong direction. Hell, you been here long enough to know the ropes. Just think you might do better in some other line of work. . . ."

Talbott stood, closing his dinner pail. "Time to git back on the job—"

Peter looked at his half-eaten sandwich. It didn't matter. He couldn't swallow, anyway. He threw it away. It sounded

149

like the boss had just given him a chance to quit before he was fired.

The remainder of the day went no better. He dragged himself home to find Joylene asleep, lashes fanned against her sallow cheeks. A meal, of sorts, was on the table; a newspaper carefully reassembled and folded beside it.

Peter sat down. The apartment, chilly in spring, was now hot and stuffy. He had little appetite, but he must eat to keep up his strength. He opened the paper, noting the date.

His seventeenth birthday would be tomorrow.

It didn't matter. He closed his mind to it and scanned the headlines. London had suffered the worst bombing of the year, an explosive falling perilously close to Buckingham Palace.

He closed his eyes, remembering a small boy who'd been certain he'd live there some day; his mother holding him, telling him tales of castles and kings. . . .

Oh, God! Oh, God—

He went to bed and lay carefully away from Joylene. Her hair was damp with perspiration, her face dewed with it. Payday he'd see if they could afford an electric fan. Maybe they could open a charge account at Ward's or Sears.

"I love you, Joylene," he whispered.

She stirred and turned toward him in her sleep.

Chapter Twenty-Four

Throughout the night, Peter worried about Joylene. She was going to have to stop working soon. And what would happen if he lost his job? He'd be too ashamed to go to Charlie again.

He had handled things badly. He knew that now. He should have stayed, faced up to his mother, insisted she get to know Joylene before condemning her. Instead he behaved like a kid, thinking just because he was man enough to love somebody, father a child, he'd be able to support a family.

According to Charlie, his mother was still adamant. Peter could come home, but he must come alone.

What if he went to the house? Talked straight to her? She'd never have to see Joylene. They could live in the servants' quarters. Maybe if she'd let him work around the place for his and Joylene's keep, he could go back to school and get some training. . . .

It was worth a try.

The next morning, after Joylene left for work, he pulled on his old school clothes. They were too tight now, sleeves and trousers too short, but they were more presentable than his oil-stained working garb. He scrubbed his hands with borax, unable to remove the grime ingrained in them.

And then he took a crosstown bus, arriving thirty minutes before his mother normally left for work.

The sight of the big house caused a lump to form in his throat. There had been happy times there, despite the restrictions of his boyhood. Now he was afraid to approach the door. If he did and were turned away, it would hurt too much. . . .

He waited behind a bush near the driveway. When his mother came out, he would ask to ride with her to the office. On the way, he would tell her—

Tell her what? That he couldn't hack the outside world? That he owed Charlie so much he couldn't ask for any more favors? That he wanted to come home?

But only if he could bring Joylene—

An hour passed, and he was at the end of his nerves. Maybe his mother was sick, or Meggie . . .

Finally, he rounded the house, scaled the garden wall, and hid behind the shelter of a lilac bush.

He held his breath as the back door opened, then began to smile.

"Meggie—"

Meggie's eyes went round, her hand going to her mouth. With a glance behind her, she closed the screen and hurried toward him, flinging herself into his arms.

"Peter! You've come home! Oh, I wish Mum was here—"

She was laughing and crying at the same time. He shook her a little, affectionately.

"Where is Mum? Is she at the office?"

"Oh, no. She went to Washington. To see the President." Meggie's smile faded as she saw his look of disappointment. And for the first time, she noticed the rest of him.

"You look awful," she said frankly. "Your clothes are funny. Did they shrink? And why are your hands so dirty?"

"I—I'm a working man now." He laughed, self-consciously. "I have to make money. Meggie—what did Mum tell you about me, why I left?"

"She said you went to school. Then Nanny told Cook it was the school of hard knocks; you got married and are going to have a baby. Are you going to have a baby, Peter?"

He reddened. "My—my wife is."

"Then I'll be an auntie, won't I?" Meggie clapped her hands in glee, then sobered again. "Did you come home to stay? Are you good-and-tired?"

"What do you mean?"

"Mum told Uncle Charlie she's sure you'll come home. She's waiting till you're good-and-tired. She thinks that—that girl will leave if you're broke. Will she?"

"No, Meggie."

"Mum doesn't like her, I guess. She said that woman will never step foot in her house. Then Uncle Charlie got mad and said—"

"Never mind, Meggie." There was a note of hopelessness in Peter's voice that he tried to hide. "Let's talk about you. How are you doing?"

Meggie launched into a description of her activities, stopping to crow with delight as she remembered that this was Peter's birthday.

"Are you going to have a party?"

He shook his head, and she insisted on going into the house to sneak out milk and cookies.

He sat quietly behind the lilac bush, soaking in the atmosphere of sun and shade, imagining what it would be like to dress in crisp whites and play a game of tennis again. Afterward, there would be a dip in the pool. It looked clean and cool, the morning sun reflected in its rippling surface.

He missed all this. But he would not give up Joylene for any of it.

Meggie returned with her snacks, and they sat on the grass, each enjoying the other's company. When he finally mentioned leaving, his little sister ran into the house once more.

She returned with two things: her piggy bank and the little toy rabbit from Peter's room.

"These are for the baby," she said solemnly.

They looked at each other for a long minute. Peter had a feeling that Meggie understood more than he'd guessed. Choked with emotion, he hugged her fiercely. She hung on to him as if she'd never let him go.

"I miss you, Peter!"

"And I miss you. Meggie—promise me something. When Mum gets home, don't tell her I was here."

Meggie promised.

She stood watching as he stuffed the piggy bank and rabbit into his jacket pockets and climbed over the wall.

Peter Carmody went home, changed his clothes, and went to work. He arrived early and listened as the men gathered, shouting cheerful obscenities to each other.

"Hey, Mac, you lissen to the news? Krauts bombin' the shee-yut outta London."

"Hell, yes. Join up myself if I didden have six kids an' a ol' battle-ax."

"We're doin' our bit, ain't we? Let's git our butts movin'. Now, where's that goddam weevil?"

Peter stepped forward. It was time for the punishing day to begin.

His Armageddon came less than an hour after the shift started. A roughneck had left a bar on the catwalk at the crownblock. Knowing Peter's fear of heights, he ordered him to climb up and retrieve it.

Peter obeyed.

Reaching the top, his hands slick with sweat and his knees trembling, he picked up the bar—and looked down.

It was a mistake. He felt a rush of vertigo and dropped the bar as he reached to grip the railing. He watched with blind eyes as the tool hurtled, end over end, hitting the earth between two workmen who sprang away as it rebounded to strike a boiler with a resounding clang.

"Carmody," Talbott bawled, "git the hell down from there."

Peter could not move; could not release his grip as he stared, frozen, at the scene below.

Talbott and another workman climbed to the catwalk, talking gently now. Reaching Peter, they pried his hands free. Between them, they moved him down the ladder, rung by rung, until they reached the rig floor.

There, Talbott's tone changed.

"Draw your time," he said. "Like to help you, but I don't want none of my men killed. Now, git the hell out!"

Peter was sick with terror and humiliation. The other workers averted their faces, not looking at him, as he drew his pay and cleared the rig.

Hardly knowing what he was doing, he walked to downtown Capitol Hill, toward the café where Joylene would be at work. He needed her—needed his wife—

He reached the door and couldn't bring himself to enter. Instead, he wandered aimlessly. He had to find work.

But who would hire an inexperienced kid?

He paused before a shop window, staring blindly through the glass. It was some time before the poster made an impact on his mind.

Uncle Sam was looking back at him, his eyes intent, a finger pointed toward Peter's midriff.

Uncle Sam wants you!

Peter opened the door to the recruiting station and went in.

Chapter Twenty-Five

*T*wo *days later Amantha returned from Washington.*

Her trip had been a success. She'd met with the President, presented her ideas, and they were going to be implemented.

He had complimented her on her good sense.

She should have been euphoric. But on the flight home she'd had too much time to think. How could she hope to help with a nation's problems when she couldn't solve her own?

She tried to bury herself in work, but Peter's blue eyes looked out at her from every page. Finally, she stuffed the papers in her briefcase and leaned her cheek against the window, thinking of Peter's recent birthday, remembering him as a little boy; the special rapport between them.

What had happened to spoil it?

She closed her eyes, hearing Charlie's voice.

"Goldang it, Amantha, Pete's too good. One of these days he's gonna bust out all over the place."

"He needs to go fishin', git him a old car to work on, git hisself dirty."

"Yer lettin' Nanny make a sissy outta him."

"He needs a job fer the summer."

"He needs some friends."

"He needs his maw!"

She'd thought that Peter would be willing to leave that girl once the novelty wore off. It would be simple to get an annulment. After all, Amantha had friends in high places. But now it had gone on too long.

Charlie had got him a job on a rig. She knew where it was located, but she hadn't had the nerve to drive by, knowing she'd give in.

She knew enough about the oil business to guess the boy was going through hell. He'd be tired, dirty, beaten—

And all because of a girl.

Again, her anger turned toward Joylene.

When she reached home, she didn't notice that Meggie was unusually quiet. After she unpacked, Amantha went to Peter's room and stood there, studying it, as if she'd find the answer to all her questions there. A frown creased her brow as she noticed the small furry rabbit he'd had as a child was gone.

It was there when she left for Washington.

She approached the shelf. Maybe when the maid dusted, it had fallen behind—

"I gave it to him."

Amantha jumped at the sound of Meggie's voice behind her.

"I gave it to him, for the baby."

"Meggie! When—?"

"When he was here. I said I wouldn't tell, but I crossed my fingers."

"Oh, Meggie!" Amantha swallowed back tears. "How was he? How did he look! Did he say—?"

"His clothes got too short. His hands were dirty, and he's kind of all bones. I gave him some cookies and milk—"

Amantha pried all the information out of her. How Peter had come over the wall and into the garden. Dear God, this was his home! And he'd come on his birthday—like a beggar—

She went downstairs and called Ryan to drive her to Peter's rig.

The sun blazed down, and shirtless men were working doggedly when the limousine drew up. Everything stopped as a tiny, modishly dressed woman approached the rig and climbed to the floor. Talbott stepped forward.

"Jesus, lady, this ain't no place—"

He paused, recognizing a much-photographed face.

"Missus Carmody?"

Amantha nodded. "I've come to speak with my son."

The man stammered and stuttered. Pete had left the field a couple of days ago. He wasn't planning on coming back.

Amantha looked at him with level blue eyes.

"You fired him?"

"Well—yes'm."

The dressing-down Talbott expected did not materialize. Amantha left the rig and hurried to the car, instructing Ryan to drive her to the nearest telephone. She had a dreadful premonition.

She must talk to Charlie.

The field line was busy.

At one end of it was Charlie Forbes. At the other, a weeping Joylene. Peter was gone. She'd seen him off on the train this morning. He'd enlisted in the army. She was crying because she was proud of him, so terribly proud.

He'd told her to call Charlie, ask him to help her return to her folks in Anadarko.

Charlie was dumbfounded. "The kid ain't old enough," he said, grasping at a straw. "Goldang it, he's only sixteen—"

"Seventeen, this week, and being married made it okay."

Charlie was silent for a moment. This really tore it! Amantha would blame the girl for what Pete had done. Wouldn't be no way to patch things up now.

"Charlie," there was a quaver in Joylene's voice, "I—I think I'd better hang up—"

His mind jerked back to the girl. Poor little thing! "Joylene—"

There was no immediate answer, only a small, incoherent whimper.

"Joylene, goldang it, girl! You all right?"

Joylene Carmody looked around the dingy little apartment that had been their first home, her's and Pete's. A blur of tears concealed the shabbiness of the place she would have to leave.

Only until Peter comes home, she thought. Just until he comes home.

"Yes, Charlie," she said firmly. "Don't worry about me. I'll be just fine."

Chapter Twenty-Six

W*hen Peter went home on leave from boot camp, it was to* Joylene in Anadarko.

Her parents, wanting to give the young couple this time alone, had loaded the rest of their sizable family into an old jalopy and gone to visit the Oklahoma City branch of the Clouds.

Thus, Peter found Joylene waiting for him alone.

He went up the front walk leading to a small frame house, and saw her standing in the doorway. He stopped, catching his breath. And then she was running, running to meet him.

"Joylene," he choked on her name as he caught her to him, feeling the softness of her; the honey-sweetness. This was what he had been dreaming of, all those nights in camp, this girl with amber skin and night-dark eyes, a white part, straight as a ruler, in shining black hair—

"Joylene!"

A car passed and she stepped a little away from him, looking at him shyly.

In his uniform, his blond locks cut short in military fashion, he was almost a stranger. There was something else different about him: a kind of confidence—

"You—you've changed a lot," she said.

"So have you." He put a hand to her expanding midsection and she blushed. There was an awkward silence, then they both spoke in unison.

"Well—"

Then they were laughing, at themselves and at each other. Like children, they caught hands and ran for the house.

Joylene led Peter back to her room, a place her father, understanding her need for privacy, had built especially for her. A section of the rear porch was partitioned off. Indian blankets served as curtains at the windows, a spread for the bed. Against one wall was a small crib, already prepared for a baby.

Peter glanced into the crib and stepped back, his face mirroring shock.

"It's only my old doll," Joylene giggled. "I wanted you to see how it would look—"

He slipped an arm around her waist, and they stood together, like proud parents.

"I think she looks like you," Peter said judiciously.

"Like you," Joylene insisted. "And it's not a she. It's a he. His name—his name is David—"

She looked up at him, seeking approval of the name she'd chosen if it were a boy: the name of Peter's father.

"I love you," he said. "I love you very much."

He drew her toward the bed, lying down, pulling her down beside him.

He kissed her ruler-straight parting, her closed lids; her full, throbbing lips. And finally his hands went to the buttons of her maternity smock, revealing the sweetness of amber flesh.

Gone were the tentative touchings of adolescence; the forlorn, frightened lovemaking of a boy half out of his mind with worry, a girl too exhausted to respond. They hungered for each other.

And there was so little time.

The days that followed were glorious ones. Sometimes they walked hand in hand, seeing the world around them with new eyes. And always waiting was Joylene's little room.

There was no talk of the war. They skirted the issue carefully. They were Mr. and Mrs. Peter Carmody. This was their home. Here, nothing dark or somber could intrude.

Only in their minds did they tick off the days. Three left. Now two.

Oh, God—*tomorrow!*

On that last night, they had to face reality.

"Pete," Joylene asked in a small voice, "where do you think they'll send you?"

"I don't know. European theater of operations, I hope. Let's don't talk about it."

"We have to, Pete. I've been wondering, shouldn't you try to contact your mother?"

"Has she contacted you?"

"Well, no, but—"

"Then there's your answer."

Joylene began to cry. "I just want everything to be right for you. Oh, Pete, I get so scared! I don't know what you're doing, what it's like—"

Now that the topic of army life had been brought up, he held her close and told her about the past weeks; how he had been a green kid, the dumb stunts he had pulled—and about his friend, Steve Meadows, whom he met on the train to Fort Sill. Steve had shown him the ropes, sort of watched over him.

"I'm glad," Joylene said. "Tell me about him, what's he like?"

Peter grinned in the darkness, remembering his first meeting with the man. He'd been sitting alone, unable to join in the camaraderie of the other recruits—who had already dubbed him "the Duke" because of his British ways.

He was feeling lost and lonely, wondering why he was such a misfit, leaning his forehead against the train window as he pondered on his problems. Then the seat beside him creaked as someone sat down.

A package of Luckies was thrust beneath his nose.

"Smoke?"

He refused and his companion lit up, then twisted, fumbling in his coat pocket. He proffered a Hershey bar.

"Here, Duke," he said gruffly.

Peter took it, his blue eyes moist at the unexpected act of kindness. He turned once more to the window.

"Heard you was a married man," the newcomer said finally.

"Yes." Peter sought for something to say. "My—my wife went back to her people in Anadarko. They're—she's Indian—"

"No kiddin'! Squawman, huh?"

Peter turned at the prejudiced-sounding statement, his eyes hot. Then he relaxed, seeing Meadows's face for the first time.

He, too, was Indian, his features bearing a marked resemblance to Joylene's.

The man grinned and extended a hand. "Steve Meadows, here."

Meadows was nearing thirty. He'd been in the military before, and when his wife left him for another man, he re-upped.

He took Peter under his wing, taught him to shoot, how to wear two pairs of socks inside his boots on the long marches, how to cope with the rigors of boot camp.

It was odd, Peter Carmody thought, that his mother should feel as she did toward Indians. Now he was married to one, and another was his best friend.

As Peter talked about Steve Meadows, Joylene felt an intense relief. Her love was a handsome prince, but with her strong maternal instincts, she sensed the young, untried boy inside him. She had worried that he would be lonely, afraid. Knowing there was someone to look after him eased her concern a little.

All that night they loved each other, knowing the smoothness of satin, the sweetness of honey, the selflessness of giving pleasure, one to the other. And when morning came they faced it almost with relief. Through the night the moment of parting had loomed before them, dark, tragic, growing in intensity.

Yet it was an ordinary morning, the sun shining, birds singing, a smell of autumn in the air.

Joylene prepared breakfast while Peter dressed and carefully packed the remainder of his gear. Then he stood over the little crib, knuckles white as he clutched its side, staring blindly down at the doll lying where his child would one day sleep.

He thought of a lesson Meadows had given him on the firing range.

162

"Don't think of it as a target. That there's a human being comin' at you. The enemy!"

Peter had turned pale and swallowed hard. "I couldn't—"

"He's goin' to kill you," Meadows added hastily, seeing Peter's obdurate face. "Dammit, he's goin' to kill your wife an' kid! Think of it that way—"

Peter knew that he would, from now on. He'd lost his courage once, on top of an oil rig. It wouldn't happen again.

He had something infinitely precious to fight for.

"Peter?"

Joylene's voice was hesitant as she stood in the doorway. He didn't turn. She moved to stand beside him and his arm went around her.

"I was just thinking," he whispered, choked with feeling. "When I come home—"

"He'll already be born and waiting for you."

"And what about his Mum?"

"She'll be waiting, too. Even if it's forever."

Finally they ate the breakfast Joylene prepared. Her cooking had improved a little, though not much. Peter praised everything extravagantly.

Then it was time to go.

Joylene wanted to accompany him to catch his bus, but conceded to his wishes.

He wanted her to stand framed in the doorway, as she'd been when he came. It would be a picture to take with him, wherever he went.

She clung to him for a frantic moment, then he put her hands away, picked up his duffel bag and went down the walk.

At the end he turned. And there she was, just the way he wanted to remember; the way she'd be waiting when he came home from the war.

He looked at her for a long moment, then went on down the street.

He did not look back.

Chapter Twenty-Seven

*T*he destination of the Forty-fifth Division, known as the Thunderbirds, was not Great Britain as Peter hoped. They proved their worth in Sicily, then crossed the Mediterranean for a massive invasion of the Italian peninsula. German aircraft swooped overhead, harassing, but otherwise doing little damage.

"Funny how you get used to those boogers," Meadows remarked, standing beside Peter at the crowded rail. "Used to get a knot in my gut when I heard that sound. Ain't much worse'n a bunch of mud daubers buzzin' around."

Peter grinned, a memory coming out of the dim past: a small boy trembling outside a privy in the oil patch; Charlie's drawling voice saying, "Goldang it, Pete, ain't nothin' to be skeert of. Them things is all bark an' no bite. . . ."

He'd come a long way from that frightened little boy. He laughed and changed the subject.

"What do you think about this operation coming up, Steve? Think it'll be worse than Sicily?"

"Hell, no. After what we been through, it'll be a piece of cake. Got us a seasoned outfit, now. Know what we're doin'."

Steve was to be proven wrong. In Sicily they'd been able to move forward through dry riverbeds, over rocky terrain. The Salerno beaches, though perfect for a landing operation, were ringed by steep hills. And there were torrential rains.

The Forty-fifth slogged forward through a sea of mud, facing a German panzer division strung in a defensive line.

Mine fields were seeded on the beaches, mortar and artillery emplacements were dug in. Deadly machine-gun fire raked the area, decimating the landing troops.

The sky was indistinguishable from the sea when Peter's regiment hit the beach to be pinned down under heavy German air attack.

The mud daubers had become hornets.

Noise.

Confusion.

Wrecked landing craft.

Scattered men and equipment.

The artillery bombardment was constant, laced with tank and machine-gun fire.

"Goddam," Meadows whispered. "Goddam!" His tension eased as Peter ran forward to drop beside him. Both flattened as a shell exploded nearby.

They were deafened by the sound. Lifting his head after a shower of mud and sand, Peter grinned at Meadows and mouthed the words, "A piece of cake?"

Meadows shook his head, sheepishly. Hell, anybody could make a mistake.

"Well, Duke—you ready? Let's go—"

The Forty-fifth moved out, fighting its way foot by foot, leaving its trail of dead and wounded. The survivors trudged through mud that weighted their boots, rain that soaked their clothing, making every step an effort. They crossed streams, holding their rifles high, emerging no wetter than they'd been before.

Persano, Eboli, Campagna . . .

Oliveto, Contursi, Campolattero . . .

Guardi, the Volturno, Venafro . . .

Pinned down for the moment in a ditch, Peter grinned at his friend. "Think we'll get medals for this, Steve?"

Meadows's white teeth flashed. "Nah, not you an' me. We're just dogfaces. Willie an' Joe, that's us."

Peter looked at Meadows, then down at himself. Both of them were slimed with mud. He began to laugh.

"Which one of us is which?"

"Hell, Duke—I dunno!"

From November first to January ninth, the Forty-fifth was in constant combat. Their ranks were decimated, Steve Meadows sick with what he referred to as "Arkansaw jitters," but which was, in truth, malaria.

It was for Steve's sake that Peter was elated when they received word that they were to be replaced and sent to Piemonte for rest and recuperation.

At Piemonte there was mail.

Peter carefully sorted the letters from Joylene as to date, reading the earlier ones first. And finally, he leaped to his feet with a war whoop.

"It's a boy! A boy! Born way back in November! I've got a son!"

The others crowded around, offering congratulations. Someone broached a bottle of whiskey and they passed it from hand to hand. Peter, who never drank, joined in as they toasted the birth of his son.

At last, half sober, he returned to his mail. In a later envelope, he discovered a photograph of the child: a crumpled baby face that bore the unmistakable print of its Indian ancestry.

His child would look like Joylene. And he was glad.

His son would never be forced into a British mold in an American world.

In the last days of 1943, while the Forty-fifth shivered in Italy, MacArthur's troops took Rabaul in tropical New Britain. Australians captured Japan's New Guinea supply base at Lae. The game of hopscotch that included the Central Pacific's Gilbert and Marshall Islands, Tarawa, Eniwetok, Kwajalein, and points north was called Operation Cartwheel.

In Italy the members of the Forty-fifth Division prepared for a mission of their own.

Operation Shingle.

Peter's regiment landed on the beach at Anzio, January 30.

The Germans held the hills that ringed the plain, their big guns booming with incessant fire. Railroad-loaded guns, referred to as "The Anzio Express," ejected their deadly missiles. The Luftwaffe screamed above the foxholes.

For the first time in their savage fighting history, the

Thunderbirds were contained, facing superior fire power, tanks—and superior forces.

"What do you think we're expected to do?" Peter asked.

"Do? Hell! Ain't nothin' we can do," Meadows said grimly. "Them krauts are gettin' ready to counterattack. And when they do, it's Katie-bar-the-door!"

Meadows had not been himself lately. He suffered from spells of fever, intermittent chills, headaches, and dizziness. Worse, his normally optimistic nature had changed. His dark eyes looked haunted.

Peter Carmody watched, waited, worried, and wondered. Crouched in a foxhole, he wrote a letter to Joylene, telling her of the coming battle, wanting her to know he loved her if he didn't come through it. There would be insurance. She must see that little David had an education.

Sealing the letter, he gave it to Meadows, asking him to see that it was delivered if anything happened to him.

Meadows did not change expression. He slipped the envelope into his pocket.

"Sure, Duke."

The Germans struck on the morning of February 16, pushing the American front back a mile. The casualties were heavy. Again they advanced, thrusting a wedge a mile deep and two miles wide into the American ranks. Cordite-scented smoke and choking dust obscured the scene as the Thunderbirds fought the Germans hand to hand.

The 179th was ordered to fall back a thousand yards. The action was tantamount to murder. Before they could regroup, the situation was one of wholesale slaughter. Peter and Meadows stood side by side, firing—firing—

Beside them a soldier named Ryan went down. Then Gregory—Miller—

Peter was weeping as he emptied his rifle time after time.

"You bastards," he kept saying through clenched teeth. "You dirty German bastards!"

Around him he could hear men crying, calling for their mothers, their wives—and the constant refrain of "Oh, God! Oh, God! Oh, God—"

That afternoon fourteen battalions of German infantry and

tanks were thrown against the shredded lines of the Forty-fifth. Heaving out of the smoke like ponderous pachyderms, the tanks bore down.

"Damnation," Meadows whispered, "look at them come!"

From behind them came the captain's shout, shrill with urgency.

"Stand, damn you! Fire!"

A spattering of shot from the decimated Forty-fifth. Then the turret guns on the approaching tanks opened up. There was a chattering of machine-gun fire as the behemoths rolled forward. The *su-wish, who-oo-mp* of bazookas.

"Get the sonsofbitches," Meadows rasped. He palmed a grenade and Peter followed suit.

"Well, Duke, here goes nothin'—"

The grin he turned on Peter faded, replaced by a look of surprise. He pitched forward. Two men just beyond him went down. A bullet nicked at Peter's sleeve as he stared at his fallen comrades in disbelief.

"Meadows! Oh, God! Steve—"

With a shrill scream of rage, Peter ran; running toward the approaching tanks in the swivel-hipped manner that had been trained into him. His mouth was wide open, his eyes streaming tears as he screamed his defiance. He reached a tank.

Up and over. Drop a grenade. Down before the explosion. Run again—

He tossed a grenade into a tank's treads. Its swiveling guns missed him. The damaged tank slewed sideways, the one behind it plowing into it broadside. Then he was up on the rear of another, slipping, climbing again, the pin on his grenade already pulled.

Meadows, recovering from the bullet that grazed his skull, pulled himself to his feet.

"Jump, Duke—Oh, Jesus!"

He covered his face as the tank burst into flame.

Peter Carmody stood in a dark tunnel. At the end of it was a small, white frame house, enveloped in a blaze of sunlight.

He left the tunnel and went up the walk. And there was Joylene, framed in the doorway.

She came to meet him and held him, his head against her warm, maternal breast.

He tasted the golden honey of her flesh, and then he slept.

Chapter Twenty-Eight

The news of Peter Carmody's death reached his wife by wire. Charlie Forbes received the message via telephone.

He'd been away from the field office for an hour or more. When he returned there was a message to call a number in Anadarko. It was a public phone booth. The caller sounded ill, and Charlie's secretary didn't catch the name. It sounded like "Jean."

How long ago? Perhaps forty-five minutes or more.

A leaden feeling in his chest, Charlie dialed. It would be Joylene, of course. Surely she wouldn't still be waiting, unless—

The phone was answered on the first ring. Joylene's voice was high, thin, like a child's. Listening to her strangled words, Charlie went gray, slumping in his chair.

"I see," he said. "Yes, I'll tell her. Goldang it, girl, I—I dunno what to say. You all right?"

The ravaged voice assured him that she was. There was a ring of steel in it that reassured him.

"Would it help if I come down there?"

"No, Charlie. I—I've got my folks."

He hung up and buried his face in his hands, sitting like that for a long time. When he finally rose, he walked stiffly, like an old man, heading for the prewar Ford that had replaced his old truck.

He was going to the town office to see Amantha. He hadn't been there since he carried other unwelcome news: the birth of Peter's child, Amantha's grandchild.

She'd refused to recognize the baby as a Carmody. The girl had probably gotten pregnant and used Peter. If it were not for her, Peter would be in school, not someplace in a war zone.

She'd blame this on Joylene, too.

Charlie parked the car and entered the Carmody-Forbes building. He opened the door that led to Amantha's suite, passing a startled secretary who raised a detaining hand.

"Amantha!"

Amantha Carmody looked up from the orders she'd been poring over, rubbing her eyes wearily.

"Why—Charlie!"

He didn't speak and she stared at him, seeing the harsh lines engraved on his lean face, the bleak sorrow in his gray eyes.

"Charlie?" It was a soft, wounded sound. "It's Peter, isn't it."

Charlie rounded the desk, taking her hands in his. She sat rigid, trembling, eyes closed as he relayed Joylene's message in his soft, drawling voice.

Peter had died in Italy, in action. There was nothing—his body would not be coming home. A special memorial service with military honors was going to be held in Anadarko. It was Joylene's wish that Amantha be present to accept the flag that would be presented.

At mention of the girl's name, Amantha jerked as if she had been struck. Her eyes opened, shock and grief replaced by a blaze of hatred.

"She killed him!"

"Goldang it, Amantha, you know better than that—"

"She killed him!" She put a hand to her head to ease its pounding. "Perhaps it's better this way. Now I can put it out of my mind—"

"You don't mean that," he said soothingly. "Come on, Amantha. Let me take you home—"

She looked up at him with blind eyes. "I have work to do, Charlie. Please go."

He headed reluctantly toward the door and she called after him.

"Charlie, please do not mention this to anyone. I have no desire to receive condolences for something that's over and done."

Charlie Forbes whirled, his eyes like sleet. "That ain't gonna give you no trouble. Kid didn't have no friends to speak of. You just go on buildin' your goldang empire in Dave's mem'ry!"

"Charlie!"

"You can throw Pete out like a piece of trash, fergit he ever was. But I ain't goin' to! I loved that kid like he was my own boy. I—"

He stopped, tears flooding the gray eyes, traveling the creases in his lean cheeks.

"Goldang it!"

Then he was gone.

Amantha's secretary, Dodie Sinclair, looked after him in bewilderment. Charlie Forbes, with his nice eyes, his ready grin and lazy, ambling gait, was one of her favorite people.

"I wonder," she said to the file clerk, "what that was all about?"

"Maybe they brought in a duster," the clerk suggested. "Or maybe Her Nibs found a mistake in the books."

They laughed. Though the office force was fond of their glamorous boss and intensely loyal to her, it was true she was a stickler for neatness, accuracy, and a businesslike attitude in all things. In turn, she worked longer hours than anyone else and was quick to reward her staff for jobs well done.

"Whatever it is, she'll be on top of it in a hurry," Dodie said. "She'll be wanting to dictate some letters. You'd better get ready to pull some files."

Dodie Sinclair was quite mistaken.

Amantha Carmody sat at her desk, deaf and blind to her surroundings as she peeled back memories like lettuce leaves, discarding those that were unpalatable until she reached the tender heart.

A little boy talking with Charlie beneath a tree in the sordid Tremenco camp. A little boy, his head bent close to Charlie's as they toasted marshmallows over a fire. A little boy with a grass blade between his thumbs, trying to whistle, emulating his friend . . .

Peter and Charlie! Why not Peter and David?

Her eyes were hot and burning, but they were dry.

Dear God, if she could only cry!

She had a sudden overpowering urge to be with Meggie, to put her arms around her, to assure herself that she still had someone. She pushed a button on her desk.

Dodie Sinclair jumped as her boss's voice entered the outer office.

"I shall be taking the afternoon off. Please cancel all appointments and order my car."

In a few minutes Amantha Carmody emerged, face very pale, but otherwise in complete control. She left an office that buzzed with curiosity and supposition.

Reaching home, she went to her study, removing her hat and gloves with hands that trembled.

She sat down behind her desk, thinking how ironic it was that she felt at ease only there, then pressed a button to summon Nanny Goforth.

She would not tell her about Peter, not yet. Not while she teetered on this verge of numbness and weeping.

Nanny's features registered shock that Amantha was home at an early hour. When Amantha asked that she find Meggie and send her to her, the old woman's face was defensive.

Meggie was being punished. She could not be allowed to leave her bedroom. Her naughtiness had earned her isolation. She was to receive only bread and water for dinner.

What had she done?

Nanny's face grew livid as she recounted Meggie's misdeeds. She'd been sent home from her private school for skipping class. In her exile, she'd cut off her braids, damaged her tweed suits, and been rude to Nanny. She had also threatened to run away.

Amantha rose and mounted the stairs, Nanny Goforth behind her. Meggie's door was locked. Amantha shuddered, recalling another locked door. She fixed the older woman with a stare until she reluctantly surrendered the key.

Meggie cowered on her big bed like a small animal at bay.

Her braids were chopped off straight, and her lovely blond hair fanned out like straw. Amantha went toward her.

"What is this all about, Meggie?"

Meggie turned rebellious eyes on Nanny. "I hate her," she shrilled. "I hate her!"

"You see?" Nanny Goforth said. "She's going to turn out like her brother. Bad blood!"

Amantha flinched and opened her mouth to speak, but Meggie was ahead of her.

"I'm not my brother! I'm not my father! I'm me! Meggie Carmody! And I'm not British, I'm American! And you can't make me be anything else! I'll run away—"

"Nanny," Amantha said firmly, "leave the room."

Snorting, the old woman obeyed. Meggie dissolved into sobs and Amantha stood, indecisive. A tray of bread and water stood on the bedside table. Amantha touched the bread. It was hard and old.

Memories of her childhood came back to her; her refusal to curtsey to a woman she did not like. The bread would sit here, as it did then, until it was eaten.

Nanny's notion of discipline.

Amantha dumped the bread into the wastebasket, then went to Meggie's side.

She sat on the edge of the bed, gathering the girl into her arms.

"We'll straighten everything out, Meggie," she whispered against the child's mutilated hair. "But, first, I've got something to tell you. Oh, Meggie! Meggie, you're all I have left! Peter—"

She could not go on. A terrible comprehension dawned in Meggie's blue eyes.

"Peter's . . . dead?"

They held to each other, rocking together in the terrible closeness of shared grief.

Later, Amantha, once more composed, went down the stairs to face Nanny. She no longer saw a trusted servant looking after her children's welfare, but a domineering old woman, querulous and demanding. Even now Amantha felt like a small naughty child as she stood before her.

"Peter is dead, killed in action," she said quietly. "I thought you would want to know."

She studied Nanny's face, seeing the fleeting expression of satisfaction that her opinions had been vindicated; that Peter had brought this on himself, as she'd expected.

Then she told her old nurse that she would be retired, pensioned off with enough to support herself in a small apartment until the war ended and she could go home to England.

It was too late for Peter, but Meggie would be free.

BOOK III

Meggie

Chapter Twenty-Nine

The war ended on both fronts. With each victory there was rejoicing in the streets. Ration books were burned. Men in Europe and Asia filtered home, released on a point system.

The loss of loved ones, the dreadful conscience-burdening memories of Hiroshima and Nagasaki, cast a shadow over those days of rejoicing. The shadows increased a determination that such events must not recur. With so many young men dead, children became America's most nurtured commodity.

America had the atom bomb. Soon others would have it, too. If catastrophe should strike again, if life should be short, then it should be merry. Money flowed freely.

What better way to spend it than on the children?

Amantha Carmody was no exception.

With the war's end, she eased up on her rigorous work schedule, delegating a lot of her former tasks to Thorne Greenberg. Thus she was still at home when Meggie came downstairs on the morning of her sixteenth birthday.

As always, Meggie's beauty jolted her. The girl wore the Northeast Pep Club uniform of pleated silver-gray skirt and crimson sweater. Her cheeks were rosy, her blue eyes sparkling as she danced into the room, her golden hair a silken cap of natural curls.

She hugged her mother and went straight to the sideboard, lifting silver covers.

"I'm starved, Mum!"

Her eyes widened as she lifted a lid to reveal a new and shining set of car keys.

"Mum! Are these—"

Amantha nodded and Meggie ran for the door. In the drive a powder-blue convertible glistened in the sun.

"Oh, Mum! Mum!"

The method of presenting her gift was probably ill-timed. Meggie laughed and chattered through breakfast, forgetting to eat. Meggie had pooh-poohed the idea of a birthday party, but there was to be a further surprise—far more exciting than the convertible, though Meggie might not think so.

It was time for school. Amantha followed Meggie to the door and watched as the girl circled the car, admiring it from all angles. She climbed into the driver's seat, wriggled ecstatically to get the feel of it. Then she inserted the key and sat smiling at the motor's smooth hum.

Seeing Amantha watching, she left the motor running and ran to her.

"I love you, Mum! It's the nicest present I ever had." The blue eyes welled with tears.

"I wish—I wish Peter—"

Her voice choked and she ran back to the car. With a screech of tires, she backed from the drive and was gone.

Amantha reentered the house. And with her was the lonely ghost of a boy with stiff shoulders and a trembling mouth.

"Mum, the other guys have cars—"

"Guy is not a proper word, Peter!"

Ah, Peter! Peter!

Would she ever get over this feeling of guilt that twisted inside her? True, Peter was reared in a restricted atmosphere, and she'd allowed Meggie a great deal of freedom. But then she'd had more time to be with her. And Peter was different. He'd been a shy, quiet, introspective little boy.

Had he changed as he grew older? She admitted to herself that she didn't know. She had not been there to watch his growing up. She could only remember his white, angry face the night she sent him to his room for the last time.

Shivering, she pushed her dark thoughts away. Peter was dead, just as David was dead. Nothing could be changed. Only Meggie was left, and they had a closeness that could never be destroyed.

Amantha had begun to live again, living vicariously through Meggie's popularity, loving the confidences exchanged at night when Meggie came in glowing from a date or a football game.

She went into the kitchen, where the cook was putting finishing touches to a birthday cake. It was small, since Meggie had vetoed a party, but it looked like Meggie; bright, happy, festooned with yellow daisies. It would follow a meal consisting of Meggie's favorite dishes.

There would be only the three of them—Meggie, herself, and Charlie, who would be equally surprised at the announcement she would make.

When Charlie arrived in the evening he took Amantha's hands and they stood apart, each inspecting the other with approval.

Amantha wore one of the new Dior creations, cut low to reveal still-youthful shoulders, the soft material of a swirling skirt revealing slender ankles above spike-heeled shoes.

Charlie, clad in a dark suit, only his hands betraying his work, was overcome.

"Goldang it, Amantha!" He searched for words. "Well, goldang!"

"You look very nice, Charlie."

Amantha was a little flustered. Yesterday she'd overheard Dodie Sinclair say that Charlie reminded her of Gary Cooper. And now she saw the resemblance.

Why that bothered her, she didn't know.

They settled in two soft chairs to wait for Meggie, sitting in silence as music from a radio in an expensive cabinet filled the room. "*If I loved you*—" The melody touched them both with memories; memories of a small Zenith with a rounded top, its voice long dead.

Amantha rose and switched it off, blushingly aware that Charlie's eyes followed her.

"I can't think where Meggie is," she said distractedly.

"You sure you ain't givin' the girl more freedom than she can handle?" Charlie asked cautiously. "Seems like it might be a good idea to know where she's at."

Amantha's nerves snapped.

"My word, Charlie! Can't you at least be consistent? I remember every word you said when—"

She stopped, appalled. Since Peter's death, they had been careful to avoid any mention of their differences. Now Peter's pale ghost stood between them.

She drew a shuddering breath.

"Meggie's a good girl. I don't worry about her. She confides in me, and I intend to keep it that way. She—she enjoys just being alive."

Another unfortunate choice of words.

The sound of a motor broke the silence. The front door opened and closed. They heard the mingled laughter of a boy and girl.

Meggie!

Amantha's heart lifted as Meggie and one of her current beaux entered the room.

"Well, miss, you're late! And look who's here. Charlie—"

Meggie looked stricken as she saw the festive table. "Mum—not a party! I thought—"

"Not a party. Just you, me, Charlie—and Dwight, if he wants to stay."

The young couple looked at each other.

"Mum, I'm in kind of a jam. Dottie made a cake and she's asked all the kids over. It's supposed to be a surprise, but Dwight told me so I could come home and change. We're all going out to the Cedars, after, to dance. Then the girls are having a slumber party. . . ."

"Of course, Meggie. You run along and get ready. I'm sure Dwight will have a piece of cake."

Dwight would and did. In fact, he had several before Meggie came running downstairs to link her arm through his. She'd donned jeans and a baggy shirt, but Amantha made no comment. She knew Meggie would wear what the rest of her friends were wearing.

When they had gone, she sank down in her chair, looking ruefully at the remains of Meggie's birthday cake.

"Charlie, do you ever feel old?"

"I just feel hungry," he said agreeably. "Now that's over with, could we bring on the grub?"

They had a pleasant meal by firelight, Charlie finishing off the cake that was a reminder of a ruined evening. Finally, he pushed back his plate, wiped his fingers on his napkin, and sighed.

"Good as that was, it ain't worth gettin' all duded up for. And that dress you're wearin' is too purty to waste settin' around the house. Let's go out on the town."

She looked at him blankly, and he continued. "Goldang it, Amantha, gitcher coat. Ain't much for dancin', but we can take in a movie. What's showin'? Got a evenin' paper?"

They found the *Times* and pored through the theater section, finally settling on a film at the Criterion.

It was a poignant, romantic picture, and Amantha was reduced to tears. Charlie's hand closed comfortingly over hers, a rough, calloused hand that somehow felt right.

When he returned her to her door, she hurried inside, filled with a kind of euphoria. She wished Meggie were here, so that she could tell her of her magical evening, their positions reversed.

My word, she thought, I've had a date! An actual date, even though her escort had been Charlie. Euphoria was replaced by depression.

There was so much in life she'd missed.

There were those among her acquaintances who pursued her, sending candy, flowers. She'd attended business dinners with many, through expediency.

But she hadn't been plied with Cokes and popcorn. She hadn't giggled through a Three Stooges comedy, or wept over a tragic love scene.

Dear God, she was thirty-seven years old! And she'd forgotten she was a woman.

Tonight she'd realized Meggie wouldn't always be there to brighten her days. And except for Charlie, she had no real friends.

Anna's Leroy had died several years earlier. She married a widower with the children she and Leroy never had. Maybelle and her husband moved back south. Edna Skaggs worked at Tinker Field, returning home to the bosom of her family. She needed no more from life. . . .

And I do, Amantha thought. Oh, God, I do! I need friendship, companionship, someone to love me.

The ache had become unbearable, like circulation suddenly returning to a deprived limb.

Amantha rose, slipped into a robe, and belted it tightly against the hurt. She went downstairs and searched in the kitchen until she found a long-unopened box of English tea.

Brewing a pot, she laced it with hot milk, her face relaxing as she pictured her mother at a tea table.

There was always lemon and sugar for Ian, white tea for Amantha; scones, berries with clotted cream. . . .

It would not be long before she was a part of the scene, once more; she and Meggie.

A plateau had been reached in the need for a constant flow of oil, now that the war was over. Within a year, with factories retooling, with a growing demand for automobiles and planes, the country's petroleum needs would accelerate.

And in the meantime, Amantha would take a much-needed vacation. She'd already made flight reservations. She and Meggie would leave for England at the end of the school year.

England! Home! The haven of her mother's loving arms. There might even be a man, one of her own kind, who—

Amantha blushed. She was daydreaming like a girl. Her place was here. And eventually she'd probably give in to Thorne Greenberg's constant proposals, marry the man and let him run the business while she sat back and grew old.

She finished her tea hurriedly and returned to bed. The trip to England was to have been Meggie's second surprise for the day. Amantha lay awake for a long time, wondering if Meggie would be pleased—or dismayed at leaving her friends.

But when she finally slept, she dreamed she was holding to a man's gentle, calloused hand; holding to it as if it were a lifeline.

Chapter Thirty

As Amantha had suspected, Meggie was not terribly pleased at losing a whole summer. Summertime was a time for swimming; for lying at poolside, toasting, surrounded by laughing friends.

It was a time for going to Springlake Amusement Park, riding the Big Dipper, spinning crazily in the Bubble Bounce; zipping down the steep wooden slides in the fun house with a burlap bag for a sled. . . .

For dancing, hotdogs and hamburgers, indulging a root-beer passion now changed to cherry Cokes . . .

The powder-blue convertible must be left behind. And there was a growing transition from Dwight to Philip.

Philip was dreamy. What if he forgot her during the summer?

England didn't have much to offer in exchange for what Meggie must leave behind.

Loving her mother, and having a naturally happy disposition, Meggie didn't sulk. And finally discovering she was the envy of her friends who had been nowhere—but nowhere!—she decided the trip might not be such a hardship after all.

She dived into the holiday arrangements with her usual enthusiasm, insisting Amantha had to have an entirely new wardrobe; bright sleeveless prints, sandals . . .

Amantha protested, considering many of their purchases vain and frivolous, but Meggie held her ground. Her mum was still young and pretty. And she wasn't British anymore, she was an American! This was 1947—and a real vacation! Why not be extravagant and splurge?

Coming in from shopping with her daughter, spreading colorful unbusinesslike garments out for packing, Amantha began to catch Meggie's excitement. She felt young, a little giddy with the whirlwind shopping sprees.

"Oh, Meggie," she laughed, "I don't know when I've had so much fun!"

For the last several months Thorne Greenberg was left pretty much in charge of the business. When Amantha dropped in at the office, it was usually a whirlwind visit.

"Are there any problems, Thorne? Good! Then I shall see to buying some luggage."

"I have an appointment at the beauty shop."

And, finally, "I must pick up my airline tickets."

Meggie talked her into having her hair done a different way. It curled around her face, making it seem more youthful, its golden highlights accentuated. Her eyes were bluer than ever, sparkling; her cheeks stained with wild rose.

Dodie Sinclair, fighting a secretarial spread, viewed her with worship—and envy.

"Mrs. Carmody, you look like a movie star!"

It was heady praise for a woman who had spent years creating an executive image. Amantha hugged Dodie Sinclair; an impulsive gesture that was entirely out of character.

A dazed Dodie watched her leave the office.

"If I didn't know better," she said to the file clerk, "I'd think the boss was in love."

Amantha was.

She was in love with just being alive. Her daughter, Meggie, was her best friend—and she was going home at last.

The night before they were to leave, Meggie was off to a farewell party, and Amantha invited Thorne Greenberg to dinner.

Together they pored over the list of instructions she'd prepared.

"If there are any problems, ask Charlie."

Greenberg thought privately that he'd see Forbes in hell first. Though he fully intended to run things in his own way, he listened and acquiesced automatically, his mind on the

186

small gold-brown head bent over the papers, feeling a shock to his system as blue eyes raised to his.

Amantha was so many people in one: the shabby, determined young widow he'd first met; the elegant chairman of the board; and now this stunning, youthful beauty.

He had an idea this Amantha would be more vulnerable.

Dinner was announced, and he slid the papers into his briefcase, offering Amantha his arm with mock formality. After all, this was a kind of celebration. . . .

Afterward they retired to her study, completing their business arrangements. Finally Greenberg held up a staying hand.

"Enough," he said, laughing. "I've been there since the beginning, remember? Carmody-Forbes can survive a few months without you—but—"

He moved toward her, taking her hands in his, lifting her to her feet to face him.

"—But it's going to be more difficult for me. Amantha, marry me! I've loved you for so long—"

Amantha took a step backward, shaken at the intensity of his plea. His dark eyes, always brilliant with quick and vivid intelligence, were heavy-lidded, shadowed with passion.

She never dreamed he had such depth of feeling, and imagined that he considered furthering their relationship out of expediency. . . .

And her reaction to his proposal troubled her. She'd felt a surge of need that surprised her.

But was it for Thorne himself—or would any man have affected her the same way? Her emotions were so delicately balanced now, with the guilt of leaving her work, the excitement of returning home.

"Thorne, I—I can't think about it now. I'm leaving in the morning—"

"Put it off a few days. We can rush the wedding through. A short honeymoon—"

"I promised Meggie—"

He sighed and spread his hands. "Then no honeymoon. I realize we both can't leave at the same time. But I'd feel better, knowing you were going as Mrs. Thorne Greenberg, that you would come back to me."

"Thorne, I can't! Maybe when I return, we can talk about it."

His face darkened with disappointment. Then he drew a small box from his pocket. It contained a matched set of rings, glittering with diamonds.

"Please, at least wear the engagement ring—"

She was torn, thinking how wonderful it would be to just be a—a wife. To let Thorne Greenberg carry the weight of the corporation on his shoulders. There might even be more children! A boy . . .

She closed her eyes, thinking of Peter.

"You will, then?" Greenberg asked hoarsely.

"I don't want to make any promises now. Please, Thorne—"

"You'll be back in September. If you make up your mind, we'll be married immediately. Can you promise me that?"

"I—I suppose so."

His face lit up again, and he pulled her to him, kissing her gently.

"I'll be waiting, Amantha."

When he had gone, she was amazed to find herself actually considering his proposition. Perhaps the embrace had solidified her thinking. When Thorne kissed her, she'd felt absolutely nothing.

There would be no question of forgetting her beloved David. Once again, she would have a home and family.

But was it fair to Thorne?

She was so troubled that it wasn't until she readied herself for bed that she remembered the September board meeting. It would be the most important of the year, dividends being declared. It was set for the first, and her return tickets were for the ninth.

She'd intended to talk to Thorne about moving the meeting to a later date. . . .

But, after all, he knew as much about the business as she, and he could serve in her stead.

He had her power of attorney.

She tried to erase all thoughts of business from her mind.

The next morning, with Meggie instructing Ryan to start

the convertible periodically, so the battery wouldn't run down, Amantha began to have second thoughts.

From the beginning she had disliked her job, doing it only for David's sake. Then the war made it mandatory, and she threw herself into the effort of producing the fuel that powered the war machine.

Now it had been a part of her for too long. She yearned for the safety of her desk, behind which she had been invincible. The new Amantha trembled a little, feeling as if she were stepping into the unknown.

Charlie insisted on driving them to the airport, admiring Amantha in her cool print-splashed sleeveless dress.

"Goldang," he chuckled, "you don't look no older than Meggie, here."

Amantha blushed. After her trim business costume, she felt positively naked.

By the time they reached the airport, Amantha was ready to turn and run. She tried frantically to think of an excuse to postpone the journey as she sat in the waiting room, hands twisted in her lap, Charlie smoking beside her in silence.

Meggie ran from window to window in a state of chattering excitement as the great planes, one after another, lifted from the ground.

"Oh, Mum! Can I take flying lessons? I want to fly—"

At last their own plane trembled on the runway. The sound of its engines seemed to synchronize with the beating of Amantha's heart. Charlie studied the monstrous three-tailed machine.

"Constellation," he drawled with satisfaction. "Hear tell it's rough-ridin', noisy, but she'll git you-all there. Does one sixty, one seventy knots. She's the C-121."

"You know all about everything, Charlie," Meggie cried. Her words had a familiar ring, as did Charlie's answer.

He had just never bothered to stuff his head full of knowledge like some folks, so he had room up there for a little bit of everything.

A man in uniform moved to open the gate. Charlie could go no farther. It was time.

There was only a moment. Amantha turned to her old friend, eyes desperate.

"Charlie, I—"

He took her small hands in his. "You just go on, have yerself a good time. But, Amantha, come back. Y'hear?"

He bent and, surprisingly, touched his lips to her cheek; then, before she could react, turned her to face the gate through which Meggie had already danced.

Amantha hastened after her daughter, stumbling blindly up the steps that led to the interior of the plane. Meggie was already seated and Amantha leaned across her. Through the small window she could see Charlie standing where she left him. She knew he would remain there until the plane was out of sight.

She was trembling like a leaf. What was wrong with her? She'd flown many times before, making frequent trips to Washington. And Oklahoma City had never really been her home. Her heart was in England.

Then why did she have this sick, plunging feeling of homesickness? As if she were going to some far-off, alien land?

A stewardess paused beside her, looking anxiously at her white face.

"Are you all right, ma'am? Can I get you something?"

Amantha's mouth quivered, but she summoned an answering smile.

"I'm quite well, thank you."

The plane moved cumbrously forward, finally lifting into the air. Amantha looked down at the city wheeling below. It looked so flat, yet it was reputedly sitting atop an inundated mountain

Well, they were on their way. It was done.

She settled back to listen to Meggie's delighted comments.

"I love flying, Mum! I think it's dreamy! I'm going to fly a plane one day. Do you think a girl can be a pilot?"

Amantha didn't answer. She sat quietly, unconsciously stroking the cheek that Charlie's lips had touched in a brief farewell.

Chapter Thirty-One

The skies of Oklahoma, when they departed, had been blue, bright, and smiling. They landed briefly in a neon-lit New York that spread beneath them like a massive treasure chest spilling over with glittering gems. From there they flew into darkness.

It was seventeen hours before they were to reach British soil. And here the skies were not welcoming. They circled London above a sky that looked like dirty cotton wadding. Amantha leaned across Meggie as the plane descended, unable to see anything. Then, miraculously, the clouds shredded to form an opening. And directly below was Buckingham Palace, shining like a jewel, fingered by a ray of sunlight.

"Look," Amantha said in a hushed voice. "Oh, Meggie! Look!"

But Meggie, distracted by the presence of a good-looking young man in uniform across the aisle, had missed it.

They debarked in a chill wet fog that cut to the bone. Amantha trembled, not only from the cold, but from the knowledge that she was once more in the land of her birth. To think she had forgotten how miserable a London fog could be!

Shivering, she and Meggie found their luggage and engaged a cab to take them to a hotel Amantha remembered from her childhood.

For months, since she'd booked their fares, she'd talked of nothing but this day; the sights they would see. Grand old buildings, parks of incredible green, children with bright rosy cheeks and happy faces.

Instead, though rebuilding was going on at a steady rate, many streets were marred by masses of rubble where V-2 rockets had screamed down. The cockney driver cheerfully volunteered the information that the parks had been used by the "H'aye-Tee-Ess," surrounded by barbed wire, antiaircraft guns pointed to the sky. The earth was hard-packed now, and nothing grew.

The cab paused at an intersection. A newsboy tapped at the window in an attempt to sell a paper. He was a very little boy and his face was pinched, blue with cold.

"It's all pretty grim, isn't it?" Meggie whispered.

"It's because of the war," Amantha reassured her daughter—and herself. "Wait until morning. When we get out into the countryside, it will be beautiful."

The hotel of Amantha's memories was a disappointment. Once gracious and commanding, it was now in desperate need of renovation. Service people had been billeted here. One wing had caught the force of a bomb and was now a spiderweb of scaffolding. Ordinary maintenance was impossible. Meggie and Amantha were shown to the best room in the house; a massive room with four-poster beds, silken drapes, and high gilded ceilings.

The draperies were faded and much-mended. A layer of grime dimmed the walls. And the ornate gilt scrolls on the hexagonal ceiling needed touching up.

"Grim," Meggie commented again.

Amantha, close to tears, reiterated, "Wait until tomorrow."

In the morning Amantha hired a car and driver to take them to her childhood home near Cambridge. In the sunlight the devastated city was even more depressing, despite the swarms of workers intent on rebuilding. Even the countryside had taken the brunt of the Luftwaffe's bombing. The wreckage of a charred plane lay in a field. Friend? Or enemy?

Though the sun was shining, Amantha was cold, her hands and forehead clammy with perspiration.

She clasped her hands tightly in her lap as they moved from desolation into the wonderful green of the country she promised Meggie. Her heart pounded with anticipation. She had not informed her sister-in-law she was coming, wanting to surprise her mother.

She was nearly home. . . .

The hired car turned into a narrow lane with hedges at either side. Amantha leaned forward, eagerly. "Just over the rise, Meggie—"

Her voice faltered, her face going blank with the shock of one who is in a nightmare; a nightmare in which the familiar is unfamiliar at the same time. The manor seemed to have shrunk. It looked worn and unkempt, its gardens and maze overgrown and untended. At one side stood a long, weathered, barracks-type building. And spreading across the once green meadow was a little cracker-box town; at its center, the smokestack of a small factory.

Amantha pressed her knuckle to her open mouth, her teeth cutting into it until it bled. Home, as she'd known it, was gone—gone—

She bade the driver to wait, and, leaving Meggie in the car, went up the winding walk to the door, shuddering at the sight of its peeling paint. She lifted the heavy knocker that had announced guests for generations, and waited.

Amantha didn't recognize the woman who answered her summons: a tall, bony woman with tired eyes, wearing a rump-sprung tweed skirt. But the eyes that surveyed her rounded.

"Amantha?"

"Livvy? It is you, Livvy!"

Her sister-in-law, Ian's wife, had once been a laughing, gay young girl. Amantha, forgetting how undemonstrative her people were, took Livvy in her arms. And they cried together for everything that had once been.

When Amantha had her emotions under control, she fetched Meggie, dismissing the car and driver. Her heart sank when they entered the house.

The great staircase still swept upward, but the foyer was partitioned off, making small cubicles. Bunk-type beds were visible through open doorways. Amantha was to find all the large rooms similarly treated, fashioned into several tiny rooms.

It had been done during the war years, Livvy explained, for

the children of varying sex and age who were sent here; refugees from London. Many of them were orphaned, and she received a stipend from the government for their care. They were taking lessons, at present, in the barracks building. Worth Gosden—surely she remembered him—had, among others, volunteered to teach them.

"They live here?" Amantha could not keep the concern from her voice. Livvy flushed.

"We could not have managed otherwise. The death taxes, you know. And there is this and the dower house to keep. I had to sell the meadowlands to a textile manufactory. . . ."

"Livvy! I wrote you, told you that if there was anything you needed—"

Amantha's sister-in-law drew herself up. "We are no worse off than the rest of our countrymen," she said in a chilly voice. "We do not need American charity."

Amantha felt a sudden surge of anger. The snobbishness of the woman! She swallowed hard.

"I would like to see my mother."

"I will take you to her. She is still in the dower house. But I think I should explain—" Livvy flushed again as she sought for words. "She is quite . . . frail. She has lost her sight. On some days she is more lucid than others, but—"

"I want to see her."

Livvy led the way across the lawn, opening the door to the tiny structure, lifting her voice as though to reach deaf ears.

"Mother, you have a visitor."

From beyond the small foyer came a thin, reedy voice. "Is it Ian, Livvy?"

The hair prickled at the back of Amantha's neck. Meggie gasped.

"But he's dead, isn't he?"

Livvy shushed her and motioned them into a small, stuffy parlor cluttered with collected treasures of the past: heavy dark furniture, an urn of peacock feathers; a pleated paper fan in the fireplace.

In the midst of it sat a tiny, shrunken figure, a lace shawl across her knees.

With an inarticulate cry, Amantha ran forward, dropping beside the old woman, taking the fragile body in her arms.

"Mum! It's Amantha! I've come home."

"I have a daughter named Amantha," the thin voice said uncertainly. "She married a—a colonist, as I recall. Perhaps you remember her?"

Amantha was weeping now. "I am your daughter, Mum! I'm here—"

"How nice," her mother said vaguely. "When your brother, Ian, comes, we must have a nice tea. You've been gone all day, however, and your father will be quite upset when he hears."

Amantha forced her voice into a steadiness that belied her horror. "I'm grown up now, Mum. And this is your granddaughter, Meggie."

"Another guest? How lovely. Livvy, you must show them about. We are an old family, and we have lived on this property for many generations. We take great pride in our ancestry."

The thin voice droned on, and Amantha could hear an echo of David's remarks. . . .

"—Everything so damned old and holy! Great-Great-Grandfather's codpiece, Great-Aunt Fannie's slopjar—"

Tears poured down her cheeks and she put a hand to her quivering mouth. Dear God, she was bordering on hysteria!

Livvy saved her.

"We will go back to the house now, Mother. Is there anything you want?"

The prideful voice became querulous. "I want my tea!"

"I shall send Debbie to you at once. Now try to nod off a bit—"

"Wake me when Ian comes."

Blue-veined lids closed over sightless eyes and the trio of visitors slipped away.

"Livvy, why wasn't I informed! Why didn't you write me?" Amantha couldn't suppress a note of anger.

"I saw no point in worrying you," Livvy said stiffly. "There is nothing one can do. I have cared for her properly."

"And I thank you for it!" Amantha said, eyes brimming. "God bless you."

They returned to the house and Livvy set about making preparations for their stay. All the rooms were full at present. Her daughter, Debbie, would bunk in with her. Meggie and Amantha could share Debbie's bed. Perhaps they'd care to rest a bit before tea?

Left in a tiny cubicle with room enough for a bed, their luggage, and themselves, Amantha and Meggie looked at each other. Amantha burst into tears.

"I'm sorry, Meggie! Oh, God, I'm sorry. It's all changed."

Meggie put her arms around her mother. "It's all right, Mum. I saw some dreamy-looking guys outside. I think this is going to be fun."

It was strange, Amantha thought, lying on the narrow bed, her daughter beside her, that it was she—not Meggie—who wanted to go home.

Chapter Thirty-Two

Livvy's daughter, Debbie, a sturdy-limbed girl with straw-colored hair, came to call them to tea. She stared enviously at Meggie's trim print sundress with its linen jacket and neat, matching sandals.

They followed her to a small back parlor, where Livvy sat behind a tea service, already having poured for two gentlemen in the room. Her face went a dull red at the sight of Amantha's svelte silk, and she fingered the tie of the ruffled blouse that had replaced her cardigan, self-consciously.

"Amantha, you remember Worth Gosden," she began the introductions. "And this is his son, Simon—"

The two men rose and Amantha suppressed a gasp, the remainder of Livvy's words unheard. Worth Gosden, some years older than she, had been a plump, innocuous man. Now he was rather thin, his face lined with suffering, one sleeve pinned over an arm missing above the elbow.

"Worth," Amantha stammered, "I—I—"

"It is quite all right," he said quickly, smiling. "I see Livvy failed to warn you. Dunkirk, you know. I say, you look smashing! And Meggie is as lovely as her mother."

Amantha returned his smile, grateful for his ease in smoothing over an awkward situation.

"Thank you. And you have a handsome son. He was only a baby when I last saw him. Do you have other children? And—how is Bess?"

There was another embarrassing pause. Then Worth explained quietly that his wife was dead. She'd been serving as a volunteer nursing sister in London at the worst of the bombings. He spread the fingers of his remaining hand in a defeated gesture.

"I'm so sorry," Amantha whispered. Then, noting that the men were still standing, "Do sit down."

She and Meggie perched gingerly on priceless worn chairs, and Livvy poured. Tea was served in thin porcelain cups; white tea, with milk. There were scones, berries with clotted cream.

Amantha was home.

The feeling of having gone back in time was dispelled when Livvy spoke.

"I should have thought to tell you about Worth's injury and his losing Bess, Amantha. But here we've all lost someone. We have had to work so hard, to suffer such deprivation, that our mutual problems go without saying; something that you, in your new prosperous country, may not understand."

Livvy's eyes flicked over Amantha's expensive dress as if it proved her theory. Amantha's temper flared, but she closed her lips tightly to avoid saying anything she'd regret.

Meggie suffered no such qualms.

"I should think no one would understand better than Mum," she said in an overly sweet voice. "Of course, my father died when I was just a baby, so I suppose that doesn't count. But my brother, Peter, died at Anzio. And your husband, Ian, was Mum's brother, wasn't he?"

"Why, yes," Livvy stammered, "I did not mean—"

"It might have been worse for Mum without her work," Meggie went on. "I can't remember her working less than eighteen hours a day. We had to have oil for planes and tanks—to help protect England— Are you through with your tea?"

Meggie's question was directed at young Simon Gosden. At his affirmative answer, she said that she was dying for a walk. Would he show her the grounds?

They left together, much to the dismay of freckle-faced Debbie. It was clear to Amantha that the girl had designs on young Simon, just as Livvy had eyes for Worth.

Amantha might have been amused had she not felt so uncomfortable.

"Let me help you clear up the things, Livvy," she finally offered. "Then I should like to take a walk myself."

"I shall accompany you," Worth said, smiling. "As for the tea things, I'm sure Debbie will help her mother. You will excuse us, won't you, Livvy?"

Company on her walk was the last thing Amantha wanted. Yet she was happy to escape the parlor and Livvy with her envious eyes. She recalled now that she'd never liked her, even as a young girl. She had a possessiveness, along with a martyr complex that made her less than pleasant. It was that quality in her sister-in-law that helped in her decision to go to David when Ian inherited the manor. It would have been impossible to remain.

Yet if she wished to stay for the duration of her vacation, she must somehow make friends with Livvy. It would not be easy. Worth's insistence on accompanying her now didn't help matters, she was sure.

"Are you warm enough?" Worth asked when they'd stepped outside. "I shall be glad to return and fetch a wrap."

"I'm quite comfortable, thank you." And indeed she was, after the stuffy heat in the small back parlor.

"I suppose you find things quite changed?"

Her eyes filled and she blinked tears back. "Yes. Especially here. The manor. My mother—"

"Pity. But I believe your mother is happier as she is, living in the past. Livvy has done the best she can."

"I'm sure she has. It's just—I can't seem to find anything that's the way it used to be."

"Then you must dine at my home." Worth Gosden's voice was rich with satisfaction. "Nothing at Greystone has changed. Though Bess is gone, I feel I owe it to her to preserve everything as it is, for Simon's sake. Too much that was tradition has been destroyed of late. But Greystone, you'll find, is intact. One needs one's roots."

"And mine have been sadly altered." Amantha stopped, staring in confusion. They had skirted the small factory settlement and walked in the direction of the ruined tower, always a landmark. And it was not there.

To their right was the hedgerow as she recalled it. To their left should be the tumbled shepherd's cot. But the meadow grass waved, uninterrupted, as nearly as she could tell.

"Where is the tower? Was it, too, destroyed?"

He explained that it had been. The tumbled stones were scavenged as foundations for the factory's cracker-box homes, as had everything else in sight. Housing materials were still in short supply, since the large cities had suffered such extensive damage.

Amantha was shivering.

"You are chilled," he said accusingly. "We shall turn back."

She accepted his decision gladly. In seeking out the shepherd's cottage, she'd hoped to find a bit of David. The cottage was gone and David was gone.

And she hurt.

They walked back to the manor, where Worth left her at the door, reiterating his invitation to dinner the following evening. Amantha accepted and he smiled down at her. She was a small woman and he, though a small man, was much taller than she. He didn't tower above her, however, like—like Charlie Forbes—

"It was a pleasant walk," she said. "Thank you." She meant it. If he had not been with her, she still might be searching for something that was lost forever.

Worth touched her hand with his one good one, in a gesture of affection, and then was gone.

Amantha went into the house to face Livvy. Her sister-in-law's face was pale, mouth set, eyes cold and suspicious. She loves Worth Gosden, Amantha thought, wearily running fingers through her windblown hair. It was clear the woman was eaten with jealousy.

"Did you enjoy your walk?" Livvy's question had a grudging note.

"Not really," Amantha confessed. "Everything is so different. In fact, Meggie and I may return to the States sooner than we expected. I find—I find I'm quite homesick."

Livvy turned away to hide her relieved expression. "It's nice having you with us, but you know best. Is there—is there perhaps a man?"

Amantha smiled at the archness of her voice. Why not let her think so? It would make this visit far more pleasant if Livvy thought she had no interest in Worth Gosden.

"I suppose there is," she lied. "His name is—is Charlie Forbes."

Now why had she mentioned Charlie, her good old friend, when there was a perfectly legitimate romance in the offing? She should have come up immediately with Thorne Greenberg's name!

It didn't matter. Charlie would grin at being linked with her in a romantic relationship. And Livvy's face had cleared.

"Stay as long as you possibly can, Amantha."

She meant it sincerely. Now she could afford to be generous.

That evening Amantha crossed the lawn to the dower house, praying her mother would be having a lucid moment. If anything, she was more confused than she was earlier in the day. Amantha was a stranger to her.

Leaving at last, Amantha was weary and despondent. She moved to the front lawn, trying to recapture a memory of herself as a child, playing at croquet with her father and Ian while her mother watched from the ivied porch. Then, later, there was Peter, a little boy tumbling in the grass.

The child she once was had vanished. Peter was nowhere. David was dead.

For an instant she envied her mother, living in the past. She and Meggie must stay here for a time, not out of love, but through duty.

And then, thank God, they could go home.

Chapter Thirty-Three

*T*hough *Amantha had allayed Livvy's fears regarding her* relationship with Worth Gosden, her sister-in-law was less than friendly when she learned Meggie and Amantha were invited to Greystone for dinner.

"I am certain you will enjoy it," she said stiffly. "Debbie and I dine there quite often. She and Simon are very close, you know."

"I didn't know," Meggie said later as they dressed in their cramped room. She peeled off the jeans and baggy shirt she'd worn all day and rummaged through her clothes for something suitable to wear.

"I don't know about you, Mum, but I'm going to wear something that'll knock him dead! That Debbie's sulked all day, and she makes me sick with her stupid jealousy!"

Amantha didn't say it aloud, but she shared Meggie's opinion. She'd had enough of Livvy's barbed comments. And while she had no designs on Worth Gosden, she didn't intend to look like a frump.

She selected a faille that turned the palest of rainbow colors; rose, blue, mauve, according to the light. It had a sweetheart neckline that bared a smooth white throat; a tiny pointed waist with an artificial rose pinned at one side; a long, rustling skirt.

Meggie, like all her friends, wore makeup. Amantha looked at her daughter's cosmetics lying on the bureau and smiled to herself.

Why not?

She touched her cheeks with a faint blush of rose, then her lips. A trace of blue shadow intensified the color of her eyes.

"Wow!" Meggie had finally chosen a dress and turned to notice her mother. "Mum, you're gorgeous! You look like a million dollars!"

Amantha blushed. "Perhaps it is too much—"

"No, Mum. Go to it! Give that witch out there a run for her money! Those snotty remarks she's been making—Honestly!"

"Meggie!"

"I mean it," Meggie said stoutly. "She's been cutting you down ever since we got here. Just because you're prettier than she is. If she wants to get a man—"

"Meggie," Amantha was pink and flustered, "I have no intention of competing with Livvy! And I am definitely not interested in Worth Gosden!"

"Well, let her think you are. Then maybe she'll appreciate him after we're gone."

Meggie had a point, Amantha thought. She certainly had a point.

If Amantha felt a pang of guilt when she and Meggie emerged from their room, it was erased at the expression of approval with which Worth greeted them.

"I have been trying to press these two into coming along with us," he stammered, gesturing toward their hostess and her daughter. "I did not think, when I issued the invitation. The Bentley won't hold all of us, you know. But if you, Livvy, and Debbie, would like to follow in your own motor, I am certain Mrs. Wheeler can set two more places. . . ."

"Debbie and I have other plans for this evening." Livvy's voice dripped ice.

"But, Mum." Debbie's protest was overridden by her mother.

"Thank you, Worth. Another time."

Simon escorted Meggie to the car, Amantha and Worth following.

"I'm afraid I've been guilty of a faux pas," Worth said ruefully. "I suppose I should have invited them earlier."

Then, turning a little red, he added, "I must say, however,

that I am glad they had other plans. I have been looking forward to this evening.''

It was still light when they turned into the tree-shaded drive that led to Greystone. Amantha had a tiny catch in her throat at sight of the familiar surroundings. As Worth said, Greystone was quite unchanged. Across the meadows, Amantha could see a shepherd and his dog bringing the sheep into the paddock for the night. The house, itself, stood dreaming in the twilight, just as it had done for some eight hundred years: lawns cut, hedges freshly clipped, flowers spilling over a low wall.

"Oh, Worth, it's perfect!"

"Not quite. No house is perfect without a woman in it."

He would be thinking of his Bess, as she so often thought of David. "Or without a man," she whispered, reaching with affectionate sympathy to touch his hand.

Worth's housekeeper, Mrs. Wheeler, opened the door to them. White-haired and motherly, she seemed to have changed little with the years. The dinner was perfect: roast beef and Yorkshire pudding, a trifle, fruit and cheese. The table was set with fine linen, Wedgwood plates, crystal and silver.

Afterward Simon and Meggie excused themselves. Worth had made one innovation for his son's sake. At the press of a button, light flooded the lawn. The younger ones wished to play croquet.

Worth and Amantha sat in high-backed comfortable chairs. The small fire, lit for atmosphere, was not too warm in the spacious, high-ceilinged room. Amantha relaxed as she sipped at a thimble of sherry.

"I feel at home in England," she admitted, "for the first time."

"I had hoped you would."

Worth's face was shadowed. She couldn't see his eyes, but there was so much affection in his voice that she felt she was treading on dangerous ground. She began to talk, nervously casting back in her memory; recalling the time the two families, hers and his, journeyed to Brighton for the season. . . .

"You weren't much older than Meggie."

And her first ball? She'd been terrified!

"It didn't show. You were a beauty, even then."

I'm talking too much, she thought. Dear Lord, what's the matter with me? For a space, there was silence. Then he said, "Amantha, Livvy tells me you may go home sooner than you expected."

"Yes, my work—"

"Why did you come here?"

"To see my mother."

No, that wasn't true!

"I guess I was looking for something. I was happy here once. I met David here. And Peter was a baby. I—I suppose I thought there would be something of them left."

Her eyes were wet, and she was thankful for the dim room.

Worth drew thoughtfully on his pipe. "You can't go back, you know. I was in hospital with this," he shrugged the shoulder that lacked an arm, "when Bess was killed. I was told, but I felt I'd find her here when I returned. The house was empty. I went to London, to the spot where she died. I suppose I came to terms with it then. Livvy has been a great help.

"Amantha, have you thought of marrying again?"

His question caught her cold, bringing thoughts of Thorne again to her mind; Thorne, who would be waiting for her, expecting an answer she wasn't prepared to give.

A peal of laughter sounded from the lawn. Instead of answering, she rose and went to the window, pulling the drapery aside. Simon stood behind Meggie, his arms about her as he showed her how to position the mallet. She swung, ineffectually, missing the ball.

The minx! Pretending this was a game she must learn! Meggie, who excelled at any sport.

Amantha laughed softly, then flinched as Worth's sound arm went around her waist.

"Our children are beautiful together, are they not?"

Amantha had to admit that they were. Simon, with his coltish movements and shy manner, might have been Peter. How unlike Dwight he was. Or Philip. Or the rest of Meggie's retinue at home. She couldn't imagine Simon gobbling a birthday cake or jumping over the side of a convertible rather than open the door.

She smiled, recalling the noisy, laughing crew at Meggie's heels.

It was good they were shortening their stay. Simon wasn't right for Meggie. Just as Worth wasn't right for her. His arm tightened around her and she felt an urge to lean back, to settle into the security that Greystone had to offer. She drew away.

"How old are you, Amantha?"

"Thirty-seven."

"I am nearing fifty. Do you think that is too old for remarriage? For beginning again?"

"Not at all," she faltered. "I think Livvy—Livvy must be about forty-two."

"I wasn't thinking of Livvy."

Amantha stepped back from the window, away from him. "Worth, it has been a lovely evening. But we really must go. Livvy may be waiting up for us. I don't like to disturb the household. If you don't mind—"

On the way back to the manor, the air sweet with a scent of cut grass, Amantha was acutely conscious of Worth's presence beside her. She thought of her loneliness, her yearning for peace and security; the corporation that was running so smoothly in her absence, that could actually manage without her. . . .

They reached the darkened manor. Meggie and Simon ran on ahead and Worth took Amantha's hand in his, looking at her, his heart in his eyes. Thanking him once more, Amantha hastily extricated herself and hurried inside. She was certain Livvy had been watching.

She breathed a sigh of relief when the household seemed to be abed. Meggie, excited with her evening, kept up a steady stream of chatter despite Amantha's efforts to hush her. In her gown at last, the girl sat up in bed, her feet curled beneath her.

"Don't you think Simon's absolutely dreamy-looking?" she asked for the tenth time.

Amantha thought of a lonely one-armed man turning fifty.

"Looks," she said tartly, "aren't everything."

When Meggie slept, Amantha lay wakeful for a long time, recounting the evening's conversation, certain that she'd read something into it that had not been there.

Surely Worth could not be seriously interested in her. She was nothing at all like sweet, gentle Bess.

As for her own feelings, Amantha knew she was attracted to the man. But there was nothing more than deep affection—and pity.

Tonight he'd said, "You can't go back—"

Who should know better than she?

Finally she slept, to dream not of Worth Gosden, but of Peter.

It is the night of their quarrel. He turns a cold, angry face toward her. And he is not in the royal raiment of his play, but in a bloodstained uniform. She reaches out a hand to him and he turns away, to fall face down on a barren beach beneath a cold moon. The waves surge in to wash around him, and she hears a child's voice calling, "Mum—Mum—"

She reaches him, struggles to turn him over. The upraised face is coated with mud that fills his eyes, his nostrils, his open mouth. And it is raining. The mud bleeds away with the rain. His open eyes reflect the light of the flares.

It is not Peter in her arms, it is David—David—

"Mum! Mum!"

Meggie was shaking her. "Mum, what's wrong? Are you okay?"

Amantha shuddered into a waking state to find her daughter bending over her.

"I had a nightmare," she said weakly. "Did I wake you?"

"You were sort of yelling in a whisper. It scared me."

"I'm sorry. You go on back to sleep."

"Too much Yorkshire pudding," Meggie said wisely. She turned over and was asleep once more; the sleep of the young. Amantha lay awake, envying her.

The next morning, ruefully surveying the shadowed eyes

that no cosmetic aid could conceal, Amantha decided her wakefulness had not been in vain.

In the long and terrible hours that stretched from her dream until the dawn, she had managed to come to a decision.

Chapter Thirty-Four

The news that Amantha planned a two- or three-day journey to Rome dropped like a bombshell into Livvy's household. It was clear that Livvy and Debbie were gratified to be rid of their guests for a short while. Surprisingly, Meggie refused to go with her.

Livvy set her lips against any offer of hospitality until Worth Gosden came storming in from the barracks building, where classes were in progress.

"What's this I hear," he asked Amantha. "You're going to Italy?" Her expression answered his question. "I say, you can't," he faltered. "It is not too long since we were at war with the bloody people!"

"I'm going, Worth."

"Then I shall accompany you."

Livvy looked as if he'd slapped her. Amantha hastened to tell him she wished to go alone. For that matter, she lied, she had business contacts who would see to her welfare.

"I still do not like it," he said doggedly. "Two women in a place like that! You will need protection."

"And I shall have it," Amantha pointed out.

Meggie interrupted the conversation, explaining that she wished to remain behind. She was enjoying her visit, and it was dumb to spoil it. She and Simon had made plans.

Worth looked at her, his face softening. "Why do you not stay with us?" he inquired.

"Worth!" Livvy gasped. "It would not be proper! A young girl in a womanless household!"

"I don't know what you call Mrs. Wheeler," Worth said, not without humor. "My word, I have been under the impression that she—"

"Don't be an ass, Worth! You know quite well what I mean. Meggie is quite welcome to stay here."

So Meggie had her way. And Amantha, though she would like to share the experience of flying over the snow-covered Alps with her, was glad. For she was going on a pilgrimage, as Worth had gone to London. Peter's death had never been real. Perhaps, like Worth, she would be able to come to terms with her loss.

Landing in Rome, confused by the masses of shouting, chattering, gesticulating people, Amantha located a cab. Worth had given her the name of a pensione where a friend had stayed prior to the war. There was an English-speaking clerk. It was among the bits of trivia Worth kept filed tidily in his mind.

The trip to the hotel was a blur of ancient brick buildings, cracked marble, broken tile—and then a straight course through grandiose structures.

"Via Cristoforo Colombo," the driver said proudly. "Il Duce." He swept a hand to indicate its magnificence, then, cocking an eye to the rearview mirror, "Trinità dei Monti? Fontana di Trevi? Palazzo Chigi? Palazzo Farnese?"

It was apparently beyond his comprehension that one might come to Rome with intentions other than sight-seeing. Amantha continued to shake her head, and to give the name of her hotel.

Finally they entered a narrow winding street that smelled of garlic. The cab stopped before a rectangular building of scaling pink stuccoed brick, an ornate grille set in its arched doorway.

They had arrived.

Entering, Amantha found herself in a corridor with a faded red carpet. At either side were huge pots filled with lilies.

Perhaps, she thought grimly, she had blundered into a funeral parlor.

Then an ell revealed a desk, a white-haired gentleman

behind it. He stood, greeting her in Italian, but when she spoke in English, he beamed.

He was proud of his English. He had been with the Italian underground, aiding British and Americans trapped behind the lines to escape. Despite his claims, his English was broken, badly accented. His gestures and the fervor with which he made them assured Amantha that she was most welcome. If she wished anything, she had only to ask.

She made arrangements for her room and asked him to employ the use of a car for the next day. She wished to be driven to the beach at Anzio.

"For why? There is nothing of interest!" The gentleman finally gave her up as a lost cause and scribbled a multitude of notes with a businesslike air.

As she climbed a set of marble stairs, following a tiny black-clad old woman, Amantha heard the clerk speaking in liquid Italian to someone else.

"These Englisi are all quite mad," he was saying confidently. "One must humor them."

Her room was spacious, its walls festooned with frescoes of dingy cupids. The enormous bed with its canopy of silk, so old it was dry and papery, might have belonged to a Borgia. A corridor had an arched window that looked down on a courtyard where untrimmed flowering shrubs grew in profusion around a fountain, long since dry, listing to one side. At the end of the corridor was a bath, to be shared with other tenants.

Amantha decided the ornate bowl and pitcher in her room would be vastly preferable to the communal bath. She did not intend to leave her room until it was time for the journey to the beach.

She had not come here to view the glories of Rome.

There was no lock on the door. She blocked it with a chair, opening it only when the meal she'd ordered—pasta, from a trattoria across the way—was delivered.

At last she went to bed, to lie there suffering from the heat, the noise, the smells. She was certain she would never sleep. Then, like a blessing came the *ponentino,* the westerly wind rising from the sea. The smell of salt, of pines, of flowers, floated through the window to billow the ancient canopy and touch Amantha's lips, her eyes, her sleeping face, with a gentle caressing hand.

There were no dreams.

For breakfast there was fruit, a pastry, and thick, black espresso coffee.

For lunch, cheese, olives, hard black bread, and wine.

She waited with an odd serenity, as if she were suspended in space and time; weightless, thoughtless. And finally the old black-clad crone toiled up the steps to tell her that her car and driver were at the door.

Rome was a blurred backdrop as they left the city; the driver making his way through horrendous traffic, adding his imprecations and horn honking to the clamor. For a time they were stalled by an accident ahead; the involved drivers joined by other drivers and pedestrians in a battle of words and fist shaking.

Amantha was deaf and blind to the racket. It was only something to be endured, ignored. Later, she would discover she could recall nothing of the journey.

They followed the Via Severiana from Rome to the mouth of the Tiber, where it turned to hug the coastline. The driver, briefed by the clerk at the pensione, knew exactly where he was going. Had he not been here during that accursed time?

The Americans had been aided by the devil, of that he was certain. Else they could not have kept coming in the face of combined German and Italian fire.

He had not wished to return to this haunted place. But the mad Englishwoman would pay well. As a precaution, he had gone to mass this morning. He made the sign of the cross as they neared their destination, and mumbled under his breath.

Amantha had no way of divining his thoughts. All she would remember would be the back of a head, covered by a flat black cap; ears set squarely to either side; a thick neck drawn low into the collar of a frayed shirt. He did not speak English, and for this, she was grateful. No sound broke the last few moments of their drive.

When the car pulled up near the water's edge, Amantha stared about with disbelieving eyes. There was nothing here of her dream. The Roman plain at Anzio stretched inland some twenty miles; a slow rise to the extinct volcanic ridges of the Colli Laziale and the Lepini Mountains. It was an area of almost flat farmland and reclaimed marshes. At a distance of four or five miles a pine forest spread inland—the Padiglione Woods.

Amantha stepped from the car, thinking dully that she had been the victim of a hoax. This could not be the place called Anzio; this flat stretch of farms and villages leading into the hills. Men could not have fought and died here.

The only thing that fit her dream was the sea, washing in against the coast in ribbons of silver. The moon had not yet risen. It was still light.

Hesitantly, she left the car and began to walk along the water's edge, pausing at the sight of something in the water. A rusted hulk, lying on its side; a battered, twisted thing of corroded metal, everything that made it recognizable long since washed away.

A landing craft, she thought drearily. Then she had not been cheated, after all.

Her car was distant now, almost obscured by the approaching twilight, when she came upon another relic of the battle at Anzio: a burned-out tank; nothing worth salvaging, half buried in the swampy earth.

Was this all there was? Thousands of men had fought and died here; Americans, Italians, Germans. Dear God, what had she expected? That the beach would be red with blood? That she might find Peter's body and take him home?

A child's cry in the distance sent her rigid, the blood in her veins turned to ice.

Peter—

She turned to see a small dark-haired boy running along the shore, followed by other children, and an Italian mother and father. The woman had a basket on her arm.

They approached the burned-out tank and the woman took a checked tablecloth from her basket, spreading it on the ground. While the children scampered, she set out a loaf of bread; cheese; wine; all the while glancing curiously at Amantha.

A picnic! Amantha began to shiver. Dear God, a picnic! Here, where Peter had fought and died. So soon forgotten—so soon forgotten—

Her head thundering, tears spilling down her cheeks, Amantha stumbled toward her waiting car. She had found nothing of Peter here, nothing to alleviate her grief and guilt. She had learned nothing, except that life went on; that little boys picnicked where older boys bled and died.

She reached the car. "Please take me back," she gasped. The driver looked at her uncomprehendingly, and she shrieked, "Roma! Roma!"

He was happy to comply. Ghosts had moved in on him with the twilight; the ghost of a friend who died beside him, splashing his uniform with warm blood; the ghost of a man he had killed in hand to hand combat; a man with surprised blue eyes.

He put the car in gear and sped back to town as if the devil were after him.

Amantha must have paid the man, though she had no recollection of it. She must have entered the pensione and negotiated the stairs. And luckily she was too ill to bar the door to her room with a chair. For on the following day, when the English lady did not check out as she'd planned, the clerk became concerned and sent the old woman to check on her.

She returned, babbling excitedly in Italian.

The English lady was very ill, perhaps dying, ill with a fever. . . .

Amantha was not only very ill, but she was permanently immersed in her dream; a dream in which a little boy cried for his mum. And added to it was a new horror. She picnicked on the beach with an Italian family, only to find that the red-checked tablecloth was Peter's bloodstained shirt.

She knew it was a dream. If only Meggie would wake her . . .

Chapter Thirty-Five

Meggie was having the time of her life. She missed Amantha, but then her mother had been away before; trips to Washington, D.C., throughout the war; a few to California. If business was involved, she would stay until it was completed. When several days passed and they hadn't heard from Amantha, she tried to soothe Worth.

He, however, was worried. He put in a call to the pensione. There was a poor connection, and the English-speaking clerk insisted, cheerfully, that Mrs. Carmody was not available at the moment, but to rest assured she was being well cared for.

Worth didn't guess that the clerk was quite frantic. It wouldn't do to publicize that a guest became ill in his hotel.

In the meantime, Worth Gosden watched the budding romance between Simon and Meggie with approval, seeing it as a wedge in his relationship with Amantha.

Simon attempted to teach Meggie to play chess. The game was much too slow for her. She countered by teaching him poker, a fact duly reported by Debbie and terminated by Livvy.

Their intervention and disapproval of everything Simon and Meggie did had an unforeseen result.

It drove the young people from the house.

This morning Meggie defiantly donned shorts and halter top, such as she often wore at home in the summer. It created the effect she wanted. Livvy and Debbie were positively steaming. Her mother would definitely hear about this upon her return.

She felt a little guilty. Amantha had asked her to be circumspect. And that was perhaps what led her to the edge of irritation with Simon.

He was such a child, despite their difference in age. Except for putting his arms around her at croquet, he'd tried to pretend she wasn't a girl, for heaven's sake! Meggie wasn't used to such treatment. Not that she was a tease, but an uninterested male was a challenge. Even now, with so much of her exposed, he kept his gaze averted as if he were embarrassed.

"I swear, Simon," she said as they walked along past the factory town and into the meadow, "compared to the boys I know, you're just plain dumb!"

His face reddened. "I'm sorry you feel that way, Meggie."

"Oh, I don't mean dumb-dumb! But there's so many things you don't know. You can't skate, you can't swim, you can't do the Lindy. You haven't even seen any movies: *The Best Years of Our Lives*, *Mrs. Miniver*, *National Velvet* . . .''

"I can't help that, Meggie."

"You don't even know the Pepsi Cola commercial," she taunted, dancing away across the grass. "*Pepsi Cola hits the spot—Twelve full ounces, that's a lot—*"

"Meggie!" He caught up with her, catching at her arm. "You must remember, I am British. And with the war, Mum being killed, my father maimed, I—"

Meggie was instantly contrite. Her blue eyes filled with tears.

"Simon, I'm sorry! I've been acting like a witch!" She paused, swallowing, seeing the darkening expression of need in his level gaze. "I—I—"

"Meggie!" His voice was low, filled with yearning. "Meggie!"

She didn't move, her lips slightly parted as he pulled her to him, touching his mouth to hers then springing back, guiltily.

"You don't even know how to kiss," she said in a tone of wonder.

"I am willing to learn."

She put her arms around him, pressing close, feeling the boy's dry kiss change to something entirely different; the

216

shudder that ran through him, his thundering heart freed from its stiff British control.

When she pulled away at last, he looked dazed. "My word," he whispered, "oh, my word—"

She knew how he felt. Her own knees were trembling. To conceal the fact, she sat down on the grass. He walked away for a moment, then returned to sit beside her, pulling her blond head against his shoulder. His voice, when he spoke, was hoarse with feeling.

"Meggie, will you marry me?"

She jerked a little in surprise. He meant it! He actually meant it! She'd gone steady—sort of; she'd kissed lots of boys and become adept at getting out of awkward situations, but this was her first real proposal.

Marry Simon Gosden? She hadn't thought beyond the moment of knowing he was attracted to her; that she had cut out that cat-clawed Debbie. But this! She was at once flattered and appalled.

"Will you, Meggie?"

"I don't know," she whispered. "I don't know—"

"I shall wait for your answer. Of course, we won't marry for several years. My father says—"

"You've discussed this with him?"

"Of course. And I shall speak with your mother upon her return. We must do things properly, you know. And—Meggie," his face was deeply red, "we must take great care. For a moment there, I quite forgot myself. I don't want to do anything to hurt you, Meggie."

In any other place, among the crowd she ran with at home, his statement would have sounded ludicrous. But here it was part of the natural order of things. A blue sky smiled down. Fat lambs grazed against a hedge in the distance. It was as if they were in an enchanted circle, caught up in an old-fashioned past.

"We'd better go back to the house now," he said soberly. He helped her to her feet and she went along with him, stumbling a little, turning her ankle on an indentation in the grass.

"Ouch!" she said. Then, "Look, Simon, there was some

kind of building here once." She could see the vague outlines of a small square. "We were right in the middle of it."

"I recall it," he said vaguely. "A shepherd's cottage, I believe. All tumbled down. Oh, Meggie—"

He held out his arms, wanting to kiss her again, but not quite daring to. Instead they took hands and raced back toward the manor.

That night, pretty, thoughtless Meggie, who had made a career of doing as she pleased once Nanny's firm control was removed, could not sleep.

She thought of Simon's proposal, of herself as mistress of Greystone; of balls and lovely gowns, herself at a hunt breakfast in a scarlet coat; on the sidelines at a polo match in a lacy-brimmed hat, cheering her husband on. . . .

She had a notion Simon had little interest in such things. She'd probably spend her life at a stupid tea table. Lemon? Milk? Sugar?

Dumb! Dumb! Dumb!

She missed her blue convertible. Philip was going to get a motorcycle. She wanted to learn to fly, a thing that would be beyond Simon's comprehension in a wife. And yet—

Oh, how she wished her mother would come back!

The next day Amantha did just that. She was still feverish, exhausted from her illness, but she defied the orders of the doctor the clerk had called in. Uncertain as to diagnosis, he had treated her for everything he could think of, shrugging his shoulders and speaking rapid-fire Italian that the clerk translated as clearly as he could.

Perhaps the water? Yes, most certainly the water. She was not accustomed to the water of Rome. Or perhaps a bacterial infection. Had she eaten fish? No? An unwashed fruit? Perhaps she had a nervous collapse. A type of brain fever.

Amantha thought of a game Meggie played. An object was selected and the players had to search for it. As they neared it, the prompter would say, "You're getting warm."

The clerk translated her words and the doctor lifted his bushy brows, then his face cleared. Clearly the patient was babbling about the humid weather. He ran his fingers inside his starched collar.

"Indeed," he answered amiably. "But the *ponentino* will come. . . ."

Perhaps it would, but Amantha would be gone. She rose from her bed and dressed. The clerk at the pensione, against his better judgment, called the airport and made arrangements for her flight, then arranged for a taxi to take her there.

She flew over the Alps, her body burning with fever, thinking of the coolness of snow. A few times she drifted back into her dream, but she pushed it away, thinking of Meggie.

She must concentrate on reaching Meggie.

In London she managed to find a car and driver, telling him how to reach the manor. Remembering nothing of the drive, she finally found herself standing before the door of her old home.

Livvy answered the knock, her face blotching with anger at the sight of her sister-in-law.

"It's about time you came back," she said harshly. "I refuse to take responsibility for that daughter of yours—"

She paused in her tirade, her expression puzzled.

"Amantha? My word!"

Amantha began to crumple and Livvy caught her in strong, angular arms.

"Debbie! Meggie! Come quickly!"

Amantha was abed for three days. In those days she grew to like Livvy a little better. She was a competent nurse and did everything possible to make Amantha comfortable, despite the masses of flowers and candy arriving from Worth.

Livvy, Amantha decided when she was able to think a bit more clearly, was her own worst enemy.

Finally, on a Saturday, Amantha was able to sit for a while in the parlor. Worth called, announcing his intention to take her for a drive the next day. Livvy balked.

"She's not well enough."

"Balderdash," Worth said gaily. "Fresh air will do wonders for her. I shall call at two."

Livvy averted her face, but not before Amantha caught a glimpse of a tear.

He's going to ask me to marry him, she thought. And Livvy knows it.

If he did, what would her answer be?

It would have been no before her trip to Anzio. But her experience there had taught her how short life could be; how, once it was over, it was like the burned tank, gradually buried in the earth, eventually to disappear without a trace that someone died here. Like the careened landing craft that would finally merge with the sea . . .

Amantha wanted love, security, a home.

When Worth arrived to pick her up, she was waiting. They went first to Greystone for tea. And she experienced the sense of timelessness she'd felt before. They chatted about inconsequential things, and she smiled wryly to herself. The notion that he would propose had been only in her mind.

Odd that she should feel a sense of relief.

"Now," Worth said, "we are going to take that drive."

They did not go far, just down a winding country lane that led to a long, pleasant ivy-covered structure.

"Greystone Farm. It is part of the property. Have you ever been inside?"

She had not.

He helped her from the car, and they entered. It was a charming place of many rooms with blue Dutch tiles and white-washed walls; an enormous walk-in fireplace in both parlor and kitchen.

"It's beautiful, Worth."

He smiled delightedly. "Then you think Meggie will like it?"

She jerked in surprise. "Meggie? I don't understand!"

"I am giving it to them as a wedding gift." he said complacently. Then, "Oh, my word! Hasn't Meggie told you? She and Simon—"

Amantha stared at him, incredulity in her eyes, still unable to speak. The words, when they came, burst forth in a single breath.

"She's only sixteen—"

"They intend to wait for two years. Give the girl time to

grow up a bit, get some stability. By that time they will know each other much better.''

"Worth, we're going home as soon as I am—"

His good arm went around her. "No, Amantha. I want you to be my wife. It will work out perfectly. The two of us, Meggie and Simon near. Grandchildren—"

Amantha's mind was whirling. This was why Meggie had been so quiet since her return. Simon was wrong for Meggie! Wrong! Meggie was like a bright butterfly. She couldn't survive trapped in a staid British setting.

And, dear God, neither could she!

"Give me time," she whispered. "Let me talk to Meggie. We'll discuss this tomorrow."

"Of course, my love."

Worth kissed her tenderly on the cheek.

And, as with Thorne Greenberg, she felt nothing.

Maybe she was incapable of love.

That night Amantha waited until she and Meggie prepared for bed, seeing the thin, childish body only just now reaching the curves of womanhood; taking note of the worried expression on the face of a girl who had never known a care.

She turned away and hung her dress in the wardrobe.

"Meggie, do you want to talk to me about—anything?"

She sensed the girl's sudden tension.

"Sure, Mum. I guess so." Meggie sounded frightened and terribly young.

"Worth—Worth told me about you and Simon, today. Is it settled between you?"

"Not exactly." Meggie sounded reluctant and Amantha felt a wave of relief.

"Do you love him?"

"I—I like him very much."

"But do you love him," Amantha persisted. "Do you love him enough to change your life to suit his? You would have to, you know. And it would be a very quiet life. Simon is—"

"Dull," Meggie finished for her.

Amantha stared at her daughter, aghast. Meggie's lips trembled. Tears stood in her eyes. Then she began to giggle.

"Dull!" she said again. "I couldn't marry Simon anymore

221

than you could marry Worth. We don't belong here, Mum. But how am I going to tell him?''

Amantha held her daughter close, thinking of having to face Worth on the morrow.

"That's something we're each going to have to work out for ourselves," she said.

They went to bed and lay quietly for a long time. Finally, Meggie asked, "Mum, you asleep?"

"No, Meggie."

"I was just thinking about Simon. He drives like an old maid. That really bugs me!"

"I know what you mean. Like Worth. He never changes anything. If he married again, Bess's picture would still hang in the same place on the wall."

"And Simon's such a chess nut. I can't sit still that long."

"Even Worth's clothes are out of date. Those knickers, that plaid cap . . ."

"I could never wear shorts and halters again. Mum, Livvy made me feel like I was . . . dirty. I don't think Simon liked them either."

"Worth would die of apoplexy if I drilled a well on his front lawn."

"Dull," Meggie reiterated, sleepily.

"Dull," Amantha agreed.

Dear God, she couldn't wait to get home.

Chapter Thirty-Six

The next morning they both overslept, rising guiltily to find breakfast kept warm for them. Livvy and Debbie were not there. A note said they'd driven into Cambridge for supplies and would not be home in time for tea.

The note was terse. Amantha had an idea that the journey had been hastily arranged. If she and Worth came to some sort of agreement yesterday, Livvy didn't want to hear it.

Poor Livvy. How she and Meggie had upset their lives!

It was just as well that they were absent. There was much to be done. When they had finished breakfast, Simon appeared and he and Meggie were off for a walk, Meggie looking pale and quite unlike her normal exuberant self.

But she would be able to handle the situation. Amantha had faith in her wise child, now experiencing her first taste of growing up.

About herself, she was not so sure. She had the magnetic pull of her childhood to contend with.

Over breakfast she and Meggie had discussed alternatives. Meggie insisted that Amantha needed a vacation, and that she herself would die of embarrassment if they cut their trip short.

"We might tour the rest of England."

Meggie grinned, a sad, crooked little grin. "Nope, I think we ought to put a little distance between us and . . . people."

Amantha had to agree.

They settled on Bermuda.

"We won't let anybody know where we are," Meggie said enthusiastically. "We'll get suntans, pick up some guys—"

"Oh, Meggie!"

"I mean it," Meggie said stoutly. "Not anything serious, of course—just mess around a little. You need to have some fun."

The decision had been made. Now Amantha must burn her bridges.

She made the necessary phone calls to handle the arrangements, then cleared the breakfast things; a chore she had not done for herself in a long time. The equipment in the kitchen was antiquated.

It would be easier for Livvy if it were modernized. No wonder she always looked tired and cross.

Finishing the dishes, she looked at her reddened hands, thinking back to a small shack in the oil patch—how she scrubbed clothes on a scrub board, hanging them out in the icy winds of winter, the red dust of summer.

Finally, she crossed the lawn to the dower house. Her mother's mind seemed clearer in the mornings. Perhaps she would be able to get through to her—and to say good-bye.

The old woman sat in her chair, an emptied tray of dishes and crumbs beside her. Her eyes were brighter this morning, but she was petulant.

"I want Livvy," she said crossly. "I've quite done with this!" She gestured toward the tray. "I do not wish it sitting here all day!"

"I'll take care of it, Mum."

"But I want Livvy! Where is she?"

Sighing, Amantha carried the tray to the kitchen, washed up the dishes and put them away. Then she returned to kneel before her mother, taking the thin hands in her own, willing her to listen.

"It's me, Mum. Amantha. I want to tell you—"

"Your language is atrocious! It is I. I shall have to speak to Nanny—"

"Very well, Mum. It is I." Tears clogged Amantha's throat as she tried to find words for what she must say. "I am leaving, Mum, eventually returning to the States. I called for reservations this morning. I came to say good-bye."

Her mother nodded, eyes suddenly focused. "That dreadful

man," she murmured. "But you would marry him. You always were a willful child. However, there is Peter to consider. Have you thought about him? Taking him to a place where he will be reared as a savage?"

Dear God! She'd gone back to their last parting. She was remembering when they'd gone to David.

"Everything will be all right, Mum. Peter is . . . safe."

"This will upset your father, you know. You have always been his favorite. But I have Ian—"

Tears ran down Amantha's cheeks, falling on the withered hand she held. Her mother jerked it away. "Do not snivel, Amantha, it is unbecoming."

She looked past her kneeling daughter.

"Where is Livvy? I want Livvy!"

Amantha rose, touching her lips to the faded cheek.

"I will send her to you, Mum."

It wouldn't matter if a few hours elapsed. Her mother had lost all concept of time.

Walking disconsolately back to the manor, Amantha considered her debt to her dead brother's wife. It was clear there was a strong bond between Livvy and her mother-in-law; that Livvy would not relinquish any of her responsibility toward the older woman, and would accept no financial help.

There had to be a way around her obstinacy.

Amantha reached the house and went upstairs to pack, unable to avoid shedding a few tears. She'd had such hopes for this reunion, only to find herself a stranger here.

In a short time Meggie appeared. She was in a similar case. Amantha paused in her packing, looking up, and Meggie laughed, at the edge of hysteria.

"Oh, Mum, your nose is red. Is mine? Aren't we dumb?"

Amantha touched her own face, then smiled ruefully. "I guess we are. You—you've talked to Simon, then?"

"He's mad at me, Mum. We had an awful fight. I let him think it was because of Philip. He said he should have known I was only leading him on; the way I dress, the way I act. He said I wasn't like Debbie. She has character. He wouldn't even kiss me good-bye."

Her blue eyes held hurt. Meggie had worked out a scenario

where, after she told him it couldn't be, he would take her hands and say, "I shall always remember you—"

"Debbie's more right for him. And she's fond of him," Amantha told her.

"Yes, but I don't like her. I hate to see her win!"

Her words jolted Amantha. Meggie, unknowingly, had made her aware of a side to her own nature. In her years of struggling in a man's world, she'd become competitive. Was she reluctant to face Worth, fearing she'd hurt him?

Or was it because she hated to lose him to someone else?

Livvy had Amantha's home, her mother, and now Worth Gosden would be there for the taking.

Amantha made a wry face. She and Meggie were more alike than she thought.

"Debbie didn't win, Meggie. You were strong enough to give him back to her. I wish I could make Worth feel like Simon. . . ."

She stopped, her eyes falling on Meggie's clothes. She'd removed them from the wardrobe, ready to pack them. Suppose she borrowed shorts and halter—

Or the tennis outfit, with its wraparound skirt . . .

"Meggie, do you think this would fit me?"

Meggie giggled, her quick mind working with Amantha's. "Try it on, Mum. And fluff your hair out. Put on lots of makeup . . ."

Laughing like schoolgirls, they worked together. Amantha, viewing the finished product, was appalled. The short tennis dress was backless, little panties under a skimpy skirt. She looked no older than Meggie's friends at home.

Meggie leered at her. "You've got nice legs, sweetie!"

Blushing, Amantha drew the wrapped skirt around her waist, covering her nudity. The skirt and the piping on the tennis dress were blue, picking up the color of her eyes. Meggie insisted on painting her nails the purple-red affected by the teenage set at home.

"You look great!" Meggie said gleefully. "But the question is, will you scare him off—or have to fight for your virtue?"

Amantha prayed that Livvy would not come home until it

226

was over and done. She and Meggie laid their plans. When Worth came in for tea, Meggie would tell him her mother had stepped out into the garden.

At the proper time Amantha slipped out a side door and into the mass of luxuriant growth the unkept garden had become. She was trembling inside. This was a ridiculous idea. But it just might work. Worth was the product of generations of ingrained, stuffy morality. If he saw that she was nothing at all like Bess—or Livvy—

At any rate, it was too late to alter her plans.

She removed the wrapped skirt, feeling the sun on her legs. She hadn't realized they were so long. She'd always been considered a small woman.

Setting her lips, she tossed the skirt over a hedge and walked to a bench where she sat, knees pressed primly together.

This would never do. She must pretend she was Meggie. She tried to assume her daughter's relaxed attitude.

Oh, lord, she couldn't go through with this!

She half stood, intending to retrieve the skirt. Worth's footsteps sounded on the walk and she sank back again.

He stopped at sight of her, holding back a spray of errant blossoms with his good arm, eyes rounding—in appreciation, or consternation?

"My word," he whispered. "Had I not just left Meggie, I would have thought—"

"I should have changed," she blurted. "But I thought it best that you see me as I am at home. I've tried to pretend I was a proper Englishwoman like—like Livvy, but it's impossible to masquerade. And it's also impossible that we—that we—"

"I've been thinking along the same lines," he said quietly. "I came to withdraw my impulsive offer of yesterday. After I had the opportunity to consider it at length, I realized it was not wise.

"I am certain you would miss your—" he studied her and she blushed "—Your business connections, your tennis, your parties, your friends. As for me, I rather prefer the status quo. I do not think I could alter my life to suit yours."

The sprig of flowers snapped in his hand. He dropped it to the ground.

"So, Amantha, if you will release me from my foolish request . . . ?"

"Of course, Worth." Her tone sounded forlorn and she hated herself. "It has been pleasant getting to know you again. And thank you."

He gave a mock salute, turned and went down the path. Amantha wiped at her eyes, not knowing he had doubled back until she looked up to see him standing, the wraparound skirt in his hand.

"Do not forget this," he said with a crooked smile. "Meggie would never forgive you if you left it behind. She looks very nice in it. Quite like her mother, if I may say so."

"Worth!"

He had known all the time. He was laughing at her. Amantha drew her knees together in an agony of humiliation.

With several strides, he reached her, his hand going under her chin, lifting her swimming eyes to meet his own.

"I knew what your answer would be, after the scene between Meggie and Simon this morning. Did you think he would not tell me?

"The boy is angry, upset. And perhaps it is for the best. He and Debbie will start seeing each other again. She's a bit prickly, but more suited to life at Greystone Farm. They will appreciate each other more, now—"

"Oh, Worth!" She could see that his smile covered a pain that was rigidly controlled. "I wish—"

"I know what you tried to do," Worth said quietly. "I thank you for it. You do not belong here, tied to an old man with one arm."

He lifted his hand to stifle her protest. "It was only a dream, and I am grateful it lasted for a little while. I think you are a very gallant lady."

Pulling her to her feet, he held her close for a moment, touching his mouth to hers.

"Good-bye, Amantha. I shall not be seeing you again. I will go out through the side gate. I am not up to confronting Livvy just yet."

He was gone. Amantha lifted her eyes to see that Livvy

had returned. She was standing at an upstairs window, looking down.

Dear God, she would be furious! Amantha wouldn't have had this happen for the world!

Chapter Thirty-Seven

*W*hen *Livvy sent word that she wished to see Amantha in* her study, Amantha braced herself for the occasion. She had changed from Meggie's tennis outfit into a blue silk she might have worn at the office, and scrubbed her face clean.

She mounted the stairs, her feet lagging a little, feeling like a naughty child about to be punished. She knew that Livvy had misunderstood what she saw from the window, but how to explain? She did want to part on friendly terms.

She pushed the door open to find Livvy sitting behind Amantha's dead father's desk; the smell of musty leather bindings and mildewed paper strong in the room, a memory from childhood. And surprisingly, Livvy did not look angry, but defeated. Her eyes were red-rimmed, her hair straggling from its lop-sided bun, but she attempted an awkward smile.

"Come in, Amantha. I thought perhaps you had something to tell me."

It was clear she believed Amantha and Worth had come to an understanding. And it was equally clear that the thought was destroying her.

"Only," Amantha said, "that Meggie and I were discussing our return to the States."

The dawning hope in Livvy's eyes made her almost pretty, until Amantha mentioned repaying the debt she owed her for her mother's care; establishing an account in a London bank in Livvy's name. Then she was adamant again.

"I have only done my duty," she said primly.

To hell with duty, Amantha thought. If American money

wasn't good enough for her stiff-necked sister-in-law, she'd try a little polite blackmail.

"A pity," Amantha murmured. "That leaves me only two options. I can fly Mum to the States with us—"

"No," Livvy said sharply, her face paling. "This is her home! She wouldn't be happy anywhere else!"

"I do have a responsibility," Amantha said gently. "I can give up my work, settle here, marry again . . ."

She hadn't said she would marry Worth Gosden, but the inference was there. She watched Livvy's face move from fear to defeat—and, ultimately, capitulation.

Livvy looked down at her desk. Finally she raised her eyes to Amantha's.

"If you insist, I suppose I could accept a small honorarium—"

Amantha herself would set the amount, taking care of it when they reached London on the morrow. And it would be an ample sum. She would see to that.

It wouldn't repay the debt she owed her brother's wife. But, in leaving now, she was giving her a chance at a very fine man.

Amantha rose to leave, looking down on her sister-in-law's bowed head. "You look nice in that blue sweater, Livvy," she said gently. "Did you know it's Worth's favorite color?"

And then she left, quietly closing the door behind her. In the morning she and Meggie would go. And behind her Amantha would leave another closed chapter. Home was no longer here, and she only regretted leaving her mother.

But Livvy had proven to be a better daughter than she.

Late that evening Amantha and Meggie sat on the porch of the old manor. The night was sweet with a scent of grass. Fragrance from some night-blooming flower wafted from the garden.

"I'm going to miss this," Meggie said a little mournfully. "It's different. Everything's been here such a long time."

"And at home everything is new. Which is better: to build something yourself or to be content with what someone else has done?"

Meggie grinned. "Mum, I love you!"

The hired car that was to take them to the airport arrived

the next morning at six. The household was still asleep when they slipped out, leaving a thank-you note on the sideboard. Amantha could imagine Livvy's relief when she found it. The trip to London was a silent one, but, once airborne, the mood of both mother and daughter lightened.

At one time, catching a hint of sadness on Amantha's face, Meggie twined her fingers in hers.

"What is it, Mum?"

"I was thinking about my mother."

"And I was thinking about mine. Mum, when you were my age, did you think your mother was old?"

"Yes," Amantha admitted, "I suppose I did."

"I used to, but I don't anymore. I found out on this trip that you're not. Life's too darned short! I intend to spend mine having a ball!"

"You have a point, Meggie."

Meggie grinned. "I sure do! Look, Mum, when we get to Bermuda—let's check in under assumed names. Mandy and Meg, the Smith sisters! Don't even let your office know where you are. Let's just have us one helluva time!"

"Meggie!"

"I mean it," Meggie insisted. "You game?"

Amantha thrust out a hand to shake her daughter's. "Game," she laughed.

When the big plane landed and its passengers debarked, Amantha's eyes were sparkling like blue seawater; her cheeks were pink with excitement.

She almost succumbed to a safe and uncomplicated form of life, settling in to grow staid and old. Now she wished wistfully for a time to be young. As young as Meggie, open to enjoyment, looking for adventure.

"Can I help you, miss?"

A man in a white linen suit smiled down at her. He took her small carry-on bag and escorted her toward the terminal. Amantha glanced back, looking for Meggie.

She needn't have worried. The resourceful Meggie had attracted a man of her own.

Chapter Thirty-Eight

*O*n the sixth of September, Amantha and Meggie left Bermuda for home. They both looked wonderful—and knew it. Surely they had been told enough times. Amantha's skin had taken on a creamy tan; Meggie's was more golden, a shade darker than her hair, with a dusting of freckles she detested.

"Didn't we have a great time?" Meggie kept insisting. And Amantha had to admit that they did.

It had been pleasant, enjoying the sun and the sea; exciting to be surrounded by a bevy of admiring young men who had no intentions more serious than being good company.

"Are you going to let yourself get all caught up in work again?" Meggie asked, wistfully. "Golly, we've had so much fun—"

"I won't," Amantha said. "I promise. Charlie's been handling the field all this time. Thorne can take care of the office."

Thorne Greenberg, to whom she had promised an answer—

Amantha was silent as the plane taxied to the terminal, weighing the pros and cons of marriage to Thorne. She didn't love him, true. But she hadn't loved Worth, and she'd almost made a dreadful mistake. At least Thorne was an American, a partner in business. His concerns were hers. . . .

"We're not supposed to be home for a few more days," Meggie said. "Can't we keep them just for us? Not let anyone know?"

Amantha agreed, and was amused when Meggie called Philip the minute they reached the house. Then she called

Dwight. Within an hour a group of Meggie's friends had descended and they were off in the blue convertible.

Amantha gave in to an overwhelming desire to call the office.

Dodie Sinclair answered, lowering her voice to a frightened whisper when Amantha identified herself.

"Thank God! Have you talked to Charlie?"

"No—"

"Call him immediately! No, don't come into the office! I—I can't talk anymore—"

"Dodie! What's the matter? Tell me—"

Realizing she was talking to a dead line, Amantha hung up.

She dialed the field office. There was no answer. She redialed, tapping a table impatiently as the distant phone rang.

Something was terribly wrong. And she intended to find out what it was. Finally, leaving the phone, she called for Ryan.

She would go to the oil patch; the place she hadn't seen since she moved from the shack she'd shared with David. She'd sworn never to visit it again, but there had been something in Dodie's voice—

She had to find Charlie!

She worried all the way. The tires of the limousine whispered on pavement, then on blacktop. Finally Ryan slowed and Amantha sat up straight, trying to orient herself.

Ahead was a chainlink fence, its gate open. Above it arched a sign: Carmody-Forbes. And before her, a green meadow dreamed under a bright blue September day. The land had healed. The pumpjacks were painted, almost silent, like bright birds dipping their beaks and lifting their heads to drink; caged; surrounded by flowers.

Charlie's kind of flowers, zinnias and hollyhocks.

He'd emulated the beautification projects of the city.

She left the car and approached the neat field office that stood on the site of the old camp. It was neat and painted, a pretty little cottage, with more of Charlie's plants blooming around it.

The office was empty, its interior rich with the scent of

Charlie's pipe tobacco. She felt a wave of affection at the hint of his presence. He had probably gone to the cabin.

She walked across the meadow, still marveling at what Charlie had done. When she reached the bottom of the deep-cut gorge, she stood silent for a moment. Pecan trees arched overhead. She heard a jay, a mocking bird. There had not yet been a frost, but here and there along the winding red-amber stream was a splash of scarlet. Sumac. Poke. A persimmon tree dangled its golden fruit like little lanterns.

A squirrel became a still life for an instant. It eyed her curiously, then went on about its business. Perhaps Charlie had tamed it. Perhaps it sat on his shoulders and stole from his pockets . . .

Everything was as it had been. All it needed was Charlie—and a little boy.

She must put these things from her mind. Right now the important thing was to locate Charlie and find out what the devil was wrong with Dodie Sinclair!

The woman was an excellent employee, but a bit giddy in an old-maidish way. Probably she was making something out of nothing.

Amantha reached the cabin, feeling a touch of nostalgia when she knocked and entered.

Charlie wasn't there.

She hurried back down the path, stopping when she reached the stream. There was no more she could do at the moment, and there was a spot she wanted to see.

Then she would never return to the oil patch again.

She followed the creek that ran like a red ribbon until it reached a deeper pool. Here, Charlie and she had cut a sapling. He'd told her how to construct a fishing pole for a small boy who hopped from one foot to another in delight.

Then Charlie had made a fire on the clay bank. . . .

She paused, shaken to see the remains of a fire in the very spot; charred, scattered wood and ash. The traces of that night were still here!

She passed a hand across her eyes. It couldn't be. Too many years had passed. The creek would have risen, become a thundering torrent in the rains. But she could almost perceive the scene; Charlie's head bent close to Peter's as they squatted over the coals, the stars winking on, the soft air filled with fireflies.

Charlie; a Peter Pan who never grew up, in this, his Never-Never Land.

Peter's face enthralled as he listened to Charlie's tales—

Peter's face! She could see it now! She had looked for him in England, where he was born; at Anzio, where he died. And there had been nothing.

Her memories had been here, waiting for her to come—

She began to cry, tears coming faster than she could wipe them away. Then she made her way back toward Ryan and the car.

As she neared it, a battered old truck drove up, two people spilling out of it. Charlie's long legs scissored as he loped across the meadow to meet her.

"Amantha! Goldang it! Well! Goldang!"

For a moment she thought he was going to sweep her up in his arms. And, surprisingly, she wanted him to. Instead he stopped short and just wagged his head at her, grinning.

"Girl, yer a sight fer sore eyes."

Then the grin faded. "I been tryin' to git aholt of you. All hell's busted loose. We gotta talk some." He looked uneasily at the young man he'd brought with him.

"You go on down to the fishin' hole. You know where it is. Git a pole at the house. . . ."

His companion was an Indian boy. Indian! And on Carmody-Forbes property. Amantha stared after him as he walked away.

"Charlie, does that boy work here?"

"Nope."

"Then what is he doing on the grounds? I issued orders—"

"Goldang it, Amantha, shut your mouth!" Charlie's face was dark with anger. "Kid's a friend of mine. And I live here, remember? Reckon I can invite anybody I choose!"

"It's your affair," she said stiffly.

"Durn right it is! And now we got more important things to talk about. Like where the heck you been?"

"Does it matter?"

"It did. It mattered one helluva lot! But it's too late now to do anything—"

"Charlie, what in heaven's name are you talking about?"

"Come on," he said. He took her by the elbow and guided her toward the field office. Inside, he pushed her toward a chair and poured a cup of steaming coffee for each of them.

"Drink up," he said grimly. "Yer gonna need it!"

Then, without any attempt to mince words, he launched into his story.

Thorne Greenberg called a special meeting of the board shortly after Amantha left. He announced that he and Amantha were to be married upon her return from Europe. Then, intimating that it was Amantha's suggestion, and using her proxy, he managed to push through a vote to lease a vast amount of land at an exorbitant price—and to purchase half interest in a refinery.

"Charlie! I didn't—" Amantha was white, her cheeks blotched with red.

"Didn't think you did!" Charlie's voice gentled a little.

"Fire the—the—!" She stopped, swallowing an expletive.

"May be a mite hard to do, under the circumstances. You better calm down and listen to the rest of it.

"The expenditures rules out dividends for this year. Smaller stockholders, hearing of it, were in the mood to sell. And Greenberg bought. His holdings amounted to a few shares more than each of them held singly. If they didn't vote together—"

Charlie shrugged to indicate the hopelessness of the situation.

"But he couldn't, Charlie! He doesn't have that kind of money!"

Charlie Forbes's face was gray, his eyes dark with pity, and Amantha felt a cold finger of chill touch the nape of her neck.

"He had him some help, Amantha. Went off to Tulsa to talk to a feller, and Dodie got suspicious. We went down to the courthouse and done some checking.

"The land we leased and the refinery all belonged to the same comp'ny, a new outfit, set up as a front. Done some more diggin' and come up with some names.

"Thorne Greenberg's one. The other'n is—"

"David's father!"

The words burst from Amantha's lips and she put a hand to her mouth, stricken as Charlie's eyes confirmed her fears.

"I do not make mistakes," she had told her father-in-law. And now she had. For a few short months of freedom, she endangered the empire she'd built in David's name.

"I'll get lawyers," she said sharply. "We'll fight this—"

"Greenberg ain't done nothing illegal," Charlie reminded her.

Amantha stood, shakily. "Don't tell anybody you've seen me," she said quietly. "I'm going home."

On the drive back she cradled her aching head in icy hands, going over and over what she knew. Thorne's actions had been a masterstroke of business. She might even have admired the smoothness of the operation, had she not known the reasons behind it.

David's father was still out to break her, and she'd be damned if she'd let him do it!

Chapter Thirty-Nine

Reaching home, Amantha dialed Thorne Greenberg's private line.

Her voice, when he answered, was the light, slightly teasing tone she'd adopted in Bermuda. She listened to it, amazed, as if it were that of a stranger.

"Thorne?"

"Amantha! Where are you?" He sounded a little frightened, wary.

She was home, she said. She didn't plan to come into the office this week, but she was dying to see him.

"You've thought over my proposal?" The wariness was gone. He sounded elated. "Then we'll just jump in and surprise everybody! Does that suit you, sweetheart?"

"Why don't you come over tonight. We'll . . . make plans."

He arrived promptly at seven, carrying both flowers and candy, and wearing a big smile. Amantha thanked him, put the flowers in water, and led him into her small study, where a fire dispelled the September night's chill.

Thorne looked at her fondly, rubbing his hands together. "This is cozy," he said. Then he reached out to her, his heart filled with passion.

"I've dreamed of this—"

Amantha moved behind her desk, studying him. Why hadn't she seen the avarice in those dark eyes, the greedy thinness of his mouth. For years she had placed her trust in this man.

She shivered a little as she remembered she had almost talked herself into going further—and becoming his wife.

"Thorne," she said quietly. "You're fired!"

His impassioned look faded, his face reflecting shock—then guilt.

"I don't understand. . . . Of course, you're putting me on! You can't mean—"

"But I do."

"Now, see here!" He began to bluster. "I don't know what you're trying to do, but it won't work."

"I think it will!"

He placed his fists on her desk and leaned toward her, his mouth twisted in a snarl. "All right, so you know! I should have known that red-necked bastard would go running to you. But you can't fire me, you bitch! I'm a major stockholder!"

Amantha reached down behind the desk, lifting the rifle with which she'd faced David's father years ago. She pointed it at him, the barrel steady.

"You are a stockholder," she said calmly. "And I am president of the board. I cannot keep you from attending meetings. But if you step one foot on Carmody-Forbes property at any other time, I'll blow your damned head off!"

She backed him to the foyer and out the front door. There, he tried to regain his bravado.

"You won't always be president of the board," he threatened. "There are those who will fall in behind me—"

She fired at his feet and he took off running.

She stepped inside and slammed the door, explaining to the servants who converged that she'd shot at a . . . snake.

"You should have called me, Mrs. Carmody," Ryan said.

"Thank you, Ryan, but I kill my own snakes."

Returning to the den, she put the rifle away, trembling now that the ordeal was over. Finally she managed to pull herself together enough to think.

Her brief summer idyll was over. She had been stupid to think the business could run without her.

She would make no more mistakes.

240

Thorne Greenberg had betrayed her to the enemy. But Charlie's behavior had hurt her even more.

The thought of an Indian boy, fishing where Peter had fished, sharing a fire, enjoying Charlie's friendship, was the ultimate betrayal.

Chapter Forty

In the years that followed, Amantha was unable to keep her promise to Meggie. Every day was a battle to put Carmody-Forbes back on a paying basis. She talked the stockholders into reselling the leases and the interest in Thorne's refinery, at a loss.

Greenberg fought her at every step.

It's like fighting the devil, she thought wearily. Every time she thought he was defeated, he popped back up again. She knew she had the board with her, but some of her shareholders were aging.

One day, it might be a totally different story.

Meggie was far too busy to notice her mother's defection. Philip had been replaced by a laughing young man by the name of Ricky Van Holsten, and the two of them were always together, their photographs appearing in the newspaper; boating on Lake Overholser; at the Beaux Arts Ball; linked with every social event.

Amantha was not displeased, nor were the elder Van Holstens. These were their children, these bright, scintillating young stars with so many interests in common.

They graduated from high school, attended the prom together; Meggie in yards of floating chiffon on the arm of her young godlike escort.

That summer they both took flying lessons. Though Amantha was nervous, she gave her approval.

These were children of another age, a far cry from her own

upbringing. Occasionally she thought of their trip to England and of Meggie's brief involvement with Simon.

He would have been wrong for her. So wrong.

It was Charlie who worried. Several times, Meggie—now with a newer convertible—was arrested for speeding. And one day a small training plane buzzed the oil patch, giving the top of a derrick a near miss.

He went to see Amantha.

"Them kids need a good talkin' to," he said soberly.

"They're just normal. High-spirited, maybe—"

"Still need a firm hand once in awhile."

"Oh, Charlie!" Amantha laughed. "You just can't seem to make up your mind. One minute, I'm too strict—" Her laughter faded at the memory of Peter— "And the next, I'm too lax. Meggie's just enjoying life. And I trust her."

Charlie shrugged. "It's your funeral," he said morosely.

It was only a figure of speech, but it bothered her until she shut it from her mind.

Ricky and Meggie vetoed all suggestions to attend eastern schools. They both chose the University of Oklahoma at Norman, living in fraternity and sorority houses, coming home on weekends if their social schedules permitted.

"It's wonderful, Mum," Meggie said happily. "I'm having a ball!"

Looking at the pretty gossamer creature her daughter had become, Amantha saw herself as she might have been, had things been different.

There would never be hardships for Ricky and Meggie. The world was theirs. When they graduated from the university, they would marry. Toiling over columns of figures, Amantha would sometimes find her mind far off in the future, planning a wedding.

But Ricky and Meggie didn't wait. As with everything else, they acted on impulse. In their second year of college, they eloped.

Though Amantha was sadly disappointed, her dreams of a beautiful ceremony gone, she hugged her daughter and her new son-in-law.

"Please be happy for me, Mum," said a misty-eyed Meggie.

"I am," Amantha said. "Oh, Meggie, I am!"

The Van Holstens were equally pleased. Along with Amantha, they chipped in to pay for a beautiful apartment. Amantha tried to give Meggie the family silver she'd brought from England, pawned to Anna, and redeemed.

Meggie shook her blond curls. "Thanks, Mum, but no thanks. It's so stuffy. It would just sit there and disapprove of me—like Simon."

"Who is Simon?" Ricky asked, a hint of jealousy in his tone.

"I'll never tell!" Meggie giggled. He reached for her and she danced away until he caught her, kissing her into submission.

Something, Amantha thought, smiling to herself, that Simon Gosden would never do.

Ricky was given a job in his father's office, and again the two became an item in the social columns, this time as a couple. On weekends they were always at the airport. Five days a week Meggie played house like a little girl, cooking, polishing, dusting. Again she was having a ball. And when the doctor confirmed that she was pregnant, she was delirious with joy.

She and her husband went immediately to Amantha, Ricky's arm proudly around his wife, both of them certain they'd invented the process.

"You're going to be a grandmother," Meggie teased. "Oh, Mum, isn't it wonderful? I hope it's a boy! I want to name him Peter."

Pain squeezed Amantha's heart, but she managed a smile. "You'll be a good mother, Meggie."

"You betcher boots," Meggie drawled, in a parody of Charlie. Then, in a flurry of excitement, the young couple ran off to tell the Van Holstens.

Amantha longed for someone to share her news with. If only David were here.

On impulse, she reached for the phone to call Charlie, then drew her hand away. They'd grown apart since she learned Charlie sponsored that Indian boy, Dave Meadows. According to Dodie Sinclair, who thought it a wonderful gesture, Charlie was "helping the kid through school."

Let them have each other, Amantha told herself. If Charlie was trying to prove something to her, he could go to hell!

Meggie's pregnancy was uneventful. She was prettier than ever, glowing with happiness. Her only disappointment was in being grounded the last several months. Her obstetrician would not allow her to fly.

But those months were a whirlwind of preparation, of baby showers given by adoring friends. One room of the apartment the young Van Holstens occupied was converted into a nursery; filled with enough equipment for a dozen babies.

"I hope it's twins," Meggie laughed.

Amantha thought of Meggie's birth, how she'd sold her silver service to Anna, in order to pay the doctor and hospital; how her gifts had been a cradle and an electric gyrator.

Now she knew it had been a happy time, despite the hardships—but she wouldn't want it for Meggie.

Even the baby's birth was uneventful. Meggie—blue eyes rather stunned that pain, which she'd never known, had found her at last—came through it like a trooper. The baby was a girl, a perfect little round-headed creature with a shock of black hair and deep blue eyes.

Back in her own bed, holding her daughter in her arms, Meggie was ecstatic.

"We're going to name her Ellen, after Ricky's mother," she said, a little sheepishly. "The next one we'll name after you.

"And, oh, Mum, now I'll be able to fly!"

If anything, Meggie's zest for living increased. Amantha's gift to the young couple was a full-time maid. Ricky Van Holsten was given a promotion, though he was rarely at work, but at home, doting over his wife and baby.

Amantha, too, found it difficult to stay away. She found herself leaving the office earlier, having Ryan drive her to the apartment, warming herself at the happiness contained in those rooms.

Once, when she arrived, she ran into Charlie, just leaving.

"Purty little thing," he commented on the baby. "Sort of puts me in the mind of Dave."

To Amantha, there was no resemblance. Ellen was a solemn child, her great eyes seeming to wonder over the world she'd been born into. She's not like Peter, Amantha thought, holding her; nor like Meggie. Ellen was herself.

Meggie adored her. To her, little Ellen was like a doll, to be picked up and put down at will. Her life was perfect—except for the dumb doctor, who still insisted she be grounded for a month. She ticked the days off on the calendar, longing for the freedom of flight.

And finally the day came.

Meggie gave a multitude of instructions to the maid, kissed little Ellen, and insisted on dropping by Amantha's office.

"Look at me, Mum!" Clad in a pink flight suit, Meggie spun for Amantha's approval. "My figure's all back! And today we fly! Golly, now I have everything! It's so great, just being alive—"

A memory of Charlie's long-ago warning tugging at her mind, Amantha asked, cautiously, "Do you think it's wise for both of you—I mean, if something should happen—"

"Then you're stuck with the kid," Meggie said, laughing. "Don't worry, Mum! Ricky and I are going to live forever!"

With a hug and kiss, Meggie danced out of the office, a grinning husband following her.

Amantha tried to return to her work, but visions of her lovely daughter wouldn't leave her alone. She paced the office for awhile, then gave up and called for Ryan to take her home. After all, it was the weekend. She'd have lunch, then drop by and check on the baby. . . .

As they approached the house she frowned. A number of vehicles were parked along the curb, a police car among them. Leaning forward, she tapped Ryan's shoulder.

"What is this? Do you know?"

"There was nobody here when I left to come after you."

They turned into the drive and Amantha stepped out. A flashbulb went off in her face, blinding her, and there was a chatter of voices that made no sense.

"I need a comment, Mrs. Carmody."

"How did you feel when you heard—?"

"The records say you had a son. Could you tell us—?"

A gruff voice interceded. "Dammit, leave her alone! Let me get her into the house. Mrs. Carmody, are you all right?"

Now she recognized the police chief. She had met him often, socially.

"What—what is this, Bob?" she asked, her mouth stiff.

"Oh, hell! You don't know! I was afraid of that."

He maneuvered her into the house, closing the door against the reporters, and seated her in a chair.

"I hate to have to tell you this. They're dead, ma'am, both of them. Their plane crashed and burned."

"It's your funeral," she heard Charlie's voice saying in her mind. *"Your funeral—your funeral—your funeral—"*

"Ma'am." It was the maid, Delia, her voice weak from crying. "Mr. Forbes just got here. He'd like to know if you want to see him."

Charlie? Want to see him? She wanted him to put his arms around her, to hold her and never let her go. But then what was left of her would shatter into a million pieces.

She couldn't bear to face him. He had been right and she had been wrong.

"No," she whispered, "not now. Please—please tell him just to go away."

BOOK IV

Ellen

Chapter Forty-One

By 1970 *the deaths of the young Van Holstens, like that of* Peter Carmody, were drifted over with the sands of change. The peace so lavishly promised at the end of the Second World War had never been realized. There'd been cold wars, hot wars, and brush fires; an endless verbal conflict with Russia; Korea; the race for supremacy in space; Vietnam. Oklahoma City was growing, bursting at the seams.

Everything changes, thought Charlie Forbes. He was lounging comfortably in one of Amantha's big chairs, long legs stretched out, pipe in hand.

Everything changed but Amantha. Now in her sixties, she was still beautiful, youthful-looking. Too little and frail to have such a commanding presence.

He couldn't help being proud of her; the way she picked up the pieces after Meggie's death. She'd whipped the faltering company back into shape, hanging on with guts and grit. Her old enemy, her father-in-law, was dead now, but that durn Greenberg was still on the scene.

And now there was this goldang oil crisis. Things got more complicated every minute!

He listened as Amantha laid her cards on the table.

A pipeline, carrying half a million barrels of oil daily from Saudi Arabia, crossed Jordan, Syria, and Lebanon. It had been accidently cut by a bulldozer. The Syrian government refused to allow it to be repaired unless exorbitant fees were paid. It was blackmail. People on the east coast of the United

States would be without heat. Factories would close. Jet fuel would be rationed.

"Carmody-Forbes will increase its production to take up the slack," Amantha said. "I want to open the wells we've shut down because of expense versus operation. And then—"

Charlie sat up straighter. "Goldang it, girl, you don't know what yer gittin' into! Them wells has just been settin' there. We'd have to use floodin', gas repressurin'—and there no tellin' if any of it'll work!"

"Then we'll put down new wells beside them."

Charlie shook his head, mournfully. "Know what'll happen then? After we shot our wad? We're gonna pay them A-rabs off!"

"Syrians, Charlie."

"Don't make no difference. We're gonna pay 'em off, an' they'll start pourin' oil agin. Then where we gonna be? Holdin' the bag, that's what! And what you gonna tell the stockholders when they git shook up over dividends?"

Amantha rubbed her forehead. "Sometimes I wonder why we're involved, Charlie. We're getting old."

Not Amantha, Charlie thought. Mebbe me, but never Amantha. The creases in his lean face were deep, now; the wrinkles that fanned his gray eyes didn't go away when he wasn't smiling. There were white threads in his sandy hair, in the brows above his direct gaze.

But Amantha was just the same, trim and neat, her ash brown hair unfaded. Maybe her complexion was a little softer now, the softness of a ripened peach, but it didn't hurt her looks.

It was only in her eyes that there was a difference. But would everybody see the sadness behind the blue, like shadows in a clear pool? Maybe he saw it because he knew it was there.

"We can always quit, Amantha. Throw in th' towel. Like you said, ain't no reason. You know Ellie don't want no part of this."

It was true. The Van Holstens, shattered by their son's death, felt they were too old to cope with a child in the house again. The care of Ellen had fallen to Amantha.

And Amantha was unable to face being a mother again.

Overwhelmed by responsibility, she tried to do her duty. The tiny room next to Amantha's office, which she'd used as a lounge, became a nursery, and then a playroom, as small Ellen accompanied her to work.

Ellen grew up with the oil business. She'd been swung into the air by oil tycoons. She even had a collection of core samples, polished cylinders showing the earth's strata.

But Ellen had opted to be a schoolteacher, delighted with her kindergarten class. And she'd shown no interest in any of the men to whom Amantha had introduced her; men with knowledge of business and oil.

There was no one to take Amantha's place.

If only Peter had lived!

"Somethin' on yer mind?" Charlie, intuitive as always, was studying her.

"I was thinking of Ellen," she lied.

"You can be proud of Ellie," Charlie said soberly. "She's a good girl."

Chapter Forty-Two

Ellen Van Holsten was a good girl. Early in childhood, she'd begun to think of herself as second best in Amantha's affections. Not that she lacked love and attention, or that there was anything in Amantha's—Nana's—behavior that suggested she was less than perfect. But somehow she'd always known she couldn't fill the dancing slippers of Meggie, pretty, laughing Meggie, whose photographs were everywhere.

Though she had vivid memories of her childhood, she could not remember being in Nana's arms as she stood at a graveside where two coffins were placed, though they contained little more than a drift of ash.

Later she would remember the improvised nursery off Nana's office; the big, echoing empty house to which they returned at night. There was a dim memory of sparse visits to the home of her paternal grandparents; of trying to make herself small at the table, while the Van Holstens talked over her head about his golf and her bridge. She always went home laden with expensive gifts, but she knew they were glad to see her go.

Home, to where pictures of Meggie, her mother, smiled down from every wall. There were also photographs of a boy with serious eyes like her own.

"Is that my father?" she'd asked once.

Nana went white and frowned. "That is Peter," she said shortly.

She'd learned early that Nana didn't want to talk about Peter. It was different with Meggie. Nana wove stories of the enchanting creature she had been, until Ellen visualized a fairy princess. Still, it was Peter to whom Ellen was drawn; his photograph she talked to in her loneliness in the big house.

"Hello, Peter, Peter, pumpkin eater," she would whisper when her grandmother wasn't present. She fancied his serious eyes lightened a little, and he smiled. To his picture she confided her secrets and her dreams.

"When I grow up, I'm going to have as many children as the Old Woman in the Shoe. But I only want a little house. Not a big one. A very little house, so we can all be cozy and warm. A house like Uncle Charlie's."

For Charlie still lived at what he called the oil patch, in the cabin his grandfolks had built. Sometimes he would come to "borrow" her, taking her home where they would dine delightfully on bologna sandwiches with midget pickles and cocoa with marshmallows, talking grown-up talk.

It was Charlie who explained about Peter, telling her it hurt Nana to talk about him, since he died in the war. And, like Nana, he talked a great deal about Meggie. Ellen wondered if, with Uncle Charlie, she might be second best, too.

These visits were exciting, but they, too, were not to be discussed with Nana. She once lived here, long ago. But she didn't like the fascinating pumps that pulled oil from the ground, nor the grassed over slushpits that pocked the meadow.

Nana didn't like Indians either. So Ellen's acquaintance with Charlie's friend, Dave Meadows, must not be mentioned.

Ellen kept the various parts of her life separate, like having two pockets in a smock and a handkerchief in each. And, being second best, she tried mightily to please. She loved Amantha and knew Amantha loved her in return. But they did not share their innermost thoughts.

Sometimes Ellen felt guilty, feeling closer to Charlie Forbes and his Indian companion.

A lonely, introspective child, she wrote poetry and developed a talent for drawing. In grade school, few people linked solemn, big-eyed little Ellie Carmody Van Holsten with the wealthy, glamorous president of Carmody-Forbes. In high school, after trying to draw her into social activities, her fellow pupils finally gave up and forgot she existed.

When Nana worried that she didn't date at all, Ellen knew she'd failed once again to live up to popular Meggie.

It was like the children's poem. She was grave Alice, and Meggie was laughing Allegra.

She longed, wistfully, to be someone other than herself.

Instead, she was shy, lanky, coltish, taller than Nana at fifteen. Her treasured compliments came from her teachers.

"Your verses are perfect for children," one said.

Her art teacher praised her talent for drawing; small sketches that might illustrate a child's book.

Maybe she should be a writer, illustrating her own work.

Then she heard an author speak on Career Day. Writing was a lonely profession, he said. She visualized herself working alone in the big echoing house, and shivered.

Studious and shy, she had little interest in boys. Ellie was happiest in the company of children. She enrolled in the State Teacher's College at Edmond, adjacent to the city, with the goal of becoming a kindergarten teacher.

There she carried an incredible number of hours, went to school in the summer, graduating with honors in three years. And now she had a semester of teaching behind her.

In the presence of little ones, she was happy and fulfilled. Her only misery came from the knowledge that Nana was disappointed in her. She'd wanted her to take business courses and an interest in Carmody-Forbes.

To Nana, the childish finger games, "Here is Thumbkin, here is Thumbkin," were ridiculous. And the little dances, "Put your right foot in, put your right foot out, then you do the hokey-pokey . . ." were foolish.

Nana could not know what it was like, growing up an only child, waiting in the nursery-playroom at the office, then going home to a house where nothing welcomed her.

Sometimes, when children tugged at her skirts, reiterating the constant, "Teacher, teacher," Ellen remembered her visits to the Van Holstens, the gifts that were lavished on her in guilt for their lack of love. Then she would scoop the children up, black, brown, red, or white, and hug them.

Now it was Friday. No more school until Monday. The weekend stretched before her with nothing to fill it. From her window, she could see the lights in Nana's study stretching across the lawn. She felt a compulsion to go down and talk to her; a need for human companionship.

Her face lit with a smile that made her almost beautiful as she neared the open door. Uncle Charlie was here.

Her smile faded as she heard his words. "Ellie's a good girl."

A good girl. Mediocre. Ordinary. Maybe, Ellen thought dismally, she was even a little dull. Not elegant and brilliant like Nana. Not ethereal and effervescent as Meggie had been. There were many beautiful words to describe beautiful people.

And Ellie was good.

She started to retreat, but Amantha had glimpsed her. "Ellen, come in. Look who's here."

Charlie uncoiled his long frame and took Ellen's hand. His gray eyes expressed his liking. Maybe just being good was enough, if Charlie liked her.

She smiled back at him and he thought how pretty she had become, in a serene way. Never hold a candle to her mother or Amantha, of course. But nice—

"We been tryin' to work out some problems," he drawled. "Run smackdab into a stone wall. Why don't you set down, tell us about them kids you're teachin'?"

Amantha rose. "Not tonight, Charlie. I'm exhausted. And I want to keep my mind on the things we discussed. I don't want to rush you off, but—"

Charlie's brows went up, then he grinned and ambled toward the door. "Guess I can take a hint. Be seein' you."

Amantha turned to Ellen. "I'm going on to bed. I must go into the office in the morning. It's a Saturday. Why don't you come with me? Jon Kidderton will be in. You know, he is advising me in corporate law. You've met him—"

Yes, Ellen had. Kidderton was a small man with slicked-down hair and a pinched nose; a man who wouldn't mind marrying Carmody money, even if it included a too-thin, rather dull girl.

"I have plans for tomorrow, Nana. I'm sorry. I'm going to

Lincoln Park Zoo, to do some animal sketches for my class. I'm reading the Just-So stories, and they—"

She paused. Nana wore that look of disappointment again.

"It's quite all right," the older woman said. "But I do think you might find the business side of the company interesting, if you would try."

Not as interesting as children, Ellen thought. No, never as interesting as children. A set of accounts didn't laugh like silvery chimes or reach out with tiny hands to tug at your heart.

Amantha left the room and Ellen dawdled. She picked up the framed photo of Peter, her lips forming her old silly rhyme.

"Peter, Peter, pumpkin eater—"

What had he been like, this little boy with the serious eyes? Had he wandered through these empty rooms as she did, maybe longing for a little house like Charlie's? Was he lonely, too?

He couldn't have been. He had his sister, Meggie. Ellen looked at her mother's picture, seeing her laughing eyes and merry lips. Meggie, who had never known what it was to feel inferior; to take second place.

Chapter Forty-Three

The next morning Ellen rose, donned a pair of slacks and a matching smocklike shirt. Her pregnant shirt, she called it, secretly wishing it were true. It was her favorite top, allowing freedom of movement.

She went downstairs, finding her grandmother already gone, ate a piece of toast, drank a cup of coffee, and put an apple in her pocket. Then, with her sketchpad and charcoals, she hurried out to her Volkswagen, grateful for a lovely, lovely day.

Wheeling out of the drive, she traversed the area around the capitol and headed down Lincoln Boulevard. She'd chosen this car herself, with an eye to gas mileage. Odd, that even in this she'd disappointed Nana. She had, of all things, suggested a blue convertible.

Ellen reached the entrance to the zoo, parked the Volks, and went straight to the elephant's pen. The elephant, Judy, was an old friend. She could have sketched her from memory; maybe even with her eyes closed. But it was better here in the sun.

Judy was out of her quarters, rummaging in the scattered straw with her trunk. On impulse, Ellen tossed her the apple she carried. Then she sat down to draw, frowning. It wasn't coming right. . . .

A giggle aroused her from her absorption. Two small children, a blackhaired boy of about six, a little girl, possibly four, were hanging on the fence.

"Look, Daddy," the boy said, "Judy looks like a fat lady in back, like her pants are falling down!"

Ellen grinned. The charcoal moved in her hand, and suddenly her drawing had character; a ludicrous figure, seen from a child's eye, with an impish charm.

She was suddenly conscious that the little girl had moved from the fence and was standing beside her. The child pointed at the drawing and laughed.

"It's a n'efelant," she said.

"Sara!" A man's deep voice intruded. "Come here! Don't bother the lady."

"But she drawed a n'efelant," the child insisted. Her brother left the fence and ran to join his sister, peering at the drawing with delight.

"Sara! Jonathan! Ma'am, I'm sorry!" A man's hands closed over those of the children. "I'll get them out of here. C'mon, kids. Let's go see the monkeys again."

"It's all right." Ellen looked up, her eyes following a lean body clad in an air force uniform to a pair of deep brown eyes. She was suddenly shy.

"Don't wanna see monkeys," Sarah said, positively. "Wanna watch the n'efelant!" She and the boy ran back to the fence, and the man sank down on the bench beside Ellen.

"Do you mind, miss? I could use a rest. Those two are a handful."

"I can understand that. I'm a kindergarten teacher."

"You should be an artist. You're good."

He took a pipe from his mouth and lit it. Ellen was suddenly reminded of Charlie.

Into the silence that followed, his son's voice rang out. "Look Sara! She went potty!"

Indeed, a steaming pile of dung had been deposited on the straw of the enclosure. The father's face turned red.

"My apologies again," he said ruefully. "My mother does her best, but she can't keep up with them. I've got to work out some other arrangements."

She looked at him, curiously, and he hastened to explain. His name was Collins. "Joe Collins, at your service, ma'am," he said with mock formality. His ex-wife hadn't liked having kids much. He'd spent a year in Nam, and while he was gone, she dumped the children on his mom and left him for one of his friends.

Ellen made a little sound of pity, and he grinned, crookedly.

"Just as well. They're better off without her."

Now he was home on terminal leave. His discharge was coming up next month. Then he had an engineering job lined up in California. He was making the most of his leave, getting reacquainted with his kids. . . .

Watching him as he talked, listening to his slow, melodic voice, Ellen wondered what kind of woman could leave this charming man and those precious young ones. She wouldn't, that's for sure!

Her cheeks turned a little pink, and she looked away.

"I shouldn't be bothering you with my problems," he said, guiltily. "Hey, kids—"

They came running, having had their fill of watching Judy. Ellen couldn't let them go. She broke in quickly before Joe Collins could lead them away.

"Do you know how the elephant got his trunk?"

The boy was big-eyed. "No."

Ellen reached out to put an arm around Sara. With children, at least, she was comfortable.

"Well, once upon a time, by the great, gray-green, greasy Limpopo River . . ."

The boy cuddled close at her other side, and Joe Collins looked down at them, with an aching yearning that made a lump in his throat.

The story ended. Jonathan's attention was diverted to a small black boy, pink tongue licking at a raspberry snow cone.

"I wanna snow cone, Daddy. Can we have a snow cone?"

"I want one, too, Daddy. Ple-e-ase?"

"Of course," he said reluctantly. "Would you like one, too, miss—I don't even know if you're a miss, a Mrs., or a Ms.—"

"Its miss," Ellen smiled up at him. "Ellen Van Holsten. Ellie, if you like. And, yes, a snow cone sounds great."

"Ellie," he said in that deep, musical voice that gave her

the shivers. "Yes, I like! Well, come on, gang. What are we waiting for?"

The children ran ahead, screeching like small parrots in their excitement. Ellen and Joe Collins followed more slowly. It seems so natural, Ellen thought. As if it's all real. As if I belong here with this man and these children. Like the rest of my life is something I dreamed—

She learned that he had a degree in engineering, and that he liked to work with his hands. He learned that Ellie's parents were dead, and that she'd been brought up by her grandmother; that though she loved Nana, she could understand the children's problems.

"Nana?" He looked at her, a question in his eyes.

"My grandmother. They call them that in England."

Her explanation was lost as he dashed forward, expertly retrieving Jonathan from the top of a fence surrounding the bear's cage. He was mopping his brow when he returned.

"Say, listen, when they get tired of this, why don't we go over to Springlake? We can grab a hamburger, let the kids go on the rides."

"Wonderful," she said happily. "It sounds absolutely wonderful!"

That night Ellen drove her Volkswagen home. Her shirt was stained with mustard. She'd ridden the merry-go-round with Sara until she was dizzy. Joe couldn't have guessed she was being a child herself.

And, best of all, it hadn't ended. Joe asked her if she could swim. And that was one thing she could do, having grown up with a pool all to herself in the backyard.

Joe had a friend who would lend him a boat. He'd like to take the children out, but was worried at the thought of handling the two of them. And tomorrow was Sunday. Would Ellie care to—?

"I'd love it," she said recklessly. Sunday was church, sitting white-gloved and stiff beside Nana. Sunday was a heavy meal of beef and Yorkshire pudding; perhaps a game of Scrabble afterward. Unless Nana decided to work.

Ellie prayed that she would.

Nana was still sleeping when Ellie rose at five. She went to the kitchen and packed a basket of fruit and cookies, thinking longingly of Charlie's bologna sandwiches. Then she drove to the parking lot at the capitol. Joe wanted to pick her up, but she'd explained it would be easier this way. He'd looked confused, but it was surely better than meeting Nana. She would disapprove of a divorced man with two children.

He was waiting when she got there, the children yawning in the back seat. He, too, had brought a basket of lunch, plus a Thermos of coffee. He looked with approval at her white middy blouse and slacks, promptly dubbing her captain of the ship.

It was a beautiful day. The boat with its white sails skimmed like a bird over the waters of the lake. The sun glinted down, tipping each ripple of the murky water with gold. Hair blowing in the breeze, hand to the tiller, Ellen felt a sense of power and well-being.

"I am the master of my fate," she quoted, laughing, "I am the captain of my soul."

"And you are a very pretty girl," Joe ad-libbed, "who makes my fam-i-ly seem whole! See, I'm a poet, too."

Their eyes met, and for a moment there was a stillness between them. Ellen drew a quivering breath.

"I think the children are getting hungry," she said hastily. "I'll get out the food."

That night he returned her to the parking lot. Leaving his children in his Ford, he insisted on unlocking the Volks and seeing her into it. They stood in the lot, the capitol looming beyond them, and he looked down at her. She was windblown and sunburned, her white middy and slacks rumpled and stained, but she looked beautiful to him.

"I can't let you go like this, Ellie. Can I see you tomorrow?"

"I teach tomorrow."

"I don't mean in the day. I'm asking you for a date. I want to pick you up at your door, take you out."

"But your children—"

"Mom can watch them. She won't mind."

But Nana would, Ellen thought miserably. Nana would

mind very much. It didn't seem to matter. She gave him her address. He would pick her up at six.

When she rose the next morning, her grandmother had still not left for work. Breakfast was in the dining room, kept warm beneath its silver covers. Ellen said good morning to the elegant woman at the head of the table, then busied herself at the sideboard. She took time helping herself to a rasher of bacon, eggs, toast from its rack.

But finally, she had to face her grandmother.

"Where were you yesterday?" the older woman asked mildly. "I had thought we'd attend church."

"I was . . . sketching," Ellen said. She hated herself for dissembling, but at least it wasn't a lie. She had taken her sketchbook along to amuse Sarah and Jonathan.

"Oh, may I see?"

Face afire, Ellen brought her drawings: a sailboat that looked as if it were flying; a humorous fish, its goggle-eyes above the waterline, a silly grin on its gaping mouth; two children beside a man at a tiller . . .

"Who are these people?"

"Just a family I met."

Satisfied, Amantha blotted her lips daintily with a napkin and rose to go. "I shouldn't be so tardy in leaving, but I haven't seen you for some time. I'll be late coming home, tonight. A business affair—"

Ellen sagged in relief.

"And do put something on that face of yours, child. You look dreadful. I can't understand it. Meggie never burned—"

Later, dabbing her crimson face with lotion, Ellen wished she could be like her dead mother for just one night. She left for school, looking forward to the coming evening and dreading it at the same time.

Nana's words echoed in her ears. "You look dreadful—dreadful—dreadful—"

Chapter Forty-Four

When Joe Collins called for Ellen that night, he didn't notice her appearance. He looked past her at the interior of the big house with a stricken expression.

"Good lord! This is a mansion! I never dreamed—"

Ellen felt compelled to apologize for her luxurious surroundings. "If you like large houses," she said deprecatingly. "I prefer small ones."

He was still looking back, his face gloomy as he helped her into the car, removing a rag doll and a toy plane and tossing them into the back seat.

"I guess I've acted like some kind of nut, plying a girl like you with hamburgers and snow cones."

"They happen to be my favorite foods."

"Yeah, sure! Along with caviar and hummingbird's tongues on toast!"

She laughed. "Would you believe roast beef and Yorkshire pudding?"

His expression relaxed a bit, but he still looked worried.

"I asked you out, and you're stuck with me. But I did something stupid this morning; bought something that almost cleaned me out. I thought I'd get my pay in the mail, but I didn't."

He thrust his hand into his pocket and she heard the jingle of coins.

"I've got enough to take us to dinner, but no movie. Or we can go to the movie and pretend we're not hungry. Maybe there's enough for some popcorn. . . ."

"Do I make the decision?"

He spread his hands. "You've heard the options."

"I would like to have a hamburger and go for a drive, maybe out to the lake."

He grinned. "You're on! As bright as you are beautiful."

But he was still not at ease as they pulled into a drive-in, ordering hamburgers and Cokes to go.

"I feel like a fool," he confessed. "The way you act with kids, I thought—well, I guess I thought you were a nice, sweet girl, living on a teacher's salary. I drove past your house three times, sure I'd goofed on the address."

"It's not my home. It's Nana's. She's Amantha Carmody, of Carmody-Forbes."

Joe whistled. "I've seen her name in the papers. Look, Ellie, if you don't want to go out with me, if you want me to take you back, just say so."

Her temper flared. "You asked me out! If you want me to go home, then, d-damn it, I'll go!"

He looked at her in shock, then his mouth curled in an amused grin. "Why, Miss Van Holsten! Such language! What if the children were here?"

"I've heard worse in my kindergarten class!"

They both laughed, and the tension eased between them.

They drove to the lake and parked, looking out over the flat expanse of shimmering water; the small brushy islands that were said to be inhabited by snakes. Tonight they looked like moon-silvered castles.

A car filled with teenagers pulled in beside them, then drove away.

"I guess we've got their place," Joe said. "And here they were, probably all set for a little necking."

"I've never done that," Ellen said, her face hot. "I've always wondered what it would be like. I didn't date in high school. In college, I was too much of a grind. . . ."

"You've never parked with a guy? A girl with your looks? We'll remedy that!"

Joe leaned to touch her lips with a gentle kiss. It turned into something more. With a muffled moan, he pulled her to him and she pressed against his strong body, her own body throbbing, the lake blotted out by a shower of stars.

Finally he pushed her away and clutched the wheel with whitened knuckles.

"Well, that's what it's like, Ellie. Now you know."

"Joe?" It was a question. Her mouth was trembling. He slammed his hand against the wheel and sat for a moment with his head bent. When he raised it, his eyes glittered with self-mockery.

"I want to show you something. Maybe you'll get a kick out of it. I told you I blew all I had on something this morning. Well, this is it!"

He reached into his pocket and took out a small jeweler's box.

"It looked like a big deal until I saw where you live. Then I knew it was peanuts."

He opened the box to reveal a matching set of rings: a small diamond, a plain wedding band.

"I was dumb enough to think you might marry a poverty-stricken family man you only met three days ago. Big joke, huh?"

"Oh, Joe! Joe!" Ellen was laughing and crying at the same time, reaching for him. He looked at her in bewilderment, then they were in each other's arms, holding tightly, his mouth hot on hers, his hands roving, touching—

This was what I was waiting for, Ellen thought. This night! This man! All these years, somewhere in my mind, I knew—

"Love me," she whispered. "Oh, Joe, love me! Then if I wake up tomorrow, and this is all a dream—"

Her plea brought him to his senses. He pulled away and sat, eyes closed, his knuckles white on the steering wheel. Finally he looked at her, disheveled and glowing in the moonlight. He managed a painful smile.

"Nothing doing. We're not going any further until I put both rings on your finger." He paused. "The rings are new, by the way. It's only the groom that's a little used."

It hurt to think there had once been someone else. But the children made up for it. Joe's children, her children.

He pulled her head against his shoulder, and she leaned

against him, content, watching the moon spread a golden path across the lake while they made their plans.

There was much to do. She had to talk to Nana. He must inform his mother, Sara and Jonathan. There would be the blood tests, license, arrangements with a minister or justice of the peace. They'd marry as soon as his discharge was final. Then she and the children would go with him to California.

Finally he drove her home. Amantha's long black car was under the portico. Joe held Ellen for a minute, looking beyond her at the house.

"Do you want me to go in with you?"

"I think I'd better talk to Nana by myself."

He released her, reluctantly, his eyes still on the gracious old mansion.

"Real estate's pretty high in California," he said dismally. "And it'll be a while before my pay starts adding up. We might need to rent a trailer for a while—a mobile home. . . ."

A mobile home! She'd seen them. They were like little houses. She would have a little house, crowded with love and laughter.

The thought strengthened her for her coming ordeal.

Amantha Carmody had left the business dinner early; she was concerned about Ellie. She had done her utmost to maintain a balance in their relationship; not strict as she'd been with Peter, nor too lenient as she'd been with Meggie.

As Charlie said, Ellen was a good girl. Amantha sometimes wished she behaved in a more normal fashion, dating a little, having friends in. But, aside from a total lack of interest in such things, Ellen had never been a problem.

For the last few days, however, the girl had been . . . different. She'd seen little of her but what little she'd seen was . . . bemused. She came home purposely to talk to Ellen, surprised and a little alarmed when she found she'd gone out.

A long hour dragged by. Amantha seriously considered calling the police. She would look a fool. Ellie was, after all, in her twenties. It would be impossible to explain she was worried only because it was out of character.

The front door opened and shut, and Amantha breathed a sigh of relief. It was cut short when Ellen appeared in the doorway. Her eyes were bright, her hair flyaway, and she looked as if she had been mauled.

The look of bravado she wore reminded Amantha, painfully, of Peter.

"Nana, I'm going to get married."

After her initial shock, Amantha was filled with questions. Who was the man? When had they met? Where—?

The answers were worse than she could have imagined. The fellow was military, on terminal leave. They'd met three days ago.

At the zoo!

Oh, dear God!

The worst was yet to come. The man was divorced. The father of two children.

"This is insane," Amantha choked. "I absolutely forbid it! You can't—!"

"But I can," Ellen said, her gaze level. "I'm of age. You can't stop me."

"I can write you out of my will. If he's marrying you for your money—"

"We don't want anything from you, Nana. We're going to live in California. He has a job, but even if he didn't— Oh, Nana, can't you understand? We want to build something that's all our own."

Amantha's anger faded, turning into a sick despair. She'd quarreled with Peter. And Peter was dead. Meggie had been allowed all the freedom in the world, and she was gone.

She had failed them all.

For the first time she thought of what Ellen meant to her; Ellen with her talents, her level head. Ellen, perhaps more like David than the others; who knew exactly what she wanted from her life.

She must not lose her, too.

"Nana, are you all right?"

Amantha realized she had been pressing her palms against a forehead that threatened to explode.

"I shall give my approval, Ellen. But only on one condition. I insist on a proper wedding. You owe me that."

Ellen was beside her, arms around the tiny figure that seemed suddenly shrunken and old.

"You're right, Nana! You're right. I do."

Amantha sat long into the night, thinking of the long hard years she'd battled, building a monument to David's name. She thought of Charlie's words.

"We can always quit, Amantha. Throw in the towel. Ellie don't want no part of this—"

She'd built her little empire, and it would stand only as long as she was strong enough to keep control. How long would that be?

All she could do was keep on trying. After all, she had nothing else to do with her life. She had worked far too long.

Chapter Forty-Five

*A*mantha braced herself for her first meeting with Joe Collins. To her surprise, she discovered she liked the young man. Though he had an easygoing manner about him that reminded her of Charlie, he was well-educated and ambitious for his family.

An engineer?

She seized on that. Why not take a job with Carmody-Forbes? He could gradually learn the business, and then—

"I'm not that kind of engineer, ma'am."

That could be remedied. Some further schooling, along with experience in the business end.

He shook his head. "I'm not much for business. I want to build things, Mrs. Carmody. Things my kids can look at after I'm gone and say, 'My dad did that.' "

"And we don't think it's a good idea to work for relatives," Ellen chimed in.

Amantha made one more try.

It might be more sensible to delay the wedding for a year. Joe could go on out to California and get established first—

"No way," Ellen said, inelegantly. "Where Joe goes, I go."

Amantha looked at her oddly, then acknowledged defeat. They decided upon a wedding date.

"Whew," Joe said as he and Ellen left the house. "That dainty little lady is something else! She looks soft and sweet, but she's tougher than a boot! How'd you ever get the nerve to buck her for a jerk like me?"

"I love you," Ellen said honestly.

Amantha watched them go, the stiffness going out of her shoulders.

She had to admire Ellen. If she'd had Ellen's courage, she would have had five more years with David. Ellen knew what she wanted.

And Joe Collins, too. He wanted to leave something memorable behind.

She smiled, wryly, thinking of her own contribution to the future: a number of six-thousand-foot holes in the ground.

Plans for the wedding began immediately. It would be a huge affair, most of the guests being Amantha's acquaintances; oil men, attorneys, senators, legislators, and business contacts. To the list Ellen added her school principal, a number of teachers, the parents of some of her students.

Ellie had asked a teacher-friend to be matron of honor; two others to serve as bridesmaids. Little Jonathan would be ring bearer, Sara, flowergirl.

Charlie Forbes would give the bride away. And Joe, out of deference to Ellie, asked Dave Meadows to serve as best man.

"I will not have an Indian in my house, Ellen," Amantha frowned.

Ellen glared back. "This is my wedding, Nana!"

Amantha said nothing more.

The next six weeks were pure chaos. The oil crisis demanded long hard days at the office, and Ellen insisted on finishing out her teaching year. Invitations must be sent. And wedding gifts began pouring in.

A room was set up with tables to display the gifts as they were unwrapped and tabulated. Silver candleholders from the White House occupied a place of honor.

"They will look well with the service I brought from England," Amantha said. "It will be yours now."

Ellen looked at the massive set on the sideboard. Her eyes welled with tears and she hugged her grandmother.

"You're a dear, Nana. I know what that service means to you. I just couldn't take it. It belongs here, with you! But the thought behind it, the idea that you want to give it to me, is enough. Oh, Nana! I love you!''

It was plain that Ellen thought Amantha would live forever. And this was no moment to discuss the fragility of humanity. The silver had been lovingly, generously, returned, and Amantha must accept it as such.

But she revised the legacy she'd leave the world. In addition to six-thousand-foot holes, there would be an antique silver service nobody wanted.

The candleholders were soon surrounded by a sea of crystal; priceless Oriental vases; a complete selection of Frankoma pottery; chests of flatware; piles of linens.

One table was covered with an odd display. Ellen's kindergartners each had made a plaque, the shape of their hands impressed in plaster of paris, using the tops of round oatmeal boxes for molds.

"What in heaven's name are you going to do with those?" Amantha asked.

Ellen smiled. "Hang them on my walls. Aren't they precious?" They were her favorite gift.

Next in line was a tastefully framed original painting, a stylized version of Indian symbols, done in the style of Acee Blue Eagle, Oklahoma's great Indian painter.

It was signed, "David Meadows."

"I thought he was an attorney," Amantha said, sourly.

"He is, but he paints, too. Isn't it beautiful."

Amantha would be glad when it was out of the house.

The Carmody home was turned inside out; carpets cleaned, windows washed and shining. The wedding cake was ordered, a mammoth, many-tiered creation. Cleaners, seamstresses, and caterers milled through the rooms that final week.

And then the wedding day dawned, blue and clear.

As Amantha helped Ellen dress, she thought of Meggie; her own dreams for such a day when her daughter married. But Meggie had eloped.

And Ellen was marrying a divorced man.

She gave a final adjustment to Ellen's veil. She looked lovely, innocent, virginal.

"Are you happy, Ellen? Are you sure?"

"I've been sure from the minute I met Joe, Nana."

Amantha's eyes were wet. "I like him, Ellen. I'm only sorry he was married before. You—you deserve better."

"It doesn't matter, Nana," Ellen said honestly. "It could be worse. I could marry a man who'd had lots of girls. Or one who would cheat on me. I couldn't stand that."

Amantha flinched, thinking of David.

The music had begun. Leaving Ellen, Amantha went downstairs to sit in the front row; a fragile, straight-backed little woman in a gown the color of wild roses.

The groom took his place, the best man at his side. Joe Collins was pale, looking young for the father of two; frightened.

Amantha's eyes left him, studying the man who stood with him.

Dave Meadows, in his late twenties, was all Indian, representing everything she hated. But she had to admit he was a presentable young man; taller than Joe, squarely built, he dominated the scene.

It could have been worse, Amantha thought fiercely. Ellen might have chosen—that, to marry.

The music changed, and everything proceeded smoothly. The matron of honor—Amantha couldn't recall her name—was a surprise. Without her glasses, her hair loose around her face, she looked more like a socialite than a schoolteacher. The bridesmaids followed, pretty but anonymous as the guests awaited Ellen's appearance.

Joe's children, for once, were beautifully behaved; awed at their part in the ritual. Sara, adorable as she scattered rose petals, brought small murmurs of appreciation from the audience.

And then the bride—

Ellen was a vision; floating in a mist of veiling, an ethereal creature with a halo of happiness around her. Her small hand rested in the crook of Charlie's arm.

Charlie!

Amantha had never realized he was such a handsome man. He had just been . . . everpresent; standing by her in the early days of her marriage; being there when Meggie was born; when David died; bringing the news of Peter's death. . . .

Charlie was always there when she needed him. That had not been too often of late. She thought she'd grown self-sufficient; able to handle everything by herself.

But I haven't, she thought forlornly, and I'm not.

Oh, dear God! Here she sat in the midst of all her friends—and she was lonely!

The words of the ceremony drifted over her like wisps of fog.

"Who gives this woman—"

Charlie's voice; "Her mother and I do."

And soon it was over.

There were photographs to be taken; Ellen and Joe coming down the aisle together, with their attendants, without their attendants, cutting the cake. . . .

Champagne punch graced a long table, lavish with canapés. A bar had been set up in one room for the lusty oil tycoons who preferred their liquor straight. Moving toward the table where tea was being served, Amantha smiled, noting there were not many takers.

The men crowded the bar; Dodie was already giggly on champagne and flirting outrageously with Charlie. Amantha halted. The Indian, Dave Meadows, was studying her silver tea service, touching its engraved surface with a gentle hand.

At least she would know whom to suspect if it came up missing!

As if she'd spoken the thought, the man's head jerked up. Seeing her eyes on him, he flushed red beneath his copper skin.

"I have been admiring this," he said quietly. "I've never seen anything like it. A family heirloom, isn't it?"

"Yes," she said. "It is."

"It's priceless." He touched the ornate tray with a reverent finger.

That made two people who thought so! Herself and a—a damned Indian!

"It's very old-fashioned," she blurted. "I have been considering selling it." Her sentence ended on a note of horror.

She had done no such thing! Where had the notion come from?

The dark face above her showed consternation. "Don't do that, ma'am! This should be handed on down in your family."

Except nobody wanted it, she thought wryly. They were anachronisms, she and her silver.

"Amantha Carmody," a voice interrupted.

Grateful for an excuse to do so, Amantha turned her attention to an old friend.

"Why, Senator! So glad you could come—"

It seemed an interminable afternoon; smiling, smiling, uttering social platitudes to this person and that. Then it was time for the bride and groom to go. In a shower of rice, they ran for Joe's car, a rather incongruous touch considering the sumptuous wedding. It was an old Ford. And attached to it was a U-Haul filled with wedding presents.

After their departure, the guests filtered away. Only Charlie remained.

Amantha felt drained, exhausted.

"You all right?" Charlie asked.

"Very much all right." Amantha managed a smile. "Could you use a cup of coffee, Charlie?"

"Well, now, I reckon I could."

They made their way into the kitchen, past the dining room with its crumbs and spills, and soiled cups, plates, and glasses. The help had been given the remainder of the day off. This would have to wait until morning.

Charlie sat down while she prepared the coffee, yanking off his tie, putting it in his pocket, and unbuttoning his collar.

"Glad it's over," he said gloomily. "Goldang thing was about to strangle me."

He lit his pipe and stared at her through the smoke, his gray gaze still concerned.

"You ain't got nobody to worry about but yerself now, Amantha. What you plannin' to do?"

"Just as I've always done. What else is there?"

"Well," he grinned, "you might take off a day and go fishin'."

She laughed. "Don't be silly, Charlie!"

"How about a little vacation? Trip to England?"

"There's nothing there for me, now. My mother's dead. My sister-in-law is married again."

"That ain't such a bad idea."

She stared at him. "What?"

"Marryin' agin. Retirin'. Givin' up this rat race."

"You're talking about me, Charlie? Me?" Amantha laughed again. "For one thing, I—I'm no spring chicken. My work is my life. And—there'll never be another David."

"Figgered you'd say that." Charlie gulped the rest of his coffee and stood. "I gotta be goin'."

He gripped her hand and she held on, suddenly not wanting him to leave. His touch was warm, comforting, just as it had always been. She wanted to rest her head on his chest, like a child.

"Thank you for taking David's place, today," she said. "I don't know how I could have managed without you. All these years, and you're still David's good friend."

His grip loosened. "Your friend, too, I hope."

"Of course, Charlie."

His eyes looked wet. "Well, goldang it! Can't stand here jawin' all night. You better git to bed—"

She saw him to the door, then went wearily up to her room. There was something on her pillow—

She picked up a whimsical drawing; a sketch of an old car, elongated, as if speeding. It pulled a U-Haul behind it. There was a man at the wheel, a woman at his side, the vague suggestion of a veil blowing in the wind. Children spilled from the two rear windows.

"Just Married" was printed on the side of the car, with the inscription, "California or Bust" beneath it.

At the bottom of the page, Ellen had penciled, "I love you, Nana. And don't worry. I'm the happiest girl in the world."

Ellen had guessed she'd be lonely. She'd taken time from the happiest moment of her life to think of a sad old woman; to leave a little bit of herself behind.

BOOK V

Amantha

Chapter Forty-Six

*A*mantha Carmody *snapped out of her reverie as the No* Smoking and Fasten Your Seat Belts signs snapped on. Surely they hadn't reached Oklahoma City.

The familiar skyline set against a flat plain assured her that they would soon be landing.

Her journey backward into time had kept her fully occupied. And why not? It had been a long life. She'd almost made it through the entire list of her memories—up until Ellen's wedding two years earlier.

But nothing of much import had taken place since then. Just work, and more work. Ellen was expecting a baby. And there had been that spell last month.

She rubbed her temples. They were aching much in the same manner as they had that day. It was so humiliating! She had blacked out, right in the middle of a stockholders' meeting. All she remembered was waking in Charlie's arms, just wanting to close her eyes again and rest.

Stress, her doctor had said. And that was ridiculous. There was no more tension than there had been at other times in her life. He recommended rest, but that was impossible, with the trip to Washington looming ahead.

Not that it had been so successful! She hadn't really accomplished anything.

And now this lapse into memory, which had blotted out her entire journey.

It wasn't like her.

It was easily explainable, however. It had been a defense

mechanism, something to keep her from thinking. The reporter's words had jolted her more than she wanted to admit.

Charlie selling out?

He wouldn't! Oh, dear God, he wouldn't!

But he had threatened to!

After she'd had that fainting episode, he'd faced her down.

"Goldang it, Amantha, this is it! You been workin' yer fool self into the ground, and I ain't gonna put up with it no longer!"

"It's none of your affair what I do, Charlie."

He looked as if she'd struck him, and was quiet for a moment.

Then he said, "If yer bent on killin' yerself, I don't aim to help you do it."

Without Charlie's vote, Thorne Greenberg would have the majority of the board with him. Amantha would be unseated. Thorne would make the decisions. It would no longer be a family company, but a vast, sprawling, wheeling, dealing conglomerate.

It looked as if Charlie had meant what he said.

"Mrs. Carmody?"

The stewardess leaned over her. The plane had landed and was nearly emptied—another lapse.

Amantha unfastened her seat belt and reached for the briefcase beneath the seat in front of her, her head pounding almost beyond endurance.

Her misery didn't keep her from casting a quick glance toward the reporter who had accosted her. He had drunk himself into insensibility.

"We'll have to pour him off," the stewardess laughed. "But I thought you'd want a head start."

"Thank you," Amantha said.

In the terminal she went to a telephone. First she called Charlie Forbes. She was back from Washington, she told him, crisply. And she needed to talk to him. He was to go immediately to her home.

She debated calling Ryan to pick her up. But then she would have to wait. And her head hurt so.

She called a cab.

As it drove through the city, she was suddenly struck by the recent changes. The traffic was heavy, landmarks had altered in these last years. She was a stranger in a strange land.

Even her house seemed different, too large, somehow forbidding.

The sun was beating down, but she was freezing. Shivering, she managed to pay the driver and turned to go up the walk.

The front door was locked, and she fumbled for the key. Her fingers seemed to be all thumbs.

Finally she gave up and leaned on the bell.

The little maid, Delia, answered the door.

"Why, Mrs. Carmody," she exclaimed, "we didn't expect—"

Her sentence ended as Amantha Carmody stumbled over the threshold and collapsed in her arms.

"I'm all right," she kept saying as the servants led her to bed. "I am perfectly all right! No, you will not call Doctor Skillern. I will not allow it!"

Once in bed, however, her iron will deserted her. Her fever soared. And when Charlie Forbes arrived, she was in delirium.

It was Charlie who sent for the doctor; Charlie who laved her hot face with cool water until the physician arrived. Charlie who waited outside the door, frantic, until the man had completed his examination.

"Durn it, Doc, what is it?" he snapped when he emerged.

"Nerves, fatigue, stress." Doctor Skillern was tight-lipped as he put his stethoscope away. "She's under sedation, now, and she'll be all right as long as she behaves herself. But these things are warning signals. If she doesn't slow down—"

"She will, Doc. And I'm gonna see she does it, if I have to hawg-tie her!"

He saw the physician out, then returned to sit by Amantha's bed.

She looked so little and lost, tossing and turning, fighting the drug she'd been given to make her rest.

Charlie took hold of the small hand that picked nervously at her covering. "Goldang it, Amantha, take it easy. Ain't nothin' needs doin' right now."

283

"Thorne—Thorne—don't let him—"

"Thorne ain't gonna do nothin', Amantha."

Presently she slept, only to wake, clutching at Charlie like a drowning woman.

"Oh, Charlie, I dreamed—I dreamed—"

Tears spilled weakly down her cheeks as she babbled her feverish nightmares.

Meggie was playing under the shack in the oil patch. A black funnel swooped down, and the house spun—

"You seen *The Wizard of Oz*," Charlie comforted her. "On the tee-vee. You got it mixed up in your head."

"Then Peter—Peter fell into the slush-pit. You rescued him, and he didn't have a face—"

Charlie was silent. He didn't have an answer for that one.

Amantha dozed again, to wake, her face a mask of horror.

"David! I can't move him! Help me! Charlie-e-e."

Then, patiently, she described David's killer over and over. An Indian man with yarn-wrapped braids; his features copper-colored—

Charlie held her, kissing away the tears that stained her cheeks, consoling her as he would a sick child. When she drifted into what appeared to be a normal sleep, he managed to catch a few winks.

When he opened his eyes, she was looking at him, her blue gaze clear and lucid.

"I've been out of my head, haven't I? I seem to remember saying stupid things. . . ."

Charlie turned a dull red. He hoped that was all she remembered.

"You had some bad dreams, I reckon."

"The doctor was here, wasn't he? I suppose it's a virus?"

"He's comin' back this mornin'. You better ask him."

She struggled to a sitting position. "Charlie, I've got to talk to you—about Carmody-Forbes—"

He stood. "Ain't got time right now, Amantha. Got to run out to one of the leases. I'll come back later on this evenin'. You stay in bed, y'hear?"

He was gone before she could say anything further.

She lay back, trying to recall what had happened in the

night. She was certain Charlie Forbes had held her, kissed her, that she had felt warm and safe in his arms.

But that, too, like the memory of babbled nonsense, was probably a dream.

Charlie did not go to the lease. He went home, changed clothes, then sat in Doctor Skillern's office until he could see him.

Hypertension was a tricky thing, the doctor told him. Amantha's brief breakdown had been like a relief valve. She had driven herself until mind and body rebelled.

A few days of bed rest and she'd be good as new—until the next time. In Skillern's opinion, it was about time she relaxed and enjoyed life.

Charlie left, assured that his plan of action was probably the best one. But first, he intended to try an alternative.

He went to a travel agency.

When he arrived that evening, Amantha was already up and working at her desk. Wearing a soft pink robe, her small feet encased in fluffy slippers, she looked like a little girl.

"Thought you was s'posed to be in bed," Charlie said from the doorway. She looked up guiltily.

"I couldn't sleep. I had to go over these papers. Charlie, I want to ask you—"

For once, Charlie took the offensive. "You ain't askin', Amantha. Yer listenin'! You an' me, we been around a long time. We're not gittin' any younger. Mebbe we both oughta be put out to pasture. It's time to re-tire! Mebbe we could—"

"And maybe we couldn't! If you want to quit—"

Charlie stopped and drew a deep breath. This wasn't any time for arguing. "Let's just whoa up, a minute. I got somethin' to show you."

He spread an array of travel brochures before her. If she didn't want to retire, how about a nice long vacation? "Look at this here!"

He held a brochure at a distance and began to read.

"Find romance on the sands of Blue Hawaii. . . ."

"I'm a little old for romance, Charlie," she said wryly.

"Okay, then how about, 'Thrill to the music of the Islands.' "

"I'm a little old for thrills, too, I believe."

"Goldang it, Amantha, you're younger'n I am! If this sounds good to a ol' strip of dried up rawhide like me—"

Charlie would never grow old. She looked at him affectionately, his lined brown face, the gray eyes that still held youth beneath a thatch of silvering hair.

Peter Pan, lured by the promise of the tropics.

And he should have the opportunity to do as he wished.

Since the reporter's comments, her emotions had ranged from numb shock to anger at Charlie's rumored defection. Then, last night, Charlie had been there to pick up the pieces, just as he had through the years.

She remembered a discussion she'd had with Charlie when David was sick. She'd asked if their struggle, working long hours, scrimping and saving to start their own business, was worth it.

"It's what Dave wants," he'd said simply. "Me, I'm too easygoin'. Just a lazy old countryboy."

It was Charlie who wanted out! After all these years of loyalty, he deserved it.

Now he was looking at her strangely. "I got somethin' to say to you, Amantha. I been tryin' to get up nerve enough fer a long time—"

Amantha looked down at the paper in front of her, and held up a staying hand. "I've been listing my assets, Charlie. I'm prepared to buy your stock—"

Charlie stood, his eyes like sleet, his face harsh with an unfamiliar anger.

"And you can go to the devil, Amantha! It ain't fer sale! But I can sure as hell give it away!"

Chapter Forty-Seven

*A*mantha was stunned when Charlie slammed out the door. There was, however, one redeeming facet to their conversation. It was clear Charlie didn't intend to sell out, in spite of his ridiculous comment.

It made it easier to follow Doctor Skillern's orders. While she didn't intend to remain in bed, she would do what little work she could accomplish at home for the next several days. And, apparently, a special meeting had not been called, or she would be informed.

No one had considered the loyalty of Dodie Sinclair to her employer. Dodie called on Amantha the evening of the next day. Seeing Amantha, she burst into tears.

"You look just the same! I was afraid!"

"I'm quite well," Amantha said humorously. "The reports of my death are grossly exaggerated."

Again, Dodie wailed. When she had herself under control, she produced a letter. "I didn't know what to do. Charlie Forbes said I wasn't to mail your copy. But I was afraid you might walk into a—a hornet's nest. . . ."

Amantha plucked the letter from Dodie's fingers, smoothing it on her desk. The expression in her blue eyes turning to horror, followed by a blazing anger as she glanced at the beginning lines, then at the signature.

Thorne Greenberg!

"I am certain you will share my sorrow that our venerable chairman, Amantha, lies at death's door," It began.

Death's door? Venerable? "The sonofabitch!"

Dodie jumped at the unexpected word Amantha uttered; Amantha Carmody, who had never been less than a lady. But she couldn't blame her.

"Yes," she agreed weakly, "he certainly is."

The letter continued, extolling Amantha's virtues as a pioneer in the oil business.

"Though most of us have deplored the lack of initiative and imagination which has kept Carmody-Forbes a small, family-type operation, we must agree that it has been stable."

"Shee-yut!" said the elegant Amantha Carmody.

Dodie blanched.

The writer went on to say that, unfortunately, the recent dwindling of dividends indicated new blood was needed; new ideas. No longer could a company of Carmody-Forbes's type remain static. There were fresh areas to be explored; the field of petrochemicals was booming. An alliance with a company such as Co-Chem would pull Carmody-Forbes into the majors. And the stockholders would profit. They would no longer need to rely on obsolete management methods.

Amantha's lips moved, but in her fury she was unable to find an appropriate word.

"Crap?" Dodie put in, timidly.

"Thank you, Dodie."

Amantha returned to her reading. Greenberg concluded by saying that he was calling a special meeting of the board. He asked that all members attend or send their proxies.

The agenda would include a motion to expand the corporation's interests, and—regrettably—the election of a new president of the board.

Amantha looked at the date set for the board meeting. Tomorrow morning! Now, she knew why Charlie worked so desperately to get her to retire! Even to leave the country!

The letter was a well-worded piece of slander, and she would face an inimical board. But there was nothing Greenberg could do—not as long as she and Charlie voted together.

But would he?

"Don't tell Forbes I showed you this," Dodie begged. "I wouldn't have, if you'd been really sick."

"You did the right thing, Dodie. And please don't let

anyone know I've seen it; especially Thorne. I'll be in for the meeting.''

After Dodie left, Amantha went through her wardrobe. The blue suit echoed the color of her eyes. A rose blouse would give a blush to her cheeks—and dear God, she needed that!

Now she must get some sleep, so she appear well and rested tomorrow.

The next morning she dressed, viewing herself in the harsh light of day. She still looked twenty years less than her age.

How dare Thorne depict her as a senile old woman!

She would show them!

As she had planned, she was first on the scene. She sat in her chair at the head of the conference table, looking down its shining length with satisfaction.

Dodie Sinclair was the next to arrive. She looked pale and frightened, but when her eyes fell on Amantha, she beamed.

''You're going to knock 'em dead!''

''I shall try,'' Amantha said dryly.

''There's one thing I don't understand,'' Dodie said, troubled. ''I just heard something I can't believe. Mr. Greenberg said that Charlie—''

She quieted as Thorne Greenberg entered. He was clearly discomfited at Amantha's appearance, but smiled and complimented her on her recovery. .

''I feared your mind might have been affected,'' he said solicitously.

So that was what his tack was going to be!

''But you look lovelier than ever,'' he added gallantly.

''I wish I could say the same for you. Those pouches beneath your eyes! Are you sure you are feeling well?'' Amantha's gaze moved to his paunch. ''You seem to have put on weight.''

''I believe I'm in fighting trim,'' he said nastily, his eyes narrowing.

''That's nice. So am I.''

The other members of the board wandered in. After an initial flash of surprise, they averted their eyes.

He's got them in his pocket, Amantha thought grimly. Look at them!

Jorge Kempe! I paid for his wife's heart surgery!

Burl Oskins! Ten kids, and I sent everyone a birth gift, a graduation present, a check when they married.

Philomena Jordan! She said I was her only friend when her husband died!

Shelby Hillard! Just about as stable as the Oklahoma wind! He'd find out who was leading the parade, then jump in front of it.

She studied the faces around the table, thinking of the past. She'd initiated benefits before they were enforced. And most of the people here had taken advantage of them. Now that their dividends had lessened and Thorne was making promises of pie in the sky, they were ready to throw her to the wolves. . . .

She looked at her watch. It was time to begin, but the chair at her right was still empty. Where in God's name was Charlie?

She met Dodie's eyes. They seemed to be trying to signal a message to her. What had she been saying when Thorne walked in?

Thorne Greenberg was smirking. "Would you call the meeting to order, Mrs. Carmody?"

"In a moment." How could she be so calm, when she was seething inside? "We have one more chair to fill, I believe."

All heads turned as the door opened and a man entered.

"Now," Amantha began, "we can—"

Her voice trailed off in disbelief.

David Meadows!

Dear God, what had Charlie done!

Meadows's eyes touched hers in a brief bewilderment. She knew he hadn't expected to see her here. Then he caught himself and inclined his head toward the board, introducing himself.

"I now hold Charlie Forbes's stock," he said in a deep, rich voice. "My name is Meadows. David Carmody Meadows."

Amantha shrank as he came to take the chair beside her. The pieces of a puzzle had come together.

Thorne Greenberg was equally stunned. "Carmody?" He blurted. "You're not—?"

The newcomer looked at him levelly. "My father was Peter Carmody, decorated posthumously for his actions in Italy. Meadows is my stepfather's name. He was also a hero."

Amantha began to tremble.

Peter's son! No! Oh, dear God, no!

He was an imposter! A woods colt Joylene had foisted off on Peter! There was no resemblance to her blond, English child! Meadows was all Indian! He had no right to the Carmody name!

She lost all control, turning to accuse him, to tell him he had no right to be here! No right—

And then she saw his eyes. They were not brown, as she had believed, but blue. Not the sky blue Peter's had been, but like David's—David's eyes in a copper-colored face.

How could Charlie have done this to her?

They were all staring at her; blurred images around the table. She had to pull herself together—

For a moment, she looked at the gavel in her hand as though wondering what it was. Then she rapped for attention.

"The meeting Mr. Greenberg desired is called to order. I suggest we dispense with formalities and permit him to speak."

Thorne, too, had recaptured his aplomb. His face was wreathed in smiles as he made his pitch, directing it at the new arrival.

Its content was much the same as his letter. He bowed to Amantha as the grand old lady of oil; the queen mother, so to speak. Her efforts had made Carmody-Forbes possible.

It was time she rested on her laurels, took a well-earned vacation to recover from the illness that struck her down when her work proved too much for her.

Having delivered his poisonous comments, Greenberg got down to business.

The company was no longer profitable as far as its stockholders were concerned. As he mentioned in his mailing, he intended to propose a merger with Co-Chem, an up-and-coming concern, with forward-thinking ideas.

He produced a flip chart, rattling off names of products, volume, profit margin, advertising, plans for expansion.

"I requested those who favored such a merger either be present or send their proxies. I'm happy to say the proxies we've received are unanimous in favor of it. Now, I would like to call for a vote from this board. Miss Sinclair—"

Dodie moved to the board on which votes were normally tabulated. Amantha's voice stopped her. Amantha stood, gripping the table's edge.

"You've had your say, Thorne. Before this goes to a vote, I demand mine. I am still chairman of this board!"

"Of course." His acquiescence was that of a gentleman humoring a sick old woman.

Amantha's voice was calm, controlled, as she continued.

"Mr. Greenberg mentioned my part in keeping Carmody-Forbes stable. I submit that this may be the very reason he desires this merger. I understand he also holds shares in Co-Chem. And since he is allied with it, I am sure he sees the advantages he will gain through a merger.

"A large and debt-ridden company will gain through association with a smaller one of good reputation."

"Mrs. Carmody—"

"You will wait until I have finished, Thorne! You have intimated that I am an old woman! It is true I have been here for many years. And that is the very reason I oppose this merger!

"How many of you remember Mr. Marland? He built up one of our largest oil companies single-handed. His people had decent housing, good working conditions, excellent pay and benefits. I patterned this company on his at a time when such action was not compulsory.

"I followed his lead, except in one matter. He allowed himself to become involved with a New York trust. He found himself removed from his chairmanship. The people who worked for him, who were his trusted friends, who depended upon him, lost their jobs on the day the trust took over. I do not wish this to happen to our employees.

"It is true that our profits have lessened. But we are debt-free. Our problems are due to the times we live in. And times change—"

"My dear lady," Greenberg interrupted, "you have just made my point! We live in a world based on credit. If we keep up with change, we must dare to gamble."

There was a murmur of assent. Amantha sank down into her chair. She had done all she could do.

"Take your vote."

"Kempe; one hundred fifty shares. Aye."

"Oskins, three hundred. I vote yes."

"Jordan, ninety-five. Yes."

"Simkiss, five hundred shares. I'm all for it. After that last dividend—"

Shelby Hillard, as Amantha had guessed, did not differ from the majority.

Around the table it went. Meadows had his head down and she couldn't see his face.

He would vote against her, of course. It was retribution—

And Thorne Greenberg was smiling.

"Well, Mr. . . . Medley, how say you?"

Dave Meadows jerked his head up.

"The name is Meadows," he said coolly. "David Carmody Meadows. And I vote nay!"

Amantha was dazed. The faces at the table blurred and danced. It was going to be all right! It was going to be all right!

Through the haze she could hear Thorne's voice, ugly with frustration. "Speak up, Mrs. Carmody. There is no doubt as to your preference. But you must say it!"

A large, square hand pressed Amantha's beneath the table, and Amantha managed a faint, "Nay."

There was no mention of an election of officers. Greenberg grabbed his charts and papers and stalked out. The room emptied quickly, the others not wanting to face the friend they'd almost betrayed. Only Dave Meadows and Dodie Sinclair remained.

"I'll take care of her," Dodie said, nodding to Meadows to go. "She hasn't been well."

She helped Amantha to her car. "You going to be all right?"

"It's just the . . . relief," Amantha told her.

But it was more than that. It was a youngish man, with a copper-colored face and David's eyes—and name.

Peter's son. And he had voted with her.

Chapter Forty-Eight

*A*mantha went home to a house that was suddenly too big, too ornate, too opulent. It was beautiful, yes, and had been included on tours of the city's finer landmarks.

But was it a home?

That seemed unimportant now. Amantha flexed nervous fingers, wondering where to begin.

First she called her attorney and asked him to come to her immediately.

Then she phoned the office, asking Dodie to find Meadows's home number.

Last she put through a call to Meadows himself. She would like him to visit her this evening, if possible.

She handled her business with her attorney, then waited for Meadows's arrival, fussing over her clothes like a girl. As if his approval made any difference—

Yet, when he arrived, she managed to maintain an outer shell of calm; the formidable Amantha Carmody, not to be bested in a deal. No one would have guessed that her heart was beating rapidly, as she saw her husband's eyes in a dark face:

"Would you like a drink? Something from the bar? Coffee? Tea?"

"Coffee, please."

Her cup rattling in its saucer betrayed her nervousness. She might as well stop shilly-shallying, and get to it! She lifted her eyes, bracing herself for the shock she still felt.

"You voted with me this morning. Why? Did Charlie make it a condition of the sale?"

"No, ma'am."

"Then why?"

He flushed a little. "I guess I had two reasons. First, I didn't trust Mr. Greenberg. Second, I approve of your type of management. The way you built the company after my grandfather's death . . ."

"I suppose you got all this from Charlie?"

"Mostly from my mother, I think. She and my dad didn't have long together, but I guess she repeated everything she knew about you, so I'd have some kind of background."

"What did she say about me," she asked in a low voice. "Did she tell you the reason I never acknowledged you?"

"She said you were a real lady," Dave Meadows said softly. "She said you loved my father so much you couldn't bear to be reminded of him. But there was something more, wasn't there?"

Amantha bent her head, biting her lip to keep it from trembling. "Yes, there was more. . . ."

"It doesn't matter now. The money you sent each month paid for my education, and there were the birthday gifts, the Christmas presents. I knew you thought of me. I used to wish I knew you."

Money? Presents?

Charlie!

Pain laced around her heart, squeezing it as she opened her mouth to deny the reports of her generosity. But she couldn't speak. His eyes were shining. David's wonderful eyes, returned to life after all these years.

"I've got to tell you something else," he confessed. "Charlie didn't exactly sell me his stock. He gave it to me, for the sum of one dollar and other considerations. But I suppose you know all that."

Charlie, Charlie!

Their tension finally eased, David Meadows told Amantha about his Cherokee wife. He had a child named Peter. There was another on the way. If it were another boy, they planned to name it Steve. A girl would be Meggie.

Peter, according to David's mother, was a darker replica of the first Peter. He had the idea he wanted to go to England when he grew up.

"Can you imagine? A British Cherokee?"

Another Peter, head filled with dreams. "I'm going to live in Buckingham Palace—"

"I have a gift for your son," Amantha said, in a choked voice. "I suppose it is really for you, to go later to him—"

Opening her desk drawer, she took out a sheaf of official-looking papers.

They were the legal consignment of Amantha Carmody's stock to David Carmody Meadows and his heirs.

David was pale beneath his copper-hued complexion. "I don't understand," he stammered.

"I'm too old to fight anymore," Amantha said. "I'm not doing you any favors. I'm handing you control of a company divided within itself. You'll have to keep it from sinking, face the stockholders. . . ."

"I'm not certain I can handle it." He looked stunned. Then his features settled into forceful lines. "I can. I will! For your sake, for Charlie's! For my children!"

"You will manage," Amantha said.

For a moment she thought he was going to hug her. And for a moment she almost wished he would.

"I—I don't know what to say," he said finally. "Thank you isn't enough."

"There will be times," Amantha told him, "that it is a very thankless job."

"But I want to do something—"

She lifted her chin. "Just bring my—my great-grandchild to see me."

David Carmody Meadows looked down at the small woman standing before him; a woman who had just handed him a fortune along with her trust.

"You're a great lady, ma'am! Do you know that?"

It was on the tip of Amantha's tongue to answer, "No, I'm just a damned old fool!" But she swallowed it back. "Thank you, David," she said graciously. She blinked rapidly. If he didn't leave soon, she was going to cry.

When he had gone, she reached for the telephone and called Charlie. He answered, trepidation in his voice. Dodie had told him about the meeting this morning. He hadn't expected Amantha to be there. And he was pretty sure, even though things turned out okay, that she was now madder than hell.

Her voice didn't give him a clue. She just said she must see him immediately, despite the hour. He grabbed his hat and headed for town.

While she waited, Amantha sat down at her little desk. Taking out pen and paper, she began a letter. It was addressed to a girl she had seen only once, on a high school stage, long years ago; a girl who had married her son and borne his child.

She folded and sealed it as the doorbell rang to announce Charlie's arrival. She let him in, her face noncommittal.

"Hello, Charlie."

She turned and he followed her to her study where she took a position behind the desk, leaving him to stand, turning his hat in his hands.

"Well, Charlie, you've done it, haven't you?"

He held out an apologetic hand. "Amantha—"

"I never dreamed you'd let me down, Charlie. Not after all these years!"

His face was agonized. "I didn't mean—"

"And then to let an Indian take your place! You couldn't talk me into retiring. You tried to drive me out."

"Goldang it, Amantha! If you'll listen—"

"Do you know what hurt me the most? Do you want to know what the worst of it was?" She stood, her eyes luminous with affection.

"The worst was knowing you deserted me! That you wouldn't be sitting beside me again. I knew I couldn't live without you, Charlie!"

She came to him, around the desk, putting her hands flat against his chest, feeling the thunder of his heart, seeing an amazed delight dawning in his gray eyes.

"Charlie, why didn't you ever marry me?"

His voice was hoarse as he answered, "Goldang it, Amantha— You never asked."

"I'm asking you now."

His calloused hand went around the nape of her neck, up under her hair. He pulled her tight against his gray workshirt. She could feel him trembling.

"Goldang," he whispered, "Goldang! I never figgered on nothin' like this!"

He let her go. "This ain't right, Amantha. You're still the boss at Carmody-Forbes. I ain't nobody no more—"

Amantha turned to her desk, picking up her copy of the document she'd had drawn up earlier in the day.

"You bought the boy out!" His eyes were bleak and accusing.

"Read it," Amantha said.

He read, his jaw dropping. Then the papers fell to the floor and he reached for her again. This time, she put up a staying hand.

"Charlie, I proposed to you, and it wasn't fair. You've always gone along with anything I suggested. I—I suppose I forgot for a moment that I was old. I—I'm not holding you to anything."

"Hush your mouth, girl," he said softly. "I've loved you since the minute I saw you waitin' there at the train. Little scrap of a thing with big, scared eyes. I wanted to put my arms around you, hold you, just like this—

"Ain't nothin' changed none. Just didn't figger a ol' lazy countryboy like me would ever have the chance—"

He held her by both arms, his gray eyes serious, almost black with emotion. "Amantha Carmody, you bein' maybe the beautifulest lady I ever seen, the onliest one I ever had a hankerin' for, but a gabby woman that never lets a man finish a sentence— Now, supposin' you let me finish sayin' what I tried to say the other day.

"Amantha Carmody, I love you more'n anything in this here world. If you'll marry me, I'll keep care of you for the rest of my natural born days.

"Well, Amantha, there's the deal. What you got to say?"

"Yes, Charlie!" She was crying now. "Yes! Yes! Yes!"

All these years! All these lost years!

She reached up to touch his face, seeing the love in kind gray eyes beneath a shock of silvered hair. She had loved him always, and hadn't known it. Ever since she sat on a clay bank, watching a small boy fishing in an amber pool. . . .

Even then Charlie had been her true husband; a stand-in for David, whose attention was focused on oil. She had successfully managed a business, but Charlie had been the head of her family.

"Still got a couple tickets to Hawaii in my pocket," he said. "Ain't turned 'em in, yet."

"Then we shall use them."

He bent to touch his lips to hers. And she knew she had waited many years for this moment. Her arms tightened around him.

She would never, never let him go.

Chapter Forty-Nine

O*ne week later a wedding was held. A wedding that set* Oklahoma City on its ear. Amantha Carmody, the acknowledged first lady of oil; small, elegant, cultured—and her very silent partner, Charlie Forbes, one of Oklahoma's own.

It was something out of a fairy tale; the ploughboy capturing the hand of the princess. And it was such a sudden thing.

"You reckon they're talkin' about us?" Charlie asked as they read over the newspaper accounts. "Way we're rushing into this thing, looks like a shotgun weddin'. S'pose they'll figger we been foolin' around?"

"I won't tell if you won't," Amantha sparkled up at him.

"Mebbe," Charlie said, hopefully, "with all this talk, none of the weddin' guests will show."

They did, coming in droves. Amantha's business and social acquaintances; the governor, a dozen or more legislators, and a horde of Charlie's old friends: roustabouts, drillers, wildcatters, their best clothes still smelling of oil.

Downstairs there was standing room only. Mingling with the guests were reporters from the *Daily Oklahoman and Times*. WKY and KOMA had television cameras set up at strategic points, and roving radio interviewers were moving among the crowd.

It must look like a political convention down there, Amantha thought.

She had wanted to keep the wedding small. Had even

suggested having the ceremony in the meadow at the oil patch, against a background of Charlie's zinnias and hollyhocks. He had gently vetoed the idea. The weather at this time of year was too chancy.

His decision proved to be wise. Last night the temperature plunged, bringing a chill that cut to the bone.

This morning was bright and blue, but the flowers would be withered; the foliage along the creek flaming; persimmons touched with frost and sweet to the taste.

Perhaps I'm like a persimmon, Amantha thought as she dressed for the ceremony. It had taken the chill of years to take away all touches of bitterness, to produce this sweetness that melted her bones.

In the meantime, it had been a perfect day, beginning with a phone call from Ellen. With the children in school, they hadn't been able to make the trip. But they would all be waiting in L.A. to see Amantha and Charlie off in style.

And among the telegrams and congratulations arriving to-day had been a small, inexpensive, but very important envelope. It contained two letters, one from Joylene Meadows, the other from her husband, Steve, accepting the hand of friendship Amantha extended—after all these years.

She prayed that, somewhere, Peter knew.

And now it was time. Amantha surveyed herself in the mirror. Her dress was a Dior creation, cut low to reveal shoulders that were still smooth and young-looking. It was tiny-waisted. The soft material of the skirt revealed slender ankles.

The gown was so old it was back in style again. She'd worn it on the eve of Meggie's sixteenth birthday. And as she and Charlie—dear, beloved Charlie—waited for the girl to come in, the radio had played "*If I Loved You.*"

Amantha smiled at the memory as she pinned on a scrap of veiling that matched its delicate blue. She would come to Charlie as a proper bride, trusting in a strong arm to lead her to the altar.

With a last look at the past—Meggie smiling down from

the walls, David enshrined on the bedside table along with
Peter's faded photograph—she left the room and went to the
head of the stairs.

David Carmody Meadows waited there for her. Her single
attendant, Dodie Sinclair, had already begun to descend the
steps with her escort. Poor Dodie! Often a bridesmaid, but
never a bride.

There was still time, Amantha thought. It was never too
late for love.

She placed her hand in the crook of young David's arm.
Together they walked down the stairs, the tiny exquisite
woman, her huge, strongly built grandson towering over her.

Amantha did not see the sea of upturned faces. Only
Charlie.

He looked pale and serious—and frightened! As nervous as
Joe Collins had been.

Then they were standing before the minister.

"Who gives this woman?"

And David Meadows said the words Amantha wrote into
the ceremony.

"David Carmody and I do."

Amantha's eyes were on Charlie. Please understand, they
begged. With these words I am setting David to rest. I am
coming to you freely—

"Do you, Amantha, take this man—?"

Take him? Charlie, who had stood beside her in need and
in plenty; who was her friend in her young years; a comfort
when her life was shadowed; the love of her winter?

"I do."

"And, Charles—"

Not Charles! Charlie! Charlie, with his lanky frame, his
slow drawl; his innate, homespun wisdom—

"I do."

It was over and he bent to kiss her. For a space they were
alone. Then a strangled sob from Dodie pulled Amantha back
to reality. Amantha stood on tiptoe and whispered into Charlie's
ear.

"You didn't say goldang once," she teased.

In the flurry of congratulations that followed, Amantha found time to meet Susan Meadows, shy, and far along in pregnancy, and young Peter—her great-grandson. Looking at the little boy, a darker image of his grandfather, Amantha was too choked with emotion to speak. She could only hold him close, swallowing her tears.

"The silver service you sent us," David's wife said timidly. "It is lovely. I want to thank you—"

"I wanted it," Amantha said sincerely, "to stay in the family."

Now she was free of the past. There would be someone else to carry on.

Too soon it was time to leave for the airport. Amantha and Charlie ran for the limousine, Ryan driving. And Dodie, romantic Dodie, produced a shower of rice.

"Goldang," Charlie whispered in mock fright, "we throwed the durn stuff at Ellie, and she went and wound up pregnant! You don't suppose—?"

"Charlie," Amantha laughed, "you're an old fool! But I love you!"

They reached the airport and boarded their plane, Charlie insisting she sit next to the window. When they were airborne, she looked down at the city wheeling below, amazed, as always, that a city built on a mountain could appear so flat. Now it sprawled over miles; overpasses, wide thoroughfares; its downtown area in the process of receiving a heart transplant.

She had come here on a train; frightened, uncertain. She was leaving, confident and secure, to soar above the city with the man she loved.

But in the interim, Amantha Carmody Forbes had helped to build that city. And the time had passed so swiftly. She could shut her eyes, see tall derricks, flares burning in the rain, and blowing dust. She could hear the sound of Waukesha engines pumping the black gold from the earth, like the beating of her own heart.

Those days were gone. And with them, the wildcatters, the greatest gamblers of them all; the squalid oil camps; the sudden gush of oil spewing skyward to drift with the wind.

She and Charlie had been a part of it all. And someday no one would remember. But they had done well.

Now they were headed toward Hawaii, a place of warmth and sun. Would they remain there for the years allotted to them? Or would they return?

As Charlie said, they would "play it by ear." They were free to do as they pleased. "No strings."

But there were, she thought. There were ties that could not be broken. And it was possible that predictable weather would pall; that they would long again for the taste of red dust blowing in their faces.

And they would come home.

But not to the big house near the capitol, with its echoing empty rooms; a house David Meadows's growing family might be able to fill—but to a small cabin by a stream at the edge of an oil patch, where sumac bloomed scarlet in the fall.

Amantha woke from her reverie. A stewardess was bending over them, with the special smile the young reserve for the old. She had seen Amantha's hand clasped in Charlie's, the Hawaiian brochures on his lap.

"So you're going to Hawaii," she said archly. "Let me guess! A golden wedding!"

Charlie grinned at her. "Betcher boots," he said.

"Well, congratulations." Another professional smile, and she moved on down the aisle.

"She's lovely, isn't she," Amantha said wistfully.

"I kinda lean to the older girls myself." He slid an arm around her and she leaned against his shoulder with a contented sigh, looking with him at the travel brochures.

"Find romance on the sands of blue Hawaii."

"I've already found it, Charlie. I found it in an oil patch in Oklahoma."

He picked up the next and studied it. "Thrill to the music of the Islands."

"We might try this one," he said with a mock frown. "I may be an old man, goldang it, but if push come to shove, I think I could work up a thrill."

His teasing stopped and his face grew serious, his eyes smoky gray as he looked down at her.

"You happy, Amantha? Really happy, I mean?"

"I'm the happiest woman in the world."

Sun glinted on the wings of the plane as it soared high above the Oklahoma border, heading toward summer, leaving winter behind.

With special thanks to:

Helen Eckroat and *Oklahoma Today*
Penn Wood, Christian College, Oklahoma City
"Curley" of Texas Flange Incorporated
The Permian Basin Oil Museum, Midland, Texas
Walter Hague, Oklahoma City, Oklahoma
Joe Truitt, Tularosa, New Mexico
Don and Mary Cole, Odessa, Texas
Mr. & Mrs. C. R. Seery, formerly of Oklahoma City
Helen Vandergriff, Harrah, Oklahoma
J. K. Blickenstaff, Oklahoma City
And my son, Smokey, and family, in Odessa, Texas

About the Author

Aola Vandergriff, born in LeMars, Iowa, spent her formative years in Oklahoma City, Oklahoma. *Red Wind Blowing* sprang from her interest in oil and the "very special breed" who produced it.

Her credits include a book of poetry, more than 2,500 short stories and articles, and eighteen novels published worldwide and in several translations.

A teacher and lecturer, she taught "Writing to Sell" at American River College, Sacramento, California, and was an editorial associate with *Writers' Digest*.

Home is an adobe hacienda in a haunted canyon above the village of La Luz near Alamogordo, New Mexico. Though she travels extensively to research her novels, she is active in political and civic affairs.